Praise for the novels of Christopher Darden and Dick Lochte:

The Last Defense

"What do you get when you combine a shrewd former prosecutor . . . with one of the smoothest, most urbane mystery writers ever to come down the mean freeways of Los Angeles? A blockbuster legal thriller like this—crammed to the gills with pith, moment, racial insights, courtroom chicanery, sexual shenanigans, bizarre police behavior, and countless other delights. . . . Can be read as a modern *Candide* or even a *Faust*—the usual suspects being greed and pride. Or you can just take it at face value, and hold on tight for a smashing ride."

—*Chicago Tribune*

"Nonstop action from courtroom to barroom to bedroom. . . . Amid the simmering stew of sex, drugs, alcohol, violence, and courtroom pyrotechnics are a stable of memorable characters. . . . Darden and Lochte make a formidable team. . . . A fast ride with a jolting, surprise finish." —*Publishers Weekly*

"Exciting and engrossing. . . . This crime-fiction dream team's most satisfying work yet . . . worthy of legal-thriller masters such as Steve Martini and John Lescroart. . . . Crackles with lawyer lore and inside jokes, all smartly tucked into its complex story. . . . Moves with propulsive force towards its satisfying finale."

—*OC Metro*

continued . . .

"A wildly entertaining roller-coaster ride through L.A.'s legal corridors. . . . [Darden and Lochte] make a great team."

—*Booklist*

"Will appeal to fans of John Grisham. . . . Fast-paced, hooking the reader from the early courtroom drama to the strong climax."

—*Midwest Book Review*

L.A. Justice

"High-octane. . . . This novel is just the kind of frenzied page-turner many authors aspire to and few deliver. Darden's legal smarts and Lochte's sure prose touch work well in tandem."

—*Publishers Weekly*

"An exciting, topical legal thriller." —*Chicago Tribune*

"A story that twists and turns. . . . Kept me delightfully off-balance, eager to see how the pieces would fit together."

—Laura Lippman for *The Baltimore Sun*

"The authors will keep you guessing." —*Houston Chronicle*

The Trials of Nikki Hill

"This literary dream team has a knack for dialogue and characterization that keeps you caring about the players. . . . Darden knows the L.A. legal system like the back of his hand."

—*Entertainment Weekly*

"A whiplash plot. . . . Darden makes good use of his own extraordinary experiences in re-creating the roller-coaster ride. . . . One heck of a closing." —*People*

"A smooth murder tale loaded with insider information. . . . Darden and Lochte are a seamless writing team. . . . You could hardly ask for more from a legal thriller."—*Arizona Daily Star*

"A genuinely suspenseful crime novel with a charismatic heroine and a cast of well-drawn supporting characters. . . . The verdict: highly recommended for fans of Grisham, Turow, and Court TV." —*Booklist*

"In fifteen years as a senior prosecutor, Darden has seen it all . . . a fascinating journey. I've been in those corridors, those courts, those meetings, and those dramas—and he makes them real. I loved this book."

—Gavin de Becker, author of *The Gift of Fear*

ALSO BY CHRISTOPHER DARDEN & DICK LOCHTE

The Trials of Nikki Hill

L.A. Justice

The Last Defense

LAWLESS

CHRISTOPHER
DARDEN

& DICK LOCHTE

AN ONYX BOOK

ONYX
Published by New American Library, a division of
Penguin Group (USA) Inc., 375 Hudson Street,
New York, New York 10014, USA
Penguin Group (Canada), 10 Alcorn Avenue, Toronto,
Ontario M4V 3B2, Canada (a division of Pearson Penguin Canada Inc.)
Penguin Books Ltd., 80 Strand, London WC2R 0RL, England
Penguin Ireland, 25 St. Stephen's Green, Dublin 2,
Ireland (a division of Penguin Books Ltd.)
Penguin Group (Australia), 250 Camberwell Road, Camberwell, Victoria 3124,
Australia (a division of Pearson Australia Group Pty. Ltd.)
Penguin Books India Pvt. Ltd., 11 Community Centre, Panchsheel Park,
New Delhi - 110 017, India
Penguin Group (NZ), Cnr Airborne and Rosedale Roads, Albany,
Auckland 1310, New Zealand (a division of Pearson New Zealand Ltd.)
Penguin Books (South Africa) (Pty.) Ltd., 24 Sturdee Avenue,
Rosebank, Johannesburg 2196, South Africa

Penguin Books Ltd., Registered Offices:
80 Strand, London WC2R 0RL, England

Published by Onyx, an imprint of New American Library, a division of Penguin Group (USA) Inc. Originally published in a New American Library hardcover edition.

First Onyx Printing, January 2005
10 9 8 7 6 5 4 3 2 1

Printed in the United States of America

For my son, Christopher Allen Darden, Jr.
CD

For Alex B-Z, who found his Hogwarts
DL

"Every lawyer has a secret . . . maybe more than one."

PROLOGUE

TUESDAY, MAY 11

The "suspicious vehicle" some unknown party had reported to the LAPD at approximately 9 p.m. was parked at the rear of a derelict minimall on Pico and Velasco. Its sharklike snout was facing a dark, seldom-used alley that good neighbors had turned into their own private garbage dump.

When Officer Joe Mooney eased the patrol car close enough to light up the area, he saw that the vehicle was a bronze-colored Trans Am. An old one. Early eighties, maybe. Covered by a layer of grime. Papers and other alley trash had collected around the wheels like dirty chickens coming home to roost.

"Looks abandoned," Joe said.

"Abandoned? Looks like it's taken root," his partner, Emmylou Paget, said. "How long you figure it's been here?"

"They boarded up the mall about four months ago," Joe said. "I don't see it being here that long. Somebody would have called it in before tonight."

"You think so?" Emmylou asked. "They aren't exactly alley-proud around here. One piece of crap car isn't gonna ugly up the neighborhood any more than an abandoned mall."

A lot of the cops at the East Pico Station found Emmylou's surly 'tude hard to take, but Joe, who had seen all types in his fourteen years on the force, was amused by it. He figured it was her way of compensating for looking so goddamned cute. He'd never tell her that, certainly not using the word "cute." She'd draw down on him. But that's what she was, barely an inch above the LAPD height requirement with the face of a cute little girl. She also happened to have the body of a woman, but as Joe continually had to reassure his wife, Gerry, he'd never given any serious thought to fucking Emmylou.

It didn't have anything to do with race. There were white chicks who worked his bone, time to time. He guessed it was because they were partners, and he didn't want to mess that up by fucking her or, even worse, having her tell him to go fuck himself. And, of course, there was his marriage to think about; he loved Gerry, and their little babygirl, Janet, was the star in his sky. Any way he looked at it, knocking boots with Emmylou was a lose-lose situation.

"Hey, Mr. Asleep-at-the-Wheel," she shouted at him. "You wanna take us in a little closer so I can ID the plates?"

"I thought all you superwomen had X-ray eyes," he said.

He slowly moved the car forward until the searchlight chased the shadows from the front of the Trans Am. That still didn't do the trick. A sheet of newspaper had wrapped around the license place.

"Fucking great," Emmylou said.

She started to open her door, but he told her to sit tight. "I'll clear the plate," he said, putting the idling car in park. "You call it in."

She stared at him. "Something wrong?"

"No," he lied, not knowing how to explain the vibes he was getting off the Trans Am. Maybe it was all the talk of terrorism in the air, the expectation of when the next deadly demonstration would take place. He doubted it would be a spot as rundown and deserted as this.

The night air was on the edge of being chilly but that didn't stop the alley from smelling like rotting garbage and urine. Despair perfume.

From what he could see past the tint and dust on the Trans Am's windshield, not to mention the greasy fast food wrapper caught under the wipers, the car was empty. But why were the tires still on it and the windows unbroken? His hand drifted toward his police special, but he didn't draw the weapon.

Instead, he did a deep knee bend and, almost daintily, stripped the newspaper from the Trans Am's license plate. Rising, he continued to stare at the vehicle, searching for some clue as to what it might be doing there. Or why it was creeping him out.

He backed away toward the patrol car and, eyes never leaving the Trans Am, slipped in beside Emmylou. She was waiting to hear if the plate rang any bells. "How goddamned long does it take to punch in some numbers?" she asked.

He barely heard her. He was too focused on the still vehicle. It definitely wasn't the usual jacked-and-abandoned situation. Even though the car looked cherry underneath the dust and dirt, it was too old to be worth a pro jack, and joyriders wouldn't have bothered tucking it away.

Joe's brown head was shaved close to the bone, but that didn't stop the hairs-standing-straight-out tickle at the back of his neck—his cop sense, working overtime.

He was not surprised when the hit on the plate turned out to be bad news. The car belonged to a fellow officer named Dwight Baskin. He and his wife, Eleanor, had been on the Missing Persons List for nineteen days.

Emmylou signed off and said, "Shit," her anger appropriate at last. "You know Baskin, right? Big, good-looking dude. They gave him the fucking Medal of Valor."

Joe had met the guy, had no feelings about him one way or another, though rumor was that Baskin had a heavy hand when it came to perps of color.

"Think he's dead in there?" Emmylou asked, eyes wider than usual.

"Either he is or he isn't."

"Don't go mystic on me, Joe." She reached for her door.

"Hold on," Joe said. "Backup's coming."

"Screw backup," she said. "Baskin could be in the car. Maybe not dead. Maybe wounded."

She was out and approaching the Trans Am before he could get his door open. She took the right side of the vehicle, shining her flashlight through the passenger window.

"He's in there," she called out eagerly.

As she reached for the door handle he shouted, "Don't!"

But he was too late.

"Baskin," he heard her say. "What the fuck . . . ?"

She threw herself to the ground a nanosecond before shots rang out.

They lit up the Trans Am's interior in strobe effect, showing Joe a bulky figure in motion behind the wheel. Then the muscle-car's engine roared to life.

The headlights flashed on, catching him dead center, blinding him.

He sensed the vehicle leaping toward him. He'd drawn his weapon automatically, but there was no time even to lift his arm. He hopped backward, one foot sliding out from under him on a piece of discarded Styrofoam. He hit the ground hard and rolled away from the sound of the car.

The Trans Am rocketed past, its wheels inches from his face. Turning sharply, it crashed into the front of the patrol car, shattering the left headlight and buckling the fender. Its driver—Baskin, presumably—backed away from the damage and peeled off down the alley.

Lying on his stomach, arms straight out, blinking away the light spots, Joe took aim and emptied his police special.

The Trans Am wobbled and made an abrupt right turn into the concrete wall surrounding the dead mall. Its horn wailed once and fell silent just as the left blinker light began flashing, accompanied by an electronic *bing-bing-bing*. Steam seeped from the crumpled hood.

Getting to his feet, Joe felt the adrenaline rush subside, leaving in its wake a sore shoulder and a pain in his left knee like the jab of a twelve-inch nail.

Emmylou was ahead of him, gun on palm, moving in on the mess.

"You okay?" he asked, limping after her.

"Sure," she said. "I love being shot at and rolling in dog shit."

Then she added, "Aw, hell."

"Baskin?"

"Used to be."

Coming up behind her, Joe saw that Baskin had done a header into the windshield, shattering it and smearing it with his blood. He was slumped forward, just to the side of the steering wheel, head resting at an unnatural angle.

"See the weapon?" Joe asked.

"Naw. But he won't be using it anymore."

She started to open the driver's door. He pushed her

aside before she could touch it with her bare hand. Using the flap of his jacket, he pressed the release button on the handle.

As the door swung open, an ugly mixture of smells rolled out—blood, sweat, and feces; scorched rubber; gunsmoke; stale food; and an unfamiliar metallic scent that cut through all the rest. Wrinkling his nose, Joe reached in, carefully clicked off the pinging blinker. He pressed his forefinger and middle finger against Baskin's neck.

No sign of life beneath the still-warm skin.

He backed away, shaking his head.

"At least he won't have to give back the medal," Emmylou said. "Looks like he's been living in the goddamned car. A year ago, this guy was on top of the world. What the fuck happened to him?"

"Nothing I wanna imitate," Joe said. "You see anyplace I hit him? Or was it just the crash? I was aiming for the tires."

"No way to tell right now, Joe," she said in a soft voice he'd never heard her use before. "Whichever, it was righteous."

"I was aiming for the tires," he repeated. Logically, he knew that dead was dead. Still, he wanted it to be the crash and not a stray bullet that killed this valor-honored cop.

He walked to the rear of the car. He was relieved to see that he'd put his shots where he'd wanted. The Trans Am's right tire was flat to the rim.

He noticed something else: the collision had popped the lock on the car's trunk. Using the barrel of his police special, he lifted the lid.

"I'm gonna go call in," Emmylou said, "tell 'em we found Baskin."

Joe stared into the trunk at a bent and twisted decaying object encased in plastic wrap. Fighting to keep his dinner down, his eyes starting to water, he called out to her, "Tell 'em we probably found Baskin's wife, too."

DAY 1

TUESDAY, JUNE 15

CHAPTER

ONE

"What made you decide to study the law?" Mercer Early asked the intense young man seated at his table. Kennard Haines, Jr., blinked behind his rimless glasses. Sidone Evans, the other member of their party of three, seemed amused by Haines's hesitation.

They were on the final cup-of-coffee phase of their lunch at The Pantry, a crowded downtown L.A. restaurant owned by an ex-mayor of the city—Mercer, a junior partner in Carter and Hansborough, the most powerful black law firm on the West Coast, and Evans and Haines, C&H's two newest associates.

"I suppose my father was a big influence," the young man finally said in what some might have assumed to be an affected British accent. Mercer knew it to be the real deal, the result of the boy spending the first seventeen of his twenty-two years in England, where his father had served as chief counsel for Altadine Industries. Ken Haines, Sr., was now an advisor to the White House, adding considerable caché to Junior's apprenticeship at the firm.

Sidone's family credentials—father a beat cop, mother in family planning in Detroit—were not quite as impressive, but her top-of-the-class performance at the University of Michigan Law School had opened the firm's doors to her.

In the several weeks that both associates had been kicking around the office, Mercer purposely had tried to build up some immunity to Sidone's beauty, which was a match for her academic standing. It wasn't that she was too young—maybe six years separated their ages—or that either of them was otherwise hooked up. He'd learned a hard lesson in the importance of keeping his personal life out of the office. And, of course, there was always the possibility of a potential sexual harassment suit, which was definitely to be avoided. So he was forcing himself to look past those ripe lips and alert bright eyes when he asked, "What about you, Ms. Sidone? What made you go for the law?"

"You first," she said.

He smiled. "Now that's a lawyer's answer. No sense giving anything away unless you have to. Points."

Kennard Haines frowned. "I didn't realize this was a test."

"Testing isn't my game, Kennard. The test comes when you step into the courtroom and anything you say or do, any blink of an eye or stutter or deep sigh may turn off a jury. You get a failing grade and your client gets screwed."

The boy looked sullen, but that was okay. Sullen faded quickly. Arrogance, stubbornness—those were things that could become a problem.

"Well?" Sidone asked. "I'm still waiting for your answer."

"Why'd I study the law?" he said. "I could say it was the money. Or the power. But the fact is: if you're a black *man* in this country, it doesn't much matter if you're a brother sleeping in the park or you're Denzel Washington, odds are the day will come when some cracker cop will be on your butt about something. When that happens you damn well better know more about the law than anybody else in the room."

"Sometimes it's smarter not to let them know how smart you are," Kennard Haines said.

"Example?" Mercer asked.

"On a visit to Manhattan, I just happened to be walking near a liquor store minutes after it had been robbed. So I got picked up, along with every other black man in the vicinity. There were quite a few of us. But I guess I was the only one using phrases like 'racial profiling,' so the police shoved me around a little more than the others. It might have gotten a lot worse if my dad hadn't had a friend in D.C. Metro make a call on my behalf. I could have saved myself some bruises by just keeping mum."

"Well, yeah. I didn't mean to suggest you should fly in the face of adversity," Mercer said. "Sometimes *keeping mum* is the smart play."

Noting Sidone's smile, Kennard said, "I'm sorry. I'm not big on slang. What should I have said? 'Keeping zipped'?"

The young woman shrugged. "I don't know. 'Chilling,' 'going baltic,' 'marinating.' Don't worry, Ken. I think you're at that point where uncool turns cool."

He grinned like he'd been paid a high compliment.

Mercer was starting to like the boy. When they were headed out of the restaurant, he decided another compliment wouldn't hurt. "If I *had* been testing you at lunch, Kennard, know what would have earned you the most points?"

The boy shook his head.

"You may be the only graduate of the Yale Law School I've ever met who didn't feel it necessary to mention that fact every couple minutes."

Kennard Haines, Jr., grinned. "I figured everybody knew," he said.

On the drive to the Criminal Courts Building, Sidone said, "Mercer, it would've been lame for me to ask you about the trial in a public dining room, but is now okay?"

"Sure."

"The client, Julio Lopez, was a fugitive from justice, right?"

The statement was correct, if a bit lacking in detail. Lopez had been convicted of murdering his stepfather, Arne Vargas, the owner of a popular Olvera Street bodega, who had been the young man's caretaker and molester for nearly ten of his nineteen years.

Deputy U.S. Marshals Tom Kinderman and Jim Hubble were transporting Lopez to Wayside Park, a facility about sixty miles north of the city, when their prisoner complained of stomach pain and asked if he could relieve himself at the next opportunity. Hubble had laughed at the notion. The more simpatico Kinderman had pulled into the nearest service station.

When Lopez somehow managed to fit through a small window at the rear of the lavatory and disappear into the wind, it was Kinderman who took the heat, and Kinderman who eventually tracked down Lopez to the San Pedro warehouse where he'd been lifting and hauling in the guise of an illegal named Luis Gordo.

It was Kinderman who confronted Lopez in a dark alley near the warehouse.

And it was Kinderman whose skull Lopez crushed with a lead pipe.

"Our client was a fugitive, sure enough," Mercer agreed as he maneuvered his Benz through the thick, slow midday traffic. "That's because I wasn't his attorney then. To my knowledge, I have never lost a trial where the client was truly innocent."

That innocence had come to light several months after the verdict, when another of Arne Vargas's young victims, a busboy in his establishment, left a suicide note in which he confessed to the crime. By itself, the note would probably not have been enough to get the guilty verdict overturned. However, a search of the dead boy's room disclosed the missing murder weapon, a knife smeared with Vargas's blood and skin particles, and a jar containing a noticeably absent body part of Vargas's afloat in alcohol.

Unfortunately, neither Lopez nor the lawmen pursuing him seemed to have received the news in time.

"Even if he was innocent of his stepfather's murder," Sidone said, "there is no question that he offed a deputy U.S. marshal."

"And, according to *Tennessee* v. *Garner,* a person must submit to even an unlawful arrest if the peace officer is acting under an existing fugitive warrant," Kennard added.

"You two have been talking about this, eh? That's good. And you disagree with the plea?"

"Not exactly," Kennard said. "It's just that the deputy marshal was performing his duty. The client admits killing him. We can't see a jury eagerly accepting this as an act of self-defense, no matter what the exigencies."

"Well, let's check out those exigencies. Suppose you're on the run from a crime you know you didn't commit and Deputy Marshal Kinderman draws down on you in an alley. What would you do?"

"I doubt I'd grab a pipe and hit him with it. I'd try to run, maybe. If that were not possible, I'd probably put up my hands."

"Even if putting up your hands meant spending a life behind bars? Suffering the same kind of sexual molestation that had turned your childhood into a nightmare? All for something you didn't do?"

"We're not arguing about Julio Lopez's motive," Sidone said, coming to Kennard's defense. "Sister Justice definitely had something in her eye during his trial. But that didn't give him the right to off a deputy marshal who was acting under the rule of law."

"The opposite of what Julio Lopez was doing," Kennard said.

Mercer had forgotten what it was like to be so fresh and so trusting in the rule of law.

"Okay," he said. "Putting aside man's natural instinct for self-preservation, what you both seem to be hung up on is the fact that the deputy marshal was just doin' his duty. Correct?"

They nodded.

"So you see where my defense is going?"

Sidone smiled. After a few seconds, so did Kennard. Points for them both.

CHAPTER TWO

Mercer's full dance card ordinarily kept him from volunteering for pro bono work but Julio Lopez's situation had intrigued him the moment C.W. Hansborough, the firm's senior partner, mentioned it during a briefing meeting.

The accused, with his tragic history, was the sort of system-battered client Mercer had in mind when he turned in his deputy district attorney ID and moved to the other side of the courtroom. And he was eager for a genuine challenge.

In his three years at Carter and Hansborough, he had been the attorney of record on that many murder trials. His first had been the most difficult—the defense of a reputed racist LAPD vice detective accused of slaying a black narcotics dealer. By comparison, the others had nearly qualified as slam-dunks, requiring only a minimal effort to tear apart cases hastily constructed by overworked or, in one instance, incompetent prosecutors.

Mercer was too young and too ambitious to stroll when he could run. And Elena Howard, the prosecutor assigned to the trial, was guaranteed to keep him on his toes. Thanks to an unblemished track record, she was considered a rising star in the D.A.'s office. With her dark skin, straightened hair, sharp protruding cheekbones and eyes set unusually wide apart, she resembled a sleek panther. She moved like a panther, too, with a grace that suggested languorous assurance, as if considerable power and speed were being purposely held in check but could be unleashed at any moment. She shared another trait with the jungle cat: a ruthless dedication to the job at hand.

Her case was essentially as Mercer's two associates had described: Lopez, a convicted murderer, had brutally slain the officer of the law assigned to apprehend him. The fact that Lopez's conviction had been overturned had no bearing on the act, since neither participant had been aware of it.

In the few weeks since the trial had begun, Mercer had chipped away at the prosecutor's case without doing any substantial damage. In his cross-examination of the investigating officers, he had underlined the fact that his client had turned himself in. He pushed the coroner, Dr. Ann Fugitsu, into admitting that the victim's braincase bone had been unusually fragile, a so-called eggshell cranium.

Elena Howard had put Antonio Fuego, a coworker of Lopez's at his late stepfather's bodega, on the stand, primarily to testify to the accused's quick and violent temper and general lack of character. Fuego had stated that Lopez had been a member of a local Hispanic gang, a charge the prosecutor also had mentioned during her opening statement.

Lopez had explained to Mercer that he'd grown up with and been close friends with gangstas—that was part of living in East L.A.—but he had never been a member of a gang, nor had he participated in any gangland activity.

Mercer had pushed that point in his cross-examination of Fuego, actually getting the witness to recant his earlier claim.

As an afterthought, he'd asked Fuego when he'd learned that Lopez had been officially declared innocent of his stepfather's murder.

"It was on the news in the kitchen at dinnertime," Fuego had said. "Six o'clock. Seven."

"Do you find it odd that by ten o'clock that night, the news still hadn't reached Deputy Marshal Kinderman and his partner?"

Fuego blinked and looked at Elena Howard, who by then was on her feet with an objection.

Baby steps.

But he was getting ready to make a major leap. The victim's partner, Deputy Marshal James Hubble, had taken the stand the previous day. Elena Howard had moved him slowly through Lopez's escape, through his and Kinderman's attempts to pick up the trail, to Kinderman's discovery of the supposed alien using a name similar to one in a comic book they'd found among Lopez's effects.

Mercer assumed that the deputy D.A. would spend the afternoon eliciting Hubble's detailed description of the events that took place on the night of the fatality.

Then it would be Mercer's turn.

When he and the associates arrived at courtroom five, Lopez was already seated at the defense table, his posture good, his eyes bright. He looked like a man without a worry in the world. These would be positive signs to put before a jury in most murder trials. But in this one, where the accused had already copped to his participation in a death by violence, they suggested arrogance, disdain, and, worse yet, a serious lack of empathy for the family, friends, and associates of Deputy Marshal Kinderman.

"Afternoon, Julio," Mercer said, taking his seat beside his young client.

Lopez nodded.

"You look like you're daring the jury to put your ass away," Mercer whispered.

"They'll do what they want. I can't be anything but what I am." He frowned. "The Kindermans are here, right? I can feel 'em on the back of my neck."

"They're here." Mercer had seen the late deputy marshal's wife and his teenage children sitting in the first row. Hoping for what? he wondered. Vengeance? They might have to settle for justice.

Or what the jury considered justice.

He looked at Lopez's peers. The jury members seemed to have enjoyed their lunch, except for the show business agent who, ever since his buzzing cellular had been confiscated by a sheriff, appeared to be suffering from separation anxiety. Several others were yawning. The middle-aged assistant pharmacist from Silver Lake polished her glasses idly. The parking lot attendant in the muscle shirt picked his nose with a couldn't-care-less 'tude that Mercer halfway envied. The county had recently changed its rules regarding jury duty, disallowing most excuses from serving. But, as far as Mercer could tell, there had been no discernable upswing in either quality or quantity.

The yawning, polishing, and nose-picking ceased with the arrival of Judge Elizabeth Beaudry, an overweight but not unhandsome woman at the border of middle age who wore her gray hair in a bun that would have looked old-fashioned during World War II. Her judicial manner was old-fashioned, too—impartial, tolerant, and smart.

Without much preamble, she jumpstarted the proceedings, with Deputy U.S. Marshal James Hubble returning to the witness chair.

Hubble moved with the hesitancy of a man who had tried once to exceed his limitations and would never make that mistake again. His flat, pale face conveyed permanent self-doubt. The lid of one watery blue eye drooped a little. Hastily combed, dank brown hair was dignified by a supreme cowlick at the crown, probably the result of day-long hat wear. Ditto the raw red stripe across his forehead. His uniform, though freshly pressed, seemed at odds with his slumped body.

"Deputy Hubble, before lunch, you were telling us about your arrival at the warehouse in San Pedro," Elena Howard said. Her velvety purr of a voice underscored her feline appearance. "Would you describe the events as you remember them?"

Hubble slapped his chest pockets, looked momentarily overwhelmed. Then he ducked a long-fingered hand into the pocket of his trousers and withdrew a flat notepad.

Judge Beaudry regarded him skeptically as he searched the notepad for a specific page, found it, and nodded as if he'd won a personal battle with himself. He took a deep breath and released it in a long, noisy hiss. "Before I get into the specifics, I'd like to make a statement," he said in an unexpectedly rich, well-modulated baritone. "Can I do that?"

The only sign of Elena Howard's surprise and possible annoyance at this request was a second's hesitation. "Please," she said.

"It was Tom Kinderman, and Tom alone, who located the accused. It was a hell . . . a remarkable job of tracking because Lopez covered his trail so completely." Hubble stared at the Kinderman family. Then he blinked, dropped his eyes and added, "I just wanted to get this in the record. Tom was one of the best lawmen I have ever seen in action. His death is a great loss, not only to his friends and family, but to everyone who knew him."

The comment had absolutely no relevance to the trial and it certainly did Lopez no favors, but objecting to it would give it weight and probably turn the jury against Mercer. So he bit his tongue and wondered why Hubble felt it necessary to lie about his feelings for his partner.

"On the evening of January ninth of this year, at approximately seven-fifteen," Hubble said, consulting his notes, "Tom—Deputy Marshal Kinderman—and I, were following a lead that we hoped would result in the capture of . . . Mr. Lopez." He gestured toward Mercer's client with his chin, keeping his eyes averted.

"You went to the East Channel docks," Elena Howard said, moving him along.

"Yes. At about"—he drew the notepad closer—"eight-forty, we arrived at . . . the East Bay warehouses just off San Pedro Road. A foreman informed us that Luis Gordo, the name he—Mr. Lopez—was using at the time, was just finishing up at Building Four.

"We got a fix on him from the entrance, made sure he was our man. Then we went out to the vehicle . . . and waited."

"Why wait?" Elena Howard asked. "Why not just arrest him?"

Hubble cleared his throat nervously. "Deputy Marshal Kinderman thought it would be better if we, ah, approached him when he was alone."

"Because he might pose a danger to the other workers?"

"Leading the witness, Your Honor."

The judge sustained Mercer's objection and Elena Howard reworked the question. "Deputy Marshal, can you tell us why you waited for Mr. Lopez to be alone for the arrest?"

"We, ah . . . sort of like you said. We didn't want to possibly involve the other workers."

"You and Marshal Kinderman have to wait long?"

"Maybe fifteen minutes. Lopez's team went off the clock at nine. They punched out and headed for a parking lot a ways down the road. We were worried Lopez might be getting a lift, but, judging from how they were grouped walking and talking, he was a loner.

"Turns out he didn't even have a car. He kept walking along San Pedro. There's this vacant warehouse that's got walkways some people use as a shortcut to the bus stop over on Harbor Boulevard.

"We were on foot. Tom—Deputy Marshal Kinderman—whispered for me to follow Lopez. He was gonna get ahead of him by double-timing it down the walk on the other side of the warehouse. We'd have him bottled up and could close in."

"But that didn't work."

"No," Hubble said, lowering his eyes again.

"Describe what happened for us."

"The defendant picked up a lead pipe and hit Tom with it."

"Mr. Lopez has claimed that Marshal Kinderman failed to identify himself," Elena purred. "Is that your recollection?"

"No, ma'am. Tom ID'ed himself."

"The accused would have recognized him, in any case. Correct?"

Hubble nodded and had to be reminded to reply vocally for the court record.

"What happened after Marshal Kinderman was attacked?"

Mercer objected to "attacked."

"I'm not sure what word defense counsel would prefer," Elena Howard said. "Assaulted? Beaten? Murdered?"

"Your Honor," Mercer said to the judge, "if Ms. Howard is asking, I'd say 'stopped' would work for me. Mr. Lopez *stopped* the deputy marshal from shooting him."

"Point made. Continue, Ms. Howard," Judge Beaudry said.

"After Marshal Kinderman fell to the ground, *mortally wounded,* what happened?"

"The accused ran away."

"You didn't try to stop him?"

"I was more concerned about Tom."

"Deputy Marshal Kinderman died in your arms, did he not?"

"Yeah." The witness's eyes flicked in the direction of the Kinderman family.

"Thank you, Deputy Marshal Hubble," the prosecutor said and glided to her chair. She smiled at Mercer and purred, "Your witness, counselor."

CHAPTER THREE

Mercer stood. He took time buttoning his jacket and adjusting his tie, all the while concentrating on the yellow legal pad on the tabletop as if it contained the secrets of the universe. Actually, the only things on it were a crude caricature of Hubble and a bunch of doodled arrows.

When he'd tested the patience of judge and jury as much as he dared, he strode purposefully toward the man in the witness chair, studying him like an insect on a pin.

Then he grinned. "How you doin', Deputy? Feeling okay today?"

Hubble frowned. "I guess, considering the circumstances."

Mercer's face shifted into seriousness. "It must be painful, recalling these events."

Hubble said nothing.

"I was very impressed by your comment about Deputy Marshal Kinderman's excellence as a lawman. How'd you put it? One of the best lawmen you'd ever seen?"

"Tom was . . . the best," Hubble said.

Mercer nodded. "So I was wondering: why had you put in for a new partner?"

Hubble blinked. "Wha-what makes you think I did?"

Mercer walked briskly to the defense table, pulled a sheet of paper from his briefcase, and carried it to the witness. "This look familiar?" he asked.

Hubble squinted at the Xeroxed page.

"I object, your honor," Elena Howard said. "If this is new evidence—"

"I hadn't planned on putting it into evidence, Your Honor," Mercer said. "Just a memory jogger."

"Might I see it?" Judge Beaudry asked.

Mercer complied. The judge glanced at the page and returned it. "Please proceed."

"Would you describe the contents of this letter for Ms. Howard and the jury?" Mercer asked Hubble.

Mercer held the paper out, but Hubble didn't bother taking it. He said, "It's my request for a new partner."

Elena Howard would not be denied. "Since Mr. Early admits the request isn't evidence, then I object to this line of questioning as irrelevant."

"It goes to the character of this witness, Your Honor," Mercer said. "Just a little while ago, Deputy Hubble was telling us under oath how fond he was of his late partner. Now it seems he didn't want to work with him."

"I'll overrule Ms. Howard's objection, Mr. Early. But don't take that as a signal to spend the rest of the afternoon on the subject."

"Thank you, Your Honor. Deputy, was there a problem between you and Deputy Marshal Kinderman?"

"Nothing specific."

"Reason I ask, the date on your request is not that long after my client managed to take leave of you and Deputy Kinderman at that rest room. Only natural for me to wonder if the one thing had anything to do with the other."

Hubble said nothing.

"Did it?"

"Tom and I had been partners for almost seven years," Hubble said. "I just . . . I wanted a change."

Mercer looked at the man shifting on his chair and experienced the feeling a poker player gets when he knows he holds a pat hand. "Deputy, are you familiar with a Ms. Coral Redmann?"

All color fled Hubble's face, even the red stripe from his hatband. Mercer knew precisely what was going though his whirring brain. Coral Redmann was a hooker Hubble visited at least twice a week. The deputy marshal was a man who engaged in pillow talk. About his wife. About his job. About his partner.

Hubble licked his lips and ignored the Redmann question in favor of the previous one. “Tom took a lot of heat about losing the prisoner. We both did. But he . . . the thing is, he had colitis. This problem with his colon.”

Carter and Hansborough’s chief investigator, Lonny Hootkins, had turned up Redmann, who, for a paltry five grand, had emptied the Hubble portion of her memory bank. Aside from the deputy marshal’s fondness for what she called “side-saddle sex,” the key bit of information she passed on was that his partner had been driving him crazy with his obsession to find and recapture Lopez. Mercer had been cross-examining Hubble with the confidence of a lawyer who knew precisely where he was headed. But this colitis business was coming from left field, giving his own bowels a little tweak.

“Deputy, could we stay on subject,” he said. “Tom Kinderman’s obsessive behavior.”

“You asked me and I’m trying to tell you,” Hubble said. “He had colitis. That’s why, when we were transporting your client to Wayside, Tom went along with his complaint about needing a toilet. When he found out Mr. Lopez was playing us, he took it very personal.

“I tried telling him Mr. Lopez had no way of knowing about the colitis, but it was like . . . I don’t know. He wouldn’t listen to reason. He really went off on it.”

“Your Honor,” Elena Howard said, “if Mr. Early is trying to establish that Deputy Marshal Hubble may have been a bit exuberant in his praise of his fallen colleague, had in fact wanted to dissolve the partnership, I am willing to stipulate to that fact. Can we now move on to something more substantial?”

Judge Beaudry smiled at that. “Mr. Early?”

“My client’s statement is that he acted out of self-defense, Your Honor. It would seem to me that the motivation and mental attitude of Deputy Marshal Kinderman would be considered substantial evidence.”

“Objection overruled.”

“Deputy, could you give us a clearer understanding of what you meant by saying Deputy Marshal Kinderman ‘went off on it’?”

“I don’t mean to imply he was loony or anything. He was under a lot of pressure. We both were. But we were carrying a full case load and he was so hung up on Lopez, the other work wasn't getting done. We had a . . . an argument about priorities. It got so, if you didn't agree with Tom one hundred percent, he thought you were being disloyal."

"By priorities you mean he was spending too much time obsessing about my client?"

"I guess."

Mercer strode to the defense table, where he deposited the white sheet.

Returning to the witness, he said, "According to logs and records, attempts to notify you and Deputy Marshal Kinderman of my client's exoneration began at three that afternoon and continued on until it was assumed you'd both gone off duty. Your radio was off. You weren't answering your cell phones. Why was that, Deputy?"

"We . . . Tom decided we should run silent. We had a job to do. He didn't want to get . . . distracted."

"Was this *running silent* your usual routine?"

"Not usual, but we'd done it before."

"What about failing to inform anyone at your headquarters that you had located a wanted man and were planning an arrest? Had you done that before?"

"No." Hubble could no longer meet his eyes. He seemed to be concentrating somewhere in the middle of Mercer's red tie.

"Your decision or Deputy Marshal Kinderman's?"

Hubble hesitated and with an expression of self-disgust said, "His."

It was time to drive the spike into the prosecution's case. Mercer hoped he wouldn't hit his thumb. "In your opinion," he said, "did Deputy Marshal Kinderman have knowledge of my client's exoneration before you and he approached him that night?"

The courtroom was so silent Mercer could hear footsteps along the hall outside, then the scrape of a chair being moved back and Elena Howard's voice. "Objection, Your Honor. Any answer would be hearsay."

"I asked for the witness's opinion, Your Honor. The opinion of a man who'd partnered with Deputy Marshal Kinderman for seven years."

"Overruled. Please answer the question, Deputy Hubble."

"I . . . yeah, he knew. We both did."

Suddenly there was a buzzing throughout the courtroom. Or maybe it was just in Mercer's head.

"What were you thinking?" he asked. "If he knew my client was no longer a fugitive, why go out to the docks?"

"You got to understand: Tom devoted months to finding Mr. Lopez. He'd put everything else on hold—his work, his . . . family. Then, just when all that effort and time was about to pay off, we hear that the guy's off the hook. It was like they changed the rules in the middle of the game.

"Worse than that. Lopez had made us look like donkeys. Tom said we couldn't just bend over for the guy. We decided to give him a scare. Shake him up a little."

"You did that, all right," Mercer said. "So what you're telling us is when you and Deputy Marshal Kinderman went after my client that night, it wasn't in any official capacity. You were just two armed dudes out for payback."

"We weren't gonna hurt him. Just goof on him a little."

"My client didn't know that. And, in point of fact, sir, you don't know what was in Deputy Kinderman's mind either. That night, he was a rogue lawman with a gun in his hand—"

He was cut off by Elena Howard's objection. "If Mr. Early wants to fantasize about the late Deputy Marshal Kinderman's motives, let him do it in his closing statement."

Judge Beaudry agreed.

Hubble sat slumped and broken in the witness chair, but Mercer was not moved. "Deputy Hubble, on the night of your partner's death, did you lie to the investigating officers about your motive for approaching my client?"

"I . . . no. They assumed . . . I just didn't correct them."

"And when my client turned himself in and was put back in prison, you still didn't correct the assumption that you and Deputy Marshal Kinderman had been acting in an official capacity?"

"No. I didn't."

Mercer turned to the judge. "I'm finished here, Your Honor."

Elena Howard seemed to have lost none of her self-confidence. "Deputy Marshal Hubble, to get back to the purpose of this trial, I ask you again, did Deputy Marshal Kinderman identify himself to the accused?"

"Yes."

"To your knowledge, did the accused believe Deputy Marshal Kinderman was there to arrest him as a fugitive from justice?"

"Objection, Your Honor," Mercer said. "Deputy Marshal Hubble has no way of knowing what was in my client's mind."

"Objection sustained."

"Deputy Marshal, did your partner ever say or even imply anything that would lead you to think he meant to physically harm Mr. Lopez?"

"No ma'am."

"Did *you* mean to physically harm Mr. Lopez?"

"No way."

"Did you witness the accused wield the blow that ended Deputy Marshal Kinderman's life?"

"Yes."

"Did you see or hear anything that could have provoked the accused's violent attack?"

Hubble hesitated for only a second, then said, "No."

"Thank you, Deputy Marshal," the prosecutor said and walked briskly to her chair.

Mercer had only one final question for the deputy. "If you were walking down a dark path and a man suddenly appeared with a gun in his hand, would you consider that sufficient provocation for defensive action?"

"Tom—"

"Answer yes or no, please."

"But—"

"Yes or no."

"Yes."

Mercer returned to his seat. He watched Deputy Marshal Hubble slink from the courtroom toward a dismal future. *Well-earned,* he thought.

"Ms. Howard, you may call your next witness," the judge said.

"I've no more witnesses, Your Honor. The prosecution rests."

"Mr. Early, are you ready to call your first witness?"

"Actually, Your Honor," Mercer said, "we feel Mr. Lopez has spent enough time behind bars for an innocent man. Therefore, the defense rests, with the hope we might move directly into closing statements. Assuming Ms. Howard is prepared."

Elena Howard graced him with a brief feline smile and turned to the bench. "The prosecution is ready, Your Honor."

Without a moment's hesitation, she approached the jury. "You must clear your mind of all the mumbo jumbo Mr. Early has been spreading in a vain attempt to excuse his client's violent act of murder. There is no excuse for murder.

"Whatever Deputy Marshal Kinderman's motives may have been that night, Mr. Lopez, by his own admission in the official record of his police interrogation, truly believed the deputy marshal was there to arrest him. That said, he had three alternatives at his disposal. He could have surrendered himself. He did not. He could have tried to run. He did not. Instead, he made the third choice: he stood his ground. He picked up a lead pipe and used it to crush the skull of a deputy U.S. marshal.

"Mr. Early, attempting to defend the indefensible, has grasped at a drifting straw—the possibility that Deputy Marshal Kinderman's motives for confronting his client may not have been pure. Well, we will never know for certain what the deputy marshal's motives may have been. Does this pose a problem for you? Not at all. Since the deputy marshal's motives were unknown to the accused, they can have no legal bearing on this case.

"Mr. Lopez's motives are very much on point, however. His actions speak for themselves. If the accused honestly believed he was in danger, wouldn't he have run instead of taking the time to pick up a weapon and wield it? No, the attack on Marshal Kinderman was an aggressive act, not a defensive one. The fact that the marshal did not survive it, while Mr. Lopez is in this courtroom today, hale and healthy, should be all the proof you need to find him guilty as charged."

She'd spoken for not more than a few minutes, but she'd made an impression on the jury. Hell, she'd made an impression on Mercer. Still, as he looked into a dozen relatively alert faces, he saw some confusion. Confusion was good. It was a first cousin to doubt. And doubt of course was Julio Lopez's ticket to freedom.

"Ms. Howard has told you that there is no excuse for murder," Mercer began. "This is an indisputable fact. But it's a fact that is meaningless in this case, since the prosecution has neglected to prove that what my client did was murder.

"So let's look at a few facts that should help you make some justice. Fact one: Julio Lopez was proven innocent of murdering his abusive stepfather. What's that got to do with Deputy Marshal Kinderman's death? Well, please note I did not say he was *found* innocent. A jury, not as alert or discerning as yourselves, found him guilty. Why? Because they believed that the pain and humiliation his stepfather had put him through should have been enough to push him into murder. But it wasn't. Even though Julio Lopez suffered in a way most of us cannot comprehend, he did not so much as raise his hand against the man who mistreated him so badly. Why? Because Julio Lopez is not a violent man. Because Julio Lopez is not a murderer.

"Fact number two: we have it on the word of Deputy Marshal Tom Kinderman's partner of seven years that he had become obsessed with finding and recapturing my client. So obsessed that when he learned that Julio Lopez's conviction had been overturned, that Julio was, in fact, an innocent man no longer subject to his jurisdiction, he still insisted on pursuing and harassing my client.

"Fact number three: fully aware of Julio Lopez's innocence, and acting far outside the law, Deputy Marshal Kinderman surprised my client on a darkened walkway with a gun in his hand. He knew my client was a man as innocent as you or I and still he approached him with a drawn, fully loaded gun. Why? Did he, in his obsession, intend to use it on my client? We only know what he told Deputy Marshal Hubble, that he wanted to frighten my client. To 'shake him up.'

"Well, he did shake Julio Lopez up. As any normal person would have been shaken under those circumstances. Julio Lopez saw a figure leap from the shadows pointing a gun at him. Perhaps the deputy marshal identified himself. Words shouted at such a moment tend more to confuse than enlighten. My client didn't want to die. He grabbed the closest weapon he could find—a piece of pipe—and struck out at his attacker.

"Even then, he did not strike to kill. There was no way he could have known that Deputy Marshal Kinderman's skull was paper thin, that one blow would prove fatal. Just as there was no way he could have known that Deputy Marshal Kinderman was only trying to 'shake him up.'

"All of these facts lead to only one possible conclusion: Julio Lopez was not trying to kill. He was trying to survive."

"What happened to the plan to put Lopez on the stand?" Kennard Haines asked as Mercer drove the two associates to the Carter and Hansborough building on Wilshire Boulevard.

"The same thing that happened to the plan to put on the character witnesses," Mercer said.

"And the expert on blunt head trauma," Sidone Evans said.

"Him, too," Mercer said. "The thing that happened was Deputy Hubble. The man made our case. Least I think he did."

"But not to put on even one witness . . ."

"You've got to be a little flexible, Kennard," Mercer said. "Usually, you want to save your best witness for last. Leave the jury with that testimony fresh in their minds. Hubble turned out to be better than any of the witnesses we had lined up."

"I think it would have helped for the jury to hear our client," Sidone said.

"Maybe," Mercer agreed. "But Julio wasn't acting exactly jury-friendly today. And Elena Howard wasn't about to let him slide."

"I think it may have made him more sympathetic," she said, "if he'd been able to tell them that, instead of identifying himself, Kinderman was screaming and cursing and calling him a spic."

Before Mercer could reply, Kennard said, "I see the problem there. We want the jury to think Lopez was frightened, not angry."

Mercer smiled. "You guys seem to—"

He was interrupted by the beep of his cellular.

As he withdrew it, checked the number, and flipped it open, he noticed he was only a block away from the office. He listened for a few seconds and told them, "Jury's in. Want me to drop you off at the firm?"

They didn't.

CHAPTER FOUR

One of Carter and Hansborough's supermodel-wannabe receptionists was still on duty at a few minutes after 6 p.m. when the trio finally made it back to the offices on the 42nd floor. Her name was Ondine and she was one of the few black women Mercer had ever seen beautiful enough to carry off blond hair—or maybe a blond wig, he was never sure about such things.

She paused in her personal phone call long enough to tell him that senior partner C.W. Hansborough wanted to see him immediately in the conference room.

The associates moved off to their tiny rooms, where only a year before Mercer had been hanging his diploma. Now he headed for the partners' wing where he occupied a large airy space that had once served as the office of a co-founder of the firm, the late Robert H. Carter.

Carter's son and namesake, commonly referred to as Bobby, the firm's other senior partner, was taking time off following an abortive run for political office. His temporary retirement meant that Hansborough had become quite dependant on Mercer, a fact not overlooked by the other junior partners.

All of them were gathered in the conference room. C.W. was at the head of the table. The others occupied leather and chrome chairs to his left and right—the sleek Eddie Baraca; Wally Wallace, overweight and sweating through his expensive Boss jacket; the nakedly ambitious Joe Wexstead; and Devon Olander, a slightly flashy thirty-something recent addition to the firm, who was an expert on divorce, spousal abuse, child custody, and other legal matters of the heartbroken. She was also, according to water cooler rumor, sharing C.W.'s four-poster.

Conversation stopped when Mercer entered the room. C.W. indicated that he should take the empty chair at the end of the table. "Congratulations on Lopez," the senior partner said.

"Good thing you scored, Mercer," Wexstead said. "Eight weeks seems a mighty long time to spend pro bono."

"Not like we aren't getting paid," Mercer said. "But maybe we should take a vote. Find out how many of you feel I've been fritterin' away the firm's hours."

"A win is still a win," Devon Olander said, "even if it is pro bono."

"I'm not sure if that'd be a 'yes' vote or not. Anyway, the point's moot and Julio Lopez is free as a bird."

"And you need work," C.W. said, sliding one of the firm's sea-green folders down the length of the table to him.

The typed label read: NUNEZ, ELDON. Under the name was a notation: LAPD.

Mercer recognized the name. Two nights before, a pair of LAPD officers, responding to a report of a gunshot, entered an apartment on Arabella Street in West Hollywood and found fellow officer Eldon Nunez in a state of shock seated near the body of his gay lover, an architect named Landers Pope.

Someone had fired off a cap into Pope's noggin, probably as he slept. Since Nunez was at the scene, mentally broken, chewing on the barrel of what turned out to be the murder weapon, he was the most likely suspect.

According to every newscast Mercer had heard or seen, Nunez had handed his brothers in blue the gun, butt first, muttering, "I couldn't do it. I tried but it was no use. He wouldn't let me."

The television talking heads, all mouth and no hard news, had had a field day speculating on what Nunez had been trying to say. Was he bemoaning his inability to kill himself after blowing away his life partner? Or could he have been suggesting that he had tried and failed to stop an unknown killer from escaping?

Adding to the murder's newsworthiness was the fact

that the victim was the godson of District Attorney Dana Lowery, a universally unloved despot whose angular figure, white-streaked jet black hair, and abrasive personality had prompted the deputies and clerks in her office to refer to her as "Cruella."

It had been part of Lowery lore that Pope had been the only human being to witness her soft and gentle side. As she notified the media shortly after the announcement of the murder, "Landers was more a son than a godson. I can assure the people of Los Angeles: his murderer will be punished to the full limit of the law."

"You didn't want this jewel?" Mercer asked Eddie Baraca, the firm's other criminal lawyer.

Eddie gave him a shark's grin. "I can barely lift my briefcase now. And, as Lopez proved once again, Mercer, you are the Big Dawg when it comes to lost causes."

"Damn right," Mercer said. "A gay black non *compos mentis* cop who stands accused of popping a cap in the golden godchild of one of the most powerful and vindictive biatches in the county, that's par for the course for Mercer Early."

Wally Wallace, the only one in the room who didn't pick up on the sarcasm in Mercer's voice said, "Right on, brother."

"You don't want to make light of this, Mercer," Joe Wexstead warned in his singsong voice. "It'll be our first chance to show the Police Officers Guild what this firm is made of."

Leave it to Joe to remind him that his defense of Officer Nunez would be scrutinized by POG, which had recently awarded Carter and Hansborough a lucrative contract to handle a large portion of the legal needs of its members.

"POG won't be expecting miracles," C.W. said. "But it would be nice if we gave them one, right off the bat."

"Why don't I have a sit-down with Officer Nunez," Mercer said, "before we start talking miracles?"

"Quite right."

"I want to use Sidone and Kennard on this."

"I see no problem with that," C.W. said.

"You know how to pick 'em, Mercer," Wexstead said. "That Sidone is finer than frog hair. Wouldn't mind putting in some late nights with her, myself."

Mercer opened his mouth to tell Joe what he thought of him, but even though one word could have done the job, he was too weary to bother. He turned to C.W. "If you can spare me here, I'd like to catch 'em before they leave and get 'em started. I'll be seeing Nunez in the morning."

"Go," C.W. said.

Closing the door to the conference room, Mercer heard Wexstead telling the others, "That man sure knows how to play the angles. Our lovely D.A. starts sharpening her knife for him, it'll be handy having a friend in the White House."

It took him a second to realize that the weasel was talking about Kennard's father. Calling him a friend was a stretch.

Still, if push came to shove, having the son of Kennard Haines, Sr., at his table surely wouldn't hurt.

DAY 2

WEDNESDAY, JUNE 16

CHAPTER FIVE

The appealing possibility that his new client might not have murdered Landers Pope disappeared early the next morning, as soon as the prison guard led Eldon Nunez into the room. It was a small space, but Nunez, an inch or two taller than the six-foot-one lawyer and maybe fifty pounds heavier in his bright orange jumpsuit, closed it in even more.

He entered cautiously, his large bald head twisting from side to side, rolling eyes taking in every crevice. Mercer stood and offered a hand. "Officer Nunez, my name is—"

"I killed 'im," his client interrupted him to say. "I killed Land." He ignored the lawyer's extended hand.

Mercer looked anxiously at the guard.

"I'll be right outside, counselor," the guard said, grinning. "Lemme know when you get tired of hearing your client confess. He's been doing it ever since he got here."

"Thanks," Mercer said through clenched teeth as the guard made his exit.

"I killed 'im," Nunez said. He took a few steps backward until he was leaning against the wall that separated the room from the corridor.

"Why don't we sit down and you can tell me all about it," Mercer said.

"I'll stand." The big man moved in twitches, almost like an automaton. "Comfort makes you careless."

Mercer shrugged and perched on the metal table. He

told Nunez his name and that he would be representing him in court. "Okay if I call you Eldon?"

"I saved Land," the prisoner said.

"I'll take that as a yes. So, Eldon, tell me about saving Land. That's Landers Pope, right?"

"I couldn't save myself. He wouldn't let me. But that's fine. I'll be saved. Not as nasty as I thought."

"Here's a plan, Eldon. Why don't we take it one idea at a time? That all right?"

"I killed Land."

"Since that seems to be a given, let's start there. Tell me about that night."

"Which night?"

"The night you killed Land."

"That's not where to start. We start with the other night."

"Okay. What night would that be?"

"The night the music died." Nunez smiled. " 'Bye, bye, Miss American Pie.' "

Mercer had a vague memory of the song, but he had no idea what significance it had for Nunez.

"Death is like a virus," Nunez said, sobering. "One person dies, then another two, then another four . . ."

He suddenly straightened, pressed back against the wall, his face turned toward the door. A few seconds later, Mercer heard the faint sound of footsteps in the corridor.

"Why don't you come on over and sit down?"

"I'll talk from here."

"Okay. Tell me about the night you killed Land."

"That night. Okay." Nunez's face softened. His skin was the color of milk coffee, but the orange jumpsuit made it look darker. "We had us a nice dinner alone at Hugo's. Land's idea. I was against it. Too many people. Too many strangers. One li'l bomb can bring a place down, you know. I saw pictures of this bar in Tel Aviv." He shivered. "And the viruses . . . Did you know him?"

"Landers Pope?"

"No. The other."

"What other?"

Nunez went quiet.

After a seemingly endless period of silence, Mercer said, "You were saying you and Land had dinner at Hugo's. Then . . . ?"

"I didn't want to go. I knew the danger. I'd seen the danger. But Land had been so good to me, trying to make me feel better the last few weeks when it got so bad I thought I'd lose my mind."

"You were sick?" Mercer asked.

Nunez smiled, but it was not the kind that warmed a room. "I was . . . suffering from too much knowledge."

"About what?"

"Any pro bodyguard will tell you. If somebody's determined enough, they will get to you."

Mercer was beginning to feel breathless trying to follow his client's rapidly shifting thoughts. "Who wants to get to you?"

Nunez grinned again and winked. "You, maybe."

"I'm your lawyer, Eldon. I'm on your side."

"What would you say if you weren't? Doesn't matter. I don't need a lawyer. I'm guilty, brother. Ask anybody."

"I'll leave that to the D.A. What did you mean you *saved* Land?"

The prisoner's yellowed eyes started to fill. "Couldn't save myself."

It was like chasing a fly that could move in any direction. "By 'save,' you mean 'kill'? You couldn't kill yourself?"

"Don't mess with my mind, brother. Save me. You can do it."

"You saying you want me to kill you?"

"Don't want you to do nothing. Do nothing and save me."

"I don't get it, Eldon," Mercer said.

"The world is a shit hole," Nunez said, nodding now as if responding to some beat only he heard. "Jesus put us here for a reason. Put Deadeye Dick here to save the metal man."

"Who's Deadeye Dick? You?"

"Shuteye Dick, that's me."

"And the metal man? Land?"

"Wrong question. No answer."

"Tell me the right question."

"Questions don't matter. God put me here to save Land. Put you here to save me. 'Less you lyin' to me."

"I want to save you," Mercer said. "That's why I'm here."

"Wastin' your time and mine *here*. Jesus says time is precious. So much evil out there. Fighting. Wars. Terrorist attack. The battle for the world has been lost to Satan's hoard. People behave like pigs. The end is coming."

Great, Mercer thought. On top of everything else, the client was a doomsday preacher. "Was Land sick? Is that how you saved him by killing him?"

"Sick? You talking about AIDS?" Nunez scowled. "My boy wasn't sick, fool. I'm not sick. The fucking world is sick."

"You get no argument from me on the state of the world, Eldon. But there's not much we can do about that at the moment. Can we stay focused on the night Land died?"

Eldon Nunez's eyes glazed. He said nothing.

"Why did you kill him, Eldon?"

"Why do you have to ask me this question, when I've answered it a hundred times or more."

"Humor me."

"I did it to save him. Why else? I loved him."

"Save him from what?"

The prisoner's head dropped. "You not gonna be any help." He moved to the door and hit it flat-handed. "Lemme out."

Mercer heard the rattle of keys. "You said that 'he' stopped you from saving yourself. You're talking about Landers?"

"Nonononono." Nunez slapped the door again.

It opened; the guard stood there, looking a bit bemused. "You rang?" he asked Nunez.

"Who stopped you, Eldon?" Mercer asked.

Nunez paused at the door. "Only one crime God don't forgive, brother. I thought ever'body knew that, even smart-ass lawyers."

The guard gave Mercer a final don't-he-beat-all? head-shake and led the prisoner away.

CHAPTER

SIX

LAPD Chief of Staff John Gilroy stood at one of the windows in Police Chief Niles Ahern's office in Parker Center, staring down at the traffic and pedestrians six floors below. It reminded him of a scene from one of his favorite movies, *The Third Man*. The villain of the piece, World War II profiteer and murderer Harry Lime, played by Orson Welles, is on a Ferris wheel in war-torn Vienna with the hero of the film, Holly Martins, played by Joseph Cotten. Martins asks Lime how he could live with himself after selling watered penicillin to hospitals, and Lime points to the people in the amusement park down below, calling them "dots."

"If I said you could have twenty-thousand pounds for every dot that stops, would you really, old man, tell me to keep my money?" Lime asks. "Or would you calculate how many dots you could afford to spare—free of income tax ..."

The scene was intended to show how callous the character was. But John Gilroy thought that Lime's statement seemed to carry a degree of logic. He watched the dots down below—more like little windup toys, really—trailing along in front of the building. Twenty-thousand pounds in the postwar years would be worth what today? A hundred thousand dollars?

His musing was interrupted by the return of Chief Ahern from the crapper. The little man's face was ruddy and he smelled of bay rum. "Feel ten pounds lighter," he said. "Escobar not here yet?"

"It's a long walk from the end of the hall," Gilroy said sarcastically. "Want me to go fetch?"

Ahern gave him a wintry smile as he tucked himself behind his desk. "He's a big boy. He can find his way."

As Gilroy lowered his lanky frame into a comfortable leather chair, he saw the chief cock his head to one side, a gesture that could mean trouble. "You think his appointment was a mistake, John?"

"Not at all," Gilroy lied. He hadn't remained the little man's chief of staff for five years without knowing when to lie. "He's a bright guy. Record as clean as a hound's tooth."

"Kept a cool head and proved his leadership in some pretty hairy command areas," the chief said.

Gilroy nodded and let it go at that. In truth he felt that Eduardo Escobar, a man eleven years his junior, was an overly ambitious opportunist who'd understood early on how eager the Department had been to promote a man of his heritage and who now at only thirty-one fucking years old was an assistant chief. And breathing down his, Gilroy's, neck.

"Well, before our *amigo* gets here," the chief said, "anything new on the gangbanger front?"

Awhile back, at Gilroy's suggestion, the chief had made a loud public declaration of war on street gangs. Some of the more cynical members of the media thought the war might have been a ploy to shift attention away from yet another inappropriate, potentially disastrous show of force by the LAPD. Talk show pundits wondered if such a "war" would accomplish anything more than a few short-term arrests.

Four months later, it appeared as if the war was a good one. "Gang-related murders and bank robberies are way down," Gilroy told the chief. "Not much activity out there, and what there is, we've been mopping up. Things have been particularly quiet."

Chief Ahern nodded. "I'd love to read all the details in the paper one of these mornings. Let's not keep it a secret, huh?"

"Consider it done," Gilroy said.

"Any movement among the Jack-key-sus since that punk—Alamo or whatever the hell his name was—bought the farm?"

The chief's reference was to the recent death of Luis Almador, who'd been the leader of the militant Hispanic gang known as the Jaquecas. "All's quiet in Little Meh-hico," Gilroy said.

"Anything new on Alamo's death?"

"Almador." Gilroy knew better than to correct the little man, but it slipped out. Only thing to do was cover the mistake with information. "He was diagnosed with hepatitis C. Mother dying of cancer. His leadership being challenged by a punk they call Bolero. I might have taken that seven-story jump myself."

"Think maybe this Bolero pushed him?" the chief asked.

"Always that possibility."

"What do the investigators say?"

"I thought an investigation would be counterproductive. A gang leader gets murdered, he becomes a martyr and the gangstas get stirred up. A leader kills himself, it confuses the troops, fills 'em with self-doubt. Cools 'em down."

"Interesting theory," the chief said. "Well, if the Jack-key-sus are staying chilly, you definitely made the right move. But we are keeping an eye on this Bolero?"

"Of course," Gilroy said. He looked at his watch. "Should we reschedule this?"

Before the chief could answer, his assistant, Molly, buzzed him to announce the arrival of Eduardo Escobar.

The recently appointed special assistant entered the room gracefully, apologizing for keeping them waiting. He was a short man, about the size of the chief, but considerably more athletic. He had the poise, self-confidence, and smartly attired look of a young man on the move.

John Gilroy hated his guts.

He decided to do a little cage rattling. "Eddie, I understand there's some kind of problem with the convention."

Chief Ahern was suddenly on alert. "A problem with the IACP?" In just a few months, the LAPD and the LASO, the sheriff's office, would be co-hosting a conference of the International Association of Chiefs of Police, a world-class law enforcement event with more than twenty thousand members expected to attend.

"No problem," Escobar said. "A minor scheduling snafu. Joey Brooks at the Staples Center is a bit of a drama queen, wouldn't you say, John? He's a friend of yours, is he not?" He gave Gilroy what seemed like a genuine smile.

"Anyway he's all calmed down and everything's under control. You give me a job, Chief, it gets done."

"This goddamn convention's gotta go smooth as a baby's butt," the chief warned. "The whole world's gonna be watching."

"It'll run like clockwork. Is that the reason for this meeting? I thought we were here to discuss Nunez."

"Right." Chief Ahern's chickenlike head wobbled to face Gilroy. "What's going on there, John?"

"He's being represented by Carter and Hansborough."

"The black firm?" Ahern looked puzzled.

"They've got a contract with POG," Gilroy said.

"I know about the goddamned contract," the chief said. "I just don't know why they're using them on Nunez."

It took Gilroy a beat too long to figure out what the chief was asking. Escobar got it right away. "Officer Nunez is black," he said.

"Really? I'd'a thought otherwise."

Gilroy and Escobar exchanged glances in a rare moment of mutual agreement: the chief was something of an asshole.

But a dangerous one.

"John, you understand what my initial feelings were about the Nunez mess?"

"Yes."

"As I was telling John, I don't want this Nunez comin' off looking like a crazy man. We had a confab with that public affairs lieutenant. What's his name, John?"

"Rockland. Andy Rockland."

"Right. Lieutenant Rockland says the whole thing's a clusterfuck at best, but we've got to try and minimize the publicity fallout. Keep it all in line."

"Has anyone told this to the district attorney?" Escobar asked. "She's all over the news."

"Right. Mourning the loss of her dong-lickin' godson," the chief said. "Some loss. Like the world doesn't have enough fag interior decorators."

Gilroy and Escobar exchanged glances again.

"The broad has been told to zip it," the chief continued. "But she's a loose cannon. Always has been. Nothing we can do about that. But we can do something about Nunez."

"Any doubt he killed the D.A.'s godson?"

"Not from what I've heard," Gilroy said. "Every second sentence out of his mouth is a confession."

"So what exactly do you hope to do about him?"

"Like I told John, we sedate him. We drug him. I don't give a shit. I just don't want to see an LAPD officer actin' like a loony-bird in court."

"If he's that crazy, will there be a trial?"

"The D.A. seems hell bent on one," Gilroy said. "Frankly, at this point, considering the media interest, I don't see how it can be avoided."

"Then . . . ?"

"Our concern is that Officer Nunez's mental state may be, ah, *incorrectly* attributed to on-the-job conditions," Gilroy said. "Post-traumatic stress. The constant pressure of the work. All very negative stuff, as far as the force is concerned. Bad PR. Recruitment goes to hell. The rank and file starts stayin' home with headaches.

"Therefore, the murder was a crime of passion, of gay passion, if you will," the chief said. "Temporary insanity, prompted by jealousy. In other words, a personal crime, having everything to do with Officer Nunez's lifestyle and nothing to do with his occupation."

"Any evidence to back that up?" Escobar asked.

"The investigation is ongoing," Gilroy said. "Kerry Barnard from POG will be meeting with his lawyers later today."

"You sure Kerry's with us on this?" the chief asked. "He's gone against us in the past."

"He sees this as being a matter of morale, ergo pro rank-and-file."

"You go with him to C&H, make sure we're all on the same page. And John, I sure don't want any TVs in the god-damn courtroom. No cameras at all. As few press as we can get by with."

"It seems as if John has this pretty much in hand," Escobar said. "Did you have anything specific for me on this, Chief?"

Ahern blinked. "Oh no. I guess not," he said. "Thanks for dropping by, Eddie."

"No prob."

When the door had closed behind Assistant Chief Escobar, Ahern wagged a finger at Gilroy. "Dammit, John," he said in a half whisper as if he expected Escobar to be lurking just outside the door, "you shoulda informed me Nunez was black. I thought he was Mex."

Gilroy had assumed that with the news coverage, the video footage, the photos in the paper, the chief might have gotten the word. "I should have mentioned it," he said.

"It's the only reason I wanted Escobar here, to get a Mex viewpoint. But I couldn't hardly tell him that. I covered all right, didn't I?"

"Smooth as silk," Gilroy said.

CHAPTER SEVEN

"Your man may be a whack job now," Lonny Hootkins said, "but up till about a month ago, his brothers in blue at Midtown Division considered him a damn good officer."

Hootkins had been a damn good officer himself until, in a state of near-exhaustion after a foot chase and capture, he'd mumbled some sarcastic comment to a reporter about the then-Operations chief at Headquarters Bureau. Forced into early retirement, he'd opened a one-man detective agency where he established a reputation as a man of honor, a rarity in that line. Recently, he'd hired on at Carter and Hansborough as the firm's chief investigator.

Of average size and girth, with a frizz of white hair on an otherwise bald black pate and rimless glasses that gave him the deceptive appearance of somebody's peaceful stepfather, he leaned back in his chair and waited for the others in Mercer's office to ask the next question.

Sidone Evans was first up. "What turned Nunez?"

"Nobody knows, exactly. His old partner quit the force over a year ago and since then he's been cruising solo. So nobody at his division paid a hell of a lot of attention to him. No idea if something was eatin' on him."

"They know he was gay?" Mercer asked.

"I got the impression it was one of those don't ask, don't tell sort of deals, but everybody knew. Probably why he drove alone. I'll check in with the ex-partner. Tonight, I'll see what I can suss out at the Holbrook Inn. Midtown cops drift to the bar there, coming off duty."

"What about his relationship with the victim?" Kennard Haines asked. "Were they having problems?"

"We're looking into that, of course."

"And his upbringing?" Kennard said.

Hootkins grinned. "Whoa down, young man. I just got handed the job this morning. You didn't want me to go without breakfast?"

Kennard blinked and looked slightly embarrassed.

"I should have a pretty complete background on both client and vic by Monday," Hootkins said.

"So all we have now," Mercer said, "is that the client killed his lover to save him, whatever the hell that means."

"Sounds kinda Son-of-Sam-y," Sidone said.

"Not exactly," Kennard said. "David Berkowitz shot and killed strangers because he was told to by the devil. Eldon Nunez may be just as demented, but he had a specific target in mind. And it sounds as if he's a Christian lunatic, taking his orders from the Almighty."

"The first thing we've got to find out is just what his mental state is," Mercer said. "Melissa's got the shrink list and is setting up an exam. She's also arranging for faxes of the police reports and coroner's findings."

He faced the two associates. "Odds are we'll be using one of three pleas: insanity, temporary insanity, or diminished capacity. You understand the differences?"

"Insanity," Sidone said. "Severe stuff. No control. Can't distinguish reality from fantasy. Tony Perkins in *Psycho*."

"Temporary insanity," Kennard said. "Same as insanity only temporary. Can't think of a movie, but Harvey Milk and the Twinkie defense."

"Close," Mercer said. "I think the pitch on that one was that the Twinkie's sugar in Dan White's bloodstream diminished his capacity. But dim cap and temp insanity are in the same ballpark. Anyway, you two know what you'll be doing for a while?"

"Just a guess," Sidone said, "but we'll probably be reading insanity, dim cap, and temp insanity case histories until our eyes pop out."

"The firm will pay for better glasses if you need 'em," Mercer said.

"You figure the client's gonna be *compos mentis* enough to sit through a trial?" Hootkins asked.

"I'll be disappointed if he is," Mercer said.

An hour later, he was sitting in C.W. Hansborough's multiwindowed corner office, the high-ceilinged room bathed in evening amber light, listening to LAPD Chief of Staff John Gilroy explain why an insanity plea would be damaging to the Department, while Police Officers Guild rep Kerry Barnard sat in silent affirmation.

Gilroy's feeling was that such a plea would suggest to the public that the LAPD placed too high a demand on its officers.

"We would very much prefer—and I think Kerry is with us on this—that you consider using *temporary* insanity."

"Officer Nunez suffered a break," Mercer said. "A snap. Shot Mr. Pope. Then sorta snapped back."

"That's exactly what I mean."

"The only problem I've got with that," Mercer said, "is I spent some time with Officer Nunez this morning, and there has been no snap back. The man is still very definitely a few rap songs short of a full CD."

"Do you have a background in psychology or psychiatry, Mr. Early?" Gilroy asked.

"No. But if somebody keeps babbling on about how he killed a man to save him, I don't think you need too many psych courses to peg him as loony tunes."

"Have you heard of Dr. Grace Medina?"

"A shrink?" Mercer hazarded a guess.

"A respected psychiatrist in our Behavioral Science unit," Gilroy said. "You might say she's part of the Department's team. Like this firm."

"Actually," C.W. said, "our contract is with POG."

"Of course it is," Gilroy said.

"And it's the client whom we serve. There may be rare instances when what's best for the client may not totally fit tongue and groove with the Department's wishes. Or even with POG's wishes, though that's a bit harder to imagine."

"This doesn't strike me as being one of those instances," Gilroy said. "What's good for Officer Nunez is good for the Department as well."

"We're with the Chief's office on this one," Kerry Barnard said.

"That's why we're here," C.W. said. "So we'll understand all points of view." He nodded to Gilroy. "You had something to tell us about Dr. Medina?"

Gilroy took his time replying. He seemed to be reappraising C.W., as if reminding himself that the outwardly agreeable black man in the big leather chair was, after all, a lawyer and not just any hair-splitting, litigious asshole but one who had helmed a very successful firm for the last couple of decades.

Gilroy cleared his throat and said, "Dr. Medina spent some time with Officer Nunez today. She believes his delusional behavior may be the result of some specific emotional crisis. Probably personal, having to do with his homosexual relationship with the man he killed."

"*Says* he killed," Mercer corrected.

Gilroy's thin lips formed a very small, very brief smile. "You doubt him?"

"Well, the man is crazy," Mercer said. "I'm not sure how much stock we should put in anything he has to say."

"Dr. Medina has a somewhat more positive opinion about his current condition," Gilroy said. "She also feels the act of violence may be an example of *temporary* insanity brought on by jealousy or . . . something of that sort."

Mercer mulled that over, saying nothing.

"Dr. Medina feels he may be suffering a chemical imbalance caused by the trauma resulting from his impulsive act. She has prescribed medication that should make his attendance in court a bit more comfortable for him."

"Uh-huh," Mercer said. "So, bottom line, Nunez is going to be on Planet Nine in court while I build his defense around temporary insanity caused by trouble in his little gay home?"

"Won't this work for you?"

"Sure," Mercer said. "It'll work even better if I get some evidence of this 'trouble.' "

"I believe our detectives have uncovered a witness or two who might be willing to testify to arguments. Jealous outbursts. I'll make sure you are provided with names and contact information."

Gilroy stood, nodding to Barnard. "I imagine Kerry has

to get back to his office. I know mine awaits. Whatever else you need, gentlemen, don't hesitate to call."

He and Barnard shook C.W.'s hand, then Mercer's, and were on their way.

"If I ever need a good silent partner, I know who I'd pick," Mercer said.

C.W. chuckled. "Kerry's long suit is hammering out raises. Don't make the mistake of underestimating him."

"Both of those guys are whiter than white," Mercer said.

"Not a lot of soul showing on the surface," C.W. said. "You have any problem with a temporary insanity plea?"

"No," Mercer said. "But that may be 'cause I don't know anything about what happened the night Landers Pope died." He stood. "Are all our dealings with the LAPD gonna be this hands-on?" he asked.

C.W. shrugged. "My guess is we may have many of these little chats with John Gilroy with or without Kerry Barnard."

CHAPTER EIGHT

Detective Lionel Mingus wanted his dinner.

It had been a long day, the last two hours of which he'd spent at his desk at Parker Center, hunting and pecking a report on a case he'd closed that evening. On the way home, he'd picked up a Stymie's Choice from Roscoe's Chicken 'n' Waffles. He'd barely swallowed one huge bite of smothered chicken livers and grits when the phone rang.

He answered it immediately. The woman he lived with, Bettye Hiler, had been working for a couple of months at All That, a ladies boutique in the Fox Hills Mall. The move there from the downtown wholesale clothes store where she'd been clerking was a step up for her—in take-home pay and, maybe more important, in self-confidence.

That was the good news. The bad news was that her boss demanded that his employees inventory the merchandise every Wednesday. This meant Mingus not only ate alone on those nights, but with his knowledge of just how mean the streets could get after sundown, he didn't rest until she walked in through the front door.

The call wasn't from Bettye in distress.

Mingus's relief quickly segued into wariness when Captain Roy Jacquette, head of the LAPD's Robbery-Homicide Division, began describing an officer-involved murder and arson in the Fairfax area. "I need you here in twenty," Jacquette told him.

"I just put in a ten-hour day today, Captain," Mingus

said, looking at the gravy congealing around the chicken livers.

Jacquette ignored the complaint, gave him the precise address, and clicked off.

For a few seconds, Mingus considered sticking the plate of food in the fridge. Then, with a "Fuck that," he picked up his knife and fork and finished the meal.

The bungalow just off Fairfax had been reduced to a smoldering ruin by the time he arrived. Somehow, firemen had been able to extract a woman's body from the blaze. Before the techs zipped the body bag, Mingus got a glimpse of a semi-charred corpse with a caved-in forehead.

"Head wound do it?" he asked.

"Mighta been the smoke," a tech named Jamie Lu said. "Or a combination. Dr. Saleem will have the answers." Saleem was the assistant coroner. He and Mingus had a relationship best described as spotty.

Captain Jacquette was standing next to his shiny black Lincoln a few yards inside the barriers that were keeping the gawkers and the media at bay. He was jawing with a big sexy blonde in a gown that made her look like she was expecting dinner and maybe even dancing.

He waved Mingus over.

"Detective McRae," the captain said to the blonde, surprising Mingus, who'd assumed she was just another of his big-tit side dishes. "This is Detective Mingus."

"Hildy McRae," the blonde said, offering a very pale, very firm hand. "Roy . . . Captain Jacquette has been telling me how much he thinks of you, Detective."

That was a fairly fresh opinion. Several years before, Jacquette had kicked his ass out of Robbery-Homicide—with some justification, Mingus had to admit, since he'd been hitting the sauce pretty hard in those days. The detective's new elevated status had less to do with his sobriety than with the fact that he had been significantly involved in the trackdown and arrest of a respected civic leader who'd engineered a series of murders.

Two of the victims had been cops working out of Robbery-Homicide. As payback for his efforts, the captain had invited Mingus, who'd been miserable as a member of the Rat Squad in Internal Affairs, to fill one of the vacated slots in RHD.

"Detective McRae joined the team today," Jacquette said. "She's been on the job six years working homicide for Las Vegas Metro."

"Hope you don't mind teaming up with the new girl," she said.

Mingus wasn't sure how he was supposed to answer. Instead, he shifted his eyes to the captain, who said, "Detective McRae will be partnering with you, Mingus. Maybe permanently. At least you'll be working together on this."

"What exactly might *this* be, Captain?" Mingus asked.

"That ash heap of a house is the property of Joseph Mooney, a patrolman working out of East Pico. Neighbor saw him take off in his SUV just before the place went up. Looks like he popped his wife in the head, torched the house, and booked."

"Any idea what might have set him off?" Mingus asked.

"Not a clue," his new blond partner said. "According to his sheet, Patrolman Mooney was a solid performer."

"Detective McRae will give you the full rundown of what we have, which is damn little." The captain was backing away from them as he spoke, heading for his sedan. "Find the son of a bitch, Mingus. And you, Detective McRae"—he smiled—"welcome to the City of Angels."

The two detectives watched the sedan inch-worm through the crowd. "There goes one smooth swinging dick," McRae said. "I wouldn't want to get on his bad side."

Mingus, who had experienced that bad side, said, "I first saw you two together, I thought you were his dinner date."

"I was. Until this went down."

"Oh."

"Now I guess I'm all yours," she said, staring at him in a way that made him uncomfortable. Particularly when she shifted her view to his crotch.

In an effort to move things back to business, he said, "Maybe we should see what the neighbors got to say about the Mooneys, huh?"

She gave him a funny little smile that he interpreted as: okay, I'll play the cop game, if that's what you want. But then you'll play my game. "Sounds like a plan," she said.

The neighbors in the predominately Jewish section of

the city described the Mooneys, Joe and Gerry, as people who kept to themselves. Mingus figured that could mean they didn't go to Temple, or they preferred barbecued pork ribs at home to Kosher dinners at Cantor's. Or maybe it had something to do with that long-ago but never forgotten "Hymietown" slip of the Reverend Jesse Jackson's.

The Solomons, who lived next door, said that there had been arguments recently. Mr. Solomon, who was more concerned about the smoke damage to his house than the death of a neighbor, punctuated every sentence with "the crazy bastard could have burned us down."

A young rabbinical student with red dreadlocks trailing from his black hat asked them if the little girl was okay.

"The Mooneys have a kid?" Mingus asked.

"A little girl, yes. Janet. Five or six. Friendlier than the rest of the family." The young man's pale face turned to chalk. "Oh, merciful God. Don't tell me she was in the house?"

It took Mingus nearly an hour to discover that Janet Mooney had not been claimed by the fire but was spending the night at the Baldwin Crest home of her aunt and uncle, Dr. and Mrs. Paul Johnston.

Olivia Johnston was a thin, nervous woman, so shaken by the news of her younger sister's death that her husband, a doctor of internal medicine, felt compelled to sedate her.

"The doc's a fast man with a needle," Hildy McRae said as she and Mingus sat alone in the Johnstons' ornate living room. "Maybe I can hit him up for a shot of B-12."

She smiled, to show him she was kidding. Mingus smiled back, but filed the comment away, figuring it must have come from somewhere.

"If she freaked like that just from hearing her sister died," McRae said, "what the hell will she do when we tell her the whole story?"

"We don't know the whole story." Mingus's energy was ebbing away and he wanted desperately to put an end to the night. "Not sure how you worked it in Vegas, but here we only tell the family what they need to know."

"You don't think they need to know their brother-in-law is armed and probably dangerous? Suppose he shows up for his daughter?"

"That's why we got the officer outside watching the house," Mingus said. In truth, he hadn't quite made up his mind how much to tell Dr. Johnston. The doctor had informed them that Joe Mooney dropped off his daughter earlier in the evening because "he wanted some time alone with Gerry."

Assuming that the man was setting up to murder his wife, the fact that he'd parked the little girl indicated he had no homicidal plans for her. Still, they were in the dark about what had prompted the death of Geraldine Mooney, so they had to assume she and the other relatives could be in danger.

Paul Johnston seemed almost too relaxed for the situation when he joined them in the living room. Mingus thought he looked more like a jazz musician than a doctor. A successful jazz musician. He was a big black man, an inch or so under Mingus's six-three, with gold-rimmed granny glasses, a pencil-thin moustache, and large hands that he moved in graceful gestures. He was wearing gray slacks of some material that shimmered as it caught the light, a black, loose-fitting shirt, and gold chains at his wrist and neck. He smelled of peppermint. "She's resting now," he said. "Can I get you detectives something?"

McRae gave Mingus a look, but instead of asking for a shot of B-12, she rose and said, "Thanks, but we've got to get going. Okay if we look in on the little girl?"

"She's asleep," Dr. Johnston said.

"It's procedure," Mingus said, getting to his feet. "We'll try not to wake her."

She was in a bedroom that belonged to an older girl, judging by the posters on the wall featuring Nelly, Lil' Kim, Missy Elliott, and others beyond the scope of Mingus's limited knowledge of the contemporary music scene.

She was sleeping peacefully in the center of a full-size bed covered by a pink and white duvet, a lovely child dark as night. Dark as Mingus. She was one more reason to believe the bromide about black being beautiful. The detective harbored unpleasant childhood memories of members of his own race taunting him about the darkness of his skin. Just looking at Janet Mooney made that weight a little easier to carry.

"Satisfied?" the doctor said a bit testily when they had returned to the living room.

"The bedroom belongs to your daughter?" McRae asked.

"Lana is at Gold Arrow Camp for the month. She's fourteen."

"You and Mrs. Johnston prepared to care for your niece for a while?" Mingus asked.

"Joe should be coming for her soon." The doctor frowned. "You said that Joe escaped the fire. I'm a little surprised he hasn't called. The poor guy must be going through hell. We should prepare one of the guest bedrooms."

"We haven't been able to locate your brother-in-law," Mingus said.

"My God. You mean it's possible he doesn't even know . . . ?"

"Hard to say. You have any idea where he might be? Any friends? Other relatives?"

"I've never met any of Joe's friends. I've heard him mention his partner. Emmylou something."

The detectives were familiar with the partner's name. Emmylou Paget. The phone had gone unanswered at her home. "Family?" Mingus asked.

"Somewhere in South Carolina, I think. Look, this fire that took Gerry, it was an accident, right?"

"At this point, we really don't know."

"My God. You're not thinking that Joe . . . He's the straightest arrow I know. Granted, he's been a little odd lately, but—"

"Odd, how?" McRae asked.

"Nothing extreme. A little moody. Depressed."

"Trouble at home?" Mingus asked.

"Not that I'm aware of. If anything, it was the job. You people in law enforcement see the world at its worst. I think it's getting to Joe. He looked unhealthy when he dropped Janet off. Eyes bloodshot. Hand tremor."

"You ask him about it?"

"I'm a doctor. Of course I did. He said he'd been having trouble sleeping. Then . . ." He paused, frowning.

"Then?" Mingus prodded.

"He started talking about terrorism. How the city was unprepared. Something had to be done."

"That kind of worry hooks him up with about ninety-five percent of the country," Mingus said.

"Joe seemed to be a little more affected by it than most of us. Just this past Sunday, at dinner here, he began a diatribe about plagues. Nuclear devastation. It was all very disturbing to my wife. Hell, it was disturbing to me.

"Gerry told him to lighten up. And he did. Still, it was all quite unlike Joe. I can't remember him ever bringing his job to our home before."

"And this evening he was back on topic with the doomsday talk?" McRae asked.

The doctor nodded. "But he wasn't . . . I mean, he was lucid. In control. Just worn down. You think he's dangerous?"

"We're still trying to figure things out," Mingus said. He handed the doctor a small white card. "My home phone is on the back. I'd appreciate your calling me if you hear from your brother-in-law."

"If? Surely he'll be coming here for Janet."

"Just to cover all possibilities, we'll be keeping a police officer out front. If your brother-in-law shows up, let the officer deal with him."

"My wife is very high-strung. This won't be good for her."

"Any way she could maybe go visit somebody for a while?" Mingus asked. "Take the little girl with her?"

The doctor frowned. "You can't believe Joe would . . . ?" He seemed to deflate, sink into himself. "We've a condo at Big Bear, a timeshare thing that's not being used right now. I suppose we could spend a few days there."

"Does Joe Mooney know about the condo?" McRae asked.

"Yes, but he's never been there. We've invited them, of course. They're homebodies." He frowned, realizing how inappropriate the word had become. "This is a nightmare. A policeman parked out front."

"It makes sense to be overcautious."

"What happens to your practice, if you take off?" McRae asked.

"My partner can handle things. At least for a while."

Mingus suggested they leave for Big Bear first thing in the morning. He dutifully wrote down the address and phone number of the condo, along with the doctor's cellular number. "With your permission, we'd like to monitor calls coming here and to your office."

"God, I can't believe this is happening," Dr. Johnston said. "Do what you must here, but I won't have you interfering with my office procedure."

"Okay. Your receptionist will have to tell callers something to explain your absence. Where was the last trip you and your wife took?"

"We spent New Year's in Maui."

"Then have her tell people you've gone back there for a visit. Something like that."

The doctor nodded.

"Mrs. Johnston employed?" McRae asked.

"She retired some time ago." He sighed. "I'm going to have to tell that little girl about her mama. I'll muddle my way through that. But what in God's name do I say about Joe?"

"Say her daddy will be calling her soon," Mingus said.

"You think that's true?" Dr. Johnston asked.

"The truth is, we don't know what her daddy's gonna be doing," McRae said.

CHAPTER

NINE

Officer Emmylou Paget lived alone in a small cottage on the Venice Canal. The place had been painted recently: gray with pink trim on the door and windows. As least that's what Mingus could make of the colors in the moonlight.

There were no lights inside the building and no one answered the buzzer. In the distance, he could hear geese honking on the canal. The air smelled faintly brackish.

"Nobody home," McRae said, shining her light through the small glass panel on the cottage's front door.

Mingus stuck a business card in the door jamb. "That's all the damage we can do tonight," he said. "We'll hook up with her tomorrow at East Pico, see what other folks there can tell us about Mooney."

Back in his sedan, heading out of Venice, McRae asked, "Where would you go if you killed your wife, Lionel?"

"I don't have a wife," he said. "And we don't know for certain that Mooney killed his."

"Well, I wouldn't want to judge him guilty just on the strength of him being ID'ed running away from the scene of the crime, leaving his wife dead or dying and his house on fire."

"Point taken, Detective," Mingus said.

She smiled. "The guys in Vegas Metro called me Hildy or Hildy Mac. That work for you, Lionel?"

"Sure. Make it Hildy."

"Good. It looks like we'll be spending some time together

so I might as well get something out in the open at the jump. One of the reasons I came here was personal. I made the mistake of getting involved with a fellow detective. He was a big, handsome black man like yourself. Only he was married to this real cunt, and the whole thing turned into a three-ring horror show. So I'm glad to hear you're not married."

"I'm close enough," he said.

"What's that mean? Engaged? Cohabiting?"

"I'm living with someone," he said, trying not to show his annoyance at her poking around his personal life.

"But you're not legally married."

"No."

"Well, all right, then," she said. "I'm glad I changed the sheets. Turn left at the next light."

He frowned at her. "Sleeping with your partner is a lousy idea," he said.

"Don't knock it till you've tried it," she said.

It was just shy of 1:30 a.m. when Mingus arrived at the cozy apartment he shared with Bettye Hiler. She was in bed, watching some comedy show on BET. She clicked off the set and lifted the covers to show him that she was naked and waiting. "Get on in here, baby," she said.

"You up kinda late, huh?" he said, taking off his jacket.

"I only been here about fifteen, twenty minutes. Mr. Palmyra took us to dinner after the inventory."

"Smells like a few drinks were involved, too," he said, sitting on the side of the bed to pull off his shoes without untying them.

"One or two," she said, giggling. "We was in this I-ty place—you know, statues and opera music and plastic grape vines wrapped around everything. They kept fillin' up our glasses with vino."

"Who all was at this dinner?" he asked, sliding under the covers, feeling a little thrill when her knees touched his.

"Etta—girl works with me—and Serena, the cashier, and this sales guy named Morris. And Mr. Palmyra." She reached out and ran her hand over his chest, pausing to draw a ring around his right nipple.

Trying to ignore the lightning bolt that traveled from his tingling breast to his dick, he asked, "Salesman ever put the moves on you?"

"Morris? He's knocking boots with Serena."

"What about Mr. Palmyra?"

"He touches my ass ever' now and then, pretendin' it's not intentional."

"That the fuckin' truth? And you don't bust him on it?"

"Not for just a little ass pat," she said. "Not if that's all he's after."

Mingus went silent, recalling that just a few minutes before, sitting in the parked car near the entrance to Hildy McRae's apartment building, his new partner had suddenly pulled up her dress, showing him what he'd be missing by not coming upstairs with her.

"I don't know what the Vegas dress code is," he'd told her. "But here most cops use underwear. Seems a little more . . . professional."

She ignored the comment, taking his big right hand and drawing it to her. He offered no resistance as she placed it on her pale, warm, cleanly shaved crotch.

She moaned and in the sound was a note of triumph that brought him to his senses. Had he been drunk with either booze or youth he would have taken her in the car right then without worrying about the stick shift or AIDS or what it might do to their working relationship. But he was sober and old enough to keep his hormones in check.

"Smooth," he said, withdrawing his hand. "Barber do that for you?"

"Come on upstairs, I'll give you a closer look."

"Not a good idea," he said. "Not gonna happen."

There was a flash of anger from her, then a resigned shrug. She smoothed her dress over her knees. "Just being friendly," she said.

"Friendly is fine. Wouldn't do for me to have my mind on that smooth pussy when I should be working the case. So let's keep it at friendly."

She got out of the car. Before shutting the door, she said, "You know, Lionel, sometimes not fucking can be even more of a distraction on the job."

He watched her strut to the apartment building. At the door, she turned. The light in the lobby behind her transformed her dress to cellophane. He could see the outline of her impressive body as she blew him a kiss.

That image returned while he was lying in the bed, pressed against Bettye. She said, "You don't have to worry about Mr. Palmyra, but I sure do appreciate what a little bit of jealousy does for you, baby."

He didn't correct her.

DAY 3

THURSDAY, JUNE 17

CHAPTER

TEN

"First, it was Baskin, a Medal of Valor officer," Chief Niles Ahern was whining early the following morning. "Now it's Mooney. John, would you please tell me exactly what the fuck they're feedin' 'em at East Pico."

John Gilroy blinked at the note of accusation in Chief Ahern's whine. To make matters worse, Eddie Escobar, typically nonplussed, was smiling at him insolently.

The chief was referencing recent events at the East Pico Division where a well-liked Medal of Valor winner, Officer Dwight Baskin, had experienced some sort of mental break, murdering his wife and then packing her in the back of the family car and driving around with her corpse for nearly three weeks. He'd been killed trying to escape capture.

Now it appeared that the man responsible for Baskin's death, Officer Joe Mooney, was emulating him by murdering *his* wife. He was currently at large.

Chief Ahern's chickenlike head was cocked to one side belligerently. "You understand the question, John?"

"Jacquette's got a top guy on Mooney's trail. Lionel Mingus."

"Who he?"

"The detective who put Barry Fox away," Gilroy said.

"Oh? Yeah? That boy's good."

The "boy" was in his forties, but Ahern was pushing sixty and Gilroy preferred to think his boss was using the term to describe age rather than skin color.

"One officer losing it and killing his wife is a tragedy," Escobar said with a smile. "Two officers doing it—three if you count Eldon Nunez killing his boyfriend—it starts to look like a pattern."

"Shades of Fort Bragg," Gilroy said.

"What was it at Fort Bragg—four soldiers killed their wives?" the chief asked.

"And one more soldier got bumped off by his wife," Escobar said. "I was real interested in the whole thing."

Chief Ahern scowled. "The army wrote it off to extreme stress, right?"

"Except for the homicidal wife," Escobar said. "Though she may have been under stress, too, of a different kind."

"Wasn't there talk about an antimalaria drug the men had been given in Afghanistan?" the chief asked.

"Lariam," Escobar said. "It's been a few years, but I think that's the name of the drug. Causes psychotic episodes. They found it in a couple of the soldier boys. But when they didn't find it in the others, they threw out that theory."

"I don't suppose we got any evidence of drugs here?" the chief asked.

"Not so far. We'll have to wait on Mooney's capture to be sure, but there's been no hint of it in his record."

"What about Nunez?" Escobar said. "Gays like their drugs. Ex is pretty common, no?"

"The only drugs in Nunez are the ones being used now to sedate him," Gilroy said. "Let's not add Nunez to the mix. He's got no connection to East Pico. No links to either Mooney or Baskin or—"

"Here's the goddamned bottom line," Chief Ahern interrupted. "None of these cases are linked, get me? I don't want to hear any more talk about drugs or mental stress or spousal abuse or any of that crapola about us pushing the men too hard. I won't have the goddamn media hounds gnawing on that bone. Understand?"

"We don't have that much control over what they gnaw on, sir," Gilroy said.

"Well," Escobar said, "we could whip up some kind of psychological study proving the majority of the force is mentally fit. Statistics scare the hell out of reporters, keep 'em off balance."

"Now that's thinking. Get that going, John. And don't let up on the drop in gang activity," the chief said. "I know the bastards hate good-news stories, but let's jam it down their throats."

"I'll get right on that, sir," Gilroy lied. He was conscious of Escobar's grin. In an attempt to wipe it away by regaining some of the chief's esteem, he added, "Detective Mingus has suggested that Mooney may not have murdered his wife."

"Yeah?" Chief Ahern brightened.

"He's broadening his investigation to cover the possibility that the killing and arson were performed by some unknown perp seeking vengeance on Officer Mooney."

"Good goddamned boy, Mingus," the chief said. "A murder totally unrelated to the thing with Baskin and to concerns over spouse abuse. I love that enough to want it on toast."

"I understand Mingus and some new hottie from RHD are at East Pico right now," Escobar said. "Lots of officers at the division believed Dwight Baskin was a god. Mingus may think one of them decided to avenge his death."

"John, make it clear to Mingus that an avenging cop has no place in my favorite scenario," the chief said.

Escobar stood. "I'd better get back to work."

"Right, Eddie. Thanks for all your help."

Help? Gilroy thought. All the bastard did was stir the chief up. Now he was ducking. He couldn't let Escobar get away clean. "Eddie, what's up with Giuliani?" he asked. "True he dropped out as convention keynote?"

"What?" The chief was glaring at Escobar.

"Yeah. He had a schedule conflict," Escobar said. "So I booked Colin Powell instead."

"Oh," the chief said, calming down a little. "He's . . . good. Good idea."

Left alone with Gilroy, he said, "You don't think Powell will be a turn-off?"

Gilroy couldn't bring himself to feed the chief's doubts, even though that would put Escobar on the spot. "You mean, because he's a Republican?" he asked.

"No. I . . . Oh, you're joshing me. Well, I suppose Powell will be okay." He scowled and asked, "Don't you have work to do, John?"

"Oh yeah," Gilroy said, getting to his feet.

CHAPTER

ELEVEN

"Lot of smokin' street legal iron warming up down there," Jerry Lin said to Mercer and Hootkins, pointing to the collection of colorful vehicles causing a din on the Irwindale Speedway's 1/8th mile dragstrip. Two movie cameras—a Panaflex and a handheld—stood ready to capture every clutch-grinding, wheel-spinning moment.

On a normal business day, the speedway's grandstand would be filled to capacity. That afternoon, with the site being rented as a location for the cable cop series *Black and Blue,* the five hundred seats were empty, except for the lawyer, Hootkins, and Lin, who were sitting in the top row, and a smattering of television crew personnel down near the track.

"You have any idea why your old partner would have jumped the rail?" Mercer asked Lin.

"Naw. Eldo was always a pretty cool customer. Never let any of the bullshit get him down."

"What bullshit are we talking about?"

Lin made a little "humph" sound and turned to Hootkins. "You were on the force, right? You know what bullshit goes down, an officer don't exactly fit in."

Hootkins gave an almost noncommittal nod.

"I remember one afternoon Eldo and me come off duty, a bunch of the assholes were sittin' around, kinda waitin', you know. Some comedian Superglued rubber dicks—what do they call 'em, dildos?—all over his locker."

"How'd he react?" Mercer asked.

"He tore one of 'em loose and started suckin' on it. Moved right up in their faces, suckin' away. They couldn't take it. They got up and left. Joke over."

"How pissed off was he?" Hootkins said.

"He wasn't angry at all. Soon's they left, he shit-cans the rubber dick, tells me it don't no way compare with the real thing, and we both laugh like hell."

"You gay?" Hootkins said.

Lin smiled. "No. I hedero. Longtime married man. Got kids, nine and twelve. Private school, now."

"You had no problem teamin' up with a gay?" Hootkins asked.

"It gives 'watchin' your back' a whole new meaning." Lin laughed. "That's Eldo's joke. Naw. He was a good partner."

"Why'd you pull the pin?" Mercer asked.

"Why'd I quit? Well . . ." A plump, unshaven guy whose Levi's were being dragged down by a ring of keys the size of a pineapple shouted for quiet. This demand was followed by a loud buzzer.

"Hold on," Lin whispered. "This won't take long."

Another even scruffier kid snapped a clapper in front of the Panaflex. The cameraman began swinging the instrument to the right until it was aimed directly at a vehicle that had been chopped and pounded into a hot rod funny car as it rolled along the drag strip.

The show's two lead actors in white jumpsuits and helmets were strapped to its bucket seats, portraying, in turn, Officer Marcus Blue, the black member of the cop buddy team, and Officer Sandy Black, his blond, blue-eyed soul brother.

"See Blue is black and Black is white," Lin whispered. "*Black and Blue*."

"Got it," Mercer whispered back.

A pot-bellied guy in a sand-colored bush jacket and tan slacks yelled "Cut" and the funny car stopped about two feet shy of the camera's lens. Its doors opened and the two actors got out to be replaced by two other performers in identical-looking jumpsuits and helmets.

"Stunt doubles," Lin whispered.

The Panaflex was repositioned and again came the demand for quiet, the buzzer, the clapper. The refurbished car revved up and zoomed down the track.

A wheel flew off. The vehicle tipped and rolled. It exploded in a fiery flash, replete with plumes of smoke.

Mercer was halfway to his feet when Lin gestured for him to sit back down.

The lead actors stumbled out of the smoke. One ripped off his helmet to display a bloody forehead. The other fell to the ground.

"Cut and print," Bush Jacket said, lighting his pipe.

"Movie magic," Lin said. "Gonna be awhile before the smoke clears. Where were we?"

"You were telling us why you quit the force."

"Yeah. Well, you know how Hispanics are the biggest non-white segment of the population? Then come your African Americans, then, what, Japanese, Chinese? Vietnamese way down on the list. That's how it works on the LAPD, too. Way down on the list. I got no future there.

"This TV producer, doing a show about a policeman who uses martial arts. *Copsocki*. Ever see it?"

"Missed that one," Mercer said.

"This producer is strolling around division and see me. I'm a cop. To him I look Japanese. He ask if I want to visit set, tell 'em how to make it more real. I'm about to tell him to go jump a lake when he say something about fi' thousand dollars a week.

"And here we are. This my third police series."

"You see much of Officer Nunez after you quit the force?" Hootkins asked.

"We friends. Play basketball every other week on Tuesday nights. Maybe once a month, we go out to eat. Me and Hana. Him and Land. Two couples having dinner."

"He and his, uh, mate get along okay?" Hootkins asked.

"Sure. Fine. Very close. All this shocking. Hard to believe."

"When was the last time you saw Officer Nunez?" the detective asked.

"Several weeks. Maybe three. He cancel basketball. Say he have too much on his mind."

"He tell you what?" Mercer said.

Lin shook his head. "No, but it was the work, I'm pretty sure."

"What makes you think so?"

"He say—and this right after he tell me he has much on his mind—he say, 'You a lucky man, Lin. Things where you work now all fake. Catsup blood and blank bullets and happy endings.' He say he got to deal with real things and it ain't pretty. It get him down."

"He wasn't more specific?" Mercer said.

"He usually happy man so I ask, what's the matter? Something happen? He say, 'Death is everywhere, moving like a cloud, touching people we love, people we hate. Everybody.' "

"He used those exact words?" Mercer said.

"Oh yeah. I remember 'cloud.' Poetic. Then he say he'll call me when he feel better. I never hear from him again. I think I go visit him in prison."

"That'd be nice," Mercer said, though he doubted Nunez would know who the hell Lin was. He'd spent a few minutes with Nunez earlier in the day and the client was so drugged he looked like he was auditioning for a zombie movie.

"What'd you think of Landers Pope?" Hootkins asked Lin.

Lin frowned. "I never get to know him too well. Quiet man. Not much to say. Eldo talk for them both. Hana, she say she think he very handsome. Like a young Brad Pitt, know who I mean?"

"Yeah," Hootkins said. "I've seen Brad Pitt."

"Almos' pretty. I notice when we at dinner, people in room—women, men—they all give him looks."

"Did he give them looks back?" Mercer asked.

"No," Lin said. "Only one he sees is Eldo."

"Thanks for your help, Mr. Lin," Mercer said.

"Anything I can do for Eldo, you call. You gentlemen want autographs of the stars? I can get 'em."

Mercer couldn't think of anything he wanted less, but Lin seemed so eager to demonstrate his status on the set, he said, "Sure, if you don't think they'd mind."

"Mind? No. They my pals." Grinning, he nearly ran down the steps in his eagerness.

As Mercer and Hootkins followed him down, the detective leaned in close and said, "Autographs? For a lawyer, you can be a real pussy."

"Spread that around and I'll sue your black ass," Mercer said.

"Sure you will," Hootkins said, chuckling, "hard-hearted customer like you."

CHAPTER TWELVE

Officer Joe Mooney had struggled through the day waiting for dark. Daytime was the worst. On constant alert. Listening for the slam of a car door. A footstep. A key in the lock. Afraid to make a sound himself. Night was a little easier, except that moving around the house, eating, thinking in darkness wore him out.

He couldn't concentrate. His mind was too full of images for him to sort out. That was the problem. He had to focus on his next move. But he felt so overwhelmed.

Back before . . . when he had a life . . . he'd spent the occasional night lying in bed with eyes clamped shut, worries chasing sleep away. Thoughts all jumbled together. What if there's a bullet I don't dodge? And Gerry gets sick and isn't able to handle things? What happens to Janet, then? And Janet's cough just keeps lingerin'. Maybe it's not just a cough. Maybe it's . . . no, that's bullshit. It's just a cough. Where the hell we gonna get the money to pay for her college? Where do we get the money for next month's mortgage?

And on and on. Worries appearing and disappearing like nightmare flash cards.

Those times, he would eventually fall asleep and on waking would smile at how foolish his fears seemed in the light of day.

Now there was no letup. The fears not only spilled over into the day, they intensified. Daytime meant activity. Cars driving by. People on the sidewalk, talking. Sometimes they paused on the walkway and he held his breath, cowering in the darkness he had made by closing the bedroom blinds tight.

Anybody could just walk right in the back door. He'd had to break the lock. Walk right in and find him and . . . kill him? Torture him? Inject him with something that promised a lifetime of pain and suffering?

Make him tell them where Janet was.

He should have been stronger. His little girl was in danger. He could have stopped that if he'd only been stronger. She was with her aunt and uncle, but that was not comforting. What could Gerry's sister or that blowhard she married do to keep them from getting Janet?

He'd played it all wrong and he didn't know how to fix it. He'd just have to gut it out long enough to make some plans.

There were enough canned goods in the house to last awhile. And the water had been left on. He tried to remember how long the owners would be gone. He could bring up the mental image of the posted order for patrols to keep an eye on the place while they were out of the country. But he couldn't zero in on the specifics.

He wondered who'd be on patrol. Would they just do drive-bys, or would they stop and give the premises a thorough check? See the broken back door. Come in. Shit.

Suppose it was Emmylou who found him?

Emmylou.

He had tried to tell her what was going on, but she just didn't get it. Nobody did.

He was the only one who realized the danger. And he had no idea what to do about it.

Maybe it wasn't too late to save Emmylou. . . .

At the moment, Officer Paget was about nine miles away in a no-frills bar near her cottage in Venice, sharing a corner table with Detectives Mingus and McRae, doing Stoli shooters and talking about him.

It had been her day off, but McRae had succeeded in getting her to pick up her phone and agree to the meet. With some reluctance.

"Of course Joe ran," Paget was saying, in reply to one of McRae's questions. "Who the fuck wouldn't run in that situation?"

Mingus had been surprised by her appearance. She looked like a high school girl. But after spending a half hour with her, hearing her language and watching her slug down the booze, he was put in mind of midgets who resembled kids until they were well past middle age.

"Innocent people don't usually run," McRae said, her tone more casual than challenging. After observing her interrogation technique, Mingus had to admit she might have a little something more going for her than tits-and-ass. He'd decided to let her do most of the talking—she was better at it than he—while he spent his time studying the behavior of the person being questioned.

"Innocent?" Paget asked with just the hint of a slur. "Who the hell is innocent these days? The way things work now, if you look at some pimp sideways, forget to treat him with proper *respect,* you get your jacket pulled. So some lowlife seeking payback on Joe does this fucking awful thing. And Joe knows he's suspect number one and that nobody's about to go looking any further.

"What would you do?"

"Me," McRae said, "I'd be out looking for the perp who did it. You think that's what Joe's up to?"

Paget blinked and frowned. "Truth is, I don't know."

"He hasn't tried to call you?"

Paget shook her head. "No. I wish . . ."

McRae waited until she was sure Paget wasn't going to complete the thought, then said, "You wish he'd call, right?"

"Yeah. But he won't. I fucked that up, too."

"How?"

"I should have been more understanding."

McRae leaned forward and placed her hand over the smaller cop's. "Don't go there, Emmylou. None of this is your fault."

Paget withdrew her hand and sat upright in the chair. "You don't know that," she said angrily. "It damn well is my fault. I knew he was carrying a heavy load. All that bullshit from Internal Affairs wore him down."

"I'm not sure I know what you mean," McRae said.

"The Baskin shooting was as righteous as it gets. Even the IAG Rat Squad had to admit it."

Mingus, a former member of the Squad, said, "Mooney talk much about that night? His feelings about it?"

"He took down a brother cop," she said. "How the fuck should he have felt about it? It's been tearing him up. Called it the worst experience of his whole career. Sent him runnin' to the shrink."

"A Department shrink?" Mingus asked.

"Doctor Grace Medina. A fucking waste of time, she is." She leaned forward, changing her voice to parody Dr. Medina's. "'And what do you think that dream about eating a banana really means?' "

She shook her head and slipped back into her natural way of speaking. "A lot of fucking good she did Joe. Or anybody else." She downed her drink.

"If you hear from Joe . . ." McRae stopped when she saw the hostility in the small woman's eyes. "Try to find out if he's all right. That's our main concern, his welfare."

"Yeah, sure it is," Paget said sarcastically.

Outside in Mingus's sedan, McRae said, "Funny how people try to put themselves in other people's shit. She wants a piece of Mooney's trouble."

"She thinks he killed his wife," Mingus said.

"Doesn't everybody?"

He sighed. "I guess so. Anyway, I believe her when she says he hasn't been in contact."

"I'm with you. But he's got to be talking to somebody. His daughter's not available. His in-laws."

"The wife's being buried in two days," Mingus said. "Maybe he'll turn up there."

McRae gave him a look. "He cracks her skull and sets her and the house on fire. And you think he'll show up for the funeral? You still don't believe he killed her, do you?"

Mingus didn't really know what he believed.

"Is it a black thing?" she asked.

"Is your believing he killed his wife a woman thing?"

"It's been a long day, Lionel. Why don't we just call this a draw. You up for dinner?"

"It's waiting for me at my place," he said. "Cooked by my woman."

"Bon appétit," she said.

* * *

Emmylou staggered down the narrow Venice street toward her darkened cottage. She was glad she'd walked to the bar. Not much chance of a DUI, if you were on foot.

A big vehicle, a Range Rover of some odd metallic color, roared down the street catching her in its headlights. It stopped, its front bumper only inches from her.

She stood there, squinting into the bright headbeams and cursing the driver.

Two men leaped from the Range Rover. They wore dark suits. One was white, one black.

The white man, taller than the other, stopped Emmylou's hand from reaching the pistol in her purse. He avoided her kick and wrapped her struggling body in his arms.

The driver killed the Range Rover's brights as the white man stifled Emmylou's scream. The black man joined them, did something tricky to Emmylou's neck, and she went limp.

The white man carried her effortlessly to the Range Rover, followed by the black man.

They drove away.

Joe Mooney stared at the departing vehicle. He was standing in the shadows beside Emmylou's cottage. He blinked and rubbed his eyes. Had the kidnapping been real, or another one of his vivid fantasies?

He realized that he was holding his police special. So it had been real. He could have threatened the men. Or shot them. He could have stopped them from taking his partner.

But maybe he would have missed. Or maybe his gun wouldn't have fired. They would have taken him with Emmylou. Or killed him on the spot.

He hadn't done anything to help her. Hadn't tried to stop them. Hadn't even thought to check their license plate.

At least he could phone in the crime. Anonymous call. Tell them that a policewoman had been abducted.

But suppose they were able to trace the call. Or they recognized his voice. And they found out where he was and caught him. And put him in prison. What would happen to Janet then?

He snuck back to his SUV and began the return trip to

his temporary safe house, eyes continually shifting from the road to the rearview mirror to make sure he wasn't being followed.

He was worthless. Less than worthless.

But he was alive.

There was still a chance he could save Janet.

And . . . maybe he could help Emmylou, too.

DAY 4

FRIDAY, JUNE 18

CHAPTER THIRTEEN

"Sorry if my call woke you up this morning, Mercer," Lonny Hootkins said from the other side of the picket fence that separated Mercer's garden apartment from one of the less-trammeled Westwood streets.

"No problem," Mercer said. "I had an early night. Got my eight in." He rested the morning paper on the metal table beside his chaise longue and got to his feet. He tightened his bathrobe and walked barefoot across the still-dewy lawn to open the gate for the investigator.

Hootkins entered, frowning at the large brown stain on the lawyer's bathrobe.

"It's the birds," Mercer said.

"Birds?" The ex-cop scanned the garden warily as Mercer led him to the chairs on the tiny patio. "Must be goddamn vultures."

"Doves, matter of fact," Mercer said. He pointed to where a couple of gray, pear-shaped birds were perched on a flower pot shelf just off the apartment's back door. "That's their spot. Been there ever since I moved in last month."

"They do some damage for little critters," Hootkins said.

"This isn't birdshit on my robe," Mercer said. "It's coffee. The birds are goosey. Every time I come out the back door, they fly in my face. Sooner or later, I'll get used to it."

"Be easier to kill 'em. I hate flyin' things. Birds. Bugs. Roaches the worst."

"Want some coffee?"

"I'll pass," Hootkins said, still eyeing the doves.

"We can go inside," Mercer said.

"No. This is fine. I like it out here in the early morning sun. They stay on that ledge?"

"Until you get near 'em. Then they fly away. What have you got for me, Lonny? You were a little vague on the phone."

"How far did you get in the paper?" Hootkins asked, indicating the *L.A. Times*.

"Far enough," Mercer said.

POLICE HOMICIDES NOT CONNECTED a front page headline screamed. The fact that it shared the key page with FILM COUPLE'S BITTER DIVORCE in no way diminished its importance, at least not in Mercer's mind.

In a hastily held press conference, Chief of Police Niles Ahern, reacting to the phrase recently coined by television pundits, "L.A.'s Three Psycho Cops," stated "unequivocally" that "a thorough investigation had turned up not one iota of evidence linking the murders of Geraldine Mooney, wife of Officer Joseph Mooney; Eleanor Baskin, wife of Medal of Valor–winner Officer Dwight Baskin; and Landers Pope, the, ah, good friend of Officer Eldon Nunez."

Ahern admitted that "the circumstances are a bit peculiar, in that Officer Mooney was involved in the tragic events leading to the death of Officer Baskin. That said, the two murders, though seemingly similar, have no other points of connection."

As for the LAPD's need to address the problem of spousal abuse within the rank and file, the chief hopped back on his high horse. "There is no spousal abuse problem," he was quoted as stating. "We take special care to make sure the men and women serving the City of Los Angeles are at peak performance capability. In addition to our FASTRAC program, the centerpiece of our command accountability system, we continually evaluate officers' mental and physical strengths.

"As for the Landers Pope murder, that is obviously a separate issue. Eldon Nunez has confessed to the murder of Mr. Pope. As of the moment, his motive is unclear, but it seems to be a crime that grew out of the, ah, alternate lifestyle relationship that existed between the victim and Nunez."

Hootkins said, "The chief's comments aren't doin' the client any favors. Not if they're puttin' the death penalty on the table."

"Page three," Mercer said. "The D.A. vows to drop the pill on Nunez."

"I imagine it would make your job easier if the deaths were connected."

"You got something?" Mercer was suddenly interested.

"Nothin' earth-shakin'. Just a bit o' weirdness involving something I heard last night at The Academy." The Academy was a bar and grill popular with cops in Downtown L.A. "Guy named Merrill Gibbons, white guy, drove his car down Temescal Canyon couple weeks ago. Killed himself. Accidental death, says the coroner's office."

"Gibbons was a cop?"

"A techie who worked in the coroner's office."

"And that ties in how?" Mercer asked.

"He was gay. Like the client an' his boyfren'."

"And they were saying what at The Academy? That this was similar in some way to the Nunez case?"

"No. Not that," Hootkins said, frowning. "Hell, those guys don't talk about stuff like that. Their conversation is a little more . . . basic. They put Gibbons and Pope together, all right, but they also throw in all the AIDS victims and victims of gay-bashing. Like all fag deaths are God's way of cluein' us in that butt-pluggin' is a sin."

"And this enlightened theory helps us how?"

"Their bullshit theorizin' don't help us worth jack," Hootkins said. "But them mentionin' Gibbons's death stirred up my curiosity. I got this pal, Jazey Swan, works in the coroner's. I give him a call last night and he tells me Gibbons was actin' putty damn strange days before he took his drive down the canyon."

"Strange how?"

"Freaky-deaky. Jumpy. Kept spoutin' out about the world comin' to an end. Shit like that."

"Your friend, Swan, he go along with the accidental death finding?"

"Oh yeah. He thinks Gibbons was so fucked up, another car or a loud noise even might'a got him to jerk the wheel in the wrong direction."

"Then . . . ?"

"Now we're at the interestin' part. I'm not the first guy to ask Jazey about Gibbons. Not so long ago, a fed named Arthur Pleasance drops by the coroner's. A brother, though not so's you'd notice, Jazey says. Arrogant as any white man. Pushy as hell, of course. But a little nastier than he has to be."

"Pleasance show any ID?" Mercer asked.

"It was good enough to satisfy the Dragon Lady, who asked ever'body to cooperate." The Dragon Lady was the coroner, Dr. Ann Fugitsu. "He interviews the people near Gibbon's work station, including Jazey."

"What kind of questions?"

"What was Gibbons like just before he died? Was he doin' the job? Actin' crazy? Like that."

Mercer took a sip of coffee. It was turning cold. "A fed interested in a supposed accidental death. Yeah, I'd call that curious. But not exactly helpful to our case."

"I'm getting to that. Jus' hold your horses. Once this Pleasance is finished with the stuff about Gibbons, he starts askin' Jazey how *he*'s feeling lately. Anything botherin' him. Jazey says he wants to tell the asshole the only bother he got is *him,* but that's never a good idea with feds. So he just says he's fine and Pleasance moves on."

Mercer was frowning. "You are going to tie this to our client?"

"I'm gettin' to that now. Over at Midtown, there was a mess of people asking questions about Nunez. Couple Rat Squadders. Some investigators from the D.A., a homicide dick named Sykes."

"I know him. We play b-ball."

"Yeah, well, along with him and the others, there was a fed there, too."

"Pleasance?"

"Naw. A big white dude name of Carl Ivor."

"Asking the same kinds of personal questions?"

Hootkins shrugged. "That's what I plan to find out today."

"Keep me posted," Mercer said, getting to his feet.

As he walked Hootkins to the gate, the older man said, "One other thing for you to think about: according to FBI records, Ivor is assigned to the Hartford, Connecticut, office and Pleasance is in Pittsburgh. Both of 'em are designated as being 'On Leave.' But that's amended by the three-letter designation 'OBN.' Nobody seems to know what those letters mean. All real mysterious."

"Sounds like you got a source at FBIHQ," Mercer said, obviously impressed.

"Don't ever'body?" Hootkins said, giving him a wink. "I'll check in with you later."

Mercer watched him get into his nondescript gray Volvo, then let the gate swing shut. Working on unlocking the secret of the OBN acronym—the "O" was probably "Office"—he headed toward his apartment carrying his half full cup of cold coffee.

He was a little late in remembering the doves.

CHAPTER FOURTEEN

Hootkins drove his Volvo through the oddly empty Westwood business district. It always seemed weird to him what had happened to this little community. Not that long ago, it had been one of the most popular spots in the city to see a movie or have dinner. Then there were a couple of minor street skirmishes, high-spirited kids in the main acting up, and the television newscasts made it look like the riot on Sunset Strip.

Westwood took on the aspects of a ghost town for a while, until, gradually, some customers drifted back. But the bloom never quite returned to that retail rose. Hootkins was trying to recall how long it'd been since he'd spent a dime in Westwood when his cell phone tickled his chest.

"Hootkins here."

"Yo, Uncle Lon." Chet Logan, the speaker on the other end, wasn't legally his nephew. He was the twenty-two-year-old son of Hootkins's former partner from long ago, a genial but generally fucked-up Caucasian named Charlie Logan. Logan had given up a fine, good-hearted wife and a great kid so that he could have more discretionary time to spend on whores and booze.

It had been a low-life pimp named Sweets Doremus who gave Hootkins the heads-up that Charlie had suffered a heart attack and was downtown, dead on a bed in Room 304 of the unlovely Hotel Lamarr, naked as a jay, with enough Maker's Mark in his system to keep him from feeling the fires of hell for at least a month.

That left Lonny with the unenviable clean-up task. Paying off Sweets and a bemused hooker for her time. Dressing the corpse. Transporting it to Logan's dreary apartment. Undressing it. Loading it into Logan's unmade bed. And then "finding" it shortly after his partner neglected to show up for duty the next day.

He suspected that because of the relocation of the body, the autopsy had probably turned up some inconsistencies with a peaceful passing in bed, but for reasons he neither knew nor cared to know, the official finding had been death by natural causes.

At the wake, Hootkins had listened to Logan's estranged wife talk about the difficulty of raising a boy without a father, even a no-good bastard like Charlie, and, in a haze of whisky and tears, he had agreed to help out whenever he could.

Being a bachelor, he'd had no firsthand knowledge of how to deal with a teenager. Certainly not a white one. So he treated Chet like he did the rookies—talking to him as if they were just two guys, the big difference being that he'd already made it into adulthood and knew some of the mistakes to avoid and shortcuts to take and would be happy to pass along his observations if the boy was interested.

This approach seemed to work and he and Chet developed as close a father-son relationship as he would ever experience. Certainly a better one than when he'd been on the son end of things, dodging his old man's calloused hand.

He was proud when the boy did well in school, but his feelings were mixed when Chet let himself get recruited by the FBI instead of following in his and Charlie's footsteps. He had the police officer's natural antipathy for FiBIes. But in his heart of hearts he felt that white-collar agency work was maybe a step up from walking the blue-line beat.

There was also the added perk for Hootkins of having a source inside the Bureau's D.C. headquarters.

"I just came out of a meeting with my boss about those names you mentioned yesterday," Chet was saying.

"Jesus, boy. Tell me I didn't get you in trouble."

"You didn't. Least I don't think so. He wasn't pissed or anything. He just wanted to know why I was checking up on Ivor and Pleasance."

"How'd he find out?" Hootkins asked, so concerned he pulled the Volvo over to the curb and stopped.

"He didn't say."

This was not good. "Your phone tapped, maybe?"

"I doubt it, or he wouldn't have had to call me in to find out what I was up to. My guess is, when I fed the names into the hopper, one or both must've rung a bell somewhere."

"What reason did you give for checking 'em out?"

"I said I got calls from the coroner's office in L.A. and from the LAPD wanting to know if two guys claiming to be agents were the real deal."

"He buy that?"

"I *am* in records management, old man. I field requests like that all the time."

"You're not phoning me from your office right now?"

"Dammit, Uncle Lon, you sure think highly of your protégé. I'm at a coin box halfway across town."

"Your boss tell you about *his* interest in Ivor and Pleasance?"

"He doesn't tell me squat. And I figured asking him wouldn't be a smart move. But I was planning on doing an 'OBN' search and see if other names turn up."

"No," Hootkins said firmly. "You don't do anything more except forget all about it."

"If that's what you want, Uncle Lon," Chet said. "You change your mind, give a ring.

"How's Mom doing, by the way? She tells me she's breathing better, but I never heard of emphysema improving."

"She's getting along okay," Hootkins said, painting the picture a little rosier than it was. "She's got a birthday coming up second of August."

"I have it marked, but thanks for the heads-up. About those agents, whatever they're up to, you sure as hell don't want to get on their bad side. Take care, huh? I don't know what I'd do without you."

The morning seemed suddenly brighter to Hootkins and filled with an infinity of prospects. "Right back at you, son," he said, clicking off his cell phone. As he eased his car into the traffic along Wilshire, he used the sleeve of his jacket to wipe the moisture that had formed suddenly in the corner of his eyes.

CHAPTER

FIFTEEN

"Whoever told you that is a . . . well, a liar, at least," the stocky young man named Geoffrey Bogan said to Mercer.

Geoffrey and Mercer, Geoffrey's platinum-haired life partner, Hagaar ("No other name, just Hagaar, like Madonna or Cher"), and Mercer's two associates, Kennard and Sidone, were in Moe's, a juice bar on Santa Monica Boulevard that had been "suggested" by its animated namesake from *The Simpsons* television series. The filth, rodents, and inebriates found in the original Moe's had been replaced by a clean tile floor, ice cream tables, a spotless counter, and a wall filled with reproductions of the more famous continuing characters from the show holding up bottles of Duff Beer as if saluting the establishment's quiet, well-behaved, mainly gay male customers.

The C&H associates were fading fast. They'd spent an all-nighter doing research in the firm's library. Mercer had suggested they give it up and get some rest, but Sidone had pointed out that they had the weekend for that.

So they'd accompanied him on the trip to West Hollywood to check out the list of potential defense witnesses supplied by John Gilroy. The first stop had been the client's apartment building on Arabella, where Jim Spangler, who lived directly above Nunez, told them of arguments that grew so intense it became difficult for him to concentrate on his psychic healing process.

Nina Asner, who lived with her twin brother Noel and

seven cats in a one-bedroom, said she was convinced that her brother and Landers Pope had been having an affair. "It's what lit Eldo's Roman candle," she said in a whispery voice.

When Noel returned home from The Sports Connection, however, he had assured them that "if anybody besides Eldo had been fucking Land, it was probably Nina, who couldn't keep her hands off him."

The residents of the building not on Gilroy's list who happened to be home on a Friday morning had a very different take on the Nunez-Pope relationship. "It was unusually loving," Mellisandra, a transvestite with a five o'clock shadow, told them. "There's so much coming and going in this part of town, so much ebb and flow, it gave us all heart to see the two of them in such a lasting state of togetherness."

Mellisandra couldn't begin to imagine what had caused Landers Pope's murder. "It must have been some truly horrible thing. I know Eldo is a member of law enforcement, but, still, I cannot believe he'd have the heart for such a thing."

"He says he did it," Mercer had said.

"Then a demon must have been using his body as a host."

That was about when they met up with Geoffrey and Hagaar, who were on their way to Moe's.

"I know who tell you lies about Eldo," Hagaar said, his accent a shade more Teutonic than Schwarzenegger's. "Da Spangler. Cops who come here, you know. Ask about Eldo and Land. Try to get us to say they fight. Spangler and others, they suck up to the police. Tell them what they want to hear. Bullshit! They lie. Eldo and Land, they love. Believe me."

"Tell them about that detective," Geoffrey said. When Hagaar seemed puzzled, he added, "The African American with the weird green eyes."

"Ah. Well, yes, he ask if maybe Eldo drinks too much. I say, he doesn't drink when he works. And he works most nights. He had been working the night . . . it happened."

Mercer had talked briefly with the various detectives working the case and didn't recall any "weird green eyes." He polished off the last mouthful of sweet carrot juice and said, "Tell me about the green-eyed black detective. Remember his name?"

Hagaar seemed stumped. Geoffrey said, "I don't remember any of their names."

"How many are we talking about?"

"A lot," Geoffrey said. "There were two homicide detectives, and some guys from the sheriff's department came around. And another two from the district attorney's office. And then the . . . man with green eyes. I remember now. He was the FBI guy."

Mercer spent a second replaying his conversation with Hootkins, then asked, "His name Pleasance?"

"Yah," Hagaar said enthusiastically. "But he was not pleasant. A sour man. He wanted to believe drink had driven Eldo to do that terrible thing. I don't know why. Like I say, Eldo doesn't drink."

Another name from his conversation with Hootkins popped into Mercer's head—Merrill Gibbons, the gay lab tech who'd taken a fatal car ride down Temescal Canyon. The FBI was looking into that death, too. Hc asked Geoffrey and Hagaar if they'd heard of Gibbons.

They hadn't.

Just before the lawyers took their leave, Sidone asked the two men, "What do you think happened that night?"

Hagaar shook his big silver-topped head. "Who can say? Maybe Eldo have nightmare, make mistake. Has to be mistake."

Driving back to the firm, Sidone said, "That nightmare idea of Hagaar's isn't bad. Nunez is a cop, probably sleeps with his weapon close at hand. Deep in a nightmare, he grabs the gun. *Blam*. He wakes up and . . . his world falls apart."

"Blam?" Kennard said. "How about *ker-chow?*"

"You two need rest," Mercer told them. "There's only one living person who really knows what happened that night. And he's circling Mars at the moment."

"It sounds like we can rule out a lover's quarrel," Sidone said.

"Yeah," Mercer agreed.

"So we're back to something like post-traumatic stress?" she asked.

Mercer was about to reply when his cell phone intervened.

It was his assistant, Melissa. "You know an Annie Sutter?"

The name meant nothing to him.

"Says she's an old friend."

"She say how old?" he asked, not really wanting to know the answer.

"No. But she did leave her phone number."

This was not good news. If Annie Sutter was an old friend of Mercer Early's, she could pose a threat to everything that mattered—his achievements, his career.

He took a deep breath. He told himself not to overreact. Maybe it wouldn't be a problem. Maybe she was just passing through town. He'd blow off the call and that would be that.

"You want the number?"

"You hang on to it," he said to Melissa. "Anything else?"

"Lonny left a big, thick folder full of Xeroxes he got from Midtown Division. Eldon Nunez stuff. Logs. Work histories."

Good news after bad.

He thanked Melissa and put away the phone. "Looks like you two are gonna be doing some more reading tonight," he said, informing them of the arrival of the Nunez material. "What you'll be looking for is something—maybe a specific event, maybe a series of things—that might have pushed him to the brink and over. And while you're at it, keep an eye out for mention of the name Merrill Gibbons."

He filled them in on what Hootkins had told him about Gibbons. There was silence in the car. Then Sidone said, "I'd still like to know: what's wrong with the nightmare scenario?"

"Nothing," Mercer said. "We may wind up using it."

He felt the need to check in with the client, to see if maybe he could get even a simple sentence out of him that might help the case.

He dropped the associates off at the office, then headed downtown.

CHAPTER SIXTEEN

Whoever was overseeing Nunez's medication seemed to have improved the mix. Slightly. The large prisoner had moved from walking death to a state of blissful incoherence. Sitting slumped on his chair, elbows on the table, he grinned idiotically at Mercer.

"What meds are you on?" Mercer asked.

"Askin' the wrong person, my brother. They give. I take. But it's gooood stuff."

"Some people are saying Landers Pope may have been sleeping around on you," Mercer said, hoping to shake something loose from that chemically altered mind.

Nunez just grinned. "Land was my true love."

"Then why did you kill him?"

"What makes you think I did?"

"It's what you've been telling people."

"It wasn't me."

The words hit Mercer like a jolt. "You're saying you didn't kill him?"

"I'm saying it wasn't me. Is it smoggy outside? Air seems close in here."

Mercer neither knew nor cared about the smog level. "If you didn't kill your true love, who did?"

"True love doesn't die."

"Do you know who murdered Landers Pope?"

Nunez stared at him. "You've seen your share of the dead, haven't you, brother?"

The question blindsided Mercer. Images from his past

flashed in his mind. A beautiful girl destroyed by drugs, being carried away on a stretcher. A woman fatally shot by a sociopath, her life bleeding away. His dreams on parade. "Yes," he told Nunez. "I have."

"Do the dead creep into you and take control?"

"I think about them."

Nunez shook his head slowly from side to side. "That's not what I mean," he said. "Do they . . . make you do things?"

"No, they don't."

" 'Course not." Suddenly, Nunez's round face broke into a grin. "Damn, but I'm a mellow fellow," he said, slapping the table with his big hand. He began singing, "Got no right to feel this gooood."

"Seems they're feeding you some nice meds," Mercer said.

The prisoner was scatting now. "Boo-doop-em-boo."

"But you're gonna have to stop taking 'em for a while. That okay, Eldon?"

"Ba-doop-em-baaa . . . my friends call me Eldo."

Mercer felt like he was lost in Wonderland. "Can you stop taking the drugs, Eldo?"

"Why?"

"There are things I'm hoping you can tell me. I'm not sure you can do that unless you're sober."

"I don't get sober, brother. The doctor says I get craaaa-zeeee." He lapsed into song again. "I'm craaa-zee for loooove."

"Listen to me, Eldo. I need your help."

Nunez stopped midsong. He let his head slump forward in resignation. "Okay."

"Who killed Landers Pope?"

"The Almighty. The source of all things."

Mercer frowned. "You got to focus for me, Eldo. Or I can't keep you from taking that trip to the white room."

Nunez smiled as if delighted. "Please don't," he said.

"You want to die?"

"We all do."

Mercer shook his head. "Not me."

"That's because you weren't with us."

"Us? Who's 'us'?"

"The chosen few."

"Who?"

"The band of lost brothers."

"You and Land?"

Nunez shook his big head in seeming dismay at Mercer's ignorance.

"Who then?" Mercer asked. "Merrill Gibbons?"

"Shit. I don't know. I don't know ever'body was there that night."

"There were a lot of people the night Landers Pope was killed?"

"Not the night Land was killed. The night that killed Land."

"I don't follow, Eldo. I'm sorry. Maybe I should try one of your pills."

"It's not pills. It's something else. Don't ask what 'cause I don't know." Nunez stood and once again Mercer felt a bit intimidated by his size. "I'm going to my cell now. But do me a favor?"

"If I can."

"Tell the green-eyed brother not to come here again. I don't like him. He's full of bad notions. Makes for bad dreams."

The guard opened up. "Ready, Eldo?" he asked.

"Ready for sweet Jeee-zus," Nunez began singing.

Mercer sat alone in the small box of a room, staring at the wall until a clanging door down the corridor stopped the sound of Eldon Nunez's improvised song.

CHAPTER SEVENTEEN

Dr. Grace Medina's office was on the ninth floor of a quiet building on the edge of Chinatown, several blocks away from the Far East Bank Building on Broadway where the rest of the LAPD's Behavioral Science Unit was located.

According to Mingus's educated nose, the corridor smelled vaguely medicinal. Hildy McRae, on the other hand, smelled about as nonmedicinal as you could get as she hurried along in front of him. The scent she was leaving in her wake was clean and flowery, but, coming off of her voluptuous body, it suggested to him not magnolias in bloom but very naughty hothouse sex.

She pushed through a door, setting off an electronic gong that had already faded by the time he followed her into the psychiatrist's waiting room.

Dr. Medina was at the inner door in a flash, welcoming them into her main office. She was a petite woman in a form-fitting mauve dress a little too long for current fashion. Her dark hair was worn in a short, feathery cut. It surrounded a sallow, birdlike face distinguished by glasses that looked plain enough to have been purchased at a drugstore. They magnified brown eyes that were alert and expressive.

What they expressed now was mild annoyance.

"I've only a short time before my next appointment," she said when they were seated and introductions had been made.

"It was good of you to cut your lunchtime short to see us," McRae said.

"You said it was important. Ask me your questions and I'll answer as best as professional ethics will allow."

She had a bit of a speech impediment or an accent—the word "best" sounding like "bezdt"—that she tried to mask by speaking quickly and on point.

"We understand Officer Mooney became your patient shortly after the death of Officer Dwight Baskin," McRae said.

"Correct," Dr. Medina said.

"What can you tell us about his mental state at that time?"

"A specific reply to your question would be inappropriate. Speaking in general terms, I'd say Officer Mooney was exhibiting signs of extreme stress which, considering the circumstance—his participation in the death of a fellow officer—was not of itself abnormal."

"Did he come to see you on his own? Or because the Department required it?"

"If you're asking if he was a willing and cooperative patient, the answer would be yes." She pronounced the word "yeaz."

"Were you making any progress?" Mingus asked.

"Evidently not much. Officer Mooney exhibited a profound depression. We were working toward a discovery of its source when . . . if one believes the news reports, he apparently was overcome by violent urges."

"Did he give you any hint of trouble at home," McRae asked, "any indication of resentment or anger he felt toward Mrs. Mooney?"

Dr. Medina's thin mouth turned down in what Mingus took to be a sign of regret. Her brown eyes shifted to the spotless slab of glass that covered her desktop as she considered the question.

Mingus used her silence as an opportunity to give the room a quick scan. The space was as wide as it was long, but a small rectangle along the inner wall had been sectioned off behind a closed door. A private bathroom, kitchenette or storeroom, maybe a combination of all three. Another door apparently led to the corridor, allowing the doctor's patients to depart unnoticed by anyone in the waiting room.

There were three windows, side by side, covered by closed blinds. On the dark green walls were two prints, funny-looking swirls that indicated the doctor liked pastel earth colors. He and Hildy were resting on twin soft leather chairs of a caramel color. They and a matching leather couch were worn to a patina that suggested they'd been purchased used.

Beside the couch, a polished table of dark wood held a box of tissues. There was a small black metal cabinet at the rear of the room and, on it, a thin, greenish-tinged glass vase housing one large white rose.

The doctor had covered most of an industrial-looking tile floor with a worn oriental rug of a green so deep it was almost black. The desk had a narrow side panel to her left supporting a darkened computer, a telephone, and a modern gooseneck lamp, the source of the room's soft lighting.

Judging by that and the simple dress she was wearing, the functional eyeglasses, the absence of any jewelry and only a touch of lipstick, the doctor seemed to have decided to bring the complex world down to size by sticking to the basics.

Having considered Hildy's question, she said, "Obviously, I had no hint that the officer was harboring any homicidal intent. What I'd gathered from the more recent sessions was that he felt a certain resentment toward his wife for not making more of an effort to understand his pain."

"Did you understand his pain?" Hildy asked.

"It's what I do, or try to."

"Had the officer's resentment toward Mrs. Mooney resulted in any confrontations between them that you know of?" Hildy asked. "Physical or verbal?"

Dr. Medina's eyes seemed to say she wanted to cooperate, but her lips replied, "As I said earlier, I'm not going to provide you with specifics."

"Do you believe he killed his wife?" Mingus asked.

"From what I know of Officer Mooney, it would have been possible for him to murder his wife, but highly unlikely."

"Why?" Hildy asked.

"The death of Officer Baskin had caused him almost unbearable mental anguish. I can't imagine anything that would drive him to take another life. Not even to save his own."

"Then he wouldn't have been much use in his present occupation," Mingus said.

"I think you may conclude that," Dr. Medina said.

"Have you had any contact with him lately?" Hildy asked.

"Since he became a fugitive, you mean? No, I haven't. Our last time together was nearly a week before . . . the death of his wife."

"Was Officer Baskin a patient of yours, Doctor?" Mingus asked.

"No." She glanced at her watch, a large functional circle on her wrist. "I'm afraid we've just about run out of time."

"Officer Paget sees you, though?" Hildy asked as if the doctor hadn't spoken of the time.

Dr. Medina stared at her and said nothing.

"She told us that," Hildy said.

"Then why ask?"

"She'll be here later this evening, right?" Mingus said.

"Did she tell you that, too?"

Mingus nodded. "We were with her when she decided to make the appointment."

The meeting with Emmylou Paget had been impromptu. Captain Jacquette, who seemed to have a habit of interrupting his meals, had caught Mingus in the middle of one of Bettye's breakfast specialties—a variation of scrapple, with, at his request, beef substituted for pork.

The captain, who preferred coffee and a couple of Krispy Kremes at his desk to breaking the fast with his dysfunctional family, was usually at work by seven. That morning he'd picked up an interoffice report that he assumed would be of interest to Mingus. According to an anonymous call-in the previous night, Officer Paget had been kidnapped from in front of her house by two, possibly three, men—one of whom was Caucasian, one black—who drove her away in what looked like a new off-white Range Rover.

"But the investigating officers found her at her place, safe as churches and pissed off that they'd woken her up that early in the a.m."

"Your guess is the caller wasn't just a run-of-the-mill crank?" Mingus had paused between bites to ask.

That's exactly what the captain had guessed. As a result, Mingus had picked up his new partner and headed to East Pico to find out if Officer Paget had any idea why Mooney might have made the crank call.

"I hung around the bar for about half an hour after you two left, walked home, and went out like a light," she'd told them. "Next thing I know, these two uniform dorks are banging on my door, demanding proof that I wasn't a fucking kidnap vic."

How did she explain the fake phone-in?

"Some asshole getting his rocks off."

"Odd that he got so specific about the vehicle," Mingus had said. "You don't know anybody drives an off-white Range Rover?"

"Nobody I know is that fucking pretentious."

"Think Mooney could have been the caller? Maybe he was tripping out?"

She'd blinked. "Christ. I don't know. What would make you think that?"

"The caller didn't dial 911," Hildy had explained. "He dialed here, into East Pico, a number unknown to the average asshole, but familiar to the officers who work out of here. That way, his voice wouldn't be taped. No caller ID. To us, it all spells Mooney."

"The poor bastard. What the hell was he trying to do?" Emmylou shook her head in dismay. "What he must be going through. Shit. I was feeling great a minute ago. And you two have to come along and bring me down."

Hildy had apologized.

"Shit," Emmylou Paget had said again as they stood to go. "I feel like crap. My emotions are on a fucking roller coaster ride. They've been on my ass to go see Doc Medina. Maybe I'll try to get in there today."

"We found that a little weird," Hildy said to Dr. Medina, "her wanting to see you."

"Weird?" Dr. Medina asked.

"When we spoke with her last night, we got the idea she didn't put much stock in therapy."

The doctor smiled. She shifted her brown eyes to Mingus. "When we've eaten, the last thing we want is food," she said. "But time passes and we get hungry again. Now, I really . . ."

"Could I use your rest room?" Hildy asked.

Dr. Medina hesitated, then nodded. "Do hurry, though."

When Hildy had closed the door, the doctor asked, "You've done so well for yourself, Lionel. Getting back to RHD was quite an accomplishment."

"Thanks."

"No more problem with alcohol or . . . relationships?"

"I got a handle on things, pretty much." Trying to change the subject, he said, "I like this office better than the one you had in the bank building. How'd you swing it?"

She smiled. "About a year ago, the unit expanded and space at the bank became a bit scarce. I requested an office apart and my request was granted."

"It's a better deal. The bank was always full of people. Used to be, goin' into that building, you'd get the feelin' ever'body was gawkin' at you, knowin' too much about your business."

"If they gawked at you now, Lionel, it'd probably be because you're looking so fit. Rested. And you've lost a few pounds?"

"A few."

She smiled. "Your partner must be taking care of you."

He shook his head. "She's not . . . Detective McRae and I, our partnership is strictly professional."

"Oh? I thought I noticed a—"

Her comment was interrupted by the sound of a toilet flushing, followed by Hildy's return.

Dr. Medina ushered the two detectives toward the rear door. "If you do hear from Officer Mooney, you'll let us know, right?" Mingus said.

A gong, indicating an arrival in her waiting room, momentarily distracted the doctor.

"Right, Doc?" Mingus said.

"I always do what's best for my patients," Dr. Medina said.

"Well, that was sweet," Hildy said as they waited for the elevator. "She'll call us about the time they get snow in Malibu."

"Find anything interesting in her bathroom?"

"Not a frigging thing except Burger King crap. And here's the weird deal: the traces of super sauce, or whatever they call it, had congealed on the wrapper. So, she had a *burger* for breakfast?"

"You rooted through her garbage to check the age of the sauce?" He laughed. "You are a detective, girl."

"Yeah, well, there's definitely something off about the good doctor. What kind of woman doesn't even have an aspirin in her medicine cabinet? And the vibes coming off her. Creepy, I'd call her. Very creepy."

"She's a shrink," Mingus said.

"She sure is that," Hildy said.

Dr. Medina listened at the rear door until she was convinced they had moved on and weren't lurking in the hall outside. Only then did she cross the office to greet the newcomer.

Two of them, as it turned out. She'd been expecting the tall man with the shaggy blond hair and the slightly bent nose. Carl Ivor. The other one was an inch or two shorter than Ivor, an African American, balding, tending toward being overweight.

"Hi, Grace," Ivor said, showing a perfect set of teeth, "meet Agent Art Pleasance."

The black man pursed his lips. He didn't nod. Nor did he offer a hand to shake, which annoyed her almost as much as the fact that he was keeping her from spending time alone with Carl.

"Well, has he called?" Pleasance asked.

"Let's discuss it in my office," she said.

The two men ambled in.

Shutting the door, she said, "You just missed the detectives assigned to the case."

"That would be Mingus and . . ." Pleasance turned to Ivor. "What the hell is her name?"

"McRae."

"Right," Pleasance said, easing into one of the leather chairs. "And you stonewalled 'em?"

She sat behind her desk, trying to hide her dislike of this brusque new agent who was acting as if he outranked Carl.

"I did."

"They know anything at all?"

"Not that they were willing to share with me."

"You didn't try to find out?"

"I didn't think it wise. Wouldn't quizzing the detectives tend to raise their suspicion?"

Her tone, only mildly sarcastic, caused Pleasance to study her for a few beats. His eyes were an unnatural shade of green. He was wearing tinted contacts, which she thought odd since the rest of his appearance, including a suit that could have used a press, suggested a lack of vanity. There was something chilling about the sea-green eyes on that black face. Maybe that was the point.

"Are they any good?" he asked.

For a moment, she thought he was talking about his contact lenses. Then reality took over. Were the detectives any good? There was quite a bit she could tell them about Lionel Mingus, but, in spite of everything, she still believed in the physicians' oath. And she was having a hard time being civil to Agent Pleasance. "They seem competent."

"McRae's a graduate of Vegas Homicide," Carl Ivor said.

"Which means what? Maybe she knows which side Steve Wynn dresses on," Pleasance said. "I'm more concerned about the guy."

"Mingus is an ex-boozer—supposedly sober these days," Ivor said. "Had a rep as a fuck-up but he got lucky, closed some murder cases and took down a local pol."

"*Local* pol, huh?" Pleasance's smile made him look like a predatory fish, Dr. Medina thought, only less friendly. "Well, those mutts better find some other yard to sniff around in now that the big dog has arrived."

CHAPTER EIGHTEEN

Chief John Gilroy didn't like to play on anyone else's court, which added to his resentment at having to fight the Friday going-home traffic all the way to the offices of Carter and Hansborough. In spite of this, he was impressed by the outer trappings of the firm—the Wilshire address, the smart architecture of the building, the shiny brass elevator that floated nonstop to the top floor.

Even better was the harem of beautiful women that turned the rather plush reception area into a sort of sybaritic dream world. "Chief Gilroy," the stunner at the front desk said to him, "Mr. Hansborough is expecting you. Jorja will take you back."

Jorja was zaftig and maybe seven inches shorter than his six feet, skin the color of a Starbuck's Frappuccino, face heart-shaped with accented eyes, lips a deep red, rounded breasts tossing freely beneath a white silk blouse. "This way, Chief," she said.

"I was here just yesterday," Gilroy said. "I bet I could find Mr. Hansborough's office on my own."

"Where's the fun in that?" Jorja said with a pout. " 'Sides, he's not in his office."

Hansborough was in a conference room with windows that provided a panoramic view of the city from Westwood to the Eastern end of Hollywood. With him were two men—the young lawyer, Mercer Early, and a rather sleek-looking African American whom Hansborough introduced as Edward Baraca, another junior partner.

Jorja took their orders for drinks—water for C.W., lime juice for Baraca, and ice tea for Mercer and Gilroy—and departed. The firm's senior partner got right into it. "Could you fill us in, Chief, on why the FBI is sticking its nose into the Landers Pope murder?"

The question nearly took Gilroy's breath away. He tried to hide its impact. "I . . . what makes you think the FBI is involved?"

"Two agents," Mercer said, "Carl Ivor and Arthur Pleasance, have been talking to Eldon Nunez's coworkers, to people in his building. To Nunez himself. They're not being very quiet about it. What's the deal?"

"It's the first I'm hearing of it," Gilroy said, trying to shake off his anger. Anger wouldn't help. He needed a clear head.

"Ivor was interviewing police personnel at Midtown," Mercer said. "He'd need permission for that, right?"

"Of course. But he could obtain that at the scene."

"Can you think of any reason for the FBI's interest?" Hansborough asked.

"Off the top of my head . . . Dana Lowery has been very vocal in her displeasure with our investigation. She has friends in high places. It's possible she pushed the local bureau into taking a hand."

"Ivor and Pleasance aren't local," Hansborough said. "Right, Mercer?"

"Not local."

"That is odd," Gilroy said. "But I don't see how that impacts on your defense of Nunez."

"The agents are also asking questions about a lab technician named Merrill Gibbons who died recently in an automobile accident," Mercer said. "I'd like to know what Gibbons's death has to do with our client."

"Why does there have to be a connection?" Gilroy asked. "These agents could be working on several unconnected cases."

"It'd be nice to know for sure," Mercer said. "That's why we'd appreciate your putting us in touch with these guys."

"Me?"

"I sounded out the local bureau chief, Gil Reuterman," Hansborough said. "He said he didn't even know they were in town. Of course, he may have been shining me on."

"We were hoping you could check with the captain in charge at Midtown to see if they gave him any contact number."

"I suppose I could do that," Gilroy said. "That's why you asked me to drive all the way here?"

"Actually," Hansborough said, "that's not the only reason. Mercer?"

"We're not finding any credible support to the theory that Nunez killed Landers Pope in a jealous rage," Mercer said. "Or any kind of rage. In fact, there seems to be some question now in Nunez's mind as to whether he did kill him."

"In Nunez's mind? For God's sake, his mind is a sump heap." Gilroy saw the others in the room staring at him. Softening his voice, he added, "I mean, we can't take anything he says too seriously."

"But this could be good news, right?" Mercer said. "If he is innocent and we can make the jury see it, we win and the Department wins. It's an even better verdict than the one you and Chief Ahern were hoping for."

"True," Gilroy said. "If you can convince a jury."

"Find Agents Ivor and Pleasance for us," Mercer said. "We'll take it from there."

Jorja entered carrying their drinks on a tray. Gilroy stood up, his mind clicking away. "I'll do what I can," he said, ignoring the offered glass of ice tea. He did remember to give Jorja a fleeting smile on his way out. But he was far from being in full control of himself. He wanted to scream.

He held it in during the elevator's descent to the second parking level and his brisk stride to his sedan. Behind the wheel of the supposedly soundproof Lexus, he let the animal sound of his anger rise from his throat.

He clawed his tiny phone from his coat pocket and even as he dialed the number knew that he was probably in a cellular dead zone.

Being correct on that point did not improve his humor.

He made his exit from the garage with wheels screeching. A block away from the building, he pulled to the curb and tried the number again.

This time he connected. "Yeah," he heard from the other end.

"What the fuck are you guys thinking?" he demanded.

"Who is this?"

"Who does it sound like?"

"It sounds like some crazy asshole who'd better get it in check if he knows what's good for him. What's put the burr up your butt, Gilroy?"

"We've got to talk," Gilroy said.

"So talk."

"Not on the phone. You at Rightway?"

"Why the hell would I be there? We'll come to you. Name the place."

Gilroy gave him the name and address of a kosher deli in the Fairfax area. "There's a parking lot in the back. I'll be in a silver Lexus."

"We'll be there in twenty minutes. Driving a Range Rover. They call the color White Gold. You join us. It'll be roomier."

Gilroy closed his phone. He gave the pistol on his hip a pat, then pulled away from the curb.

A White Gold Range Rover! The arrogance of these pricks.

CHAPTER

NINETEEN

When the meeting in the conference room broke, Mercer headed back to his office carrying his glass of ice tea. He was surprised to find Melissa absent from her desk, even more surprised that the desktop had been cleared and the computer screen was dark.

A glance at his watch explained everything. How the hell did it get so late so early?

He noticed that the phone's red message button was blinking an S.O.S. Evidently his day hadn't quite ended.

He entered his office, sat, took a long swallow of ice tea, and hoped it would keep him nominally alert for a while.

The message was from Lonny.

Judging by the noise in the background when the detective answered his cell phone, he was either at a convention of loud talkers or a crowded bar room. "I'm with a couple blues you're gonna want to meet," he said. "They can make some interesting connections for us."

"Where are you?"

"Swede's," Lonny said, "but we're gettin' ready to make like a tree and leaf."

"You been drinking?"

"Isn't that why God made bars? Don't worry, boss. I don't go over a brew or two. Anyway, we're grabbin' hat. This is no place to have our talk. Too loud and too up close."

He gave Mercer an address on Sierra Bonita in the Hollywood foothills. "House belongs to my new pal, Delray.

Officer Delray Parmenter. We'll be there in ten, fifteen minutes."

"Shouldn't take me much longer," Mercer said.

Passing the library, he paused to observe Sidone and Kennard through the thick glass door, yawning and rubbing their eyes as they struggled through the Nunez reports. He stuck his head in. "I forgot to mention something. It's an acronym used by the FBI."

"That'd be Federal Bureau of Investigation," Kennard said. "Can I go home now?"

"The acronym is 'OBN,' " Mercer said, ignoring the comment and the question.

"Old Black Nannies," Sidone said.

"See how easy it is? You guys work on it in your spare time," Mercer said.

He shut the door on a groan and shout of "What spare time?"

Moving on, he wondered if Kennard had made his play yet and if it had been successful. If they *had* knocked boots, he owed them points for keeping it on the way down low.

He was heading for the elevator when he heard Camilla, the night receptionist, say, "There's Mr. Early now."

He turned.

The most beautiful woman he'd ever seen was rising from a couch near the far wall. She was tall, her smoothly rounded figure neatly encased in a white linen suit. Her body was enough to turn heads, but it was the angelic perfection of her light brown face that caused him to lose track of time and place. Wherever he was, he was holding his breath.

"Mercer?" she said, as if she couldn't quite believe it.

She moved toward him. His feet seemed to have frozen to the carpet. "It's Annie, Mercer. Annie Sutter. Actually it's Annie Corey, but back in Little Rock, before you moved . . ."

"Annie Sutter," he said, as if trying it out.

"You have done some changing, Mercer," she said, "some serious growing and filling out in the last fifteen years."

"You've filled out pretty good, too," he said.

She took another step toward him. "No big hug for your old playmate?"

He'd never seen her before in his life, but he didn't let that stop him from taking her in his arms.

Damn! The smell of her perfumed hair. The feel of her body pressed against his. De-amn! His knees felt like they might be giving way. "Mercer Edgar Early," she whispered in his ear. "I guess you are glad to see me."

He pulled her closer, felt her resist and, with reluctance, lowered his arms. She stayed near him, took his right hand in both of hers. " 'You will always be my love of loves,' " she said. "Remember when you told me that?"

Hard to remember words he hadn't spoken.

Now that he had seen her, he realized how impossible it would be to carry out his original plan of ignoring her, hoping she'd go away. He definitely did not want her to go away. With a recklessness that surprised him, he heard himself say, "Annie, we should talk."

"It's why I'm here. So much to catch up on."

"There's business I have to see to right now. Could we meet when I'm through? Late supper, maybe, around nine?"

"That'd be lovely," she said.

"Come on," he said, indicating the open elevator. "I'll take you to your car."

The receptionist was smiling at them as the doors slid shut.

On the brief descent, Annie started to quiz him about his recent life, but he held up a hand and said, "Let's save all that 'til dinner."

Her powder-blue Thunderbird was parked with its top down in the visitor's section. She slid behind the wheel. "I'm at the Bel-Air," she said. "If you get hung up, call. We can make it tomorrow."

"I'll get away if I have to use a weapon," he said.

She started backing away, then braked. "Remember," she said, "I'm registered as Annette Corey."

He'd heard her mention the name before, but its significance had been lost on him at the time. "That your married name?" he asked, not wanting to hear the answer.

A flicker of pain creased her perfect brow. "George passed away in February," she said. "One of the reasons for this trip is to settle some estate matters."

"I'm sorry," he said.

"He suffered for so long, death seemed like a blessing. George was a good man. I imagine he's smiling down now, happy I've found an old friend. I'll see you tonight, Mercer Early."

She drove away, pausing at the exit to wave to him. Then she was gone.

What the hell was he doing? he wondered. Nothing that good old George would be smiling down on, that was for sure.

CHAPTER TWENTY

Mingus came alive when the shimmering off-white Range Rover bounced up from the basement parking beneath a pastel-pink, Moorish-looking apartment building. The vehicle made an abrupt right turn and roared east down Washington Boulevard.

The detective, whose thoughts had been drifting far afield from the job at hand, welcomed the rush of adrenaline. He started up his Crown Victoria and drove off in pursuit.

"Ivan Calder" had been the name on the Rover's rental agreement. It meant nothing to the Department computer. Calder's New York address on the agreement didn't exist.

Because of the Rover's tinted windows, Mingus couldn't tell how many people were inside. At least two, he figured. The ones he and Hildy had seen driving away from Dr. Medina's office building.

Hildy had been bothered by the fast food garbage in Dr. Medina's bathroom. Not only did the doc seem an unlikely Burger King customer, there was something furtive about an early morning hamburger consumed in a shrink's office.

Then there was Officer Paget's turnabout on the value of therapy. Hildy's conclusion was that Emmylou's sudden decision to visit her shrink may have had less to do with a need for a psychic massage than a desire to hook up with her fugitive partner.

Mingus didn't really see his former therapist in the role

of accessory after the fact, but went along with Hildy's request that they settle in for a while, keeping an eye out for Joe Mooney.

Instead, they'd spotted two men leaving the building and getting into an off-white Range Rover. The men fit the description of the pair who'd supposedly kidnapped Paget and the vehicle was a match, too.

Mingus made the quick decision to trail them, leaving McRae behind to continue her watch.

The Rover was big enough to make tailing it child's play. Mingus had no trouble keeping it in sight all the way to the pink apartment on Washington Boulevard, where it burrowed into a basement parking area.

He pulled over to the curb farther down the block and waited, giving the two men enough time to leave the vehicle and settle down in their apartment. Then he strolled to the pink monstrosity and cautiously descended the sharp incline to where the Rover rested in the slot nearest the stairwell.

It was locked. No surprise there.

He could see little through the tinted windows, but as he circled the Rover, he noticed a sticker on the rear bumper that provided the name of the rental company and the vehicle's ID number.

Back behind the wheel of his Crown Vic, he used this information and his cell phone to come up with the fake name and address. Progress of a sort.

He leaned back against the comfortably worn leather seat and, keeping his eyes on the apartment building, tried to get a fix on what the presence of the two men told him. They obviously were real and not the figments of some crank caller's imagination. Did this mean that Officer Paget *had* been kidnapped? If so, what had been the purpose of the kidnapping, how or why had she been freed, and why was she denying it?

Okay, the kidnapping was doubtful. Then what? Assuming that Mooney had made the anonymous call, why had he described these two men and the Range Rover? He was probably delusional. Maybe he'd seen them somewhere else. At his wife's murder? If that had been the case, why wait to make the call and why put them on the spot somewhere else? Why drag Paget into it?

It didn't make any sense.

But it had to mean something. They were connected to Mooney in some way. He didn't have reason enough to get a warrant or bring them in for questioning. He'd just have to hang and see what developed. If anything.

It hadn't been that hard to pass the time, sitting in his car alone. Well, not quite alone. There was the smell of McRae's flowery perfume.

He preferred to use her last name when he thought of her, as if that made her presence in his head less personal. It was like imagining bourbon on the back of his tongue and thinking it would make him less a drunk if he called it lemonade. She was his bourbon. His for the taking. And he was getting thirstier every day.

She wanted him. And he wanted her. Why was he fighting it? The obvious answer was Bettye. But he thought there was something more than fidelity that kept him from knocking boots with the big blonde.

He didn't trust her.

That was it. She was making it too easy for him. He wasn't exactly Taye Diggs. The only actor he in any way resembled was maybe, on a good day, Forest Whitaker. Why was the woman throwing herself at him?

He had no idea what she hoped to achieve either by fucking him or by fucking him over, but he still didn't trust her.

He was working that theme when the Range Rover emerged from the parking level and drove away.

Hanging nearly a block behind, Mingus followed the boxy vehicle east on Washington, then north to Hollywood. On Melrose, the Rover headed east again. Its destination just beyond Fairfax was a flat, recently whitewashed building identified by a neon sign that read HELLO DELI.

Mingus followed the Range Rover down a one-lane driveway to the rear of the deli where he watched it slide into the last empty parking space on the lot. Pretending to be waiting for someone to free up a slot, he parked, motor running, within a few feet of the Rover, the Crown Vic's rear blocking the off-white vehicle.

He was expecting the two men to get out and enter the deli. But that didn't happen. Instead, a man stepped from a silver Lexus three cars away and headed his way. Mingus bent down, as if searching for something on the floor of his car.

He was worried the man might recognize him.

He'd certainly recognized the man. It was Chief John Gilroy, the second most powerful officer in the LAPD.

CHAPTER

TWENTY-ONE

Some jackass was parked in an old Crown Victoria with his engine running. Gagging from the toxic exhaust, Gilroy considered drawing down on the son of a bitch and shooting him dead. He figured Early could get him off with a self-defense plea.

The Range Rover was, as expected, big and garish, painted the color of Marilyn Monroe's pubic hair. Ivor opened a rear door for him.

The pale leather interior felt and smelled new as he slid in beside Ivor. Pleasance was in the passenger seat, watching him in the mirror attached to the sun visor. A third agent, crew cut and empty-faced, was behind the wheel. Gilroy recalled he had an oddball first name. Tip. Tip Carlyle.

Pleasance twisted on his seat to face him. "Wha'da'ya think, John?" he asked, indicating the Rover's interior. "A beauty, huh?" He ran a hand along the top of his leather seat in a caressing manner. "Know what the Land Rover folks call this color leather? Parchment."

Gilroy had assumed that Chief Ahern had been the ultimate test of his self-control, but Pleasance was taking it beyond the beyond. "I don't give a rat's ass about your seat covers. What I'd like to know is what the hell are you thinking, driving around in this showboat? Why not a Hummer? That bright yellow one you can see for miles?"

"John doesn't like our taste in transportation," Pleasance said to Ivor.

"We've got five dead. One of my officers is in prison, so far gone he's drooling on his jumpsuit. Another is in the wind, crazy as a bedbug and armed and dangerous. This whole thing is busting apart at the seams. You were supposed to come in like the Wolf and put it all back together. Without anybody knowing you were ever here. Instead, you guys are sending up flags all over the goddamned—"

"We don't have time for your shit, John," Pleasance said, cutting him off. "We've got dinner reservations. At this place in Beverly Hills run by what's-his-name—you know, Indiana Jones—by his kid. So just calm down, stop your moaning. Everything's being taken care of."

"Nunez's lawyers know who you are. They want to talk to you."

"Oh? Then they're in for a disappointment."

"You're not listening. They know who you are. Christ, the homeless in the park must know who you are. What part of keeping a low profile don't you understand?"

"Low profile? We got the ticket to ride, *John*. We got truth, justice, and the American way in our inside pocket. So fuck low profile. And fuck your bougie lawyers."

Gilroy glared at him. He thought about telling him how unwise it was to underestimate the tenacity and ferocity of even the lowliest of lawyers and that the crew at Carter and Hansborough were way up at the other end of that spectrum. But he doubted that anything he said would matter to the arrogant prick.

His silence seemed to take some of the edge off of Pleasance's attitude. "Don't worry, John. Things have been falling apart, to be sure. But the fixer is here now. So relax."

"You have a fix on Mooney?"

"We've got a fix on everything. Your street rodent infestation is under control, right?"

Gilroy nodded. "The Hispanic gang activity is way down."

"We thin their herd first, then my brothers who wear the blue and red. Then the yellow bangers. All according to plan. Don't worry about a thing."

Gilroy had to admit that part of the deal was working. But Pleasance was one of those puffed-up fools who could wind up choking on his own hubris.

Well, he'd tried to caution the man. There wasn't much

else he could do. Life had been so much nicer when Carl Ivor had been overseeing the operation solo. Carl was someone you could talk to. Now, he was definitely out of favor because the breakdown had occurred on his watch.

His eyes went to Ivor. The man was keeping a game face, all things considered. It must've been a blow to the heart, taking the blame for something beyond your control and then having to toady to a strutting asshole like Pleasance. Gilroy could write the book on the demoralizing effect of toadying.

"If that's all, John," Pleasance said. "Wouldn't want you to spend a minute longer in this vehicle you seem to dislike so much. But for your information, the people at *Car and Driver,* who know a little bit about these things, they think it's hot stuff."

"I'll keep that in mind," Gilroy said as he climbed out of the oversized SUV.

Through a half-opened window, Pleasance said, "You just worry about keeping your little bossman happy, John. We'll take care of the heavy lifting. If any big, bad attorneys try workin' their lawbook mojo on us, they'll live to regret it big time, you can be sure."

Gilroy hoped Pleasance wasn't lying about the "live" part. In his experience, arrogance and ruthlessness went hand in glove. Not for the first time, he wondered if it might not have been a mistake agreeing to be their point man inside the LAPD.

CHAPTER

TWENTY-TWO

Lonny Hootkins was sitting at the kitchen table of Delray Parmenter's comfortable little cottage on Sierra Bonita when the doorbell rang.

He'd been speculating on how much the place must have gone for when Delray took it out of escrow the year before. Two bedrooms, two baths, average living and dining room. Garage attached. Yard the size of his, Lonny's, living room rug. He figured maybe three hundred grand in a down market.

He was thinking about selling his place in Silver Lake, the two-story house where he'd been born, spent his whole life. He'd been thinking about selling it since his dad passed on four years before. It was more than a single man needed, and that was what he had always been and would always be, a single man.

A single man who liked order in his life. He found Delray's house to be too damn messy. It was the kind of mess comes with kids, part and parcel. Tricycles in the dining room, along with building blocks, papers with colorful scribbles, little plastic pieces of something or other crunching underfoot. Baby shit like the bottles under the couch, rubber balls, dolls gnawed on and carelessly tossed away, and the tiny swing on a rope hanging from a living room doorway that you had to push aside to walk by.

The baby, a cute little monkey named Rosie, was down for the count in her crib. The four-year-old twin brothers, who weren't all that alike, were out at the Cineplex with their mom, who'd looked to Lonny like they'd been keeping her on the go since her head left the pillow that morning.

Delray seemed a nice enough dude, except for his hangdog manner, which was understandable, considering the circumstances. As he rose to answer the door, Lonny noted the weapon stuck under his belt.

The other man seated at the table jerked a thumb at the gun and nodded to Lonny. "That's what it's come to," he whispered. "Shit."

He was an older, balding cop named Kells Harnick who had been a rookie when Lonny first met him. Kells's inability to go along to get along hadn't helped his career any and he was nearing its end, still on patrol. He stopped shaking his head and focused on the newcomer—Mercer Early.

"Lonny, my ol' *compadre* here, don't think too highly of too many people," Harnick told Mercer after the introductions had been made. "He says you can walk on water."

"Not even in my pontoon shoes. But it's good of Lonny to say so."

"Officer Harnick tends to gild the lily," Hootkins said. "What I tole him was you could barely hold your head above water."

"I stand corrected," Harnick said with a smile.

"Something to drink, Mercer?" Parmenter asked, holding up his Corona.

The lawyer looked at the coffee cup in front of Lonny. "Some of what he's drinking, maybe."

"I went to Midtown today," Hootkins said, "hoping to meet up with Agent Arthur Pleasance. He and Ivor had been hangin' out there yesterday, talking to everybody about Eldon Nunez. But they'd moved on to East Pico."

"You happen to ask who cleared the interrogations?"

"That would be Captain Bastino at Midtown, Captain Faust at East Pico. Only they call it debriefing sessions. Anyway, I hustled my old bones over to East Pico, but missed 'em there, too."

"You didn't miss nothing," Harnick said. "That Pleasance was just another jaybird doin' his strut."

"Tell Mercer what the jaybird was after."

"Joe Mooney," Harnick said.

"Cop killed his wife?" Mercer asked.

"They don't know that," Parmenter said, placing a cup of black coffee in front of Mercer. "Not for sure."

"That fed gave you the full treatment, partner," Harnick said. "Tell 'em about it."

"Pleasance is one scary son of a bitch," Parmenter said. "He threatened me, the green-eyed fuck."

"Threatened you how?"

"Exact words? 'You go running your mouth about our little talk and, never mind your badge, we'll put you away somewhere your little girl will be old and gray before you catch sight of her again."

"What's his problem?" Mercer asked.

"Just being a FiBIe to the n'th degree," Harnick said.

"Sounds a little more than that," Mercer said. "You show him any attitude?"

"All the attitude was coming off him," Parmenter said. "Maybe that has 'em shaking in their boots back east, but out here, he's just another two-legged El Niño."

"Another what?" Hootkins asked.

"Blast of hot air," Parmenter said. "Like I'm gonna bend over and tell him something that'll put Joe Mooney further in the stew."

"He's in pretty deep already," Mercer said. "Murder and arson, him running away from the crime scene. That's gonna have to be one hell of a defense."

"If he lives to stand trial," Parmenter said.

"Like we been telling Lonny here," Harnick said, "Delray's got an interesting theory."

"These officers being accused of murder," Parmenter said. "I don't believe it. I think something else is at work here."

Hootkins locked eyes with Mercer. He got the lawyer's unsaid message: he was thoroughly pissed that Hootkins had wasted his time on some young cop with a crackpot theory.

"Maybe you'd better elucidate a little on that for Mercer," he said to Parmenter.

The young cop frowned, took a swig of beer, and began his story.

* * *

Mercer really didn't want to hear it.

He wanted to get the hell out of there and head for the Bel-Air Hotel and the beautiful, recently widowed Annie Corey.

Then Delray Parmenter said, "It all started back in March of this year, when a cop named Dwight Baskin dropped out. Him and his wife. Just seemed to disappear. They say now he killed his wife and went on the run with her in the trunk of his car."

"That's what they say," Mercer mumbled.

"I don't buy he did it."

"No?" Mercer's bullshit tolerance level was rapidly being approached.

"No," Parmenter said. "See, I became part of the story about a month and a half ago. The night Joe Mooney and his partner tried to apprehend Baskin and wound up in a shooting match with him."

"I saw the news footage," Mercer said, trying to hurry things along.

"What I'm gonna tell you wasn't on the news. See, the shooting took place on my beat. I got there quick. Gunsmoke still in the air. Mooney and his partner were standing by, waiting for the investigators and lab guys—and the news crews—and all the shit that was about to come down on their heads.

"Mooney was real broke up. I mean, Baskin may have been a fugitive, but he was still a Medal of Valor cop."

"A medal man," Mercer said, thinking out loud. "Not a 'metal' man." What was it Eldon Nunez had said at their first meeting about the medal man? What had been the context? Something like God had sent Deadeye Dick to save the medal man.

"What's that?" Parmenter was staring at him.

"Remind me," Mercer said. "Officer Mooney shot and killed Baskin?"

"He shot out Baskin's right tire and sent the car into a wall and Baskin into the windshield. It was the crash killed him."

"But it was expert shooting, right? Deadeye marksmanship."

"Night. A fast-moving vehicle about a hundred yards and opening. Mooney on the ground. Placing three in the tire. I guess you'd call it good marksmanship."

"I didn't mean to interrupt," Mercer said, showing a little more interest now. "Go on with your story."

"Well, like I said, I got there fast and I wasn't there five minutes when this forensics guy shows. Even before the detectives and the assistant coroner.

"He says he was nearby when he got the call and he's carrying the right ID. So what the hell?"

"Tell Mercer the forensic guy's name," Hootkins prompted.

"Merrill Gibbons."

"Who took a fatal drive down Temescal Canyon," Mercer said.

"You got it," Parmenter said. "See where I'm going with this?"

"Not completely."

"Well, hang in here with me. Gibbons gets there. He's screwing around near the car. The detectives come by. A couple other patrol cops. Then all hell breaks loose, because the news creeps catch the smell of blood.

"We're trying to keep everybody back from the scene. We're pushing 'em away from Mooney and his partner. Little female named Paget. Out of the corner of my eye I see this Gibbons lift something out of the goddamned death car." He took another pull at the beer bottle.

"What was it?" Mercer asked.

"Your guess is as good as mine. Metal box. Coulda been Baskin's lunch, all I know. Anyway, I probably wouldn't have thought twice about it, but Gibbons is acting fucking weird, heading off down the alley with this box. So I follow him.

"Next street over, Rubello, there's a car parked on the corner. Beemer sedan. A funky dark purple color. Window rolls down. Gibbons hands off the box and I get the hell back to the crime scene."

"Couldn't it have been a coroner's assistant in the Benz, somebody like that?"

"Could of, but it wasn't."

"You saw the driver?"

"No. But I know who he was. And I know that, even though he's a cop, he's got no damn reason to be taking evidence from this particular crime scene. He don't even work out of Pico."

"If you didn't see him," Mercer said, "how do you know who he was?"

Parmenter hesitated before replying. "There aren't many cars that color." He smiled. "Blue Violet. That's what he calls the car, the Blue Violet."

Parmenter's smile disappeared so fast, Mercer wondered if he'd imagined it. "Anyway, I know the car and who was driving it."

"You gonna tell me his name?"

"It was your client, Eldo Nunez," Parmenter said.

CHAPTER

TWENTY-THREE

Hootkins had considered prepping Mercer for Parmenter's revelation, but there was a perversity about his nature that found amusement in the observation of young folks getting the rug pulled out from under them. The lawyer proved to be a bit of a disappointment.

He didn't show any sign of surprise.

He said, "You know Officer Nunez fairly well?"

Parmenter blinked. "Yeah," he said. "We were friends, a while back."

Damn, Hootkins cursed himself. He'd been in the young man's company all evening. How had he missed that? Paying too much attention to the nonessentials. First the rowdy bar, then the house, the family, the kiddie toys. He turned to Harnick. The balding cop was staring at his beer bottle without expression.

"Did you know Landers Pope?" Mercer asked Parmenter.

"I'd seen him around, I guess. Didn't really know him."

"So your friendship with Officer Nunez predated his relationship with Pope."

"Yeah, it was over at least a year before they started up," Parmenter said, anger edging into his voice. "But that's got nothing to do with what we're talking about."

"You're suggesting that a client of mine may have performed some act that is at the least suspicious and at the worst criminal. I'm just trying to get a fix on where you're coming from."

"Where the fuck are *you* comin' from? Your man here said you're trying to help Eldo. That's why I'm talking to you."

"Okay," Mercer said quietly. "Tell me how we help Eldo."

"What the hell don't you understand? There was something they all were in on. Baskin, Eldo, and the forensic guy."

"Gibbons."

"Baskin was the weak link. When he broke, the scam started to sour and everything headed downhill."

Mercer spoke slowly, with great patience. "You have any thoughts on what the scam might have been?"

Parmenter looked at the lawyer as if he'd just dropped down from another planet, a particularly backward one. "What else could it be?" he said. "What is always the answer when people start fucking up? When the goddamn bank loses your deposit, when the postman throws your mail away, when the surgeon cuts off the wrong leg? What is always at the heart of it?"

"You're talking about drugs?" Mercer said.

"Bingo."

"So how do we get from a drug operation to a trio of cops turning homicidal at home?"

"Lemme get another brew, first," Parmenter said.

"I'll fetch," Harnick said.

Parmenter was leaning forward, looking like he was avoiding tacks on his chair seat. His eyes were into rapid blinking. The boy was definitely het up.

"Here's how I see the deal," he said, accepting a perspiring Corona from Harnick. "The drugs were muled in from Mexico by the Emmes or Jaquecas—*vatos* from one of the toxic taco tribes. That's where Baskin came in. He must have—"

"Whoa," Mercer said. "What's the connection between the *vatos* and Baskin?"

"I thought you said you knew all about Detective Baskin. He was in charge of a special gang unit out of East Pico. He spent enough time with the Emmes to get his own 13 shirt." The gang, named for the thirteenth letter of the alphabet—"M" for "Mexico"—proudly displayed the number on various items of apparel.

"I figure what happened: he took to sampling the merchandise in a big way, went off his nut, popped his wife, and took his long ride with her in the trunk."

Mercer seemed to be thinking on it. Finally, he said, "Then you figure it was drugs in the black box?"

"Or money. Or a computer disc with information about the drug operation. Something the other members of the crew didn't want anybody to find in Baskin's car."

Hootkins caught Mercer glancing at his watch.

"What about the other officers and Gibbons? You figure they went whack-happy, too?"

Parmenter frowned. "Not voluntarily," he said. "I think somebody's doing a clean-up. Closing things down by fucking with the minds of everybody involved. Getting 'em high, making 'em do crazy shit."

"You tell your theory to the FBI guy, Pleasance?" Mercer asked.

"No fucking way. He'd have laughed in my face. Worse, he might even be involved. Maybe that's what that threat was all about."

"You tell your idea to anybody else?" Mercer asked.

"Just my partner," Parmenter said, indicating Harnick. "Now you. I hope it wasn't a mistake."

"The mistake would be to tell anybody else," Mercer said. He turned to Harnick. "I don't suppose you saw Gibbons take the box?"

"I was off duty that night," the older cop said. "The flu."

"Am I on to something, Mercer?" Parmenter asked.

"I don't know," Mercer said. "Maybe. I'll have to sleep on it." He stood up. "Thanks for talking to me."

"What do you think I should do?" Parmenter said.

"What do you want to do?"

"Keep me and my family safe."

"Then forget everything you told me and let me worry about it." He turned to Hootkins. "Walk me to my car," he said.

The gray-haired investigator followed the young lawyer out of the house and across the front lawn to where his Mercedes was parked. "The boy's theory kinda falls apart since the tox report says no drugs were found in Baskin's body," Hootkins said.

"Not a trace?" Mercer asked.

"Nope. Only thing looked out of place was that the body was lacking in serotonin, which I gather is something called a neurotransmitter."

"What's that mean in bottom-line language?"

"I'm the last guy you wanna ask about medical stuff," Hootkins said. "But my man Jazey Swan tells me when these nerve transmitters aren't doing their job, a man can get pretty depressed. The well-known worried blues."

"Worried enough to go off his nut like that?"

Hootkins shrugged.

"Well, the absence of drugs is the key thing for us. It means Parmenter's theory is jive. Ergo, we don't have to worry about our client being a key player in a drug cartel. We just have to worry about him killing his boyfriend. What a relief, huh?"

"Parmenter did give us a link between Nunez and the two other cops," Hootkins said.

"A link we don't want to use, unless the contents of that black box turn out to be more innocent than it seems."

"Sorry if I wasted your time," Hootkins said.

Mercer checked his watch again. Opening the car door, he said, "It wasn't a waste. It's helping me make a little more sense out of what the client has been goin' on about. I'd thought it was all mumbo jumbo. I'm gonna try the black box on him.

"Meanwhile, see if you can convince Parmenter to keep zipped about his theory. Tell him no drugs were found in Baskin. Tell him anything to shut him down. Now that he's spilled, he'll want to beat his gums to anybody who'll listen. That won't help our cause."

"I was thinking," Hootkins said, "if there was anything at all to the drug stuff, maybe the 'B' in 'OBN' stands for 'Boo-yaa' or blow. Some drug word like that."

"That may be a little too hip for the room," Mercer said. "I don't know. We'll work on it, but right now I gotta run."

Hootkins watched the Benz drive off, Mercer obviously in one hell of a hurry, the way he was gunning it. The old man turned and headed back toward the house.

He felt strangely reluctant to go inside now that the subject of Parmenter's sexual orientation had been broached. He didn't hate or even dislike gays. He just felt uncomfortable around them, probably a little intimidated by the sex things they did, or he imagined they did. The thought crossed his mind that his old pal Kells Harnick, whom he'd known for twenty years, might have been playing for the other team the whole time.

He paused to pick up a stuffed toy that one of Parmenter's kids had left in the bushes beside the front steps. It was a weird-looking thing—a big yellow sponge with bulging eyeballs, a toothy grin, arms and legs, wearing pants and gloves and shoes.

When he grasped the sponge's stomach, it giggled. He squeezed it again and, in a chirpy mechanical voice, it said, "I had a great day today. Did you have a great day?"

"I'd call it mixed," Hootkins told the sponge, and carried it into the house.

CHAPTER TWENTY-FOUR

Hildy was waiting downtown at a restaurant just off the Santa Monica Freeway in an area popular with local Hispanics who preferred it to the tourist-rich cantinas and bodegas several miles to the north on Olvera Street. The blinking neon sign said the establishment's name was Casa Nuevo, but the only thing "nuevo" about either its furnishings or its few customers that Mingus could see was a flat television monitor in a corner of the room tuned to a soccer match on Telemundo.

The Health Department had awarded the dive a big blue "C" card that it was forced by law to display prominently in its window, a warning that the kitchen was somewhat lacking in hygiene or careless in food preservation. The deep-fat fry smell wafting from that direction accompanied him up the stairs where it added one more piquant element to the stale beer-and-booze aroma of a sinister little bar.

It wasn't hard to spot Hildy. She was sharing the room with maybe a dozen young Hispanic males whose muscle shirts and baggy black pants were similar enough to suggest a gang or, at the very least, a close kinship. They noted his presence with a feigned insolence, then, ignoring him or pretending to, they continued to converse in soft tones.

Mingus couldn't make out a thing they were saying above the loud music from the speaker system. Christina Aguilera was using her peevish nasal voice to assure anybody who was listening, and herself, that they were all beautiful.

Two of the Chicano "beauties" were huddled over their drinks, talking to the bartender, a full-bodied woman with Native American cheekbones whose jet-black bangs seemed to meld into her eyebrows. Like the waitress getting her ass massaged by one of four lads sitting at a table in a corner, she wore a sheepskin vest, open in front over tight shorts that used to be called hot pants—maybe still were, for all Mingus knew.

A Chicano style-setter, with hair dyed a lemony yellow, a droopy moustache of matching hue, and a couple of cheap gems embedded in his left ear lobe, stood beside Hildy, leaning into her so intimately it looked like he was trying to mount her from the side.

She was laughing at something he was whispering in her ear when her eyes met Mingus's in the smeared mirror behind the bar. " 'Scuse me," she said, and pushed the boy off her so that she could swing around on her stool.

He saw at once that she was high. Not falling down drunk, but close enough. It had happened quickly. She'd sounded reasonably sober twenty minutes before when she'd called to give him her location.

She waved a hand at a glass resting on the bar that contained an inch of some cloudy, greenish-tinted liquid. "You gotta try one of these, Lionel. They call it a Macaw."

"More like a Mick-ay," he said, talking loud, trying to outdo Christina. He took her arm. "C'mon, let's go. The car's across the street."

She yanked her arm free. "I'm not sure I wanna go. My new friend Ramon has been telling me about this place where they have the mos' amazing show."

The lemonhead was smiling at him, waiting for their scene to play out. And then what? Mingus wondered.

"Not jus' women but muscle men, too," she was saying. "Guys built like a *tripode*." She giggled. "Three legs. Isn't that what you said, Ramon?"

Mingus noticed her gun was still in its holster under her jacket. "C'mon. You can catch the tripod show some other night."

"You come, too, *amigo*," Ramon said to him. "I fix you up with nice *tripode. Negro grande.*" He laughed.

Mingus ignored him. He called to the bartender. "How much do we owe you here?"

"All paid," was the reply.

"Good. C'mon, Hildy. We got stuff to talk about."

"*Blanco,* if that's what you want," Ramon said. "*Chaval,* maybe. Whatever pleasures you."

Hildy turned to the lemonhead. "Don't mind Li'nel. He's shopping for a halo," she said.

She slipped from the stool, staggered a little. She reached out, grabbed the glass from the bar, and weaved toward an empty table near the back of the room. Mingus followed, growing more and more annoyed by the second.

"This isn't smart," he said when they were seated.

"Back off, altar boy. I'm not on the clock now. It's play time."

"You're drunk with a gun on your hip in a Chicano gangster pussy bar. There are better places to play."

"Like my bed."

There was an upside to this situation, he realized. An hour earlier he was thinking about doing just that, rollin' around with her on that bed. Now he realized how bad an idea that was. She wasn't just a loose cannon, she was a loose cannon loaded with shrapnel.

"How'd things go at the doctor's office?" he asked.

"What? Oh. Big fuckin' time waste. Our fren' Emmylou showed 'bout an hour after you deserted me."

"Staying there was your idea."

"Yeah, maybe. Anyhow, she showed. Hour later, the doc came out. I followed her to a place called Fong's Paradise where she picked up some food."

Mingus knew Fong's. The last time he'd been there, he'd wound up watching two men die.

"She started back to her office, but she did this weird thing first." Hildy paused, frowning.

When she didn't continue, Mingus said. "What was the weird thing she did?"

"Oh yeah. There's a park right near her building, with a statue of a guy in jodhpurs, some old movie director I guess. Th' doctess sits down on a bench and starts pullin' containers out of the food bag, openin' 'em, up, closin' 'em, and putting 'em back."

"Checking to make sure she got the right order?"

"I didn't have a clear view, but that sounds right."

"Anything else?"

"No. She carried the bag back to her office."

"How much food?"

Hildy frowned. "I don't know. A big bag and it was full."

"More than she could eat by herself?"

"Oh. I see what you're saying. Yeah, it looked like enough for two. Like maybe for her and Paget."

"Paget was still there?"

"Unless she split while the doc and I were on our walk. But you're right about the food. Too much for just one person."

"How about for three?" Mingus asked.

"Aw, shit. Maybe I did miss the big show. Well, fuck it. I don't wanna think about that now. Work's all done for this week."

"When Medina left at the end of the day, was she by herself?"

"Jesus, Li'nel. Don't you ever kick back?"

"Lemme guess," Mingus said, "you got tired of watching the building and quit at five. So you didn't see the doctor leave, alone or with others."

"I waited until fuckin' six-thirty, man. I was tired. I was hungry and thirsty. I had to pee. I didn't just take off. I went up there. The office door was locked. Dark inside. I stuck my ear against the back door and couldn't hear a sound. She musta left through some other exit. So I called it a day and why the hell not? What else could I do? I went out and found a nice clean Chinese restaurant where I had my pee and a Sapphire martini and a catfish the size of a cat.

"Then I walked around a while, trying to get my phone to work, to call you to pick me up. But the fucking phone wouldn't work. Battery, I guess.

"That's when Ramon pulled over to the curb in his lovely electric blue car with a naked blonde painted on the door and asked if I needed any assistance. He took me here, where I called you."

Hildy seemed to be sobering. She hadn't touched the drink. "And what were *you* doing all afternoon while I was pressing my butt against a stone street bench scoping the building?" she asked.

He told her about the apartment in Culver City and the trip to the deli where the FBI agents met with Assistant Chief John Gilroy.

She didn't seem impressed. "So big deal. Why wouldn't a high-ranking officer meet with FiBIes?"

"In a deli parking lot?"

"No law against it."

"When he got out of their Rover, I heard one of the feds say something about taking care of lawyers and their 'law-book mojo.' I wonder what lawyers he was talking about and why they need taking care of."

"I don't see what any of that has to do with Joe Mooney."

"Maybe it's *his* lawyers who've got the agent worried. Or maybe Baskin had a lawyer. That's something for us to kick around."

"I'm tired of work talk."

"Let's get out of here," Mingus said. "The music's too loud and the place stinks. That's without even mentioning the scumbags, like your pal Raymond."

"Ra-moan. I think he's cute. And he knows how to treat a woman."

"Sure he does." Mingus stood. "I'll drive you home."

"Then what?" she asked, staying in her chair.

"Then you get some sleep."

"That's what I figured." She tossed back the last of the drink. "I think I'll stay."

Ramon had been keeping an eye on them from the bar. She waved to him. He smiled.

"You're in trouble and you don't know it," Mingus told her. "Don't expect Everybody-Loves-Ramon over there to behave like any form of humanity you're familiar with."

She stared at him and, for a brief moment, he thought he might have gotten through to her. Instead, she said, "For a black man you don't show a lot of tolerance toward other ethnics." She laughed at him, a nasty, raw guffaw.

He waited for her to finish and said, "They're burying Mooney's wife tomorrow afternoon. We should be there, case he shows."

She seemed to be considering it, then said, "Get the fuck out of here, Li'nel, and stop bothering me."

Her words cut though the music, catching the attention of the Chicano lads in the room. Ramon sauntered toward Hildy with a fresh drink in each hand. He placed one in front of her. "Another Macabre for the *belleza,*" he said, pulling a chair close to her and sitting down.

"Thanks, sweetie," she said. She faced Mingus with the drink, held it up in a mock salute, and gulped down a good portion of it.

It was *her* life.

"See you when I see you," he said, then went down the stairs and out into the gaudy, neon-lit night.

CHAPTER TWENTY-FIVE

From his table on the patio of Hilltop House, a well-fed Mercer sipped black coffee and looked at the shimmering lights of the city. Sometimes they resembled zircons, but tonight they were the real thing.

Far below on Sunset Boulevard, a cockroach parade of cars crawled forward, stopped and crawled forward again.

Towering over the Strip, but well below Mercer's perch, a vanity billboard saluted a musician recently arrested for raping a thirteen-year-old girl. The musician's manager had hoped Carter and Hansborough might handle the defense, a dream shattered by C.W., who'd supposedly told the manager he was too old and too rich to take on a client whose music was nearly as offensive as the crime he supposedly committed.

Mercer took another sip of coffee and Jack Daniel's. He was wondering what was keeping Annie when she swept through the restaurant's French doors, looking even more stunning than when she'd excused herself to "freshen up," an improvement he'd thought impossible.

"Don't think you're fooling me," she said. "I know what you've been doing with all your questions about my life."

"I doubt that," he said.

She looked surprised. "You haven't been getting me to talk about myself all night just to keep me from finding out how you've spent the last fifteen years?"

"Well, maybe," he allowed. "But my underlying motive

was to keep you here so I could enjoy your company, even though I don't deserve that pleasure."

"I don't understand."

While waiting for her, he'd decided the straightforward approach would be the best. "I'm not the Mercer Early you grew up with."

"Of course not. You're an adult. But you don't hear me complaining."

"You misunderstand. We've never met before today. Mercer Early isn't my real name."

He'd shocked her. No question. "But . . . I saw an article about you. There can't be two people by that name who grew up in Little Rock. On my street."

"You shouldn't believe everything you read in the papers," he said. "They're trying so hard to compete with TV they don't spend a lot of time on research."

"I still don't understand."

He took her hand in his. "Your friend Mercer died in an automobile accident a few years back," he said.

Pain and grief failed to undercut her beauty. "How . . . ?"

"I don't know too much about the details," Mercer said. "He lost control of his car on a highway. Somewhere near Pine Bluff. Don't think he could have suffered much."

"God. His parents must have been . . ."

"They were with him in the car."

"Ohhhhh. All of them gone? My God. Excuse me, I . . ."

"Yeah."

He let her sit with her thoughts for a while. He knew she'd eventually get back to the subject at hand.

"I don't understand," she said finally, her eyes sparkling with tears. "About you, I mean. Your name . . . ?"

"I saw a report of the accident in the *Pine Bluff Commercial*. I liked the sound of the name. I figured he might even appreciate it if I kept it going."

"What was wrong with your name?"

"My plan was to become a lawyer. My name didn't fit the image."

It was a lie. John Parker would have been a fine name for an attorney. But at the time, he'd thought that name was on a fugitive wanted list. He'd needed a new identity and his search for a recently deceased black man his age and general description had resulted in his usurping Mercer Early's identity.

Since then, he'd learned that he was no longer being sought in connection with the drug death of a young woman in Huntsville, Alabama. John Parker's suspect status had ended long ago. But, for better or worse, he was Mercer Early.

"What's your real name?" she asked.

"How'd you feel if I told you you'd just had dinner with Alfalfa Jones?" he said.

She grinned. "Get serious. That's not your name."

"Close enough."

She frowned. "The reason I had dinner with you is I thought you were my Mercer."

"See how powerful the name is," he said.

She looked away, toward the night sky.

"I'd like to be that," he said.

"Be what?"

"Your Mercer."

She stared at him. "You'd better take me back to my hotel."

He nodded and waved for the check.

The drive to the Bel-Air was a silent one. He parked in a small area beside her ground floor suite. Two couples—the women in cocktail dresses, the men in white dinner jackets—passed them on the way to her door.

"Folks a little formal around here," he said.

"Wedding party," she said. "A whole mess of marriages at this place."

Mercer got a picture in his head of Annie and himself, standing before a preacher near one of the Bel-Air's lagoons. Birds singing. Swans doing their neck-linking thing.

Not going to be happening.

Apparently she couldn't wait to be rid of him. She already had the key in the door. Another few seconds and she'd be inside. Door shut. End of love story.

"Annie, I . . ." he began, and stopped as she entered the suite and disappeared into its darkness.

He was a bit perplexed as to his next move.

She gave him a clue. "You're gonna have to make it past that doorstep if you're gonna be my Mercer."

DAY 5

SATURDAY, JUNE 19

CHAPTER

TWENTY-SIX

Mercer awoke to the delicious scent of coffee mixed with Annie's subtle perfume. She was standing beside the bed, fully dressed, holding a full cup of the aromatic brew. "Sorry to wake you, honey," she said, placing the coffee on a bedside table, "but I've got to run and I didn't want you to think I'd deserted you."

He yawned and grinned up at her. "Oh, baby," he said. "You don't know how happy I am to find out last night wasn't just a dream."

"Even the talk was good," she said.

The talk had taken place after they'd made love the second time, the slower, more intimate second time. Resting in his arms, she'd told him about her marriage to George Corey, a widower with children her age. The children had not approved of the marriage, accusing her to her face of being a gold-digger. They'd even attempted to have their father declared incompetent.

"There was nothing slow about George's mind and they knew it," she'd told him. "But they put him through hell anyway. And a few years later, when his body started to fail him, there they were again, at his sickbed, trying to get him to sign a paper giving George, Jr., control of the business and usufruct of the estate.

"He refused and they never returned, not one visit during the long year it took him to die."

"Must have been rough," Mercer said.

"The medicine didn't do much for the pain."

"Rough for you, I mean," he said.

"Maybe, but the hardest part came later, dealing not only with the fact that he was gone, but with my inability to grieve. I just felt relieved, for him, but for me, too, and that carried guilt with it."

"I know what you mean about the guilty feeling that comes with a sense of loss," he'd said.

"You were married?"

"No. This was . . . I guess you'd call it a romance. But it wasn't that either."

"In Arkansas?"

"No," he said. "Someplace else. Where isn't important."

"Tell me about it."

He was on the verge of spilling his big secret. How he'd met the beautiful and spoiled white girl named Gisela on campus at the University of Alabama. How they'd become lovers almost overnight. How he had, in his inexperience, not realized she was a drug addict until the night in his apartment he caught her snorting cocaine.

When he stopped seeing her, she'd told him she would die without him. He didn't take the promise seriously, but she kept it, breaking into his apartment one night while he was away and overdosing on heroin. He returned in time to see her body being removed, and to hear the police inquiring as to the whereabouts of the "boy she was visiting, the one who'd supplied her with the drugs."

He ran away.

Eventually he traded in his tarnished identity for one a dead man no longer needed. Only recently, an LAPD detective named Mingus had looked into the matter and discovered that the girl's death had been declared an accident long ago with the file officially closed.

Should he tell Annie all this? He wanted to be open with her, but he thought it was too soon to be bringing up Gisela's death and what he still considered to be his cowardly behavior. "Let's save that story till we're old and gray and got nothing else to talk about," he'd said.

She'd let it go and they'd both drifted off.

But now, watching him slip into a hotel terrycloth robe, she said, "Last night, I wasn't trying to pry into your past."

"I didn't think that at all."

"It's still a little soon for us to be unloading all our baggage. I probably shouldn't have said all that about my marriage. But I didn't want to keep anything back."

"I'm not into keeping secrets from you," he said. "And it's not that big a thing anymore. But it's a long and not so pretty story. I'd rather not get into it with you about to rush off somewhere."

She nodded and looked at her watch. "I am in a hurry. Our company has a plant in some place called Van Nuys. Off the 405. I'm supposed to meet with the manager there in thirty minutes."

"You're gonna have to step on it," he said. "Lemme throw my clothes on and I'll be out of here."

"Take your time. There's breakfast waiting on the patio. And the morning paper."

"I don't have much time, myself. I'm meeting with a client."

"The one you mentioned at dinner? Nunez?"

He nodded.

"You going to get him off?"

"Sure," he said, moving close to her, taking her in his arms and kissing her. She tasted of toothpaste and coffee. He hated to think of what he tasted like. But she didn't seem to mind.

"Why don't I pick you up for dinner at eight tonight?" he said.

"Better make it nine," she said. "I may need a couple hours beauty sleep first. It's going to be a long day. Starting right now."

She gave him a peck on the lips, picked up a soft leather briefcase and purse, and headed for the door.

When it had clicked behind her, Mercer took his cup of coffee to the patio where a glasstop table held pastries and orange juice and, beneath a silver lid, a mound of scrambled eggs from which Annie had consumed a tiny section.

He sat down and did away with the rest of the eggs while scanning the contents of the Metro section of the paper. Then he took a long, hot shower, dressed, checked the label on the perfume bottle Annie had left on the dresser, and drove downtown to spend what he hoped would be some quality time with Eldon Nunez.

CHAPTER

TWENTY-SEVEN

"Is it smoggy out?" the client asked.

"Moderate," Mercer said, though he had no idea if that were true. "How's it going, Eldo?"

The client seemed twitchy, but still crazy. "I miss it," he said.

"The smog?" Mercer asked.

"The feel-goods. I'm not feeling so good."

Was he making a joke? Probably not, judging by the way he was scowling and shaking his head.

"You're still on some meds, right?"

"Raymond Burr had the chance to own all the land he walked around in a day," Nunez said. "But he was so greedy he didn't close the circle and he lost everything. That's greed for you."

Mercer assumed the reference was to some movie or television show. Its relevance, if any, to the situation at hand was lost on him. "You know Dwight Baskin, Eldo?"

Nunez blinked. He began tapping on the table.

"Dwight Baskin," Mercer repeated.

"It was the beginning of the end."

"What was? The night Baskin died?"

"The night Baskin stole the darkness."

"What is the darkness, Eldo?"

Nunez smiled and Mercer thought he saw a glint of something new in his eyes. Insanity? Sanity? "The darkness is doom."

"How did Baskin steal it?"

"He was looking for the answer."
"What answer?"
"The darkness is the answer."
Mercer wondered if Nunez might be fucking with him. "Do you remember the night Dwight Baskin died?" he asked.
Nunez blinked. Tapped the table. "Yes," he said.
All right, Mercer thought. "Were you there?"
Tapping faster and harder. "Yes."
"Why were you there?"
The question seemed to pain Nunez. His hand quieted, rested on the table top as if forgotten. "To collect the darkness."
"Was the darkness in a black box?"
"The box?" Nunez pushed back from the table so suddenly it startled Mercer. "It's not here?"
"No. Not here. What was in the box?"
"The darkness."
Damn. Mercer groped for a way of shaking him loose from the darkness-doom loop. "Describe the darkness."
"Can't. It can't be seen. It just is."
"But it was in the box."
"Yes."
"How do you know, if you can't see it?"
Nunez's eyes flashed. He made a fist and used it to pound the table. "Because Land is dead, you stupid asshole."
Mercer felt as if he might have deserved the insult. Nunez was telling him something useful, if only he could decipher it.
"Who sent you to collect the box, Eldo?"
"The doctor," Nunez said, his hostility subsiding.
"What's the doctor's name?"
"I call him Dr. D."
"Where did Dr. D. tell you to take the box?"
The big man stood up, sending his chair skittering across the floor. "I'm going now." He knocked on the door and shouted "Out!"
"Where can I find the doctor?" Mercer asked.
The guard opened the door.
"You don't find the doctor," Nunez said to Mercer. "Dr. D. finds you."

* * *

Mercer's mind was filled with buzzing bees as he stepped into a vacant elevator. A thin, intense woman joined him just before the door slid shut. She was in his face almost immediately. "I thought it was you, you ungrateful piece of shit."

"Nice seeing you, too, Dana," he said to District Attorney Dana Lowery.

"I've known you were an opportunistic prick," she said, "since the day you quit our office to sell your ass to the vermin of the world. But to defend the faggot lowlife who killed my Land, that's . . ."

She seemed to be groping for the ultimate insult.

"You know we shouldn't be having this conversation, Da—"

She was on him, pounding his chest with her balled fists. Dropping his briefcase, he closed his arms around her, pulling her against him to stop the blows.

Cursing, she writhed and wriggled trying to break free. Then she went limp and began to cry. She was actually hugging him, weeping against his chest when the elevator door opened on the main floor.

He was aware of people standing there, not as many as would have been present on a weekday, but enough, gawking at the tyrant they called "Cruella." To cut short their delight at the unexpected sight of her in tears, he hit the button for the sub basement.

There, he walked the D.A. to the vacant stairwell and waited for her to pull herself together.

They sat side by side on the dusty concrete steps.

"He . . . was . . . my world," she said. "A baby so glorious it could break your heart . . . . A little boy, handsome and polite and loving. He called me Deena." Her smile softened her face almost to the point of beauty.

Mercer knew enough about human nature, and about Dana Lowery, to realize that her mood would soon shift quickly and dramatically. She would hate herself for this display of humanity and hate him for having witnessed it and, in her mind, for having caused it.

She would berate him for as long as it took to get herself back in form. And for some reason he didn't quite understand, he would stay and allow her that opportunity.

But when the mood swing came, she did not rave nor rant. She stood, brushed the dirt and dust from her dress, and in a chillingly quiet voice, said, "Your client is an immoral freak of nature who has robbed me of my boy and robbed the world of all that is good in it. Your courtroom tricks will not save him. Nor will the threats from the gay mafia within our government. He will never see freedom again."

Mercer followed her up the stairs to the main floor.

"What threats?" he asked. "What gay mafia?"

She wheeled on him, in full fury now. "I'm talking about the calls from the fucking White House, telling me that it would be in the country's best interests to drop all charges against your client. I'm talking about some FBI hardass threatening to have me removed from office if I continue to, as he put it, *persecute* your client. But you wouldn't have any idea why a worthless, lowly LAPD cop would be getting such powerful support?"

"I wouldn't," Mercer said.

"He's gay," she shouted. "They're gay. Hell, why am I standing here telling you? As if you aren't gay, too. Fuck all of you degenerates."

She raced up the stairs, stumbling in her haste.

Mercer watched her go. As amused as he was by the absurdity of her antigay rant, he was also perplexed by some of the other things she'd said. He knew that FBI agents had been sniffing around the LAPD, but this was the first he'd heard of the bureau's attempt to stifle the Nunez trial. And, assuming that the White House interest in his client wasn't a Dana Lowery fantasy, what was behind it?

He wondered if it might not be the contents of the mysterious black box. Could Eldon Nunez's darkness wind up being his salvation?

CHAPTER TWENTY-EIGHT

Mingus, who usually was able to sleep in on weekends, awoke even before the 8:00 a.m. alarm Bettye had set for herself. He opened his eyes, got a vague fix on the time from the brightness of the room, then closed his eyes, and continued to lie, unmoving, in a pretense of sleep.

The room was cool, thanks to a controlled air unit that he could hear humming in the far recesses of the building. Outside, Saturday morning traffic ebbed and flowed, its sharps and flats muted by double-pane windows.

Beside him, Bettye shifted, the pattern of her breathing changing slightly. *Floating up to meet the day,* he thought.

He felt like he could and probably should head to the bathroom to relieve himself, but he wasn't ready for the out-of-bed experience. In spite of the events of the night before, or perhaps because of them, he was thinking about Hildy. Wondering how badly she'd gotten herself fucked up.

The alarm suddenly filled the room with music courtesy of KJAZ. He recognized Coltrane's tenor sax right off. It took him a little longer to name that tune. By the time he'd pegged it as "Lush Life," Johnny Hartman's satiny but deeply masculine voice was spelling it out.

The bed shook slightly. There was a click and Hartman and Trane were no longer in the room. He felt Bettye's weight leave the mattress and heard her tiptoeing to the bathroom. He realized his pretense of sleep was complicating her preparation for work, but he didn't feel up to morning chat.

Eventually the pretending gave way to real sleep. When he awoke again, it was after 9 a.m. and he was alone in the apartment. He sat on the side of the bed and tried to plan his day. The only thing pressing was a visit to Green Meadow Cemetery at 2 p.m. when Geraldine Mooney was being laid to rest. He had hours to fill.

Bettye had ground fresh coffee and readied the machine with water so that all he had to do was push a button. She had also made a breakfast place setting for him at the kitchen table that included the morning paper, folded and unread.

It made him feel loved. And guilty.

He spent an hour messing with a bathroom faucet, fixing the leak but at the cost of leaving ugly scratches on the chrome base from the pliers. A trip to Gold's Gym used up another hour and burned off some calories, but the endorphin kick didn't do as much for his mood as he'd hoped.

Finally, after lunch, when he could put it off no longer, he dialed Hildy.

Her cellular was turned off and an answering machine took the call.

Trying to convince himself he was only concerned for her safety, he drove to her apartment.

She didn't respond to the buzzer. A rubber-banded pack of mail forwarded from her Vegas address, mainly bills from the look of them, lay on a counter beneath the tenants' brass boxes. Not knowing when the mail got delivered, he couldn't tell if this meant she'd been out all night or had left earlier that day before it had arrived.

Or, letting his darker thoughts have their way, it might mean she was up in her apartment with her throat cut.

He shook his head, thinking that might clear away the morbid image. In a state of malaise, he returned to the Crown Vic and began driving in the direction of Green Meadow. He figured there was little chance Hildy would be meeting him there.

He arrived before the hearse and the mourners. He found a tree-shaded wooden bench atop a rolling hill that gave him a clear view of the surrounding area. If Joe Mooney arrived to send his wife off, Mingus would see him.

Leaning back against the bench, he wondered how they kept the grass so green. Must've had the sprinklers going overtime. His folks were buried in a considerably less verdant facility, not that it mattered much. When you were dead, you were dead. He always figured he'd be buried with them, but he wondered if he shouldn't discuss the matter with Bettye. He was still a young man, but you never knew when that scythe was going to swing. Especially in his line of work.

He watched the late Mrs. Mooney's burial mound being prepped and, before too long, spied the hearse and the short line of vehicles following it.

He'd spoken long-distance with the brother-in-law, Dr. Johnston, the previous day. The doctor had turned the arrangements for the funeral services over to his receptionist. His plan had been to drive in from Big Bear that morning with his wife and the Mooney daughter and go directly to the services. Afterwards, the three of them would take the drive back. "Assuming you still think that's necessary, Detective," he'd said.

Mingus had told him that he thought it was.

Looking none the worse for the drive, they emerged from a limo with a pretty teenager whom Mingus took to be the Johnston's daughter. About twenty-five others showed up for the burial. Mingus was convinced that Joe Mooney was not among them.

Nor was Hildy.

He stayed seated on the bench, checking the area, until the last mourner's vehicle was on its way out of the graveyard. Then he descended the hill and approached the freshly sodded patch with its new headstone.

"Rest in peace," Mingus said, wondering if the dead ever did.

He returned to the Crown Vic feeling depressed and aimless and began to drive with no particular destination in mind. It was four o'clock on a Saturday afternoon. He should either be chilling in some mindless action movie or focusing on what damn little information he had that might lead him to Joe Mooney. Instead, he was letting his mood drag him down.

He realized that, like a riderless horse, he was following his nose to a ramshackle, unpainted building a block ahead—The Kittyhawk Bar, the site of many a long night that had left him senseless and red-eyed and degraded and disgusted with himself.

He hadn't wet his lips at the K-hawk in years, hadn't felt the lure of a night of whisky and smoke and strange pussy since taking up with Bettye. But his mouth felt dry as sand and he longed for the cold, harsh sting of alcohol at the back of his throat.

A group of black men, even more fucked up than he, was standing around in front, talking bullshit and gesturing with their beers. They turned to stare at him as he drew the Crown Vic to the curb. He looked at their slack-mouthed, unshaven, hostile faces and drove on.

A few blocks away, he parked again.

This time he got out his phone and the small spiral notebook he kept. He found the number he wanted and fed it into the phone.

On the second ring, a machine picked up. He listened to the message. He'd heard it before. He waited until the promised beep, then said, "Dr. Medina, this is Lionel Mingus. I'd like to make an appointment. Nothing to do with Joe Mooney. This is personal. I . . . need some help."

CHAPTER

TWENTY-NINE

"I can understand where the D.A. got her theory," Hootkins said as he and Mercer strolled along the junk-strewn alley where Dwight Baskin had died. "There's an awful lot of gay folks involved in this."

"That says more about the way of the world," Mercer said, "than it does any homo conspiracy. There are a lot of gay folks involved in everything."

Hootkins didn't seem convinced but was not in a mood to argue the point. As if inclined to change the subject, he gestured toward a gap in the wall surrounding the abandoned mall. A cluster of cinderblocks rested on the other side of the wall, like the piece of a crossword puzzle. "That must be where Baskin's vehicle gave it up."

Mercer looked at the wall. A clinging vine, growing up from the alley, had taken up occupancy in the broken section. Time and nature moved on.

"The black box had to be in his car," Mercer said. "Maybe the trunk."

"With his wife's corpse," Hootkins said.

"And the tech, Merrill Gibbons—"

"The gay tech," Hootkins reminded him.

"The gay tech, Merrill Gibbons, removed the box and took it"—Mercer headed down the alley to Rubello Street—"took it to Nunez's car, which was parked there."

He pointed to an empty curb across from the alley. "And this is as far as we get, because we don't know the next destination for the box. Just that it went to a Dr. D."

"Lot of Dr. D.'s in the area," Hootkins said. "real doctors, fake doctors. I once knew a guy called himself a Doctor of Romance."

"If either of his names starts with a 'D,' be sure to tell the associates to add him to the list they're making."

"That Haines boy might be put to better use givin' his daddy a call. See if he can find out if and why the White House is interested in the client."

The thought had already occurred to Mercer. "I'll talk to him about it," he said.

They were walking to their cars when a Caddy Escalade with a tinted windshield rolled into the alley and parked, facing them.

The passenger door opened and a large man climbed out. He was white with a square jaw and a black buzz cut. He was wearing a dark suit, white shirt, and tie of alternate green, gray, and blue stripes. He stood beside the vehicle, staring at them.

"What the hell is this?" Hootkins asked.

"Least they're not Crips," Mercer said.

"Not sure I prefer the Terminator." Following the lawyer's lead, he continued walking in the direction of man and machine.

When they were within four or five feet of the car, Buzz Cut asked, "What are you men doing here?"

"I was just gonna ask you the same question," Mercer said.

Buzz Cut started to say something, but was distracted by someone inside the Escalade. "You hang right there," he ordered Mercer, then turned to the distraction and asked, "What?"

Another car turned into the alley and stopped beside the Escalade. A beige Jaguar four-door. The man who emerged from it was white and middle-aged with a smooth, tanned, unremarkable face and neatly clipped graying hair. He wore a loose brown pullover sweater, starched khaki trousers, and brown suede boots that Mercer immediately coveted.

Buzz Cut snapped to attention. The newcomer glared at him until he swung back into the Escalade. Then the vehicle backed out of the alley and drove off.

"That's some vanishing act," Mercer said.

"I must apologize for the boys," the newcomer said. "They're not as people-friendly as we'd like. But we've had some little problems with the property."

"Who would 'we' be?" Mercer asked.

"Forgive me. Fred Touey." He offered his hand. "Touey Realty."

Mercer shook the hand and introduced Hootkins and himself.

"You gentlemen wouldn't be in the market for the most undervalued piece of property in L.A.?"

"Just looky-looing," Mercer said. He scanned the mall's exterior. "How'd you know we were here? There a camera around somewhere? Or an alarm system?"

The man pointed to a spot up near the mall building's roofline. "We had to put in some of those cheap little mini-cams. Flash pictures of the property on the monitor in our office every thirty seconds."

"Probably no competition to cable," Mercer said.

Touey smiled. "Not as entertaining, but more informative. The reason for the cameras and the abrasiveness of my associate is we've had homeless people camping out on the property. Using it for a toilet. Setting fires to keep warm."

"Your associates thought we looked homeless?"

"They don't think. That's why I'm here. So, gentlemen, what can I tell you about Pico Mall?"

"I understand there was a police shootout here in this alley not long ago."

"Had nothing to do with the mall, however."

"Messed up the wall some."

"A little cement and plaster could fix that. Wouldn't take much to put the place back in apple pie order. Look, this mall has been sitting here inactive for nearly half a year. Hemorrhaging money. The owners are highly motivated to sell."

"Was this a specialty mall?" Mercer asked.

The question seemed to confuse Touey. "Specialty?"

"A food mall? A medical mall?"

"It kinda covered the waterfront," Touey said. "A little of everything. That may have been the problem."

"Would you have a list of the businesses?"

"I imagine I could put that together for you."

Touey started moving to his Jaguar. "Anything else?"

"Your boots," Mercer said, causing Touey to stop and look at him, confused. "They're very handsome. I was wondering where I might pick up a pair."

Touey looked down at the suede boots. "Tell the truth, my wife bought 'em for me. On Rodeo Drive, probably. That's where she spends her shopping time and my money."

"I got a question about your wearing apparel, too," Hootkins said.

Touey seemed amused. "Probably more of my wife's doing. She's got all the taste in the family."

"She buy you that gun under your shirt?"

Touey lost none of his good cheer as he lifted his pullover, exposing an impressive six-pack for a man in his middle years and an equally impressive Beretta Centurion nestled in leather at his hip. "I picked this up myself. Fact is, not all our properties are in the high rent district. A little armament raises my comfort level somewhat."

"Could I have one of your cards?" Mercer asked.

"Of course," Touey said. He slapped his pockets and frowned. "Hell, I left the office so damned fast . . . hold on."

He got into the Jag, popped the glove box, and poked around in it briefly. He looked at Mercer standing beside the driver's door and shook his head. "No go. But we're in the book. T-o-u-e-y. Fred Touey Realty. On Pico near Fairfax."

The Jag's engine grumbled, then lapsed into a satisfied purr. "I should have that list of the former tenants for you first thing Monday. Call or stop by."

"Thanks," Mercer said.

"I know you lawyer types don't like to be kept waiting." He gave them a wink and backed into the street.

As the Jaguar cruised away, Mercer saw Hootkins jotting down the plate number in a notebook. "I'll be real interested to see what that turns up."

"I imagine so, him being the only Realtor in the big, wide world forgets to carry a business card."

"He's also a mind reader," Mercer said. "Knew I was a lawyer without my having to tell him."

"I'll see if there's some poor soul on weekend duty owes me a favor," Hootkins said. "You gonna be at the office?"

"Till six."

* * *

The incident was not only odd, it was unsettling, Mercer thought. Driving away, he got out his cellular and was about to dial information, to see if there could possibly be a number for Touey Realty, when a street sign caught his eye. Smiling, he pocketed the phone. It was Touey Street. Good old Fred Whatever must have driven past it on his way to intercept the men in the Escalade.

Thinking of that, Mercer saw one of the large black beetles in the traffic behind him. How many could there be in that part of the city? Few enough for him not to feel paranoid.

Nearing Le Brea, he moved into the far right lane. So did the black Escalade. He made the turn. The Escalade didn't.

Maybe he was a little paranoid, after all. But was that so bad, all things considered?

CHAPTER THIRTY

Mingus stood before Emmylou Paget's pink front door, wondering if he should press the buzzer or do an about-face and go have a drink somewhere. He'd driven to Venice with the idea of sidelining his self-disgust at least temporarily by moving ahead with the investigation. He was curious about Paget's no-show at the cemetery. And a few other things. But now he wasn't sure of the wisdom of interrogating the officer solo and in his present state.

What the hell. He pushed the buzzer.

He had to push it one more time before he heard bare feet slapping hardwood in his direction. She peered out at him through the small glass panel in the door. He could see her hair was uncombed, her eyes sleep-crusted. "Fuck you," he heard her say through the door.

But she opened it. She was wearing a deep purple silk robe that she'd wrapped rather carelessly around her nakedness. "Don't you fuckers ever sleep?" she asked, stepping aside as he entered a small, orderly living room furnished in what looked like Ikea basic.

"It's five o'clock in the evening," he said.

"No shit?" She seemed genuinely surprised. "Well, it *is* Saturday. Right?"

"Last time I checked," Mingus said.

"C'mon back. I gotta get some coffee or I'll die."

She walked him past a room with a dinner table and chairs that looked like they'd never been used, into a spotless kitchen that she began to clutter with pots and pans.

Almost by rote, she loaded a Mr. Coffee and set it perking. Then she got two thick white mugs from a cabinet and placed them near the machine. Each had the same decoration—a little pink pig wearing a police cap.

"Damn, I'm starving, too," she said. "Want some eggs?"

"Thanks, but the brew will do me fine," he said.

He stood near the Mr. Coffee and watched her spray-oil a fry pan and place it on a low burner. Then she cracked four eggs into a bowl and started attacking them with a fork. Her movement caused the robe to shift, briefly exposing one small and, to his eye, perfect breast. It didn't seem to bother her and he was certainly fine with it.

"Rough night?"

"Not really," she said. She stopped beating the eggs, an odd expression on her face.

It looked like fear to Mingus. "You okay?" he asked.

"Sure," she said, and carried the bowl to the sink where she added a little water to the mix. "So, Detective, what's on your mind this morn— this evening."

"I kinda expected to see you at the funeral," he said.

"The fu . . . awww, shit. *Shit!*" She stopped stirring the eggs and stared at the floor for a few moments, then shook her head in a gesture of hopelessness and returned to her task. "Well, I don't know any of Gerry's folks anyway. Didn't know her all that well, either. Anybody show up from East Pico?"

He shrugged. "I didn't see anybody wearing a uniform. Wasn't a big crowd."

"I fucking should have been there," she said.

Mr. Coffee had done his job, so Mingus filled the cups and carried them to a wooden table for two under a window that looked out over the canal. Taking one of the chairs, he asked, "How'd things go at Dr. Medina's yesterday?"

"What makes it your fucking business?" She poured the stirred eggs into the pan.

"You met up with Officer Mooney there," he said.

"That's bullshit." She moved to the table and picked up her cup of coffee. She took a long swallow. "There *is* a God," she said, carrying the cup back to the stove.

The eggs were making a racket so she found a spatula and began moving them around.

"We both know you and he were together in the doc's office yesterday," he said, pushing the truth.

"Dream on," she said, busily scraping the scrambled eggs onto a plate.

"It'd be better for everybody if we brought him in before he did any more damage."

"Why tell me?" she said, joining him at the table with her eggs and coffee.

"Because you know where he's holed up," he said.

She stared at him. "You're shitfaced drunk, aren't you?"

"Hell, no," he answered, too defensively.

"But you've been boozing. I can smell it on you. Hell, it's almost putting me off my eggs."

He silently cursed himself. What a fuckup he was.

She seemed to relax, confident that she had the upper hand. "Where's your hottie partner, by the way?" she asked.

When he didn't reply, she smiled. "Is that the deal? Anna Nicole's off doing the dirty and it's driving you to drink?"

This was getting totally out of hand. He'd had a few drinks but he wasn't drunk. He could think straight and it was time for him to do that if this so-called interrogation was to end in anything but disaster.

He forced himself to smile. "I'll tell you where my partner is, you tell me where yours is."

She lost some of her good humor and gobbled eggs instead of responding.

He sipped coffee and stared at her.

"I got no idea where he is," she said finally.

"He didn't confide in you yesterday."

"I didn't see him yesterday. I've told you that already. Sober up."

"You saw him all right. How was that Chinese food, anyway? They do a pretty good job at Fong's as a rule."

She was frowning now. Maybe a little puzzled. A portion of egg fell off her fork back onto the plate. She didn't seem to notice.

"Don't be a goddamned idiot," he said. "You know the moment you met with him, you put yourself on the hook for anything unlawful he does from that time on. To himself, or anybody else."

"That's not—"

"Oh, but it is, Officer Paget. You're an accessory. You're hindering an investigation. The one thing you're not doing is helping Officer Mooney. And he is in desperate need of help, as you fucking well must know."

He was shaking her. He could see that.

Suddenly, she threw the fork across the room. Not at him. Not at anything. She pushed away from the table and ran from the kitchen.

He took another hit of coffee, then followed her.

She was in her bedroom, crying. It was evidently where she spent most of her in-house time. Magazines and newspapers were scattered on the floor around the bed. Dirty clothes were in little piles where she'd stepped out of them. CDs and cassettes, naked and in cases, were stacked carelessly on a counter next to a cheap all-in-one soundbox.

There were a few books on a tall narrow cabinet, but its shelves were mainly being used to hold stuffed animals and dolls. Their presence made it seem as if the room belonged to a little girl, an impression enforced by the small female huddled on the rumpled bed weeping and sniffling.

Seeing him standing in the doorway, she quickly shattered the image of youth. "Get the fuck out of my house, you fucking drunk."

He entered the room cautiously, as if it were a forbidden area. Which it was, sort of. Woman on the bed, naked under a robe. It was a situation that cried out for a partner to be present. A female partner would be particularly welcome. But he was there by himself. And he wasn't going to walk away.

"I didn't come here to give you any trouble," he said. "Just tell me where I can find Joe Mooney and I'll leave."

"I don't know where he is. Now get out."

She leaped from the bed and rushed toward him, presumably to push him out the door and out of her life. But her feet got caught in clothes on the floor and she stumbled.

He stretched out his right arm, catching her before she dove headfirst into the wall. Then, awkwardly, he withdrew his arm and took a step away. She looked at him, tears in her eyes, and said, "Just go, please."

"I won't hurt him," he said. "I swear to God."

"I'd tell you where he was if I knew," she said, her eyes tearing. "He is so fucked up."

"Fucked up how?"

"He's . . . crazy. No other way to put it. Delusional. Talks about conspiracies. He thinks there's this major plot to control all America. I don't know . . . lunatic speak."

"How did you arrange the meeting?"

"I didn't. I guess Dr. Medina must have told him I was coming in."

"Then she's been in touch with him?"

"I swear I don't know," she said. "It all seems like a dream. Joe and I sitting in her office, eating Chinese like everything was normal. Except for the crazy things he was saying.

"You were right, by the way. He was the one called in my 'kidnapping.' He really believes he saw it happen. I told him that I'd probably know if a couple of guys dragged me into an SUV and drove off with me. But he just gave me this 'so you're against me, too,' look."

"How'd you leave it with him? Still friends?"

"I . . . I don't know." She got that frightened look again. "I can't seem to . . . I remember sitting at Dr. Medina's desk, eating with Joe and talking. And . . . that's it. Until I heard you ringing the bell."

"You don't remember leaving the doc's office?"

"No. Nothing. It's . . . look, I've had nights when I drank a little too much and maybe blacked out. But I could always fill in the blanks. You know, I'd remember drinking and getting sleepy. Maybe even realizing the next morning I hadn't spent the night by myself, even before checking to make sure.

"But the only thing we were drinking in the doctor's office was tea. And I pulled a total blank until fifteen or twenty minutes ago."

"The way you downed those eggs, I'd say you slept through dinner."

"I don't remember driving here or taking my clothes off or getting in bed. Nothing."

"Sounds like you mighta been slipped some industrial-strength roofie," he said. "Throw something on and we'll go get you tested."

"No fucking way. Who'd do such a thing? Not Dr. Medina. Why would she? I can't see Joe drugging me, even as far out as he is. What would be the point?"

"If you can't remember the last twenty-four hours, something's been going on."

"Just forget about it, okay? You asked me about Joe. I saw him yesterday. He's in bad shape. I don't know where he is. End of story."

"If that's the way you want it."

She grabbed his arm. "You're not gonna put any of this in your report? Please. It'll make me look like a fucking mark."

"Anybody can get fed a drug without noticing it. I lost a gun and badge that way awhile back."

"Yeah? Was that a good career move for you?"

The badge had been used by a felon to gain entry to a woman's house. He thereupon beat and raped her every which way and left the badge behind as a gift for Mingus. "No," the detective said to Emmylou Paget, "it wasn't exactly a career highlight."

"So you get my point. Drop it, please."

"I'll forget it, if you promise to call me if you hear from Mooney again."

"Deal," she said wearily. "Now is that it?"

"I imagine so," he said, realizing that he'd learned a lot without learning anything.

CHAPTER THIRTY-ONE

"Annie who?" The speaker was a white guy in his twenties with a face full of acne scars, wearing a white shirt over tux trousers. He looked like he was getting ready for a big night. He was standing in the doorway to the hotel suite where Mercer had spent the previous night, staring at the lawyer with suspicion.

"Annie Corey."

"Never heard of her."

"Who is it, Hank?" a female voice came from somewhere in the suite.

"Some guy looking for somebody. You just get dressed. Our reservation's for nine. We're late."

Most of this conversation wasn't registering with Mercer. When Hank started to close the door, he grabbed it and held it open.

"Dude," Hank said, "you got the wrong suite."

"This is her suite," Mercer said.

"It's a hotel, man. People come and go and she went. Now back off."

"Right." Mercer backed away as the door slammed shut. "Sorry," he said to no one in particular.

At the front desk, an attractive female night clerk, surrounded by freshly picked flowers, confirmed Hank's statement. "Mrs. Corey checked out this afternoon."

Just like that.

"Did she leave me a note? Mercer Early?"

The clerk observed the line of guests or potential guests

forming behind Mercer before giving her desk a quick scan. "No note, I'm afraid, Mr. Early."

He was about to ask her to check again when reality set in. Annie could easily have reached him by phone or left a message at the office. He thanked the clerk and departed.

His initial confusion had turned to hurt. Sitting in his parked car in front of the hotel, the hurt turned to anger. He took out his phone.

Lonny Hootkins answered on the second ring, with some kind of thunderous classical music playing in the background. "Hold on a minute, Mercer," he said, "lemme turn down the box."

The kettle drums considerably subdued, Hootkins picked up the phone again and listened while Mercer sheepishly gave him an abbreviated version of the situation. When he'd finished, the old detective said, "I imagine we can find her. You can find most anybody these days. But why would you want to?"

Mercer could have given him a list of reasons, ranging from male pride to a worry that Annie's awareness of his use of a dead man's identity might somehow wind up biting him on the butt. He didn't want to get into any of that with Hootkins. He said, "I just want to find out from her what the hell happened to make her leave without a word."

The detective sighed and said, "I don't suppose the hotel let you take a gander at the home address or phone number she gave 'em?"

"I didn't think to ask."

"I'll take care of that. It'll probably tell us what we want to know. Might cost you half a 'c'."

"That's fine. How long will it take?"

"The impatience of youth. Gimme an hour."

Mercer closed his phone, once again in awe of Hootkins's facility for gathering information.

He was at home in his underwear, moodily sipping a Grey Goose and tonic and speculating on how up to date Marvin Gaye's "What's Goin' On" was starting to sound, when the detective got back to him.

"Ain't nothing easy in this world," Hootkins said.

"You couldn't get the information?"

"I got it all right, but it sure as hell wasn't worth the fifty bucks it cost."

"I don't understand."

"The phone number the lady put on the card belongs to a cat and dog hospital in Pine Bluff, Arkansas. Run by a nice, tired-sounding woman named Dr. Mary Armor who lives on the premises. She's never heard of Annette Corey or Annie Sutter or anything like that."

"I don't suppose there's a directory listing for either name?"

"You don't suppose correctly. Not even an unlisted phone. And here's the other bit of news: Dr. Armor was kind enough to tell me that the address Annette Corey gave on Atkins Lake Road would probably be in the middle of Atkins Lake."

"If she knew there was an Atkins Lake Road, she must have some familiarity with the town."

"Maybe. In any case, what we got here is something a bit different than it looked like at the jump. You say she came to see you at the office?"

"Right. She . . . thought I was somebody else."

"Who?"

"A friend of hers. That part's not important."

"It's the whole deal, Mercer," Hootkins said. "The lady checked into a hotel under an assumed name, then initiated contact with you. If she was really looking for somebody else, then her quick runout makes some sense and we probably don't have to worry too much about what's really on her mind. On the other hand, if she had her sights set on you, and was just using this mistake thing as a come-on, then this is something we've got to pursue."

"We're going to pursue it," Mercer said.

"Aw-reety. What I need now is a nice set of prints."

Mercer closed his eyes in thought. She was wearing gloves at the office, but not at dinner and sure as hell not in bed. Unfortunately, the task of running down all the prints they might find at the restaurant or the hotel room might be more than they could handle. That left . . .

"The door handle in my car should have something," he told the detective. "Maybe the metal clasp of the seatbelt."

"You gonna be home for a while?" Hootkins asked. "I'll be there with my kit.

"Oh, and jus' to clarify matters, am I billing you or the firm on this?"

"I guess that'll depend on who the lady is and what she was after."

DAY 6

SUNDAY, JUNE 20

CHAPTER THIRTY-TWO

Joe Mooney awoke in a hospital-like room that seemed vaguely familiar, though he was sure he'd never been in it before.

Well, maybe not sure.

His imagination, which had been in hibernation for most of his life, had suddenly emerged to hold sway over his thoughts to the point where he no longer knew what was real and what was fantasy.

At least he was beginning to doubt his sanity, which was a good sign, wasn't it?

He noticed his arms were bare. He was wearing a thin, sleeveless nightshirt open at the back. A hospital garment, the kind people wore when they were sick. He didn't feel sick. Just confused.

He looked at the pale green room and desperately tried to recall how he'd gotten there. He didn't have a clue.

There was a window showing a patch of gray-blue sky. A *ping* sounded in the near distance when he left the bed to stagger toward the window.

He looked out on a canyon being lit by a low-hanging sun. There were buildings scattered on the other side of the canyon, but no human life that he could see. Just vegetation.

He backed away from the window and noticed a door to his left. It led to . . . an empty closet.

Where were his clothes? His weapon?

Footsteps sounded in the hall.

The other door, the one near the bed, opened and a man walked in. Tall, wearing a spotless, starched white coat. A doctor, then, though there was something disappointing in the fact that no stethoscope hung from his neck, no gold pens protruded from the pocket in his coat.

The man had a most kindly face. "How you doing, Joe?" he asked. "You remember me, right? Dr. D.?"

Joe had never seen him before in his life. "I don't know you," he said.

"That's okay. You and I are going to get to know one another pretty well. But now I think you should go back to bed. You've had a rough time of it, buddy. You need some rest."

Joe didn't move. "Where am I?" he asked. "How did I get here?"

"That and a whole lot of other information is stored right up here"—Dr. D. tapped a spot on his forehead—"in the old think tank. But you've locked it in. We're trying to find the key to help you unlock it."

"I want to see Janet," Joe said.

"Your daughter? She's fine, Joe. Don't worry."

"She's so helpless. There are so many terrible things."

"First things first, Joe," the doctor said. "Right now, let's concentrate on getting you rested and strong."

"No. I have to see Janet."

He headed for the door.

The doctor made no move to stop him.

Joe opened the door. A heavyset man in a dark business suit stood in an otherwise unoccupied pale green hallway, facing him. Without expression, the man brought up both hands and pushed Joe back into the room.

Gearing himself for a run at the man, Joe felt a sharp pain in his left shoulder. The sting of a bee.

Dr. D. took a few steps backward, away from him, holding a hypodermic needle on high in his gloved hand.

Joe felt his legs give out.

The heavyset man caught him before he hit the tile floor. Joe was aware of this, just as he could see that the man had no trouble at all dragging his 185 pounds of dead weight to the bed and rolling him onto it.

"Anything else, Doc?" he heard the heavyset man ask.

"Not for the moment," the doctor replied.

CHAPTER THIRTY-THREE

Mingus was feeling remarkably good as he climbed the stairs to his apartment, enjoying the ache of muscles he'd overworked during a hard-fought Homicide–Hollywood Division baseball game in the park.

The previous day, Saturday, had ended much more positively than it had begun. He'd stayed off the booze after the desperation drinks and spent the rest of the evening trying to make some sense of what he'd learned from Emmylou Paget.

He'd been a little concerned that Dr. Medina had not returned his call, particularly since he now had both a professional and personal reason to spend some time with her. He'd decided that if he didn't hear from her, he'd drop by her office on Monday.

A little after nine, Bettye had returned from work with dinner from Roscoe's—a couple of Carol C. specials with potatoes and collards and cornbread smothered in butter. Later, after a more than unusually satisfying lovemaking session, he'd drifted off to a deep, dreamless sleep.

And today he was definitely on the upswing. The baseball game had been good for him, the camaraderie, the exercise, and, who was he kidding, the fact that they'd cleaned the clocks of those Hollywood assholes, 11–4. Since Virgil Sykes hadn't shown—Sykes was a churchgoing man, disinclined to hurry home, change clothes, and drive all the way to the park—Mingus had pitched. He wasn't much of a pitcher, but the team was strong enough and all he had to do was get the ball over the plate.

"Yo, Bettye. The Kevin Brown of Homicide has arrived, ready for some . . ."

He could tell from the look on her face as she entered the living room that something was very wrong.

"You left your phone home," she said, handing him the cellular.

"So I did." He placed the phone and his glove and cap on a table by the sofa.

"Woman been ringing you."

"Got a name?"

"Hildegard. Very fancy name. She pretty?"

"She's a cop. We're working on the Geraldine Mooney murder," he said.

"Oh. She didn't mention that."

"But she did mention something that's got your back up."

"Nothin' important. Jus' that you been 'workin' her pussy' nights. That's her language, not mine, as you well know."

"She's got a very unusual sense of humor."

"Seems like."

He knew she would not ask the question. But that would not stop her from worrying about the answer.

"I haven't had sex with that woman," he said, realizing that he was sounding very presidential. "And it's nothing that's ever gonna happen."

"She that ugly?"

"She looks good on the outside, but she's a mess underneath. I don't like her. I don't like working with her. And I sure don't like her bothering you."

"She wants you to call," Bettye said.

"That's too damn bad," he said. He took her in his arms. "Since the night we met," he pulled her close, "I have not strayed. You're all the woman I want or need."

She kissed his neck. Then his mouth.

They were lying in bed, enjoying that postcoital glow, when his cell phone rang in the living room. Bettye stared at him, one eyebrow raised.

He grunted out of bed, put on a robe, and walked into the living room to answer the call.

"About time you got home, Lionel," Hildy said, amusement in her voice. "I was getting tired chatting with your auntie."

"What you want, woman?"

"You know what I want."

"Don't waste my time with your bullshit."

"Wait. Don't hang up. The Johnstons are back in Baldwin Crest with Janet Mooney."

"No. They just came in for Geraldine Mooney's funeral yesterday. I guess you forgot about that, huh?"

"I didn't forget," she said. "I was . . . a little tied up." She laughed.

"Well, you didn't miss anything. Mooney didn't show. The Johnstons headed back out of town right afterwards."

"No they didn't, Lionel. They stayed right here."

"You sure?"

"Why would Roy lie? He called a couple hours ago with the bad news. That's when I phoned you and got your little lady. Didn't she tell you I wanted a callback?"

Mingus saw his Sunday taking a sharp downward turn. He was annoyed that Johnston had ignored the danger of staying in town with Mooney's little girl. He was annoyed that *Roy,* Captain Jacquette, would call McRae over him. And he was annoyed he was going to have to get dressed and go to work.

"Pick you up in twenty," he said.

CHAPTER

THIRTY-FOUR

Hildy was waiting for him in front of her apartment building.

She slid onto the passenger seat, leaned into him, and said, "Hi, lambchops. How's about a big wet one?"

He pointedly ignored the comment, put the car in gear, and drove off.

"You're beautiful when you're angry," she said.

"Jacquette didn't say why they stayed?"

"I think that's one of the things he wants us to find out."

She coughed.

Glancing over, he saw that she was paler than usual. Her eyes were puffy and red-rimmed. "You okay?" he asked.

"Okay and then some. I had quite a night. Little guys may not have much in the sock, but they sure know how to use what they've got. Are little women like that?"

"I wouldn't know."

"Gee, the way you put me down all the time, I guessed you liked 'em small."

"I don't put you down. You put yourself down."

"That's *your* story. So your woman's a big gal? Sounded tiny on the phone."

He was keeping his anger under control. He wanted to grab her by the neck, slap her silly, tell her there'd be more where that came from if she ever lied about him again, to anybody. But she'd get too much satisfaction from that, just as she would get the satisfaction of knowing she'd upset Bettye if he pushed it.

So he changed the subject, telling her about his chat with Emmylou Paget.

"So I did miss Mooney at the doc's. Well, la-de-da."

"At this point I'm more concerned about what's going on with Paget. Drugs, probably."

She was quiet for a while. Then she said, "You and your auntie ever try any enhancements when you're doing the nasty?"

Back on that.

Mingus couldn't imagine what he'd done to deserve this trainwreck of a partner.

"Try a Lovers' Special," she said. "Ex, dusted with PCP. Ramon had some last night. Now I've had my share of shit, but this was . . . transcendent."

"Let me get this straight," he said. "You not only slept with that gang boy, you did drugs with him?"

Something in his tone must have sent out a warning that she'd stepped over the line. "Forget it, Lionel," she said. "I'm just fucking with you."

That may have been true, but he didn't think she'd been lying. A Lovers' Special. Jesus. It was just a matter of time before she did herself in, figuratively and/or literally. When that happened, he didn't want to be anywhere nearby.

There was a patrolman parked in front of the Johnston home on Aladdin Street. He told Mingus all was "copasetic."

Dr. Paul Johnston seemed surprised to see them. Even more surprised when Mingus asked why they had changed their plans about an immediate return to Big Bear.

"Don't you police talk with one another?" Dr. Johnston asked.

"What do you mean?"

"We were told we could come home by your chief of police."

"Chief Ahern?" Hildy asked.

"One of his assistants. I probably could recall the name if you mentioned it."

"Gilroy?" Mingus asked.

"Exactly. John Gilroy. We were headed to the cabin when he phoned, and we turned right around. The Big Bear area gets a bit, ah, provincial in summer."

I bet it do, Mingus thought.

"It's all right, isn't it? This Gilroy wasn't being premature?"

Mingus had no idea what Gilroy had on his mind. "He's the boss," he said.

"Still no word about Joe?"

"We're working on it," Mingus said.

"Has he tried to reach you or his daughter?" Hildy asked.

Johnston shook his head. "Not to my knowledge. He must be hurt or sick somewhere. I know how much he loves the little girl."

"Could we see her?" Hildy asked.

"She's with my wife in the back."

"We'll just say hello and then be on our way."

Reluctantly the doctor led them through the house to a large, brightly flowered garden at the rear. The doctor's wife, Olivia, was seated on a chair in the shade of an oak tree, reading. Several feet away, Janet, wearing a paint-stained smock, was working on what vaguely resembled a portrait of her aunt.

Mrs. Johnston did not rise to greet them. Fine with Mingus. She nodded to them both. He nodded back. Hildy headed for the little girl, hunkered down beside her, said hello, and asked about the painting.

Mingus made a perimeter tour of the garden. It was completely surrounded by a stucco fence approximately five-and-a-half-feet high. The side sections could be accessed only from the gardens of the neighboring houses. The far rear section separated the property from a steep sloping hillside that provided a great view of the recently renamed Kenneth Hawn Park and made the garden inaccessible to anything but a mountain goat approaching from that direction.

Dr. Johnston was waiting for him at the end of his survey. "You seem concerned. Are we in danger here?"

Mingus was momentarily at a loss for an answer. As far as he knew, Mooney could turn up at their house at any minute. But he wasn't privy to whatever information Assistant Chief Gilroy evidently had. So he settled for a line of moderate doublespeak. "If your brother-in-law has made no effort to contact the girl by now, odds are he's not going to. But he's still a fugitive."

"Then why were we told to return home?"

"Because the danger has been reduced to the point where you can start easing back into your regular routine," Mingus said, knowing it was bullshit. A considerably darker reason had occurred to him.

Evidently the doctor had not picked up on the more ominous possibility. "Television and the newspapers seem to have found other interests," he said. "It's been a chore keeping Janet away from the accounts of Joe's monstrous acts."

"It's all made-up stuff," Mingus said. "Nobody knows what went on that night."

Johnston nodded, but it seemed obvious he sided with the majority opinion. As if trying to chase the bad thoughts from his mind, he shifted his attention to the garden. "Your partner seems to have made a connection with Janet. It's the first time I've seen the little girl laugh since . . . well, in a while."

Hildy and the girl were sitting on the grass. Janet was pointing up to the clouds overhead and they both were giggling like schoolgirls. "She must have children of her own," Dr. Johnston said.

"I don't think so," Mingus said.

"She should."

Mingus had to admit that Hildy did look damned maternal. He wasn't totally surprised. He'd known coke whores and killers who, in the presence of children, suddenly were transformed into human beings. It was not a permanent transformation, however.

"We'd better be on our way," he told the doctor.

It sounded as if Captain Jacquette was at a concert of some kind. Mingus's cellular was picking up a reedy soprano singing in a foreign language in the background. The captain was whispering. "I'll try to reach Gilroy later and see what the story is."

"No chance you could call him now?"

"At present," the captain whispered, "I am sitting in a school auditorium with Mrs. Jacquette, suffering through Puccini's *La Bohème*."

"The girl who's singing don't sound so bad," Mingus said.

"The girl is my son. He's appearing in the key role of Mimi. I don't know whether to be proud or throw up. But in either case, a call to Gilroy will have to wait."

Mingus folded his phone and slipped it into his pocket. "He'll let us know," he said to Hildy.

"Is it usual for Gilroy to get so hands-on in a murder case?" she asked.

"There's nothing usual about this murder case," he said. "But I'm afraid I know why the Johnstons were told they could come back."

"It's fairly obvious," she said. "They're bait."

CHAPTER THIRTY-FIVE

"Bait?" John Gilroy couldn't get a grip on what Roy Jacquette was saying. The call had awakened him from a particularly pleasant predinner nap. He hadn't quite returned from a secluded beach tryst with Catherine Zeta-Jones. He could still feel the waves slapping at their entwined bodies.

From the kitchen came the clink of glass on glass, his wife Esme pouring another drink while puttering with dinner. "I don't know what you're talking about, Roy," he said into the phone. He was thinking, *Don't go, Catherine. I'll be back with you in a minute.*

"I'm talking about the Johnstons," Jacquette said. He sounded annoyed. "Mooney's in-laws."

"I'm with you on that. What about them?" *Hold on, Catherine.*

"I'm just confirming my assumption that you brought them back here to use Mooney's kid as a staked goat."

"That's where you lose me, Roy. You think I brought them back? Me, personally?"

"You trying to tell me you didn't?"

"Why would I get involved at that level? In any case, it's your show."

Jacquette was momentarily silent. If he was searching for a diplomatic response, it must have eluded him. "Don't con me, John. I've been at this game too long not to know when I'm being handed the shit-end of the stick."

"I don't follow any of this."

"The Johnstons say it was you who told them it was safe for them to return. Denny Ordell at Central Division said the order for a round-the-clock guard on the Johnston home came from your office. So what's the play, John? Mooney gets grabbed clean and you take the credit. But if there's a fuckup of any kind, I get the fallout?"

"I swear to God, Roy, I know absolutely nothing about any of this."

"Then consider this a heads-up, because your name is all over it."

As soon as Jacquette broke the connection, Gilroy was dialing a new one.

Hearing Pleasance's voice, Gilroy jumped right in with, "What do you fuckers think you're doing?"

"John," Pleasance said in a fake friendly voice, "how lovely to hear from you."

"What have we been up to?"

"Actually, Carl and Tip and I had a few beers and watched Tiger curse his way to another win. What else on a sleepy Sunday afternoon?"

"I'm talking about using my name to get the Johnstons to bring Mooney's kid back into town."

"Not on our scorecard," Pleasance said. "First I'm hearing about it."

"I don't believe you."

"John," Pleasance said wearily, "you got to take a relaxitive. Mellow out, mon. And use your head. Why would we want 'em back in town?"

Gilroy considered the question. Pleasance was right, of course. They were the last people who'd need Janet Mooney to draw her father out. They knew right where he was.

"You there, John?"

"Yeah. I see your point. Sorry I blew."

"No problem. Look, in about an hour we're going to dinner at The Star Bar. The women are supposed to be incredible. Hard bodies. Big silicon breasts. Faces nipped and tucked to look like movie stars. Think about it, John: getting your lap danced by a ho' looks the spitting image of Nicole Kidman, only with tits."

"Catherine Zeta-Jones." The name slipped out before Gilroy could stop it.

"Yeah, might be one of those, too, with a Cheshire cat smile. Come on along. Get your bad self on."

"I'll take a rain check," he said, as if his visiting a place like The Star Bar would be anything but a fantasy.

"Your call, John."

Gilroy replaced the phone. He was in trouble. Someone was trying to screw him. The only thing he knew for certain: it wasn't Catherine Zeta-Jones.

CHAPTER THIRTY-SIX

Not being a man who kept the Sabbath, Hootkins had spent a good portion of the day working. Specifically he had tried to find a match for the nice clear set of prints belonging to Mercer's twenty-four-hour girlfriend that he'd lifted from the door handle of the lawyer's car.

So far, his cultivated network of cronies with access to fingerprint databanks had come up with zip. The fake Annie Corey was not an ex-con, nor had she served time in any of the armed forces. Duplicates of her prints were not to be found in the FBI's IAFIS—Integrated Automated Fingerprint ID System.

He had a friend at one of the larger security agencies with a spanking new Cray supercomputer that tapped into international databanks, but that marker could not be called in until Monday morning. So, with the Corey job on hold, Hootkins checked his list of paths not yet traveled in gathering material for the Eldon Nunez defense.

He put through a call to Lydia Klinger. Mrs. Klinger was the sister of Merrill Gibbons, the late lab tech who was seen removing a black box from the alley the night Dwight Baskin died.

Her voice had an old sound, though the detective's notes had her pegged as Gibbons's younger sister and he'd been in his early forties. "I don't understand what I can do to help you," she said, after he'd told her his name and that he was working for Eldon Nunez's lawyer.

"We understand your brother knew Mr. Nunez."

"I've never heard him mention that name."

"Probably a working relationship," Hootkins said. "I was hoping you might still have your brother's possessions stored somewhere. In an attic maybe?"

"What are you looking for?"

"I wish I could give you . . ." Hootkins paused because he could hear shouting in the background.

"Who the hell you talking to?" an angry male voice demanded. "Not that worthless Jew bastard Robert?"

Lydia Klinger put her hand over the phone, but Hootkins could hear her say, "No, Dad. It's someone calling about Merrill."

He couldn't make out her father's comment, but it prompted her to say, "We can at least be civil."

Her hand was lifted from the phone in time for the detective to catch her father's last words, " . . . can't hear the goddamned machine, all your yapping."

"Sorry," Mrs. Klinger said to Hootkins, speaking almost in a whisper. "What were you saying?"

"I was asking about your brother's possessions."

"We . . . I . . . most of them are still in his room."

"Get off the goddamned phone now."

"I'll get off when I'm ready." No longer whispering, she said to Hootkins, "What did you say you were looking for, specifically?"

"Anything that might have reference to our client. Would it be possible for me to take a look at his room?"

"Your client is a murderer."

"I agree it looks that way," Hootkins said. "But there are other possibilities. That's what I'm investigating."

"How could Merrill be involved? He had . . . he was gone before—"

"Shut up!" came another yell.

"Oh, you shut up," she said so softly she didn't expect her father to hear.

"Mrs. Klinger?"

"Yes. I'm listening."

"I don't want to upset you, but one of the possibilities is that our client is being framed."

"Why would that upset me?"

"We have reason to think Eldon Nunez and your

brother were working on a project together. If our client was framed, that leads to another possibility."

"Oh, my God," she said.

"Ma'am, we're just speculating here," Hootkins said. "Your brother's death probably was an accident. Still, I imagine you'd like to make sure."

The house was in the Oak Knoll section of Pasadena, an old two-story Craftsman of dark wood. Like Hootkins, Merrill Gibbons never moved out of the family home. His sister left only long enough for a brief try at marriage. She lived there with her father, a cantankerous old skeleton who now sat a foot from the TV in the overfurnished living room, nibbling on onion puffs, drinking sherry, and verbally abusing his daughter.

Mrs. Klinger was a short, wiry woman with thick ankles and black hair that she wore close to her scalp like a cap. She had on a dark blue shapeless dress with a white collar, the kind Hootkins called a grandma dress. On her wrist was a gold Cartier watch that he appraised at about four grand.

She'd been a bit surprised to discover the color of his skin, but had nonetheless welcomed him in. Old Monty Gibbons had not been quite so hospitable. "What the hell is this?" he asked his daughter, eyes bulging.

"Mr. Hootkins is a detective, Daddy. He wants to see Merrill's room."

"The hell he does. Tell him to get his black ass off my property. Im-me-git-mah."

She sighed and said to Hootkins, "He goes on like this all the time. I'm past apologizing for him."

Hootkins said nothing. He didn't want apologies from these people, or even civility. He wanted access to Merrill Gibbons's room.

"Can I get you something to drink?" she asked.

"No ma'am. I'm fine."

"Marrying a Jew wasn't bad enough. Now you invite nigras into the house?"

"Merrill's room is upstairs," she said, leading the way.

The old man continued to berate her and insult Hootkins as they climbed a carpeted stairway. "Must be tough with him always at you," he said.

"You're seeing him on a good day."

They walked past doors that opened to a large, airy, masculine bedroom; a smaller, more feminine one; and a bedroom that had been turned into an office with bookshelves and a file cabinet and a desk bearing one of the newer super-thin laptop computers.

Mrs. Klinger hesitated in front of a dark wooden door at the end of the hall. Taking a deep breath, like a swimmer leaping into a pool, she opened the door and walked in.

Following, Hootkins found himself in a bedroom even larger than the first he'd seen, running the width of the house. As spacious as it was, it seemed crowded. Heavy drapes covered three of the four walls, keeping it a permanent midnight in the room.

The fourth wall served as a gallery of bits of Americana that included portraits of Ronald Reagan; the Bushes, father and son; and Abraham Lincoln. An oil painting depicted the American flag when there were just forty-eight stars. A framed handwritten note on embossed FBI letterhead carried the signature of J. Edgar Hoover.

"When Merrill was thirteen, he sent Hoover a letter saying he wanted to be an FBI agent when he grew up. That's Hoover's reply. My brother prized it higher than gold. I wonder what it might bring on eBay?"

She sat down on an overstuffed chair near the neatly made queen-sized bed with its dark blue blanket bearing the gold letters "LAPD." She evidently was going to observe everything Hootkins did, make sure he didn't walk off with something valuable, like that Hoover note.

Fair enough, he thought.

He walked to the desk and saw nothing of note on its surface. "Anything bothering your brother in the days before the accident?"

"Just my dad. He and Merrill had really been going at it even more than usual."

"What about?" Hootkins left the desk and moved on to a high, thin bookcase that separated two sets of drapes.

"Anything and everything," she said. "Usually Merrill just ignored him, but Dad really got under my brother's skin by ridiculing his worries about terrorism."

Hootkins saw that the paperbacks on the top shelf of the bookcase were mainly pop thrillers by authors like Robert

Ludlum and Tom Clancy. "Was he worried about anything specific?"

"He feared we'd all be subjugated by a marauding force. That America would fall. He feared it more than death."

"Sounds like the old 'better dead than red' idea," Hootkins said as he examined the bookcase's second shelf with its computer how-tos, including *Using Microsoft Office, Taming the Internet,* and various dummies guides. Below that were recent nonfiction tomes: *Let Freedom Ring,* William Bennett's *Why We Fight, American Jihad,* and *Avoiding the Apocalypse.* The bottom sheves were filled with magazines like *Scientific American* and *New Scientist,* thick periodicals with names like *Forensic Chemistry* and *Journal of Forensic Sciences,* and a collection of medical tomes, some of which probably dated back to his school days.

"Not much dust," Hootkins said, straightening slowly to save his knees.

"We have a housekeeper," she said. "Do you really think it's possible Merrill was murdered?"

"There didn't seem to be anything wrong with the car. And he hadn't been drinking."

"Merrill didn't drink."

"So that leaves about a hundred other things mighta caused him to go off the road. One of them bein' murder."

"I see."

He was standing in front of a closed door. "This a closet?"

"Yes. Look inside, if you want."

It was a moderate-sized walk-in. Clothes kept in neat rows. Summer suits, sport coats and slacks near the front, heavier winter wear toward the back. Hooks holding several hats aloft, scarves, belts. A long line of shoes on the floor, also piles of more science and forensics magazines.

Five stacked cardboard shoe boxes piqued Hootkins's interest for no other reason than they seemed to have been purposely placed at the rear of the closet. The top box contained shoe shine material—polish, rags, a brush. The box under that was empty. Box number three had shoes in it, white buckskins. Box number four was filled with white athletic socks. Box number five contained another box. A black one.

Trying to hide his eagerness, Hootkins carried the shoe box from the closet and placed it on the desk. For some reason, he felt he had to ask permission to open the black box inside.

"Why not?" Mrs. Klinger said, curiosity drawing her to the desk.

Using the rubber nub of a pencil, he lifted the black metal lid. Inside was a pack of trading cards. He used the pencil to move them around. All seemed to be color photos of nude, muscled males in various stages of sexual arousal, posing alone or with one another.

Had Merrill Gibbons and the client been exchanging visual material that had nothing whatsoever to do with criminal conspiracy and murder? That possibility caused Hootkins to issue an unconscious groan of disappointment.

He turned to address Mrs. Klinger, who'd returned to the chair.

"I'd like to borrow the box for a while," he said. "See if it might have Eldon Nunez's fingerprints on it."

"Why would you think that?"

"Your brother and Officer Nunez were observed with a black box. It may not have been this one, but just on the off chance . . ."

"Yes. Take it, please. And don't bother returning it. I don't want it in the house."

He nodded. "I see the computer books, but I don't see a computer."

"Well, they took that," she said.

"They?"

"The men from the lab where Merrill worked."

"When was this?"

"A few days after his death," she said. "Something to do with a project he was working on."

"Could I take a look at the receipt?"

She frowned. "I don't believe they left one. Why would they?"

"They're supposed to. They're taking away property that has a certain value."

She relaxed. "Oh, well, that explains it. It was more like an exchange. They gave us a new laptop."

"You happen to remember their names?"

She shook her head. “No. Just that they were from the lab and needed some of Merrill’s things.”

“They took other stuff?”

“Computer things. Zip drive. Modem. Discs. Like that. They were here for a while. They left with a fairly large boxful of things. I can’t imagine they took anything of value other than the laptop, but I’m really not sure what they took. Dad was keeping me busy that day, being even more demanding than usual.”

Hootkins sighed and looked at the room again. “I won’t be botherin’ you much longer,” he said.

CHAPTER THIRTY-SEVEN

"And you're sure it *wasn't* anybody from the lab?" Mercer asked later that day when he and Hootkins were headed toward the apartment that had been shared by Eldon Nunez and Landers Pope.

"Putty sure. Gibbons's death has been officially declared an accident so I don't see any legit reason for anybody to be takin' anything from his room," Hootkins said. "I didn't want to spook the woman, but I went into it a little bit more before I left. They were two white men. Blond hair. Average height and build. Thirties. In business suits. She didn't think to ask for IDs. Not when they handed over a brand new laptop, still in the box. It definitely trumped IDs. I can't think of a soul working for the county or the city laying down anything like that. They'd have got a warrant and taken the damn machine."

"She see what they were driving?" Mercer asked.

"Course not. She was probably too busy playing with the new computer."

"So the black box was all you came away with?"

" 'Fraid so," Hootkins said. "Lots of prints on the box and more on the cards. I'll get to 'em when I can."

"Speaking of prints . . ."

"Still no hit on your girlfriend," Hootkins said, "and damned if I can figure that out. In this day and age, for prints not to be on file somewhere is a little odd."

"What hasn't been a little odd lately?" Mercer asked, as he pulled into a two-hour parking spot.

They'd already given the Nunez-Pope apartment a quick run-through on Friday. Now they were prepared to do a more thorough job. They knew they were sifting through the dregs. The rooms had been gone over thoroughly by the LAPD, the D.A.'s investigators, and all the ships at sea. But there wasn't much else to do on a restless Sunday evening.

Mercer walked down a hall to the rear of the apartment. He worked his way forward from the master bedroom—the murder scene, with a dried bloodstain the size of a basketball on the mattress—to the bathroom—a bloodred-and-onyx-tile nightmare—to an office stripped clean of computers and files, presumably by official hands, to the kitchen, where someone had unplugged the refrigerator without emptying it and compounded the felony by leaving the door ajar just enough to let the odors of sour milk and spoiled food slowly pollute the area. He turned up nothing of consequence.

Hootkins had remained in the combination living-dining room. He was sitting on a leather ottoman, picking up and examining objects from the floor—books and CDs and DVDs that had once filled shelves built into one long wall.

"Been savin' this one for you," he said with a grin as he handed Mercer a book.

It looked new. The title was *GROBC-42: The Sex Supercharger*. By a Dr. Alan Donleavy.

"Figgered with your girlfriend in the wind, it might be sexy enough to help you pass these lonely evenings."

"Damn thoughtful of you," Mercer said. He was about to toss it to the floor when a quote on the cover caught his eye. "Team Donleavy brilliantly explores the impact that nerve-transmitter signals have on sexual behavior."

He carried the book to a window where the light was better.

"I was just goofin' on you, son. If you're really in need of a sex supercharge, you oughta check out some of the movies on cable."

"Nerve transmitters," Mercer said. "Weren't we just talking about neurotransmitters?"

"Yeah. Dwight Baskin's autopsy said he'd been running low on the neuro-watchicallit serotonin, which coulda made him depressed."

"This book is about nerve transmitters, which is a weird coincidence," Mercer said. "Assuming you believe in coincidence."

He dragged a chair over to the window, sat down, and started leafing through the volume. According to a credit card receipt nestled between two pages, it and another very expensive book, *Venlafaxine and CFS Symptoms,* had been purchased by Nunez two weeks prior to Landers Pope's death.

"See if you can find this other title," Mercer said, handing the receipt to Hootkins.

While the detective poked through the pile, Mercer skimmed *The Sex Supercharger*. In spite of its exploitative title, it seemed to be geared toward a scientific rather than a general readership. Much of it was based on research into certain causes of sexual dysfunction done at the University of the Americas by Donleavy and his team of scientists. The subjects were female lab mice and hamsters, genetically bred to remove the protein DARPP-32 from the nerve-transmitter channel in the brain's hypothalamus. Without the protein, the nerve signals that prompted sexual behavior were not sent and the subjects lost interest in sex.

Injections of estrogen and progesterone failed to change the situation, but the addition of the artificial hormone GROBC-42 put that gleam back in the rodents' beady little eyes.

Why the hell would Nunez have spent nearly a hundred dollars on a textbook on nerve transmitters and artificial hormones? It had to have something to do with the lack of serotonin in Baskin's body.

"This what you're talkin' about?" Hootkins said. *Venlafaxine and CFS Symptoms* by Dr. Horace Greil was even thicker and heavier than *Supercharger*. A subhead on the jacket read: *SSNRIs' Effect on Neurotransmitters Serotonin and Norepinephrine.*

Mercer nodded. He was flipping through its pages when something caught his eye. Handwriting in the margin—*Parnell's Storage*—and a phone number with a 213 code, which suggested downtown L.A.

"Whatcha got?" Hootkins asked.

"Let's find out."

He took out his cell phone and dialed the number.

"Yes?" a male voice answered.

"Is this Parnell's Storage?"

"No."

Click.

The lawyer tried the number again. No answer this time.

Frowning, he asked Hootkins, "Ever hear of Parnell's Storage?"

"Sounds kinda familiar."

Mercer dialed information, requesting a Los Angeles number for Parnell's Storage. The electronic voice said it would be just a minute and he was transferred to a live local operator who informed him that she could find no such listing in the city.

At his insistence, she tried several suburbs. Nothing.

Frustrated, he put away the phone and said to Hootkins, "A couple more things for your to-do list. Find out what you can on Parnell's and check the listing for this phone number." He handed over the book.

"I wasn't planning on sleeping any time soon anyway," the investigator said.

CHAPTER THIRTY-EIGHT

With their work schedules, Mingus and Bettye rarely spent a Sunday evening on the town. But he wanted to do whatever he could to chase away the unpleasantness of Hildy's phone call. So they'd had a fine meal at the place where they'd met, La Louisianne Restaurant, or, as its regular patrons would have it, LaLa's.

He was putting away the final ice cream–covered bite of apple pie. She was sipping milk coffee. They were dragging out the dinner a bit, waiting for a second set by George Rose, the detective's favorite vocalist.

The members of the band were drifting back to the stage area when Mingus's cell phone began to vibrate in his pocket.

As he brought out the phone, he saw Bettye's eyes narrow. "I don't wanna hear it's that bitch again."

It was that bitch.

"I . . . Lionel . . . he . . . they . . . hurt me."

Damn. He hated her for her stupidity and for dragging him into her fucked-up life. He hated himself even more for caring about what happened to her.

"How bad?"

"Bad enough. Need . . . help."

"Okay."

Bettye watched him put away the phone. "You goin' to her," she said.

"Her boyfriend beat her up."

"Way I see it, her boyfriend was having dinner with me."

"You ever lie to me, Bettye?" he asked.

"You know better."

"What makes you think I'd lie to you?"

"Men think they can get by with it, they do it."

It hurt him that she lumped him in with her ex-husband and every other bullshit artist she'd encountered. But it was evidently what she believed and he didn't have the time or the patience to argue it out with her.

"Come with me," he said, signaling for the check. "You can see for yourself. And you can help."

Tears filled her eyes. "You'd dishonor me that much? To take me to your bitch's lair? I don't think so, Lionel."

"It isn't like that. I'm not like that," he said.

They stared at one another while the waitress toted up the bill. Mingus paid for their dinners. When he stood to go, Bettye remained seated. "I'm gonna stay and drink my coffee and listen to the music."

"How you gonna get home?"

She turned her head to a bar lined with cat daddies on the prowl. "I'll get a lift," she said.

It reminded him of Hildy's rebuff in the Mexican bar just two nights before. She'd stayed, too. He felt the warm spot Bettye had kindled in his heart start to freeze up. "Okay," he said. "Enjoy yourself."

"You too," she said.

At the door, he turned to look at her. The band members were starting to work their instruments. Bettye was dabbing at her eyes with a tissue.

He felt like crying himself.

Hildy's apartment door was open. He didn't know if she'd unlocked it or if the little punk—Ramon, that was his name—if he'd left it open when he split.

The living room reeked of marijuana and some unidentifiable tangy odor. There were several empty tequila bottles on the floor—Jose Cuervo Anejo, a pricey brand. Cushions had been pulled from a sofa. A chair was on its side.

A police special lay on the carpet. Mingus squatted and poked a pen through the trigger guard to lift it to his nose. He smelled only oil. He returned the weapon to its original resting place.

"Hildy?" he called.

"In here."

She was in her bathroom, using the toilet for a chair, pressing a towel full of ice cubes against her face. Her hair was wet and stringy. The short kimonolike robe she was wearing showed a fair amount of scraped and raw and torn flesh.

She held the towel and cubes away from her face and he saw her right eye was swollen shut, her cheek just starting to show a yellowish bruise. "Don't hate me because I'm beautiful," she said. The sarcastic laugh she began ended with a yip of pain. A cut on her lip opened up and started to bleed.

"What happened?" he said.

"The usual. Dinner and drinks with my guy. And his three amigos." He noticed her speech had improved by light years since her phone call.

"They're feeling unloved, so he gets a generous notion. Blowjobs for all. On me. I offered a different suggestion: they could all get the fuck out of my apartment. The vote went four to one against me."

Mingus was studying her wounds, trying to gauge their seriousness. "There's a gun on the floor in the living room," he said.

"Mine. Ramon left it? See, he is a sweetheart. He didn't participate, by the way. Just sat there, pointing my gun at me, while his pals played dicks ahoy. Later, he beat me for being unfaithful to him. He's such a romantic."

Mingus got out his phone.

"Put that away," she said.

"You've been raped and beaten," he said.

"That's why I called you. Jesus Christ, what good would it do for me to report this? I invited the bastards here, fixed 'em drinks. They'll say I begged them to do me. Four of them versus one of me."

"Four punks versus one officer of the law," he said. "And it's not just rape. You've got the cuts and bruises to prove it."

"Right. And what kind of cop would that make me? A bubblehead who let herself get raped and beaten by her dinner guests."

But that's exactly the kind of cop you are, Mingus thought.

"They spend a few weeks inside and I move on to some other job. I don't think so."

"Okay. Let's get you to an emergency ward."

"Hello. Haven't you heard what I've been saying?"

"You're gonna have to see a doctor. About that lump on your head and about the possibility that those boys gave you a dose of something."

"I'll do that later. When there won't be any Ex or coke in my system."

"If you're just gonna ride this out, Hildy, what the hell am I doing here?"

"I want you to go find those little bastards and avenge me. I want you to break their bones."

The request was as insulting as it was absurd, but, because of her battered condition, he held his anger in check. "Not my style," he said.

"You owe me," she said.

"Say what?"

"You owe me," she repeated. "This is your fault. You left me with Ramon the other night."

He knew the folly of trying to argue with that kind of logic. It was time for him to leave, but he just couldn't stop himself from saying, "You made your own bed, Hildy."

"That's perfect," she said, rising to her feet. "Blame the goddamned victim. *I* was the one they stuck their dicks into. Remember? *I* was the one who got beaten and pistol whipped."

He was into it now. Rolling downhill. "You drag a feral dog into your house, don't be surprised he bites you."

"You sanctimonious piece of shit. You fucking macho phony." As he turned to go she hurled the towel full of ice at his head. He ducked, but some of the wet cubes hit his right ear and neck, hard as rocks. The rest clattered against the bathroom wall.

He didn't let it slow his departure.

She staggered after him, open robe flapping behind her wounded body. "You left me to those animals. This is all your fault, you bastard!"

He made his exit without a backward look, but he could hear her screaming from her doorway. "You did this to me, you nigger faggot. You did it."

Her shouts lured some of her neighbors into the hall.

One look at Mingus on his exit march sent them back-stepping gingerly into their apartments.

He told himself that the guy who came up with that "no good deed goes unpunished" idea must have been quite a student of human nature.

CHAPTER

THIRTY-NINE

Hoping to salvage something from the ruinous night, Mingus heavy-pedaled it back to LaLa's. Their table was occupied by another couple. He took a tour of the bar area, but Bettye had evidently gone home. Or someplace else.

He hesitated just a moment too long in making his exit. The smell of liquor and the sound of laughter drew him to an empty stool. The barmaid asked him his pleasure.

"Thug Passion," he said, surprised that she'd had to ask.

He watched her pour the Alize Red and Courvoisier. "Been working here long?" he asked.

"Little over a year. You want a water back with that?"

"No thanks," he said, sending her on to the next customer. Over a year. He supposed it had been at least that long since he'd sat down at the bar. Or any bar. Taking up with Bettye had definitely put a crimp in his night life. Wasn't for her, bartenders wouldn't have to ask what he wanted to drink.

He stared at the Thug Passion, caught a whiff of its perfume, and lifted it a little too eagerly to his lips.

Several hours later, he somehow managed to unlock the apartment door and stagger into the living room. There, he discovered the couch had been turned into a bed.

Well, shit. At least Bettye was home. And she'd made up the couch, hadn't just dumped the sheets and blanket and pillow for him to mess with. They'd talk things out in the morning.

Grunting, he got rid of his shoes and coat and pants and shirt, leaving them in a pile on the carpet. He tiptoed to the bathroom, relieved himself, studied his booze-bloated face in the basin mirror, and decided that, since he would be sleeping alone, there was no need to bother brushing his teeth.

Either he was too big or the couch was too small for him to stretch out completely. Lying there, knees bent, the room swirling around him, he realized he could not have done a better job of fucking up his life if he'd tried to.

It had been nearing 2 a.m. when he'd left LaLa's. He needed to get up around 7 a.m. He wanted to have the talk-out with Bettye before she went off to work. He figured it was important to get to Parker Center early, too, to be there when the shit came down on Hildy. He wasn't going to add to it, merely make sure none of it got on him.

He was worried he might not be able to wake up when he needed to. No way could he get an alarm from the bedroom without waking Bettye. He wasn't sure he could even set the damn thing in his present condition. He'd just have to put the wake-up call in his head.

He needn't have worried.

The doorbell rang at 4 a.m., followed by heavy pounding. He sat up groggily and watched Bettye, hastily tying a robe around her, heading for the door.

"Who's there?" she asked, anger putting an edge to her voice.

"LAPD," a male voice replied. "Open up, please, ma'am."

She turned toward Mingus. "What is this?" she asked.

"Beats me," he said.

"Well, you handle it." She walked into the kitchen.

Hungover, fuzzy-mouthed, and aching in every joint, he rose from the couch. His eyes burned and his knees, which had been bent for a couple hours, felt as if somebody had jabbed them with hot knitting needles. He limped to the door and opened it.

Two uniformed black patrolmen stood there. Weapons drawn and aimed in the general vicinity of his naked chest. The shorter one asked, "Lionel Mingus?"

"Yeah," he said. "*Detective* Lionel Mingus."

"Right. I'm carrying a warrant for your arrest, Detective Mingus. I hope you'll cooperate."

Bettye was standing behind him. "Oh my God, Lionel, what have you done?"

"Nuthin'. I've done nuthin'." He turned to the officers. "What's the charge?"

The officers tensed. The big one took a step forward. "I gotta cuff you. Wanna turn around for me?"

Mingus didn't move. "What's the charge?" he repeated.

"You've been charged with rape, sodomy, battery with intent, b and e," the smaller cop said. "I mighta skipped one or two things. You loaded up, detective."

"Okay," Mingus said with resignation. He raised his hands and took a step back into the apartment. "I won't give you any grief, Officers. You got your job to do. Come in and watch me put on my pants. Then if you gotta cuff me for the trip downtown, fine."

Bettye was standing frozen to the carpet. She stared at him with eyes wide open. She looked confused and frightened. "You remember Mercer Early, baby?" he asked. "Number's in my phone. Call him and tell him I need him. Real bad, it sounds like."

DAY 7

MONDAY, JUNE 21

CHAPTER FORTY

"I didn't know you were a slumlord," Mercer said to Mingus as he and one of the firm's new junior partners, Devon Olander, escorted the detective from the Twin Towers lockup late the next day. It had taken the lawyers twelve hours to arrange bail, some of that devoted to scraping together the necessary cash and property to satisfy the bondsman, Bulldog Jack Brody.

"It's just a piece of property my uncle the judge left me," Mingus said. "A big lot he paved over. Guy selling used cars off it, pays me a grand and a half a month for the privilege."

"It's three hundred grand worth of pavement," Devon said, getting into the rear of Mercer's car, while the men took the front seats. "That and the cash impressed Bulldog Jack enough to put up the bail."

"Why'd that old judge set bail so high, anyway?" Mingus said. "Half a million. Damn."

Mercer started the car. "Got the breakdown, Devon?"

She removed a Sony palm computer from her purse, an N290 Clie, hit a few buttons, and began to recite, "Your basic rape, $50,000. Sodomy, $100,000. Brandishing of weapon, another $100,000. Breaking and entering, $50,000. An officer of the law doing any or all of these things, priceless."

"Damn!"

"Remember, there's a restraining order, too," Devon said. "You're to keep away from her."

"No problem there. I never want to see the bitch again," Mingus said. "But I guess that's gonna happen in court."

"I think we can make the whole thing go away without a trial," Mercer said, eyeing the late evening traffic.

"Yeah?" Mingus said. "How?"

"The police lab recovered enough semen from her sheets to sire an army," Devon said. "DNA, DNA, DNA. Saliva on the tequila bottles. Prints. None of that'll match yours, I hope."

"Not in this world."

"Good. They found drug residue in the apartment, too. She's saying you brought it and forced her to use it."

"I know," Mingus said glumly. "Two miserable sons of bitches who I used to work with on the Rat Squad been at me for hours about that and everything else."

"There won't be any evidence of drugs in your blood?"

"No, but there will be alcohol. I hit it hard last night."

Devon smiled. "Five Thug Passions. Four will put an elephant down. They won't find any tequila?"

"No tequila," Mingus said. "I thought I drank six."

"Not unless they slipped you one on the house. I have a copy of the bar tab."

"You been to LaLa's?"

"Establishing a timeline. And it's a good one. The singer at La Louisianne began his second set at approximately 10:45 p.m. Just prior to that, Detective McRae phoned you. Your friend, Ms. Bettye Hiler, can testify she was present when the call came in and that immediately after you disconnected, you told her that McRae said she'd been beaten. This was before you even left the restaurant."

"Bettye didn't actually hear Hildy," Mingus said.

"That would've been ideal, but, as it is, we're in good shape. Now, you're back at LaLa's at 11:52. We know that exact time, because it's when the bar lady rang up your first TP. Date and time are part of the automatic entry.

"That would suggest you left the restaurant, drove to Detective McRae's place, forced her to do drugs, raped her repeatedly, beat her, got back in your car and returned to the restaurant in just over an hour. It's a twenty-minute drive each way, leaving you with maybe fifteen minutes to be as bad as you could be. Not even Speedy Gonzales could have pulled that off."

"So, they've got a real shaky case," Mercer said. "And we haven't even started looking for the punks who did the work on her."

"There's also the lady's past history in Vegas," Devon said. "You know damn well there'll be some pretty hair-raising stuff. Hildegard McRae didn't turn into a monster overnight."

The sun was just setting when they arrived at the Carter and Hansborough Building. Getting out of the car, Devon left Mingus with a cautionary request. "Stay as far away from Detective McRae as you can. She may make an effort to phone you, to suggest some deal. Don't say a word. Just hang up. And stay at home. If you're out somewhere, she might try to track you down. Sit tight. Understand?"

He said he understood.

As they headed for Inglewood and his apartment, he asked Mercer, "She as good as she thinks she is?"

"Seems to be," Mercer said. "You holdin' up?"

The two men had met over a year ago when, together, they'd taken down a tough and powerful opponent. Since then, they'd maintained their friendship with an occasional lunch or dinner and slightly more frequent catch-up phone calls. Their bond was tight enough for Mercer to sense the detective was having trouble dealing with the situation.

"They made me surrender my badge and gun. Captain Jacquette put me on indefinite suspension. I go to trial, even if we win, my days as a cop are over."

"Like I said, I don't see it going that far. Fact is, considering what the county put you through, basically on just the word of a seriously disturbed woman, you may come out of this a wealthy man."

"I didn't sign up for the money."

Mercer nodded. "I know." He made a quick right turn and checked the rear view. A black SUV made the turn, too.

"I really fucked things up with Bettye," Mingus was saying.

"She seemed okay when she called this morning. Calm and cool."

"Cool is the operatin' word."

"What's up with her?" Mercer asked. He squinted but couldn't quite make out in the fading light if the SUV was an Escalade.

"Hildy phoned and told her we'd been hittin' the sheets. No truth to it at all, by the way."

"Bettye must know now that the woman's a lying bitch," Mercer said.

"She took it real hard. Then, I get the phone call in LaLa's, an' Bettye tells me not to go to Hildy's place. But like a pure fool, I leave the woman I love, just so I can put myself in this jackpot."

Mercer had slowed his speed to just under the limit. The SUV was not taking up the slack.

"So you're saying what?" Mercer asked. "That we shouldn't put Bettye on the stand on your behalf?"

"That's not what I'm sayin' at all," Mingus said, his voice heavy with outrage. "I'm not talkin' about the goddamn trial. I'm talkin' about my life." Then he saw Mercer grinning and he grinned, too. "Got me, Dawg."

"It's gonna be fine," Mercer said. "The woman loves you."

"You the expert on that, huh?"

The streetlights blinked on. Mercer's eyes went automatically to the rearview mirror. The black vehicle was still back there. "Lionel, check out the SUV behind us. That an Escalade?"

Mingus turned. "Shit if I can tell from this distance. He followin' you?"

"Maybe."

"Slow down. See what he does."

"I tried that. He slows down."

"Then what's your question?" Mingus said. He turned around again to observe the SUV. "It is an Escalade. What you been doin', you got folks tailin' you?"

"Actually, it's something I've been meaning to talk to you about ever since I found out you were investigating the Mooney killing."

Mingus frowned at him. "Don't tell me you're Mooney's lawyer?"

"No. Not yet, anyway. But I am representing Eldon Nunez."

"Another cop charged with homicide," Mingus said. "More to it than that?"

"I think so, and that's probably why we're being followed."

"You know who's in the Esca?"

"Best guess, at least two thugs working for a smooth white guy pretending to sell real estate."

"That doesn't sound good, not with night fallin'," Mingus said. "Specially since I got my weapon pulled. Don't suppose you're carryin'?"

"You know I don't play that game. I need a piece like a dog needs fleas."

"Then we better try somethin' else. Floor it."

The detective directed Mercer up one street and down another, the black SUV staying with them, finally telling him to drive into the Lazy Dayzee Carwash on Prairie, a few blocks south of The Forum. "A perp tipped me to this place," he said. "I was tailin' him at the time."

The carwash was lit by serious wattage, but a brother in an orange jumpsuit waved them down. "Jus' closin'."

Mingus rolled down his window and said, "We need the Dayzee Special. Now."

The brother barely nodded his head and ran to the switches.

Mercer drove forward as Mingus moved his window up again. In front of them water suddenly spurted from rows of nozzles. With a clang, the machinery took over, pulling the car into the spray. When the vehicle was halfway through the cycle, Mercer heard and felt it being freed.

"Go," Mingus said. "Take a left at the alley."

"Why a left? That's the way the SUV's pointing. They'll be waiting."

Mingus smiled. "According to Dayzee, who I had a long intimate talk with after I lost the perp, most times the chase car'll do what I did, make the U, figurin' the runner to head the opposite way."

"So we do the opposite of what seems smart?" Mercer said. "That kind of thinking got us into Vietnam."

But it worked in this case. The Escalade was nowhere to be seen when they left the alley. Instructed by the detective, Mercer made a right on Buckthorn, continuing on, SUV-less, to Mingus's apartment.

Its windows were dark.

"C'mon in," Mingus said. "I wanna hear what you got to say about Mooney and Nunez."

Mercer figured it wasn't just curiosity promoting the invite. The detective wanted company.

The apartment smelled of food. Bettye had fixed a pot of some kind of stew, left it heating on the stove for him.

She'd left a note, too, resting against the Betty Boop salt and pepper shakers on the kitchen counter. Mercer figured she must've had a real jones for the sexy little cartoon character. Betty Boop was decorating the note, too.

He could not see what the note said, only the reaction it had on his friend, a slump of the shoulders, a dulling of the eyes. Mingus folded it and stuck it in his shirt pocket.

"You up for dinner?" he asked.

"Sure."

Mingus turned off the warmer, took the stew, and stuck it in the refrigerator. "Lemme shower the jail off me," he said. "Then we can go get something to eat."

"Might be better for you to stay in."

"I been sittin' in a cell most of the day, dawg. Got to stretch my legs. We'll find some out-of-favor joint. Eat. Drink. And talk about something upbeat, like murder."

CHAPTER FORTY-ONE

The restaurant Mingus picked would not have been Mercer's first choice. Bitches' Brew was a South L.A. bar and grill owned by twin sisters, Flora and Fauna Higgins, who, in their prime, had gained a certain fame for double-your-pleasure hooking.

Now in their nonpro middle years, a little overweight but still underdressed, they held sway over a moderate, minimally rowdy fifty-something clientele that mainly stuck to the bar area, knocking back beer and booze, listening to the music of Miles Davis or MJQ or Herbie Hancock and waiting to see where the night took them.

Mingus had opted for a booth in the far recesses of the sublit room, where a bored young waitress, sorely in need of memory lessons and a better attitude, brought them food they had not ordered.

The detective seemed oblivious to the fact that he was eating a meatless casserole instead of lasagna. "I ever tell you about Bettye's ex?" he asked.

Mercer shook his head and studied his pot pie, wondering what was in it. Surely what he was chewing was not the chicken he'd been expecting.

"Ramblin' Roy Hiler is a grifter, presently spending the second of a ten-year visit to the stone house. The only thing good I can say about him is he just stole from her. Didn't beat her. Didn't try to turn her out. Didn't push her to join in his scams.

"But livin' with him wasn't exactly smooth like butter.

The first thing she said when we took up together was how happy she was not to have to worry about cops at her door day or night."

He shook his head, as if to throw off the troubling thought. "I don't blame her for leavin'."

"The note say she was leaving?"

"Pretty much."

"For good?"

Mingus ducked his head. "She wants me to give her some time to think about it."

"Where is she?"

"With a friend, note says. I could probably pin it down, but I don't know where that would get me."

Mercer thought that if he was in Mingus's position, he'd be trying to talk Bettye into coming home tonight. The woman had cooked a dinner for him. She was waiting for him to come get her. She wanted to be with her man. Unlike Annie Corey, wherever and whoever she might be.

"I figure I'll give her some time to work it out," Mingus said.

"That's one way to play it," Mercer said. It was as close as he would get to giving advice. It was never a good idea to get involved in a brother's romantic problems.

"Okay, enough of that," Mingus said. He suddenly became aware of the half-eaten dinner in front of him. He pushed it aside and signaled to the waitress. She approached the table as if she were in a slow-walking contest.

"You can take this away and bring me a slice of apple pie à la mode. Mercer?"

"Just a cup of coffee. Black. No sugar."

"I'll have one of them, too."

Watching the woman slouch off with their dishes, Mingus said, "Let's get down to business, bro. Mooney and Nunez. You tell me your dream; I'll tell you mine."

The information exchange took about forty-five minutes, with time out for Mingus to send back a slice of mincemeat pie à la mode—"Who in their right fucking mind would eat mincemeat pie in the first place?"—and for Mercer to get a cup of black coffee without a shot of booze in it.

"Seems to me it boils down to this," the detective said. "Some bad shit has been brewin' out there for some time.

The night Mooney took down Dwight Baskin, the dark stuff started to float to the surface. Maybe the black box the late Merrill Gibbons handed off to your client is the answer to everything. But not if it was pictures of guys with big dicks. I don't see that being enough to draw a bunch of FBI suits to town, even if Hoover was still callin' the shots."

"They're not just ordinary FBI, either," Mercer said. "They're listed as being off duty."

"And a couple of 'em just happen to have spent time in Dr. Medina's office building," Mingus said.

"The doc seems to be a hub. She's Mooney's shrink. She's Officer Paget's shrink. She's my client's shrink. That can't be just coincidence."

Mingus frowned. "Well, she is a department psychiatrist," he said. "A lot of officers go to her."

Mercer stared at him, wondering if he was one of those officers. "She's still one of a select group that knows more about what's going on than we do." He held up a hand and clicked off the fingers. "The doc. My client. Mooney. What about Paget?"

Mingus shook his head. "She seems more confused than us. I don't think it's an act."

"Okay, who else then?"

"The feds?"

"If they do, and you saw them meeting on the sly with John Gilroy, he'd know, too, right? Maybe Chief Ahern. So, out of this cast of characters, whom do we have access to?"

"Dr. Medina and Nunez," Mingus said.

"And one of them isn't making much sense."

"I'll call her in the morning," Mingus said.

"I'd better call her," Mercer said. "You're not officially involved anymore. And you've got to keep it on the down low, brother. You don't do anything, except put in crib time. Stay off the street. If you got to call somebody, try Bettye."

"I thought you said I shouldn't be worryin' about the rape charges."

"Don't worry," Mercer said, "but stay cautious. And stay away from public areas. Anything you say or do could wind up working against you."

"That's too bad," Mingus said. " 'Cause I been seriously thinking about stranglin' our waitress."

CHAPTER FORTY-TWO

It was night when Joe Mooney woke up in his hospital room. There was enough moonlight for him to make out the bed he was in. Turning, he saw the door outlined in light from the hall.

He threw back the coverlet and swung his legs around, preparing to get out of bed. His head felt . . . heavy. Ditto his limbs.

He sat on the side of the bed, girding himself for the ordeal of standing. That was when he heard the people in the hall just outside his door. Two of them. Their shadows stretched under the door across the polished tile.

They were arguing. He was fairly certain the woman was Dr. Medina. She had that way of pronouncing words funny, though he'd never heard her raise her voice before. He wondered what she was doing at the hospital at night. Visiting him? No. He had to remember, people had reasons for doing things that had nothing to do with him. Dr. Medina had told him that.

He was not able to figure out what she and the other person—the man—were arguing about. He heard Dr. Medina use the word "monstrous." Her complete sentence was, "What you suggest is monstrous."

What could the man have suggested?

"Control yourself, Doctor," the male voice said. "Even if we were not at such a crucial point, the ship you speak of has already sailed."

Crucial point? A ship that sailed?

"You're a coldhearted bastard," Dr. Medina said, shocking Joe. He saw one shadow slide away and heard footsteps going off down the hall.

Then the other shadow left, soundlessly. Joe guessed that person—the male, he thought—must be wearing rubber soled shoes.

Joe slid down the bed until his bare feet hit the cold tile floor. Then he pushed up and off the bed, standing there, swaying slightly, wondering why it had been so important for him to get up.

Maybe he had to urinate. Maybe that was it.

He took a step toward the hall door and groped for the light switch he thought was there.

Yes.

Momentarily blinded by the overhead light, he backed to the bed, rested against it. He noticed that someone had draped his clothes across the seat of the solitary chair. They looked clean and pressed. Even his Reeboks had been scrubbed.

His leather holster rested beside the clothes. Empty. His police special was missing.

He definitely had to piss.

It seemed to take him forever to walk the seven steps to the bathroom, open the door, do his business. He was on a return trip to the bed when the door to the room opened and the kindly-looking Dr. D. entered with a glass of something that appeared to be the sweet milk that they served at the hospital, the milk Joe thought was so delicious.

"Time to hit the road to dreamland, Joe. What are you doing out of bed, anyway?"

"I . . . had to pee."

"When you gotta go, you gotta go. But back to bed now. Chop chop."

Dr. D. waited until Joe slid under the coverlet, then handed him the glass. It was the sweet milk. He drained it eagerly.

"Oh, I almost forgot the good news," the doctor said, taking the empty glass from him. "Your daughter has been asking about you."

His daughter. His sweet baby daughter. "Janet's here?"

"No, Joe. She's with her aunt and uncle, at their home."

"Oh, right. I remember. I tried to call there. To talk to

her, find out how she was doing. The machine said they were away on a trip."

"Joe, I do believe you're sounding like your old self."

"I . . . my thoughts are clearer. Was it you just arguing with Dr. Medina?"

"Dr. Medina? Why would she be here?" He smiled. "Has somebody been dreaming?"

Joe didn't think it had been a dream, but it wasn't worth arguing about. If Dr. D. really thought he was getting better, he didn't want to alter that opinion with a stupid argument. "When can I see Janet?"

"Well, that may be a problem."

"What kind of problem?"

"The Johnstons don't want you to see her or talk to her," the doctor said. "They're . . . planning to adopt her."

"They can't do that." He sat up in the bed. "I'm her daddy."

"I'm sorry, Joe. I didn't mean to upset you. Get some rest now. In the morning, we'll see if we can figure out a way for you to spend some time with Janet."

"I don't want to sleep," Joe said. "Tell me about this adoption bullshit. Tell me . . . exactly . . ." He was struggling now to stay upright. A sudden exhaustion was making it difficult.

He couldn't . . . stay . . .

When he awoke again, it was still dark outside. His body felt rested, stronger somehow, but his thoughts were jumbled. The only thing that registered was that Gerry's brother and his wife were trying to take Janet from him. His little girl was in trouble and only he could save her.

He made it to the chair without much difficulty. He dropped the hospital garment to the floor and began putting on his pressed, clean-smelling clothes. Undershorts. Orange cotton polo. Khaki pants.

He sat on the chair to pull on his brown socks and work his feet into his white Reeboks. When he stood up again, he noticed that his holster was now on the floor beside the chair.

It was no longer empty. Someone had returned his weapon. He slid the pistol from its leather sheath, checked it and discovered it was loaded.

Right on, Mooney thought. That would be a major help in getting to Janet and saving her from the bad things—how had Dr. Medina put it?—the "monstrous" things the world had in store.

DAY 8

TUESDAY, JUNE 22

CHAPTER

FORTY-THREE

Mingus woke a little after six, an hour earlier than usual, to experience the sinking sensation of vaguely pleasant dreams being shattered by the harshness of reality.

The apartment was unnaturally quiet. No coffee beans being ground. No clink of dishes. No soft, contented humming coming from the kitchen. Just the sound of solitude.

He sat on the side of the bed while his feet searched for and found the soft leather slippers Bettye had given him for his birthday. He yawned. There was a sour taste in his mouth. His whiskers itched. The view through the window was of a dirty gray dawn. Figured.

The coffee tasted like sewer water. What the hell was the matter with him? He used to be able to brew a damn good cup of coffee. Maybe not as rich and tasty as Bettye's, but nothing like this.

The refrigerator was full of food.

He dropped a couple of frozen pastries into the toaster and clicked on the kitchen radio. There'd been a home invasion with two dead, the national security level had been raised to a yellow alert, the bodies of two Mexican American teens had been discovered in Griffith Park, apparent suicides. Bad news on top of bad news.

He spun the dial in search of music, spending a few seconds each with 50 Cent rappin' about money and death, Teddy Riley and Blackstreet offering up hot sex at breakfast time, and Elvis's daughter Lisa Marie singing through her self-induced pain, before settling on whatever station it was had the good sense to be playing Les Nubians' Afropean sound.

The smell of something burning alerted him to the fact that the toaster's timing had been set for dark—in this case, burnt black.

Dumping the inedible pastries in the garbage, Mingus decided this probably wasn't shaping up as one of his better days.

Two hours later, shaved, bathed, and dressed, he was sitting in his favorite chair in the living room, surrounded by documents pertaining to the Geraldine Mooney murder—coroner's report, crime scene interviews, sheets from Joe Mooney's LAPD work jacket. They were all copies. The originals were in their official repositories or, like the murder book, were at Robbery-Homicide to be turned over to whomever Captain Jacquette tapped to replace him and the bitch.

That decision had probably already been made, he thought. Maybe the new team would call him, maybe not. He wished to hell somebody would call. He'd never thought of himself as a people person, but the solitude was driving him loco.

The TV was tuned to MSNBC with the sound off. He grabbed the magic wand and punched up the gain just enough to bring other human voices into the room. Two talking heads were second-guessing the reasons the stock market was having as lousy a morning as he.

His late uncle Judge Frederick Mingus, a crusty lifelong bachelor who'd raised him, had left him comfortably well-off. Enough for him to put some money in the market, a small amount that grew smaller by the day. Normally this did not concern him, since it was found money, money he hadn't earned. Now, however, he wasn't sure what sort of financial obligation he'd wind up with, thanks to the bitch. He hoped it wouldn't break him.

He clicked away from the financial news and did a cruise through about 135 channels, pausing from time to time to observe a boxing match from the fifties, a quiz show from the sixties, the preparation of veal shanks, golf, race cars, various salespeople whose sincere but desperate pitches were being applauded by audiences who looked like they'd drifted down from some other planet.

Mingus checked his watch. Barely after nine. He'd been up less than three hours and already he felt like beating his head against the wall just to be doing something.

He was not going to make it through the day unless he had help. And Dr. Medina was the person who could provide it. Mercer would be talking to her about the murder. That didn't mean he couldn't consult her as a patient.

Her phone rang once, twice, a third time. She had not yet arrived at the office. Or she was with a patient. Or she wasn't picking up for any number of other reasons. With some annoyance, he waited for the click indicating that the answering machine had been activated.

He thought he'd missed the click because, after the fourth ring, a voice announced, "This is Dr. Medina."

He was waiting for the rest of the recorded announcement, when the voice said, "This is Dr. Medina. Is someone on the line?"

"Oh, yeah, Doc . . . Dr. Medina. This is Lionel Mingus. I was hoping—"

"Lionel, my God. Thank heaven you called." He was momentarily stunned by the animation and the anxiety in her voice. "I've been sitting here wondering . . . I didn't know what I should . . . and here you are. Perfect."

"What's going on?" he asked, not sure he wanted to know. He had his own problems.

"I can't just sit here," she said.

"I know what you mean."

"Some things you can justify, but not this. Lionel, Joe Mooney is on his way to kill his in-laws and possibly his own daughter."

Mingus was on his feet. "How do you know this?" he said, heading to the bedroom for the keys to his car.

"The important thing is that I do know. And now you know, too."

He tried prying more out of her as he locked the front door and ran to his car. "He may have already reached the Johnston home," she said. "He's taken drugs. Please don't kill him, unless . . ."

"Unless I have to," he said. "What kind of drugs?"

"I've told you all I can," she said, and broke the connection.

* * *

It was a fifteen-minute trip from Mingus's apartment in Inglewood to the Johnston home in Baldwin Crest. On the way, he managed to fit in a call to Captain Jacquette.

"How do you know what Mooney's planning?" the captain asked.

"I got a tip, a very reliable one."

"From who?"

Mingus didn't want to bring Dr. Medina's name into it until he'd had a chance to talk to her. "I can't . . . you just gotta trust me on this, Cap."

Jacquette was silent for a beat. Then he said, "I'm sending a team out, Mingus. I don't want to sound ungrateful for the heads-up, but you are not—I repeat not—to participate in anything at the scene. I don't even want you there."

"Who's on Mooney now?"

"Wasson and Puchinski."

Duke and Pooch. No world-beaters, but they did the job. Still, Mingus wasn't about to turn around and go home. He was only a few blocks away.

"Mingus, I gotta get goin' on this, but, for what it's worth, I don't see you raping or beating up a dame. Not even drunk."

"Thanks, Captain."

"Now get the hell home, kick off your shoes, and veg out until you're badged-up again. We'll take care of Mooney. You take care of yourself."

"Gotcha, Cap," he said. The house was in view.

The first thing he noticed when he drove up was the empty black sedan across the street. He parked behind it.

As he walked past, he saw it wasn't empty at all. A white officer Mingus didn't recognize had fallen sideways out of sight on the front seat. There was blood on his forehead and a knot the size of a jawbreaker.

The driver's window was rolled down, but because of the position of the unconscious man, Mingus had to open the door to reach a pulse. It was strong and regular. The man stirred as Mingus moved his jacket aside enough to glimpse the LAPD ID tucked in his shirt pocket.

Mingus slid the man's police special from its holster. Then he crossed the clean, deserted street.

The Johnstons' front door was ajar.

He used the tip of his right shoe to open it further. The living room was empty. He could hear someone in the rear garden talking, but couldn't make out the words.

He moved to the sliding doors. Through them he saw the highly strung Olivia Johnston seated under the tree, apparently frozen in fear. Five feet away, a tense, jabbering man, Joe Mooney, had one arm around his little girl. She was trying to draw back from him, reacting no doubt to the gun he held in his other hand.

"We are no match for the demons of the earth and the dark spirits of the sky," Mooney was saying. "They can capture us, take over our body and souls, degrade us, make us do anything."

"Daddy, please let me go," the little girl begged. "You're hurting me."

"Oh, sweet baby. I don't want to hurt you. I don't want anything or anybody to hurt you or to do anything to rob you of your innocence or purity." He was moving the gun up. "That's why—"

"Hey, Joe Mooney," Mingus called from the doorway. He'd tucked the stolen police special into his belt in back, could feel its cold barrel poking just above his ass.

"Who's that?" Mooney asked, turning himself and his daughter to face Mingus.

Olivia Johnston was behind Mooney now, but Mingus had no hope that she could somehow shake loose of her fear long enough to do anything to help the situation.

"Dr. Medina sent me, Joe. She thought you'd need my help."

"Medina? Dr. D. said I shouldn't listen to her. She's been infected. On the demon side."

"No way," Mingus said, edging toward the man a step or two at a time. "It's Dr. D. who's the bug head." He wondered who Dr. D. was and what game he was playing.

Joe Mooney frowned. "You're messing with me. Dr. D. said confusion is the first weapon in the enemy's arsenal."

"What enemy is that, Joe?"

"The . . . *the* enemy. The terrorists. The North Koreans. Al-Qaida. Destroyers of the free world. Degraders of our beloved."

"If this Dr. D. is so hot, why don't he tell you his full name?"

"What? Don't mess with me, now."

"Is Emmylou the enemy?"

Mooney blinked. "Emmylou? No."

"She sent me here, too, Joe. Her and Dr. Medina. They both want to help you."

"No way anybody can help. Gotta do this myself."

"Daddy, you're hurting my arm."

"Oh, I'm sorry, baby." He relaxed his grip and she tore free of him, backpedaling away.

He took a step toward her and as he did Mingus's peripheral vision picked up the movement of vines on the garden wall to the left. Shifting his sight, he saw the barrels of several guns resting on the wall, aimed at Mooney.

He felt more than heard the whispered command. He opened his mouth, but the "No!" he shouted got lost in the hail of bullets coming not just from the left wall but from the right, catching Mooney in a crossfire, turning him into a blood-soaked instant corpse held upright and puppet-dancing until the last shot was spent.

Mingus focused on the girl who was staring in horror at the ghastly object on the ground that a second before had been her daddy. He wanted to rush to her, to turn her from that horror, but common sense told him that the yard was still very much in play. Any motion could result in another spray of bullets.

To his surprise, Olivia Johnston stood from her chair and walked to the little girl as if nothing in the world had happened. She placed herself between Janet and the dead man. She bent down, hugged the child, pressed Janet's face to her chest. When she rose, she was cradling the little girl in her arms like a baby.

She carried Janet across the battleground to the house. As they passed, Mingus heard the woman saying, "Don't cry, sweetheart. It'll be all right."

Mingus almost believed her.

Until at least twenty armed men rolled over the walls and an arm encircled his neck in a chokehold of steel. The gun was yanked from his belt, raking his back in the process. A gruff voice close enough for him to feel the man's saliva spray in his ear demanded, "Who the fuck might you be, boy?"

CHAPTER FORTY-FOUR

"What part of staying at home didn't you understand?" Mercer asked, leading Mingus from Parker Center at dusk.

"Fuck you," the detective said. "Thank you for picking me up, but I don't need any more bullshit right now. So, thank you and fuck you."

Mingus had spent four hours at the scene being pushed around and shouted at and, finally, questioned by Assistant Chief Eduardo Escobar. "There's a piece of work," he told Mercer as they headed for the lawyer's car. "A real desk warrior. Tough as a toothpick. Shoutin'. Struttin'." He grinned. "Miz Johnston sure as hell stood up to the little weasel. He wanted to question Mooney's kid, who any goddamned idiot could see was flirting with catalepsy. Miz Johnston, who used to be an RN, told him if he didn't want his ass sued from here to Guadalajara—his ass, personally, not the LAPD's—he'd better get the fuck out of the room."

Mingus laughed. "I swear to God, Mercer, it was beautiful. This timid woman turning into the real deal." He sighed. "Then things went downhill fast. Anytime there's a fatal shooting these days, everybody does the scurry. This wasn't just SWAT taking out a perp. It's cops killing a cop, and, justifiable or not, somebody is gonna have to pay a price. And I'm stuck there with my ass hanging out."

Mingus explained that after they'd finished with the obvious questions of who he was (answered truthfully) and what he was doing at the scene (answered with the lie that he just happened to drop by), they decided to float the theory that he'd wound Mooney up, concluding that if he hadn't stepped in, the rogue cop could've been captured without a shot being fired.

"Any truth to that?" Mercer asked.

"I hope not. Mooney kept quotin' some guy named Dr. D. That's who stirred him up. Dunno what kind of doctor. Maybe a shrink."

"My client mentioned a Dr. D.," Mercer said. "What'd he do to rile Mooney?"

"Filled him up with a load of ET-terrorism bogeyman bullshit. I don't know why. Anyway, Miz Johnston took the weight off me by explainin' that Mooney was about to shoot her and the little girl when I distracted him."

The detective scowled as he got into the car. "Wonder if I coulda talked the gun away from him if they hadn't unloaded on him."

Turning the key in the ignition, Mercer said, "Maybe, or maybe Mooney would have plugged you and the girl and the auntie."

"Yeah. But damn, Mercer, I've never in my life seen anything like that and I never want to see it again. They tore that poor son of a bitch apart."

Trying to shift his friend's thoughts, Mercer said, "I got a sense from Captain Jacquette they won't be bringing any charges against you."

"I'm just gonna be a witness. No thanks to Assistant Chief Eduardo Escobar, who woulda liked nothing better than to sink his pearly whites into my ass."

"What changed his mind?"

"When Cap Jacquette finally showed, first thing he wanted to know was, who invited SWAT to the party?"

"*He* didn't?"

"No, and it shoulda been his call. So Dwyer, the hardcase heading up the SWAT team—calls himself Barbwire Dwyer, if that don't tickle your toes—he says his superior told him the order came from on high, Chief Ahern's office. At that point, my man Eduardo suddenly realizes he's got pressing business elsewhere and does a fade.

"Then Dr. Johnston showed, screaming, and after him, division chiefs, D.A.'s investigators, and a CSI crew. The media were starting to arrive and turn the place into a circus campground when Jacquette dragged me out of there.

"I spent the rest of the time in his office getting my ass chewed on for disobeying his direct order and for refusing to tell him how I knew about Mooney."

"How did you know?"

"Doc Medina told me."

"You saw her?"

"No. On the phone."

"How did she know about Mooney?"

"She didn't say. Lemme have your cell phone."

"She's not at her office," Mercer said. "I've been trying her all afternoon."

Mingus punched in the doctor's number and listened for a while. He handed the phone back to Mercer. "Not there."

"What'd I say?"

"Turn around. We gotta go to her office."

"Why?" Mercer asked.

"Cause we gotta talk to her and I don't know where she lives. Should be able to find that out at her office."

"You mean break in?" Mercer said. "Man, you must love it in jail."

CHAPTER FORTY-FIVE

They didn't have to break in.

Dr. Medina's office door was unlocked. This was not a particularly prudent way for a psychiatrist with confidential patient files to leave her establishment. Especially in that neighborhood at a time of night—approximately 7:30 p.m.—when most of the floors were unoccupied and on minimal-light status.

Mercer followed the detective into a dark reception room. In the soft light from the hall, they both saw that the inner door was ajar.

Mingus went through it. A couple seconds later, an overhead light in that room went on.

Mercer kneed the outer door shut and joined the detective who was hunkering near the filing cabinets. "Don't look like anybody's been at these," Mingus said. "But there's a desk drawer hangin' open. Looks like whoever was here knew what they were after and made short work of it."

Mingus began to pace around the room, poking into corners. Mercer was drawn to the desk. The folders on its surface were in a neat pile. The only thing out of order was the drawer that had been pulled out so far it hung down at a precarious angle. Resting in it was a small tape recorder with its cassette tray exposed and empty.

He sat down at the desk, looked at the recorder for a minute, then turned his attention to Dr. Medina's phone. He scanned its quick dial tabs, found one reading HOME.

He pressed it.

An answering machine came on just after the third ring.

"Doc's not home," Mercer said, wiping the receiver with a handkerchief and replacing it on its cradle.

"You just destroyed evidence," Mingus said.

"That's the pot callin' the kettle black."

Mercer's right knee bumped against the desk well. The wood there was not as smooth as it should have been. He rolled the chair back and discovered a little button two and a half feet from the base. There was another on the left side of the well.

"What have we here?"

Mingus strolled over, looked at the buttons. "I imagine one of 'em triggers 911. The doc deals with some hard cases."

"And the other button?" Mercer asked.

"The recorder?"

Mercer studied the machine. Two wires sprouted from it. One led up through the desktop into a small microphone hidden in the lamp. The other was an electric cord traveling down to a floor plug in the well.

"Not the tape machine," Mercer said.

Mingus circled the desk until he could follow the progress of the phone's mounting cord down over the left side of the desk. He saw that it was joined by a much thinner green wire at the bottom of the desk and that both cord and wire journeyed together into the connector box. "Looks like the left button is for 911. Now the other one . . ."

He got down on his knees and began studying the rug near the right side of the desk.

"Gotcha."

He pointed to a slight unevenness in the rug's surface. He used a finger to indicate its progress toward the right side of the desk. Then he began crawling in the opposite direction, following the unevenness toward a wall directly below a framed swirl of color.

He stood and ran his hand over the surface of the painting, then bent forward until his face was about a foot away from the spot he'd been touching. "The doc's a tricky gal," he said. "Got a leetle tiny lens here. Ain't microfibers something?"

He walked quickly to the doctor's bathroom and entered. Mercer's attention was drawn to the rectangle of light that immediately appeared on the carpet near the open door. It caught something that glittered.

He walked to the object. A pair of thin-rimmed glasses lay broken and ground into the carpet. "Found something that doesn't look good," he said.

"I bet I got you beat on that," Mingus said from the bathroom.

He was standing just past the door, not moving. He was staring down at a woman's body. The hair was matted with blood.

"Dr. Medina?" Mercer asked.

"Uh-huh." Mingus bent and touched her neck. "Been dead a while."

He stood. "That's convenient," he said.

Mercer saw he was pointing at an LAPD badge resting near the doctor's foot. "Joe Mooney's, you figure?"

"That'd make it a real neat package."

"But you don't buy it," Mercer said.

"No way."

Mercer showed him the broken glasses.

"I bet this is where she got hit," Mingus said. "Maybe running for the door. Killer caught her, whacked her with something." He looked around. "Coulda taken it with him."

"Scrape marks on the carpet," Mercer said. "Why bother to drag her into the bathroom?"

"Hell, why kill her in the first place?"

Mercer saw his friend close down a little as a possible answer occurred to him. "She warned me about Mooney," he said. "Pissed somebody off."

"Maybe him," Mercer said.

"He wouldn't have had time."

"Speaking of time," Mercer said, "we better get out of here."

Mingus went back into the bathroom.

To Mercer's astonishment, the detective moved around the body toward the room's built-in shelves, where he began digging past rolls of toilet tissue, Kleenex boxes, and sanitary napkins.

"What the hell are you doing?" Mercer demanded.

Mingus didn't answer. He withdrew a black and silver machine—the smallest video recorder the lawyer had ever seen—studied its front panel for a few moments, then pressed a thick forefinger against one of the silver buttons. There was a whirring sound, a lid flipped up and a drawer slid out offering up a disc.

Mingus removed it, using his thumb and forefinger. "The doc pretended to be old school, but she was state of the art."

"Put the damn thing back," Mercer said. "It's evidence."

"Not anymore," Mingus said, slipping the disc into his shirt pocket. He pulled some Kleenex squares from an open box and wiped the recorder before replacing it on the shelf. Then he put back the toilet paper and other objects, wiping each item he'd touched.

"You just can't help making trouble for yourself," Mercer said. "That disc could be vital evidence that you just turned to shit. Hell, it could have the goddamn murder on it."

"We got to find a disc player."

"The firm has one," Mercer said.

"Then let's go see what we got."

Mingus moved back through the office, using the Kleenex on items they'd touched—the phone, the lamp—and then turning off lights.

They were about to step out into the hall when they heard footsteps approaching, the rattle of keys, and someone saying, "I don't know nothing about that, Officer."

The two men raced back through the dark office. "Eyeglasses," Mingus whispered as they approached the side door. Mercer stepped around the broken glasses, bemused that the detective would worry about disturbing them, considering how much they'd already altered the crime scene.

They paused at the rear door, wondering if the hall was clear. When they heard the voices in the waiting room that no longer mattered.

They stepped into an empty hallway, easing the door shut behind them.

The elevator stood waiting, but they ignored it and took the stairs, five flights' worth.

On the main floor level, one exit led to the lobby and the elevator banks, a second to the service entrance. They took the latter.

Standing on the sidewalk, puffing, Mingus said, "That was close."

Mercer glared at him. "You think?" he said, angrily.

CHAPTER

FORTY-SIX

Mingus was sorry Dr. Medina was dead. It wasn't like they were close friends, but she'd helped him come to grips with some of his demons and he felt bad that he'd been unable to help her when she'd needed it.

But he was also a pragmatist. Nothing could be done about her death now, except to make sure her killer paid for the crime. Recent events—notably the slaughter of Joe Mooney—had shaken his confidence in the due process of law. He wasn't sure that the LAPD would be allowed to seek justice. That had been the motivating force behind his taking the disc.

So far, it had not shed much light on the murder or anything else. But the picture on the widescreen plasma monitor in the Carter and Hansborough conference room had been so crisp and clear Mingus had felt he was looking through a window at Dr. Medina sitting at her desk facing Hildy McRae and himself.

The sound was garbled since their voices were being bounced around the room and blunted by the wall.

"I wonder why the doc didn't work out the sound better," Mercer said. "She could have run a separate line next to the video and she wouldn't have had to use the cassette recorder."

"The DVD looked brand-new," Mingus said. "Maybe she didn't have time. Or maybe she tape-recorded everybody and only used the video discs every now and then."

The detective was studying his video image. He wasn't in

love with it. He looked fat and slow and stupid. Nor was he in any way flattered that the therapist had felt their meeting worth recording. It had begun the DVD-RW disc.

When Hildy made her exit to the rest room, he suggested Mercer speed the disc forward. The action jumped ahead jerkily and soundlessly until they made their departure, leaving the camera's eye to take in only the desk and chairs.

Mercer returned the player to normal speed. The stage stayed empty for a couple of minutes and he was about to fast forward again when the doctor escorted two males into the frame.

"These are the FBI dudes," Mingus said.

Mercer nodded. "The green-eyed Arthur Pleasance and the guy who needs a haircut, Carl Ivor. What do you suppose they want from the doctor?"

"Too bad the sound is messed up. I guess she was getting that on the tape."

Though it was impossible to make out anything they were saying, the trio's body language was clear. The shorter black man, Pleasance, was the alpha male. Controlling the conversation, expressing anger, eventually working past Dr. Medina's cool façade to put her on the defensive. Ivor seemed to be perfectly happy taking the passive role and observing the duel between his partner and the psychiatrist.

Pleasance kept the conversation going for about ten minutes, then, being obvious about consulting his watch, he pulled the plug on the meeting.

As the two men rose to leave, the camera went to black.

After a minute of watching a dark monitor, Mercer said, "I think that's it," and reached for the remote. He barely touched it with his fingers when the monitor came to life again.

A black man had pulled a chair around so that his back was to the camera. A white woman was sitting next to him, facing him. She seemed nervous, on edge. Dr. Medina was not in the frame.

"You recognize them?" Mercer asked.

"The female's Emmylou Paget. I can't tell for sure from the back, but the guy looks like Joe Mooney."

Paget seemed to be wailing on the guy, giving him hell. At one point he hopped from the chair and began pacing.

"Definitely Mooney," Mingus said.

"Could this be just before the murder?"

"No. This is probably later the same day we were there. The doc's missing, so it's when she went out for food."

"Maybe she was using the recorder like a nanny catcher, to see what they'd do when she wasn't around," Mercer said.

They watched as the couple continued to talk and argue and Emmylou seemed to grow more and more upset and frustrated.

"Okay if I whip this forward?" Mercer asked.

"Sure."

Mooney and Paget stood, sat, stretched their legs. Then Mooney rose up and grabbed her.

Mercer hit the pause and shifted back to normal speed. Mooney took his partner's face in his hands. He surprised them by kissing Paget on her forehead.

She began to cry and he held her in his arms.

They stood like that for minutes, holding one another. Mingus flashed on Mooney's mangled and bloody body and looked away from the monitor. He wondered if anyone had thought to tell Paget that her partner was dead. She'd probably caught it on the news.

"Dinnertime," Mercer said.

Dr. Medina had returned with a bag of food. While she removed the white containers and placed them on her desk, Paget laid out the paper plates. Mooney watched them both, smiling.

"Guy doesn't look so dangerous to me," Mercer said.

Mingus had nothing to add to that.

Paget loaded up their plates. As they began to dig in, Mercer said, "Damn, I'm getting hungry."

"We could go to Fong's Palace in Chinatown. That's where their food came from."

"You are some detective, Lionel," Mercer said.

Suddenly Paget's fork slipped from her fingers and she slid off of her chair onto the carpet. Mooney started to get up, presumably to assist her, but he never made it. Instead, he slumped back with such sudden force he and the chair tipped over.

Dr. Medina was on her feet in a flash, rushing to the fallen man. Checking his head, his neck, his back. Apparently satisfied that he wasn't seriously damaged, she moved on to Paget.

Again, there seemed to be no cause for concern.

The two men watched in fascination as the doctor turned to look directly into the camera, evidently realizing that it was on. She went to her desk, reached into the well.

And that was that.

They checked to make sure the rest of the disc was blank. Then Mercer did a playback on the dining scene. "The doc wasn't exactly getting busy with the chicken chow mein," he said. "Didn't eat a bite."

"Naw. She drugged the food. Hildy was following her that evening, saw her messing with the containers but didn't realize what the doc was doing."

"Medina was definitely in the middle of everything," Mercer said. "Why'd she get the video equipment? It sure as hell wasn't as a therapy aid. Blackmail?"

"No way."

"You did just see her slipping the mickey to two cops."

"I'm not saying she wasn't involved in whatever's going down. But blackmail . . . ? I don't see that. I think she rigged up the video because she realized she was in deep water and she wanted some kind of physical evidence to stay afloat."

"Then what's going on? What's the bottom line on this?"

Mingus shook his head. "I don't know. But I'm inclined to agree with you that whatever it is, it started coming apart the night Dwight Baskin cashed it in. This is all patch-up stuff and it's turning damn ugly."

"The black box is the key," Mercer said. "It's like there's a curse on it. Everybody who touches it dies or goes nuts."

"Where'd it come from? What was Baskin doing with it?"

"I don't know, but his body was short on serotonin, which I gather can send you on a real downer. I suppose the thing in the box could be the cause."

"You got much info on Baskin?"

"A file about yea thick," Mercer said, holding his thumb and finger an inch apart. "I haven't gone through it all, myself."

"I got the time, Mercer. A little reading matter might help me pass it."

Mercer led the detective to the firm's library, where, at

nine-thirty, Kennard Haines, his eyes red as fire, was going through an Alhambra phone book.

"What's up?" Mercer asked him.

"I'm working on the Dr. D. list. There're gonna be thousands of them." He sounded as if he might cry at any minute.

"We're looking for a male," Mercer said. "Probably a medical doctor or a shrink. Or maybe a cleric. Or a scientist."

"That sure makes it easier," Kennard said.

"Did you get a chance to talk to your dad about White House interest in the client?"

"Yes. He promised to look into it."

"Thank him for me." He suddenly realized that Mingus and Kennard had never met. When he'd introduced them, he added to Kennard, "Lionel would like to take a look at the Baskin file."

Kennard blinked. "I . . . I don't think it's here."

Mercer looked at the pile of file folders in a box on the floor. "I put it back there yesterday."

Kennard said nothing.

"Let me make a wild guess," Mercer said. "Sidone missing. File not here. Hmmm."

Kennard sighed. "She wanted to give it one more run-through."

"No big deal," Mercer said. "I'll print out another copy for Lionel. Then the three of us can grab some dinner, if you're up for it."

Kennard looked confused, then perplexed. Then he grinned. "Dinner sounds excellent," he said.

It took nearly ten minutes to duplicate Lonny Hootkins's impressive file on Dwight Baskin. With it in hand, Mingus decided to opt out of the dinner.

"I've got Bettye's stew back at my place," he said.

Mercer thought he understood. If Bettye decided to come back tonight or tomorrow, Mingus did not want her to find the stew there, untouched.

He turned to Kennard. "Looks like it's just the two of us."

This didn't seem to upset the young man at all.

As Mercer was walking back to his office, Devon Olander stopped him in the hall. "Was that Detective Mingus I heard?"

Mercer nodded. "We're working on another matter. Why?"

"You sure he's playing straight with us about his relationship with Detective McRae?"

"I'm sure. Why?"

"The criminalists found his hair follicles in McRae's bed."

"His hair? He's bald."

"Pubic hair."

Mercer was surprised.

"On the plus side, they also found evidence of several unidentified males. That suggests the bed got quite a workout, but the presence of his hair is a problem . . . unless he slept with her the day before, say."

"He says he didn't have sexual relations with her. I don't believe he lied."

"Well, I'm taking a short trip to Vegas to look into that bad romance of McRae's that Mingus mentioned and see what else I can turn up. Meanwhile, you might want to ask him if he can think of any other way his short ones wound up on her sheets."

Mercer said he would.

CHAPTER FORTY-SEVEN

Mingus was in his living room with the TV on. The ten o'clock news shows couldn't get enough of the SWAT shooting. Some of them featured zoom shots of Officer Joe Mooney's bullet-torn body. Sound bites of SWAT leader Barbwire Dwyer discussing the "unfortunate but unavoidable takedown" of Mooney were appearing with the frequency of commercials.

Mingus was grateful that Captain Jacquette had got him out of there before the media onslaught. He hadn't heard his name mentioned in any of the broadcasts, though he did catch a glimpse of himself and the captain driving away in the background as the Channel 9 cameras did a traveling-shot entrance into the Johnston home.

He'd been particularly concerned that, had he been connected to the Mooney shooting, the assault and rape charges against him that had rated only a small graph in the morning *L.A. Times* Metro section could have suddenly blossomed into page one bad news.

At the tail end of the show, a "This Just In" report flashed a scene of the front of Dr. Medina's building where a body bag was being rolled out. A female reporter was describing the scene, rather breathlessly. She ended with, "Among the police officers Dr. Medina had been treating was Officer Joe Mooney. There is evidence to suggest that this doctor-patient relationship may have led to her demise."

The eleven o'clock news shows were more of the same. When he grew tired of hearing the many ways that reporters and anchors could imply that Mooney had murdered the doctor without actually stating it, he replaced current events with a dumb comedy show in which a large cast of black actors behaved so idiotically it made *Amos 'n' Andy* look like August Wilson material.

Mingus sighed, turned down the sound, and picked up the Dwight Baskin file for a second look. He'd been struck by one thing that Mercer had not mentioned. The Medal of Valor winner had been in charge of a small antigang unit at East Pico Division. Because of this he had developed a profound interest in a rising star of the gangsta community—a vicious seventeen-year-old who had discarded the name he'd been given at birth, Ricardo Hernandez, in favor of the gang name Bolero.

According to Baskin's sources, Bolero had recently become the new leader of the militant Jaquecas, an organization of approximately a thousand members that was spreading out from the center of the city to various unsuspecting suburbs.

Baskin had been particularly interested in the reason for Bolero's ascendancy—the death of the gang's former leader. Luis Almador's fatal seven-story fall from the Perdido Building in downtown L.A. had been officially categorized a suicide.

Almador's family and even some of his brother Jaquecas had testified at the inquest that Luis had been depressed over health problems (he was undergoing injections to rid his body of hepatitis C), his mother's death by cancer, and the fatal drive-by shooting of his two closest friends and most trusted soldiers, Jerry Ruiz and Armando Puig.

Baskin remained unconvinced, however. He'd scribbled a note on the bottom of his copy of the official suicide finding: "Bolero did it!"

Pursuing that belief, he'd made Bolero his special project. Stalking him, pulling him in at every opportunity. One of the officer's last official acts before he went off his head was to pick up the banger's fourteen-year-old brother for soliciting, an obviously trumped-up charge meant to do nothing more than shame the boy and his family. He was trying to rattle Bolero's cage enough to prompt some kind of violent reaction that would earn the teen a long stay in the stone house.

Mingus wondered if there had been a reaction from Bolero. Nothing stupid or obvious. Some very sly scheme that had sent Baskin into cuckoo land.

He put the Xeroxed pages aside.

He knew what had been driving Baskin. He'd felt that same frustration at seeing the cockroaches disappearing into the cracks in the system. The gangs were clear evidence that justice no longer prevailed. Chief Ahern could boast that his war against them had been won and that he had the gangstas under control.

Mingus knew better. It wasn't just the ever more frequent drive-bys or the bank robberies or the dope trafficking. Gangism had spread across the country, several generations' worth by now with many of the older members having discarded their colors for suits and ties, the better to burrow into key positions of government, even law enforcement.

Maybe he was picking up on Baskin's paranoia, but he thought that it was not the impossible dream for a gang leader like Bolero to decide to mess up a cop's mind rather than do damage to his body.

Jesus, the world seemed to be getting too damn confusing, everything moving too fast. Or maybe he was just slowing down.

With a sigh, the detective pushed his weary body from the chair. He was headed for the bedroom and a night of sleeping alone when his cellular rang.

Had to be Bettye.

His mood shifted immediately. He ran across the living room to answer. But it wasn't her.

"Hey, Li'nel, I'm so horny, baby," Hildy said. "How'd you like to come over here and make all your problems go away right now, tonight?"

Controlling himself, Mingus simply clicked off the cellular. Before he took two steps toward the bedroom, the apartment phone began to ring. He lifted the receiver a few inches from the cradle. "Li'nel, you bad mutha-fu—"

He hung up.

A few moments later, another ring.

She was crazy enough to keep dialing him all night. He unplugged the phone. Tomorrow, he'd have to pick up a cheap answering machine. He figured her messages would be worth saving for IAG or the court, if it came to that.

More important, he'd need some way of knowing if Bettye was trying to reach him.

CHAPTER FORTY-EIGHT

Mercer and Kennard were having after-dinner drinks at The Jury Room, a small watering hole on the ground floor rear of the Carter and Hansborough building.

The bar had been fairly busy when they'd arrived. Now it was down to a couple of drunk granpas hitting on a table of stone sober and hostile women and another junior partner, Joe Wexstead, who was with one of the firm's stunning receptionists in a booth in the far corner, setting himself up for a serious harassment suit.

Mercer had been preoccupied by the bad news Devon had given him, but decided to put it away for the night and pay more attention to what the young associate was saying.

"C.W. asked me today how I thought the Nunez trial prep was going," Kennard said.

"What'd you tell him?"

"I said he'd have to ask you."

"That's the right answer."

"Fact is: I don't know how it's going."

"That would have been the wrong answer."

"Sidone and I have been seeing you and Lonny running in and out of the office, but I guess we're feeling a little left out of things."

"It's not intentional. We're busy gathering information, just like you. Soon we'll put it all together and see what we've got."

"My dad says most criminal trials are like icebergs,"

Kennard said. "It's easy to get hung up on the stuff below the surface."

"In this case, we got a little more hidden stuff than usual. But, bottom line, if all else fails, we've got a very legitimate insanity defense. You hear from your daddy often?"

"More from my mother, who quizzes me like a prosecutor about everything. Dad calls maybe once a week, mainly to satisfy himself I haven't been eating lotus leaves out here. Actually, he says he's worried I don't have enough friends. I tell him it's kinda hard to make friends when I got a boss who keeps me in the library 24/7."

"At least you're not alone in the library," Mercer said.

Kennard smiled. "That does ease the pain. She's fantastic. Brilliant. Beautiful. Sexy."

"And why are you here with me?"

The smile went away. "She says I'm like her brother. That's not exactly encouraging. Any suggestions?"

"You are definitely asking the wrong man," Mercer said, waving his credit card at the bartender. "I'm pretty much batting zero in that department."

In the building's underground parking, Mercer paused to watch the associate drive away in a bright red Mini Cooper, so new it still carried the dealer tags. He wondered if the recent purchase had been a move to impress Sidone. *Ah, to be gifted, young and black. And wealthy, with a powerful father.*

He was walking toward his car when a woman called his name. He recognized the voice without having to think about it.

Annie Corey was moving toward him, as beautiful as ever. "Guess who's back," she said.

He was so surprised, his mind so suddenly jammed with questions, he couldn't speak.

She solved that problem by moving into his arms, pressing against him and kissing him with a hunger bordering on desperation.

As lost as he was in the moment, he was vaguely aware of an approaching vehicle. They were standing in the middle of the car path.

Without breaking the kiss, he lifted Annie and carried her aside.

The vehicle moved forward until it was beside them.

Annie seemed oblivious to it, but it was interfering with Mercer's concentration.

"Get a motel room," someone in the vehicle called out.

Mercer angrily broke the kiss and turned to face the vehicle.

It was the black Escalade.

The muscle man with the buzz cut swung out of the passenger side. He was wearing a dark suit over a black T-shirt.

"You live in that SUV?" Mercer asked.

The man didn't answer. He opened the rear door.

Mercer moved in front of Annie, protectively, misreading the situation.

"Get in, Mercer," she said. "This is a win-win deal for you. You've got questions; we've got answers."

CHAPTER

FORTY-NINE

The smell of fresh plaster and paint permeated the black cloth hood Mercer had been wearing as a blindfold since leaving the C&H building. Because the trip had been mainly nonstop, he'd assumed it had been via one or more freeways. It had ended on a sharp downward drive.

Now he was being led from the Escalade across a dirt path and into a building with a gritty cement floor where the odors became even more powerful.

When the black cloth was removed he discovered he was in the midst of construction or renovation. The building was lighted by bare bulbs surrounded by miles of wires of various shades and sizes that would eventually be hidden in the recesses of a lowered ceiling. Most of the drywall had been prepped for painting.

He wasn't able to tell where in the city he was. Though the windows seemed to be clear, there was nothing but blackness beyond. That in itself was significant. Either the city was in the midst of a power failure or they were in an area without streetlamps or neighbors.

Annie escorted him down a dim hall to a door outlined by light. It led to a completely finished, well-appointed office. Three men were in it, seated on ergonomic chairs that Mercer assumed had to be more comfortable than they looked.

The faces were all familiar, though it was his first in-person meeting with FBI agents Pleasance and Ivor. The third man was the genial bogus Realtor who'd tried to sell him the failed mall.

He smiled at Mercer and asked him to take the empty ergo chair on the other side of the gunmetal-topped desk.

As the lawyer had suspected, the sculpted steel seat, inward angled backrest, and curved arms of the chair were blissfully relaxing.

"I'm sorry about all this secret mumbo jumbo stuff, Mr. Early," the man said. "I'm Commander Tim Sellars. To your right are FBI Special Agents Art Pleasance and Carl Ivor. I believe you know Special Agent Anne Andre." He indicated Annie.

"Not by that name," Mercer said.

"Yes. This has been one of those cocked-up deals where we ran around in circles when we should have just cut through the crap and had this talk. Saved us all a lot of bother."

"I'm all for saving bother," Mercer said. "Maybe we should start with what the hell you folks really are. You say you're a commander. I don't recall that being an FBI title."

"It's a very fluid situation we're in, Mr. Early. The folks in this room, we come from various sections of the government, brought together by pressing world conditions. Originally we were assigned to a branch of the U.S. Department of Homeland Security, engaged in research and technology. Then we were shifted over to the recently created DTRA, the Defense Threat Reduction Agency.

"Now we occupy our own little niche."

"Your niche called OBN?" Mercer asked.

The commander frowned. "Where'd you hear that?"

"I keep running into it so much," Mercer said, "I keep expecting to see it in sky writing."

"OBN is . . . one of the things we're involved in."

"What's the full name?"

That earned him a smile. "All you have to know about our operation—all I am allowed by law to tell you—is that we are assisting the DTRA and providing the military with ways of combating terrorism and all of its ugly threats."

"What do you want with me?"

"Well, you see, sir, you are interfering with our work. We'd like that to stop."

"How am I interfering?" Mercer asked.

"By poking around in matters best left alone. What are you after, Mr. Early?"

"What you see is what you get. I'm a lawyer defending a man accused of murder."

"That would be Officer Eldon Nunez?"

"None other."

"And why are you so interested in the late Officers Dwight Baskin and Joseph Mooney?"

"Put those two together with my client and you've got three top police officers who suddenly decided to kill the people closest to them. That means the district attorney's case against my client may not be so open and shut."

"Clarify that for me."

Mercer was not about to mention the black box. "Well, police work is stressful by itself. If these officers and my client had been adding some clandestine activity to the normal pressures of their jobs, that could help to explain what pushed them over the top. Obviously my concern is with Eldon Nunez."

"I can rest your mind on one thing, sir. Eldon Nunez performed no service or services for us that would have added to his stress level or pushed him into any form of antisocial behavior, homicide in particular."

"But he was working for you?"

"Next question."

"Was Joe Mooney working for you?"

"Mr. Early, these are things I cannot answer."

"I can subpoena you to answer in court."

"As a matter of fact, according to new guidelines set down by the attorney general of these United States, you can't. Now, is there anything else we can help you with?"

"You haven't helped me with anything."

"I thought I'd been rather forthcoming. If you've a question . . . ?"

"Have you tried to get the district attorney to withdraw the charges against Officer Nunez?"

"Matter of fact, we have."

"Why?"

"That's something I can't tell you. But Ms. Lowery has remained adamant. We're still hoping to change her mind."

"I don't think that's going to happen."

"Then it'll be up to you to set Officer Nunez free."

"What exactly are you trying to achieve?" Mercer asked.

"Our ultimate goal is an America free of the fear of terrorism."

"I mean specifically."

Commander Sellars smiled. "If I told you that, I'd have to kill you. Good evening, Mr. Early. Stick to your lawbooks and let us do our jobs and life will be milk and cookies."

"What's the big secret?"

"All will be made clear, eventually," Sellars said.

"Time to go," Annie said.

"No, my dear," Sellars said. "You stay. Art can accompany Mr. Early on the return trip."

She turned to Mercer. "Good-bye," she said. He thought he saw a hint of regret on her beautiful face. Or sadness. Or nothing at all.

As the Escalade strained up the slope, heading away, Pleasance said from beside him on the rear seat, "Brother to brother, how's little Annie rate, pussy-wise?"

Mercer's first inclination was to headbutt the pig. But blindfolded in a car where three men carried guns and he wasn't one of them, he decided to go the opposite route. He pretended to think over the question.

Finally he said, "It's like Fats Waller told the woman who asked him what jazz is. If you've got to ask, you might as well not mess with it."

Somebody in the front seat snickered.

Pleasance didn't have much to say after that. But he made up for it when they arrived back on Wilshire in front of the Carter and Hansborough building. He yanked off the hood, trying and failing to take some of Mercer's hair with it. "Here's the deal, *Mister* Early," he said. "The commander has just cut you a very large break. In repayment, you're gonna get on about your business like a good little lawyer and prepare to defend your client on the grounds of temporary insanity. If you so much as belch anything that sounds like NSA or DTRA or OBN, you will wind up in a little windowless cell far, far from any courtroom or any hope of release, where the only sound you'll hear will be Iranian and Arab terrorists weeping in their bloodstained beards."

"Man, your use of graphic imagery is absolutely brilliant," Mercer said. "You could be the homeland security poet of despair."

Pleasance glared at him. "Personally," he said, "I hope you ignore this warning. I hope you use your talent as a smart-ass to try and give us all the trouble you can. Then when they drag you to that matchbox of a cell, wearing the label of traitor to your nation, a broken, beaten, weeping, snot-dripping pariah, I will be there banging the drum to mark the day.

"Nighty-night, lawyer man. Sleep tight, knowing America will be safe and secure."

DAY 9

WEDNESDAY, JUNE 23

CHAPTER FIFTY

"This Commander Sellars, if that's his real name, wanted to know why we were so interested in Dwight Baskin and Joe Mooney," Mercer told Lonny Hootkins over breakfast at Rae's Diner. "How'd he know we were?"

Hootkins swallowed a forkful of pancakes. "He saw us pokin' around the alley where Baskin caught it."

Mercer checked out the diner. The place had thinned out after the early rush. The waitress was behind the counter, back to the room, studying the chefs through the rectangular order window.

The only other customers were at a distant table, two guys in Adelphia whites downing carbos before tackling another day of cable repairs and complaints. Mercer didn't think his conversation with the detective would mean much to anybody with an ear out, but he was always cautious about discussing important matters in public places.

"The alley, right," he said with lowered voice. "Well, there are any number of reasons we might have been there. Sellars seemed to know without doubt that we were investigating Baskin and Mooney."

Hootkins savored a sip of coffee. "It's been a while since your office had a visit from Ladybug. She can do her thing while I see what I can turn up using the new names of your playmates."

* * *

They met again that afternoon in the lawyer's office. Hootkins flopped onto the client chair, placed a cup of coffee on the edge of the desk, and unzipped his battered leather briefcase.

"Ladybug been in here yet?" Hootkins asked.

"While I was out. It's clean."

"Just bein' cautious," the detective said. He withdrew a couple of grainy Xerox photos from the briefcase and shoved one across the desk.

Her beauty shone through the Xerox.

"FBI Special Agent Anne Andre," Hootkins said. "Presently listed as being on duty in the San Francisco office. But if you call there, they'll tell you she's on temporary reassignment and that they're not at liberty to provide information any more specific than that. But they'd be happy to pass along any message."

"Do we know what she did before San Francisco?"

Hootkins consulted his notebook. "Out of the Academy, she was sent to a Legal Attaché office, what they call LEGAT, in the American Embassy in Amman, Jordan. There for a couple years, then they pulled her back to D.C. and put her in Investigative Services Division at headquarters."

Mercer wondered if she'd been in the city while he was finishing up at Howard Law, if maybe their paths had crossed without notice. He interrupted the detective to ask if he had specific dates.

Of course he did.

Annie had been in Jordan when he graduated. He was long gone before she took up residence in the D.C. area.

"Something about the dates strike you as important?" Hootkins asked.

"Not really. What was she up to in D.C.?"

"Initially, she was in Counterintelligence, then Counterterrorism. Last thing she did before coming west was in the bureau's Criminal Investigation Division."

"Well, that fits in with what Sellars said about all of them being drawn from various areas of government work."

"Speak of the devil . . ." Hootkins presented another grainy but identifiable photo of a figure in a police uniform. "Commander Timothy Jasper Sellars," Hootkins said. "I had a cousin named Jasper. Dead now, though.

Your Jasper was a career cop in the nation's capitol till about a year ago when he stepped down from being in charge of the First District there."

"That would definitely be the district of choice," Mercer said. "Covers the city's business and political hub. The Capitol, the White House."

"It's also got the Supreme Court, which is where the commander had the good fortune last year to nip some mad dog's attempt to blow the place up. He suddenly became the prez's new best friend and now he's out here, giving you a hard time."

"Actually, he was a gent. A lying, two-faced son of a bitch, but a gent. It was Pleasance who ruined the evening. Now there's a real sourball."

"He's got some spilled blood in his bureau file," Hootkins said. "Early on in his career, he went guns-ablazin' into an apartment filled with some admittedly bad dudes cutting up heroin bricks. No problem about them, they were illegals, but a three-year-old girl in the next apartment wound up shot to death, too."

"They kept him on after that?" Mercer asked.

"The illegals and the dope added up to a big score. The victim's mama was a coke whore who didn't have much of a voice in the matter. What I've seen of the type, she might not have even noticed. Toppin' that off, the agency was having some shifts in leadership. So Pleasance took the mildest of reprimands and moved onward and upward.

" 'Fore I forget, that number in Nunez's book is no longer in service and, according to the records, hasn't been in service for over a year."

"What about Parnell's?"

"Damn, son, I can only do five things at one time."

A fiftiesh, pear-shaped woman marched into the office. "Don't y'all get up now," she said, though neither of them had made any attempt to.

She wore her wiry white hair in an unkempt frizz and was dressed in a rumpled plaid shirt over a purple T-shirt that featured a drawing of a martini and the words, I PUT THE GODDAMN BUG IN THE OLIVE. The rest of her outfit consisted of worn and torn tan Levi's and ancient scuffed Doc Martens. She could have been used to illustrate the definition of "bag lady," even if she hadn't been toting a huge canvas carryall.

But, though Mercedes Ladybug Tyrell had zero interest in her outward appearance, she was, in fact, several giant steps up the economic ladder from homeless and carried in her bag not a collection of eccentric scavenged items but an assortment of very specific electronic devices worth well over $150,000.

She placed the bag on Mercer's desk. "This is my third . . . no, only my second trip here. Last time was back about ten months ago?"

"A little over a year," Mercer said. "I'd been dealing with some tricky people and I wanted to make sure the office was clean."

"Well, it was clean then, as I recall. But, brother, today we hit the Sneaky Pete mother lode." Ladybug began to cackle.

Mercer looked at Hootkins, whose shrug suggested that he knew the woman was a little strange, but was worth putting up with. "Foun' something, huh, Lady?" he asked.

"Oh yeah." She began rooting around in the bag. She removed what looked to Mercer like an electronic beetle, black with little wire legs. She found two more in the bag. "These little darlin's are what is commonly referred to as infinity transmitters," she said, talking faster as she warmed to the subject. "I'm not gonna fill your handsome head with a lot of jive about how they work—the ringer coils and hookswitches and all that. Main thing is, some outside party phones in, plays an electronic tone that stops the ring on this end and starts the transmitter, which then sends anything being said in the room back to the caller.

"Once was, the sneak had to hit a note on a harmonica to turn on the mike. It's why they used to be called harmonica bugs. But everything's slicker and easier now, so the sneak only has to press a specific key on his phone to get things movin'.

"It's a little trickier when the call comes in through a reception switchboard, but, lucky for your sneak, everybody in this office has also got a direct dial number."

Mercer raised his hand to get a word in. "Where exactly did you find these things, Ladybug?"

"One in the big boy's office." That's what she called

C.W. Hansborough. "One in the conference room. And one in here."

"So these could have been turned on and off at any time without our knowing? Doesn't matter if the phone is on the hook or off?"

"I knew you was smart as well as good-lookin'. See, it's the ringer coils that pick up the audio. You just have to short one side of the hookswitch . . . well, trust me. It works."

"I don't suppose there's any way of telling who planted 'em?"

"Short of catchin' 'em? Not that I know of. I mean, you don't find this stuff on a counter at Costco, but they're not difficult to come by."

"There's not much doubt who's responsible," Hootkins said.

"The arrogant bastards," Mercer said. "They just bust in and bug our offices. Probably put one in my apartment, too."

"These are strange times, son," Hootkins said, looking mournful. "Lawless times. The Constitution, Bill o' Rights, they're starting to look like yesterday's newspaper. These folks figure they got the kind of clout they don't have to bother with known rules of law."

"Maybe," Mercer said. "Ladybug, yesterday I saw this nice little video camera with a very small lens."

"All the manufacturers are makin' 'em now," Ladybug said. "Mini-this, micromini-that. There's a Hitachi Ultravision saves to a mini-DVD."

"Well, what I'm thinking is, soon as whoever placed those bugs here finds out they're gone, they're gonna try to plant new ones. I'd like to get a look at 'em."

"I could rig one of those Hitachi's in here, hidden in that," she said, pointing to the cabinet beneath the windows on the far wall. "Lay in a wide angle ultra-mini lens triggered by a motion detector. Have it in place by six p.m. Four grand, installed."

"Sounds a little steep."

"The Hitachi costs over a grand, sweetpea. Then there's the special lens. I may have to bring in a guy to do a little touch up on the furniture. And we make the whole thing happen four hours from now. Hell, you gettin' a bargain."

* * *

C.W. agreed. "It's a small price to pay, if your plan works," he said. "Any idea how long we've been bugged?"

Mercer shrugged. "Maybe ever since we took on Nunez."

The senior partner frowned. "Well, what's done is done, but it's fucking outrageous, and we're not about to let it slide. I don't give a damn if it is the government, we do not let it slide. Understand?"

Mercer replied that he understood and agreed.

"Who knows about the hidden camera?" C.W. asked.

The question caught Mercer off guard. "You mean in the firm?"

"That's what I mean. I assume everybody knows the bug lady's made her sweep. Can't be helped. But keep the knowledge of the camera between us."

"You think somebody working here bugged us? That never even occurred to me."

"People are only human. Speaking of which, with you getting deeper and deeper into this Nunez mess, what's going on with your other cases?"

"Eddie's taken over the Gavalan defense. Nothing needed on Hawes and Lundy for a while. I'm going to hand off Terrenova to Wally."

"Give it to Joe," C.W. said. "I know you don't like him, but Terrenova could get tricky and Wally's not the lawyer for tricky."

Mercer turned to go, but C.W. had one thing more to say. "I'll be out of the office for the next couple of days, so you'll be in charge. Anything earth-shattering comes up, or if our candid camera catches anybody, I'll be available by phone."

"Were you headed?"

"I'm taking a little jaunt to Vegas, catch a few shows."

"I never pegged you for a Wayne Newton fan."

"Love the man."

Mercer didn't have to ask if he was going alone. Devon was going to Vegas, supposedly on Mingus's behalf.

People were only human.

CHAPTER FIFTY-ONE

"Bastard." A *click*. Thirty seconds of silence. "Prick." *Click*. Thirty more silent seconds. "I know you're there, you macho son of a bitch. Well, fuck you."

Mingus's new answering machine had been working perfectly while he'd been away from the apartment on errands.

Much of that time had been spent in a cubicle at the *L.A. Times*, calling in a marker from a crime reporter named Manny Menendez who'd won a Pulitzer the previous year for a three-part article on the city's Hispanic gangs.

The journalist had expressed skepticism about Luis Almador's death being a homicide. "He was going though some serious shit at the time, *amigo*. And there have been a profound number of suicides among the bangers. Any shrink can tell you why. The danger, the pressure, the drugs causing wider and wider mood swings, whcrc down gets so far down that death seems like the simple answer."

Regarding Baskin's theory that Bolero killed Almador, Menendez had shrugged. "Baskin was a fucking storm trooper with an anti-Hispanic bias, you ask me. But, having said that, if anybody did help Luis jump off that rooftop, Bolero would be my first choice. He's a psycho. Know what Bolero means, *amigo*? 'Shoeshine.' Somebody who polishes, get it? Polishes people off? It's what he loves, what he's good at."

Mingus had returned home that evening to find

twenty-eight messages blowing up the machine. All but one were from Hildy, the dissenter being a telemarketer pitching credit card insurance. When he'd seen the high number of calls, he'd assumed that one had to have been from Bettye, but, as he'd just concluded, he'd assumed wrong.

He slumped on the couch, staring at the phone. It was nearly six, but she'd still be at work. Should he call her? And then what? Try to convince her of his love with the store full of demanding customers and her boss, Palmyra, slobbering next to her, hand on her ass? He'd get about as far as that telemarketer.

That's what he'd be, a telemarketer of love.

He thought about driving over to the Fox Hills Mall to deliver the pitch in person. She'd hate that. Him showing up at her work, putting their personal life in front of Palmyra and the others. It would be the act of, in Hildy's echoing words, "a macho son of a bitch."

Another option would be to drive over there and wait for the store to close at eight. Like a stalker. He should have quit at telemarketer.

The phone rang.

Automatically, he reached out, but stopped himself in time. On the third ring, the machine went into action.

He heard Mercer Early's voice and picked up.

"Stuff's been happening," the lawyer said. "How's dinner at LaLa's sound in about an hour?"

"Fine. I got a few things to tell you, too."

As much as they both liked the restaurant, it was the wrong place for them that evening. The bar was too busy and too noisy, the air too charged with sexual electricity.

The question about Mingus's pubic hair turning up in McRae's bed did nothing to calm the air. "That's goddamned impossible," Mingus said. "I never even whipped it out to take a piss at her place."

"Had to come from somewhere," Mercer said.

"I dunno, maybe she bought it on eBay," Mingus said. "All we been through, Mercer, I figured you'd take my word on this."

"You figured right."

Mingus nodded. Then he knocked back his Thug Passion

and stood. "This ain't doing it for me tonight. C'mon. I got a better idea. Place I just heard about today."

Mercer finished his drink and paid the tab. He followed Mingus out of the restaurant. "Where we going?"

"Española," Mingus said. "I was gonna suggest we head there after dinner, but we might as well eat there, too."

"How far?"

"Downtown. On Miramar."

"You sure you want Mexican?" Mercer asked as Mingus drove them toward the heart of the city. "I'm not big on spicy and they use a lot of pig in their food."

"It's not the food you're gonna have to worry about," Mingus said. "Española is where a banger named Bolero eats out on Wednesday with his folks. I've been told it's about the only place we got a chance of talking to him without him shootin' first."

"And why is it we wanna talk to him?"

"He maybe had something to do with Baskin turning crazy. I'll fill you in on the drive downtown."

Mercer didn't respond positively to Mingus's theory. "No real connection between this Bolero and Baskin's death. Just a hunch," he said. "I got a hunch telling me not to get anywhere within a mile of this psycho and I think mine makes more sense."

"But you'll check it out with me, right?" Mingus said.

"I guess. But don't expect me to be eating any pig."

That part of it worked out to Mercer's satisfaction. The Española, a large family-oriented trattoria, offered a wide assortment of dishes without pork. He ordered the pan broiled sea bass, Mingus the steak fajita plate.

While their dinners were being prepared, Mingus went off in search of the banger. He had only a vague idea of what the young man looked like. He'd assumed that a mad dog killer would stand out, but if he was among the family groups bulking up in the main dining hall, he was hidden in the camo of his own tribe.

Returning to the table, the detective passed the open door to a private room. Inside was a family of five, a somewhat dignified elder couple, a senorita in her early twenties, and two boys. The younger was fifteen maybe, a spindly, nervous kid with slicked down black hair and effeminate manner. The other was not much bigger than his brother, but his otherwise billowy silk shirt sleeves drew tight over corded biceps. He wore a red, white, and green beaded necklace.

With his glistening, randomly cut black hair, drooping moustache, and spindly goatee, there was a wild look to him as he nattered away in Spanish to his considerably more subdued, almost wary family. Broad gestures. Manic laughter. But what Mingus found most chilling were the boy's eyes—pale blue, constantly shifting but without any spark of life.

The detective checked the plates on the table to get an idea how much longer they'd be dining. When he looked up again, those dead eyes were staring straight at him. He felt like a deer caught in headlights, but he had enough presence of mind to nod politely and move on.

At their table, Mercer paused long enough in his fish-eating frenzy to ask, "Find him?"

"I think so," Mingus said, disturbed by those dead blue eyes, but trying to keep it on the jaunty side for Mercer's benefit. "No hurry. They're just on their first course. We'll catch him over dessert."

"We're just gonna barge in on him and his family?" Mercer asked.

"Kinda," Mingus said. "What's he gonna do? Shoot us in front of his mama and daddy?"

"He sure as hell isn't gonna be of a mood to talk."

"I'm a cop, Mercer. I know how to get this punk to talk. Now stop frettin' about this and finish up tellin' me about these bastards who kidnapped your ass."

Mercer had told most of it on the drive. While they ate, he brought the detective up to speed on Hootkins's background snaps and the discovery of bugs in the office phones.

"So you figure this is all one more example of homeland security gone wild?"

"That's how it seems, but . . ."

The lawyer was distracted by two young men heading toward their table. The grim look of determination on their lean faces, the red, white, and green bandanas tied round their necks, and the fact that the happy family chatter had suddenly ceased suggested to Mercer that this might turn out to be another bad night.

"Neg-ros," the man in the lead called out. He gestured upward with both hands. *"Andar."*

Mercer remained seated. "The word is pronounced 'Nee-grows,' " he said to the man. "Not that I'm recommending its use, understand."

"He don't understand," the other man said. He was in his mid-twenties. His friend was younger, maybe not even twenty. "He don't speak English. You two come with us now."

"We haven't finished our meal," Mingus said, pointing to the remaining food on his plate.

The man who understood English reached out and tipped the plate into the detective's lap. Mainly refried beans and rice, soaking into his pants. "Now you finished."

Mingus's arm shot out, grabbed the young man's shirt-front, and pulled him forward until his face was a few inches from his soiled lap. "How'd you like to lick it off, suckah?" the detective said.

He heard the metallic click and felt the gun pressed to his temple. Across the table Mercer started to rise. The man who didn't understand English kept his first gun pressed to Mingus's head while he drew a second from beneath his jacket and, cross-armed, aimed that at the lawyer.

"Solt' mi amigo," he yelled at Mingus.

The detective's knowledge of Spanish was limited, but he could figure this one out. He released the gunman's food-throwing *amigo,* who rose up angrily brushing at the wrinkles in his silk shirt.

Everybody in the place was staring at them.

"Andar," the gunman ordered.

"I think we better *andar,"* Mercer said, standing slowly, hands at chest height where the gunman could see them.

Mingus did likewise.

"It's called chilling," Mercer said to the detective as they were marched across the dining hall. "Try it sometime."

"Shut up," the man who could understand English said.

Their journey was brief, through a swinging door marked CABALLEROS, into a large, beautifully tiled bathroom that smelled of sweet disinfectant. There, while patrons quickly exited past them, eyes averted, they were instructed to stretch out their arms and touch the wall.

The man who understood English patted them down, missing the Smith & Wesson Bodyguard holstered against

Mingus's left inner thigh, possibly because he did not want to touch the refried beans–encrusted pants. Satisfied that they were not armed, he stepped back.

"Now, we wait here for Bolero. He wants to know why Crips think they can come here where Mexican families eat."

"Crips?" Mingus asked. "Do you see us wearing Crips colors? Do we look like Crips?"

"Not to me. But to Bolero, if Crips are Nee-groes, then all Nee-groes must be Crips. See, we ain't 18th Street, where they welcome blacks. Bolero don't like the black color."

"Suppose we're black Colombians," Mingus said.

Mercer scowled at him. "You didn't exactly get a real fix on Bolero's likes and dislikes before dragging me down here, did you?"

"Guess not."

"To offer another example of how Bolero thinks," the man who understood English said, "Crips are our deadly enemies and must be destroyed. Crips are Nee-groes. Therefore, all Nee-groes . . . You get the idea?"

CHAPTER

FIFTY-TWO

Bolero burst into the bathroom so full of fury he was almost shooting sparks from everywhere but his deadened eyes. He stood five-five in boots, with a narrow waist and skinny legs under his heavy weight-room upper body.

That body seemed to be vibrating. He marched toward them, drawing back his hand. Mercer tensed himself for a slap, but instead, Bolero wheeled on the man who understood English and backhanded him into the stalls. "You dumb fuckhead . . . what did I say? What were my orders?"

The man crawled to his feet, trying to overcome a combination of shock and pain and fear. "You said to get them out of the dining room, *jefe*."

"No fuss, I said. *Quieto.*"

"Sí. Quieto," the non–English speaker said, grinning and nodding his head.

"The idiot understood," Bolero said. "But the smart guy forgets the key element. Gets everybody upset. My friends. My relatives." He suddenly drew back and hit the man again. "Fuckhead!"

Bolero then turned toward Mingus and his face wrinkled in disgust. "What's that on your pants?"

"The fuckhead dumped food in my lap."

With fluid grace Bolero reached under his silk shirt and retrieved a gold-damascened .45 that he shoved against Mingus's right cheek. "Understand this, *cabrón*. I call him a fuckhead. You don't call him a fuckhead."

Mercer prayed Mingus would keep his mouth shut.

His prayers were answered.

Bolero backed away, his weapon trained on Mingus.

Mercer heard the door open behind them, but he wasn't curious enough to turn and see who'd joined the party.

"What's on your mind, black man?" Bolero said to Mingus. "Fucking O.G., walkin' right in here. Figure to bleed me out in front of the people I love, go back to your cuzz and make 'em think you still can get it up?"

"I'm no O.G.," Mingus said. "I'm a homicide cop."

Bolero frowned. He looked at his favorite punching bag. "You didn't check for a badge?"

"He got no badge."

"My man say you got no stinkin' badge," Bolero said, grinning at his joke. Then his face grew mirthless. "Somebody here's lyin' to me."

"Not carryin' a badge," Mingus said. "I got an ID in my pocket."

"Get it, fuckhead," Bolero ordered.

The man who understood English limped to Mingus and took the leather ID folder from his pocket. He handed it to Bolero who examined it and threw it back to Mingus. "Detective Li-o-nel Min-gus. Well, Li-o-nel, why the fuck you don't carry a badge?"

"That's not important. The point is, I'm a cop."

"You don't seem to understand what's happenin' here, Li-o-nel. You not the man here. I'm the man. I'm the one say what's important. I want to know what happen to yo' shiny LAPD badge. You *mordelon*?"

"I'll tell you if I'm on the take," Mingus said, "if you tell *me* somethin'."

Bolero stared at the detective as if he couldn't make any sense of him. Then he began to laugh, a high-pitched cackle. Strutting back and forth, he said to his *vatos,* "Can you believe this *tiras negro*? Fucker's got some *cojónes,* huh?"

He circled behind Mingus. Moved in close. Standing on tiptoe, he said into the detective's ear, "You amuse me, *hombre*. You offer me a deal: you tell me, I tell you. I say no to your deal and I make you a different one."

He spun around and pointed his gun at his human punching bag who'd been trying to keep a low profile behind the gunman who didn't speak English. "Hey, *tonto,* you got a clock?"

The man nodded, held out his arm to display a huge watch on his thin wrist. *"Bueno,"* Bolero said. He put the gold filigreed barrel of his pistol to Mingus's temple and said, "Here's my deal. I shoot you clean and torture your friend till he dies. Or I shoot him clean and torture you. You got one minute to decide. Starting—"

"Can I pee first?" Mingus asked.

Bolero could not believe his ears. He began to howl with laughter.

Mercer heard some of the other *cholos* laughing with their leader. He wasn't at all amused. His heart felt like it was about to rip through his chest. A bullet in the head or torture. Shit. All for some stupid fucking hunch of Mingus's. On top of that, the detective, now that he'd got them in this hopeless mess, seemed to be acting too cool for school. Damn the man.

He didn't want to just stand there, but what could he do? The loco was concentrating on Mingus, but that was no help because the only other gun he could see, held by the non-English-speaking banger, was aimed at him. And the *cholos* who'd been drifting in behind him for the show were undoubtedly armed.

"Pee?" Bolero said. "Man, you got more pressing matters to think about. And you got one minute, starting now."

Mercer saw perspiration appear on Mingus's forehead. The big man's right hand went to his crotch. What the hell was he doing?

Bolero must have been wondering the same thing. He pressed his rococo pistol harder against the detective's head. Mingus slumped and dropped his hand to his side.

"How much longer he got?" Bolero shouted.

"Thirty-four seconds."

"Count 'em down, fuckhead."

Fuckhead did as ordered. "Thirty-two . . . thirty . . . twenty-seven . . ."

The count was down to the single digits when Mingus said, "Okay, okay. I made my decision."

"We waiting."

"Shoot him," Mingus said. "I'll take your fuckin' torture."

"Whoooo-eee. Macho, macho man," Bolero sang. He

danced across the floor and pressed the gun to Mercer's head.

The lawyer closed his eyes. He was surprised when Annie's image appeared. He tried to remember a prayer, any prayer.

"Don't do it, *amigo*."

The request came from somewhere near the door.

"Huh?" Bolero replied.

"I owe this man."

Mercer opened his eyes. He saw Bolero taking a step back, scowling toward the speaker.

Moving very slowly, Mercer turned. His former client Julio Lopez, wearing black silk baggy pants, a loose black shirt, and a gang-colored bead necklace, was walking toward them.

"You know this black cop?" Bolero said.

"He's not a cop. When they had me for killing the marshal, he's the lawyer won my freedom."

"Him?" Bolero seemed doubtful. "A *negro*?"

Julio made a fist, banged it against his chest. *"Cierto."* He approached Mercer and hugged him. *"Mí amigo."*

Bolero shrugged. "What about this bigmouth cop? Okay I kill him?"

"He worked on my case, too," Julio lied.

Bolero cocked his head and studied his friend. "You boolsheet me?"

"These are good guys, Rick . . . ah, Bolero."

Bolero smiled. "Well, fuck," he said, and returned his ridiculously ornate weapon to its sheath under his shirt. He looked around the room. "You bloodthirsty *cholos* will have to settle for beer and wine.

"And you, big mouth," he said to Mingus. "You get to take your pee. We'll be in my family room when you finished. Don't forget to wash your hands."

In the stall, Mingus slumped against the metal partition and tried to calm himself. Damn, that was too close. He had no doubt that the crazy gang leader would have killed them both.

He wasn't so sure they were out of the woods yet.

He unzipped his pants and slid the gun from its weeping eye holster. He stuck it behind his belt, a more accessible location. Then he did what men usually do in a urinal.

After using wet toilet paper to clean a fair amount of crusted beans from his pants, he followed Bolero's advice and washed his hands.

The non-English-speaking gangsta was standing guard outside the private dining room. He nodded to Mingus and opened the door for him.

Bolero's family had gone. He, Mercer, and the guy who'd saved their bacon were seated at the table. The gang leader was scooping out spoonfuls of some doughy-looking dessert onto plates.

"For Señor *Boca Grande*," he said plopping a mound onto a plate and pushing it toward Mingus. "Have some of my mama's favorite, *capirotada o sopa*."

Mingus eyed the stuff suspiciously.

"It's good," Bolero said. "Trust me."

Mingus caught a dot of it on the tip of his spoon and brought it to his lips. It tasted like bread pudding.

"So?"

"It's not bad," Mingus admitted, spooning a larger amount.

Bolero reached under his shirt and brought out the golden gun, placing it on the table beside him. Mingus put down his fork and picked up a napkin that he used to wipe his lips. When he returned the napkin to his still-damp lap, he kept his hand there, just inches from his gun. He waited to see what his flaky host would do next.

"You know your lawyer friend would be dead right now," Bolero said to him, "and you would be suffering the torments of hell, if it were not for Julio."

Mingus stared at the slick-looking dude who'd saved his life. He nodded his thanks.

"I love this man," Bolero said, gesturing toward Julio. "He is as much a brother to me as my own brother. More. I appreciate what you have done for him. But by giving him his freedom, you have put him in your debt."

"They have also become my friends, Ricky."

Bolero grinned. "Jus' like the rest of my family. They keep calling me Ricky, too. Or Ricardo. Like I was some Cuban fuck, ready to do the mambo." He reached over and mussed Julio's hair. "But I love this guy.

"So, where was I? Yeah. Your deed put Julio in your debt and tonight, I canceled that debt for him, just as I have canceled debts for him in the past."

"*Mí amigo*—" Julio began.

"Let me finish," Bolero said. He looked from Mercer to Mingus. "So, the slate is clean. Now we start fresh. I want you to satisfy my curious nature, Señor *Boca Grande.* I want you to tell me what happened to your badge."

Mingus's fingertips touched the grip of his gun. "I'll tell you," he said, "if you'll tell me something."

Bolero slapped the table and cackled. "Goddamn, you some hard son of a bitch. But I respect that. Okay, deal. Tell me."

"I was chasin' down a killer a couple weeks ago and the bastard took a shot at me, point blank. It hit my badge and bent it to shit. Gave me a bruise the size of a grapefruit right here," he pointed to the left side of his chest. "The bastard was so surprised he didn't kill me he just stood there while I emptied my police special into him."

"No shit. Where was this?"

"Denker Park. The dude I blew away . . . a Rollin' Thirties Crip."

"Oh, man, I love this fucking story. You kill any others?"

"Just him that time."

"So they gettin' you a new badge, right? An' they ain't gonna charge you for it, right? Not for somethin' like that?"

"No charge," Mingus said, trying to keep a straight face. "Now it's your turn."

"What you wanna know?"

"Anything you can tell us about Dwight Baskin's death?"

"Baskin's death?" Bolero looked surprised. "I don't know nothin' about his death, 'cept a cop killed him and I danced when I heard. The fucker hated my ass.

"He kept tellin' people I killed *mí amigo* Luis. Boolsheet. Luis was a great leader, an' I loved him. But he got sick. Sick in the body and sick in the head. He had these friends, Jerry and Armando. Close friends. Tight. I swear—I don't know for sure—but I think it was him killed them. Why, I dunno, 'cause he killed himself 'fore I could ask him.

"But Baskin, that cockaroach, he blame it all on me. He blame me for everything. But he couldn't get nothin' on me so he had my kid brother picked up. Geraldo's not right upstairs. A sweet little boy. Don't mean any harm to nobody. No way he's Jaquecas. Son of a bitch put him in a tank with fuckin' animals. Before we could get him out, some degenerate had been on him. I had to take him to the doctor.

"And then Baskin follows us there. To the fuckin' *clinica*. Hangs around outside, scarin' sick people, the *cabrón*."

"What *clinica* is that?" Mercer asked.

"This place we go get fixed up when we need to." He grinned. "Without havin' to 'splain about how we come to have a bullet in our ass or a knife wound on our arm."

"The city does this?" Mercer asks.

"Not the city. Rightway."

"Say what?" Mingus asked.

"Call they-selves Rightway. Bunch of fat-cat *gringos* with more money than they know how to spend. So they pay for the *medicos* to fix us up."

"Must pay 'em a lot for them to risk their careers by not reporting gunshot or knife wounds," Mercer said.

"I guess. Maybe they feeling guilty being so rich and successful they got to give some of it back to us poor Chicanos."

"Why would they want to give it back to a gang?" Mingus asked.

"Maybe 'cause we so lovable," Bolero said. "No, seriously, they tryin' to save us from our life of crime."

"How's that work, exactly?" Mingus asked.

"If we want them to keep fixin' us, we gotta sit still for their Rightway boolsheet. It's like church talk. You know, we on the wrong way, but they showin' us the right way."

"How long's this been going on?" Mercer asked.

"A year, maybe."

"Anybody you know ever change their ways?"

Bolero grinned. "Hell, yeah. Everybody. We all good boys now."

"Where'd you say the *clinica* was?" Mingus asked.

"I didn't. The docs don't want a bunch of cops botherin' 'em, like that prick Baskin."

He stood up, put the gun back under his shirt. "Okay.

That's all you dudes get from me. That and your fucking lives. *Vamos aquí."*

He strutted to the door.

"So long, Julio," Mingus said, shaking the young man's hand. "Thanks for the pass."

"Ándele!" Bolero said and left the room.

"You saved us, man," Mercer said, hugging his former client. "But I could do with one more favor. Where's the *clinica*?"

Julio looked at the open door. "I'm not sure. Never been there. It's in this neighborhood. From what I've heard, it used to be a big storage barn and still looks like one from the outside."

"Know anything about Rightway?"

"Just what Ricky told you."

"*Amigo,* the bitches will not wait forever," Bolero said from the door. "Not even for the likes of you and me."

Julio gave Mercer the briefest of smiles and followed the little gangsta from the room.

"Well, what do you think?" Mercer asked the detective.

Mingus sat down at the table and pulled the bowl of dessert toward him. "I think that, long as I'm here, I'm gonna have some more of this cappy soap."

CHAPTER FIFTY-THREE

John Gilroy strolled among the late-night crowd that was lingering on the Santa Monica Pier, sampling every dubious delight of its carnival attractions.

The breeze off of the ocean had chilled the summer night, forcing him to zip up his midnight-blue windbreaker. The jacket had been a gift from his wife, Esme, who still labored under the misapprehension, after twenty-nine years of marriage and at least that many discussions on the subject, that he preferred sport clothes that looked almost exactly like his uniform garb.

His pier mates certainly had no problem finding outward signs to express their individuality. They all seemed young, pierced, and tattooed. For the males, gangsta seemed to be the style of the night. The women were even more of a distraction. Exotic hairstyles, gems glinting from various facial points, pouty lips painted comic book colors, nearly bared breasts, legs, bellies—all seemingly impervious to the dropping temperature. He wondered what it would be like to have one of those young voluptuous animals squirming on his bed, opening herself to—

"Enjoying the sights, John?"

"Wha—?" Gilroy wheeled to find his old friend nearly at his elbow. "Timmy. You kinda snuck up on me."

"It's my little cat feet," Commander Tim Sellars said with a smile. He turned up the collar of a handsome car coat of dark brown suede. "Kinda nippy out here, isn't it?"

"You picked the spot," Gilroy said.

"It'll suit our needs. C'mon, let's try out the wheel. Like everything else out here, it seems to be a little scaled down, but I bet it still offers a pretty good view of the coastline."

As they walked to the neon Ferris wheel, Sellars put his arm around Gilroy's shoulder and gave him a manly hug. "You know, Johnny, it occurred to me the other day that you're the oldest friend I've got."

This was not news to Gilroy. He'd spent a fair amount of time lost in the past recently, mulling over their history together: growing up in the Colony Park section of Galveston, Texas; smart boys, breezing through Parker School so fast the teachers and the other students never knew what hit them; sharing the funky apartment, and a fair amount of funky women, in Huntsville, aka Death Penalty Central, while attending Sam Houston State.

Sellars's dad, a retired Texas Ranger, generous with tales of gunplay and kick-ass bravado, had inspired their pursuit of a degree in criminal justice. It was a wise choice of careers. They did well enough in the classroom to be tapped by Alpha Phi Sigma, the national criminal justice honor society, and after graduation to be given a choice of opportunities. They decided on D.C. and the U.S. Capitol Police Department.

Sellars had had a natural flair for playing department politics and he pulled Gilroy upward through the ranks in his wake. Eventually, they'd separated, Sellars starting his rise through D.C.'s Metro Police while the newly married Gilroy went west to seek his fortune with the LAPD.

"Remember the morning we met?" he said as Sellars bought their tickets.

"I think so. But remind me."

"Hurricane Carla had swept our old place away and we'd just moved back into the new house. I happened to see you next door in your backyard. Recall what you were doing?"

Sellars paused in his financial arrangements with the ticket seller. "Johnny, is this gonna be a two-trip or a three-trip conversation?"

"Probably two," Gilroy said.

"I'll buy three just to play safe."

"You remember what you were doing when we met?"

Gilroy pursued the question as they boarded the rocking gondola.

"Playing Superman? My mom made me a red cape and I'd run around the backyard to get it to flap."

"Not that day." The gondola swung as the wheel lifted it toward the night sky. "That day you were catching dragonflies, seeing if they really got drunk on tobacco."

"It did kinda knock 'em for a loop," Sellars said. He stared at Gilroy. "Johnny, I hope to Christ you're not lookin' for some parallel between that and what we're doing now."

"The only difference is we're playing with people instead of bugs," Gilroy said.

The gondola moved up another notch. "We're not schoolboys anymore, John. And these experiments aren't just a way of entertaining ourselves on a lazy summer afternoon. This country is in peril from without and within. Two-thirds of the world hates our ass. Hell, that's probably a conservative estimate. They'll be coming here to do their damnedest.

"Meanwhile, the ethnic gangs are literally gnawing away at the foundations of this once-great country. Dr. D. is offering us a way to kill two birds with one stone."

"Dr. D. is a lunatic," Gilroy said.

"Is that what you dragged me from a martini and a surefire blowjob to hear? Of course he's a lunatic. But he's *our* lunatic."

The gondola was nearly at the top of the Ferris wheel now and both men were feeling the cold. "That's not why I wanted the meeting," Gilroy said. "I wanted to ask you, face to face, if you set me up for the Mooney shooting."

"Set you up?" Sellars seemed genuinely surprised, but Gilroy knew that his friend had Academy Award potential. "What makes you think you were set up?"

"The Johnstons claim it was I who told them they could return home, and this SWAT cretin, Dwyer, is going around telling people I ordered them to move in and take Mooney."

Sellars shrugged. "Hell, John, I don't know who was using your name, but it seems to me they did you a favor. It was a righteous takedown."

The Ferris wheel had been spinning for several minutes,

but Gilroy had barely noticed. Now he realized they were headed up, while he was experiencing a sinking feeling. "Righteous? For God's sake, Tim. It was murder. Your savior of mankind, the doctor, sent Mooney out to be executed."

"Where in the blue-eyed world did you get that notion?"

"Mooney was under lock and key at the compound."

"How . . . ? Oh, of course. Your psychiatrist friend. When I asked you about her, you said she was a pro and a patriot. A professional should have had a better grasp on the principles of confidentiality."

"You killed her, didn't you?"

"All I know is what I hear on the news. They're saying Joe Mooney killed her."

"That's crap. You had both her and Mooney killed."

"Mooney was a war casualty. Too far gone to rehabilitate. A repeat of the Baskin mess would have really let the dogs loose."

"What about the man in prison? Nunez?"

"Another of your wizard recommendations. Granted, he controlled the one person who could get the goddamned D.A. to roll over and play dead when we wanted. And he was loyal to the cause. But he sure as hell is a pain in the ass now."

"So, in return for his loyal service, he dies, too?"

"That decision hasn't been made. He never knew much and, from what I hear, he's not likely to remember whatever that was. Still, we may have to get one of our guys at the prison to make a mistake and let him have a belt or some bed linen."

"Listen to yourself. Planning a man's murder without even blinking an eye."

"I thought you understood the game, John. Look out there," Sellars said, pointing into the night. "Lights as far as you can see down the coast. Thousands of citizens getting ready to rest their heads in peaceful sleep. Now use your mind's eye to look beyond there, across this great country, and you'll see 290 million mainly law-abiding, God-fearing citizens who cherish their freedom and who are enjoying the highest quality of life available on this planet.

"Now look down there on the pier at . . . what? Maybe 200 gaudy little bugs crawling around with only sex, drugs, and music on their minds. You tell me if you wouldn't smash five or ten or twenty of them, if you knew it would save the 290 million?"

Gilroy experienced a feeling of déjà vu, but he shook it off. "You and the doctor make quite a pair, Tim," he said. You're both homicidal maniacs."

The accusation seemed to depress rather than anger Sellars. He slumped against the seat as the gondola made its final descent. "Aw, Johnny, I wanted this to be like old times, the Sam Houston Two back in action again. But Dr. D. was right. You're not really with the program."

"So what, Tim? I join the bugs? I won't be easy to squash."

"Nobody's gonna squash you, Johnny," Sellars said. "I give you my word."

Gilroy didn't actually see Sellars's hand came out of his coat pocket, was not aware of what his old friend was doing until an atomizer appeared just inches from his nose.

He saw a puff of mist leave the atomizer. The wind whipped some of it away, but he felt a chilly moisture on his nose and mouth.

His hands were in his pockets. As he tried to free one to wipe his face, Sellars trapped it and sprayed him again with the mist.

"I'm truly sorry, Johnny," Sellars said.

Gilroy felt his strength ebbing away. It no longer seemed important for him to free his hands. He'd always thought of Timmy as being his one true friend. A life of misplaced trust.

A life that wasn't really worth much, now that he thought of it.

Their gondola stopped at the platform. He tried to call out, but he couldn't open his mouth. He saw the FBI agent Carl Ivor moving toward them through the waning crowd.

"On or off?" the wheel operator asked.

"Off," Sellars said. "I could use a hand. My friend seems to be having a problem."

The operator took one of Gilroy's arms, mumbling about liability. As he felt himself being lifted from the gondola, he heard his old friend say, "John, do not worry. We're taking you to a doctor."

That was precisely what was worrying John Gilroy.

DAY 10

THURSDAY, JUNE 24

CHAPTER

FIFTY-FOUR

By 10:30 a.m. the next morning, Mercer was sitting in his sedan with Mingus and Hootkins, parked half a block away from the warehouse that housed the clinic run by Rightway.

According to the scant information available from the organization's Web site, Bolero's description had been fairly accurate but incomplete. Rightway's genesis had been a group of Beverly Hills matrons who'd originally called themselves The Ladies Who Lunch. Approximately a year before, their "good works and efforts to increase the quality of life in the inner city" had come to the attention of "the government's newly formed Department of Youth Preparedness." The DYP had awarded The Ladies "a substantial grant to create and maintain a free clinic that would serve and redirect inner-city wayward youths."

To that end, the primarily government-funded, tax-exempt charitable organization called Rightway had been founded. Its slogan: "We know the right way to heal bodies and souls."

The organization's test clinic had begun operation in February. Word of mouth alone had attracted a large roster of "contributors from both the business and religious sectors," along with "a group of the city's finest medical professionals who are donating their skills to bring about social change." For correspondence purposes, questions, and donations, one might use the official e-mail address or the equally official post office box in West Los Angeles.

As Mercer saw it, the big jokers in the deck were the lack of any participants' names and the absence of a brick-and-mortar location for the organization. Add in the fact that it was being funded through some vague government department, and the clinic seemed a sure bet to have been opened for reasons other than those presented to the public.

Finding the location had been a matter of Mercer connecting two obvious dots—Julio Lopez's description of the building as "a big storage barn" and the address of the long-defunct Parnell's Storage that Hootkins had pulled from a five-year-old L.A. phone book.

The former site of Parnell's occupied nearly half of a city block in the warehouse district. The flow of foot traffic going in and coming out of the warehouse's open front door consisted primarily of young males wearing Jaquecas colors and an assortment of bandages and casts. But there were older Hispanics, male and female, and some children seeking Rightway's off-the-books health care, too.

Mingus left the car to sample the nongangstas. Mercer watched as a middle-aged man with a broken arm ran from the detective and a woman clutched her bag of "medicine" to her chest protectively and backed away from him fearfully.

"This clinic has got quite a practice," Mingus said, getting back into the rear of the sedan. "Gangbangers and illegals."

"Whoever's fixing these bangers up is breakin' the law and doin' that right out in the open," Hootkins said. "The beat cops must know about it. Which means there's gotta be somebody with a lot of clout getting the department to keep its hands off."

"Speakin' of dudes with that kind of clout . . . ," Mingus said, pointing to a platinum-colored Range Rover that cruised past them and pulled up in front of the *clinica*.

The driver tapped the horn and almost at once Agent Pleasance exited the building in the company of a man with silver hair and a benign, almost saintly face.

Mercer turned on the engine. "Let's see where they're headed."

Hootkins had been feeling like a fifth wheel all morning. "You go on," he said to Mercer. "I'll hang here for a while and then stroll over to the station house on Olive. The desk sarge there, Wolfman Bill Bardoo, is an ol' *compadre*. He'll give me the official line on the clinic."

His feet had barely touched the sidewalk when the Benz took off. He watched until it and the Rover zipped around the corner. Then he turned his attention to the clinic.

He toyed with the idea of just strolling in. Problem was, the crowd was 100 percent Chicano. Not much he could do to keep from standing out. He checked the ebb and flow of sick and wounded for a while, then began the short walk to the Olive Street station and Wolfman.

He was just a block into it when he became aware of somebody a few feet to the rear keeping pace with him.

It was a very young Hispanic, maybe even preteen, with the letter "J" crudely tattooed into the back of his right hand. "Out fo' a stroll, ole man?"

"Nice day for it," Hootkins said.

"You in the wrong neighborhood."

Hootkins shrugged and kept walking. The Olive Street station was maybe three blocks away.

"You innerested in the *clinica,* huh?"

"Not particularly."

"You lyin' to me, nigga?"

Hootkins stopped. As many times as he'd heard it in his long life, the word still had the power to fire him up. He thought he might be able to draw his gun before the little weasel could do him any damage. Not that he'd kill a boy that young, no matter how nasty his tongue might be. Maybe shoot him in the foot or the thigh.

Then he noticed the others. Three. Standing back a few yards. They were kids, too. Wearing knit caps too warm for summer. Red, white, and green kerchiefs. Oversized shirts and baggy pants, looking like their older brothers' hand-me-downs.

They'd kill him in a New York minute, or try to, if he gave them what they considered a reason. That was the problem. He didn't want to start something that might result in his death or, almost as bad, his having to shoot four little boys, even in self-defense.

"What is it you gentlemen want?" he asked.

"You innerested in *clinica,*" the talkative boy said. "We show it to you."

The pistol under his coat felt heavy, but the boys didn't seem to care if he was carrying or not. He thought they might be less inclined to cause him to use it in a clinic full of doctors and patients. And he'd wanted to see what the place was like inside. He let them walk him across Alvarado and down the street to the warehouse-*clinica*.

CHAPTER

FIFTY-FIVE

Mercer didn't have to stay on the Rover's back bumper to keep track of the huge vehicle. Staying a safe distance, he followed it along the Santa Monica Freeway to the San Diego, where the vehicles headed north, a caravan of two. "Any thoughts on who the creeping Jesus is with the feds?" he asked Mingus.

"Nope, though the guy's face looks like holy picture material. Maybe he's the saintly Mr. Rightway."

"Never thought the feds had many saints on their team," Mercer said.

The Rover eased over to the far right and exited the freeway, turning left on Sunset Boulevard. It took Sunset to Charleville Canyon Road, then headed up and into the canyon.

Hanging far back, Mercer got only glimpses of the Range Rover as it whipped around the winding road. He kept pace with it at a distance, continuing up past woodsy homes. Eventually the upscale residential neighborhood gave way to open canyon. Rounding a bend, Mercer got a sudden clear view of the road ahead and saw to his dismay that the large vehicle was no longer on it.

He had to drive nearly a mile before finding a shoulder wide enough to make a U-turn. Then he descended the canyon road slowly, looking for the turnoff.

Mingus spotted it, an unmarked drive that seemed to be leading to open space.

The lawyer continued down for maybe a quarter of a

mile and parked the Benz so that most of it was off the road. He and the detective got out and walked to the edge of the canyon. From there they could see that the unmarked drive led down to where a lower natural plateau had been developed into a large hunk of prime real estate.

Two buildings had recently been constructed on the secluded property. The main structure was a retro 1950s Southern California ranch-style home.

Three cars were parked in front. Mercer recognized Sellars's beige Jaguar and Annie's powder blue Thunderbird. The silver Boxter was a new entry, but it was one more indication that the feds seemed to like their luxury vehicles.

The Rover was parked by the second building, a long white slab that looked even newer than the house, judging by its pristine, chalk-white paint and the fact that it was surrounded by bare earth while some foliage covered the rest of the property.

"This has got to be where they took me Tuesday night," Mercer said.

"That back building reminds me of some kinda army barracks," Mingus said.

The door to the building opened and two young men exited. They were wearing white coats, white face protectors, and thick gloves.

"Okay," Mingus said, watching the men remove their masks and gloves to light cigarettes. "So it's not an army barracks."

"Looks like they're working with some serious materials," Mercer said. "We have to get in there and find out what's going on."

"You were givin' me heat for wanting to bust into an office. Now you want to hit what could very well be considered a government or military compound? They hang people for that kind of bad behavior."

"So how do we get in?" Mercer said.

Mingus moved to the lip of the canyon. "Not only is this one hell of a sheer decline, but if that ain't enough, they figure they still got you beat."

Mercer, who was not fond of heights, leaned as far as he dared. It was enough for him to glimpse razor wire strung halfway down the slope.

"They probably saved their heavy duty surveillance stuff

for the driveway," Mingus said. "See there, where the drive levels off? A spycam on that post? Probably got pressure gauges and body heat sensitive warnings and all that shit."

"So you're saying we don't get to see what's inside?" Mercer said.

"What I'm sayin' is, it might be easier just to walk into the *clinica,* see what we can find there first. This place ain't going away anytime soon."

On the drive back to downtown L.A., Mercer tried to reach Hootkins to see if he'd found out anything at the Olive Street station. He was surprised when the call was switched to the detective's recorded message.

Mercer left his name and cell number.

No one tried to stop them as they entered the clinic, but their presence seemed to cast a pall over the twenty or so patients sitting on cheap folding chairs in a boxlike, drywalled waiting room. There were no bangers in the crowd that Mingus could see. Just probable illegals, whose Spanish conversation had been halted by their arrival and who now were looking from them to the twenty-something Chicana who sat at a battered desk, holding a phone to her ear.

She cut her conversation short and asked, "Yes?" in a tone more confrontational than welcoming.

"We'd like to see the manager," Mingus asked, showing her his ID.

"That would be me," she said. "What can I do for you?"

"Is there a doctor in charge?" Mingus asked.

She was less interested in the question than in Mercer, who was moving toward the door that presumably led to the working area of the clinic. "Señor, you're not allowed to go in there."

He ignored her.

She pressed a button on the desk and a buzzer sounded somewhere beyond the door.

Mercer grabbed the doorknob, but it wouldn't turn. He was trying again when the door was thrown open from the other side. He barely managed to twist his body enough to let his arm and shoulder take the hit.

A heavyset white man in a lab coat followed the door. Even wrapped in the loose white coat the man had that gym rat V-shaped physique—thick wrists, thick neck. He glared at the lawyer who was rubbing his arm. "Sorry. Were you standing there?" he said.

"Cops," the receptionist said, bored now.

The lineup of patients watched the interplay like spectators at a bullfight.

"Local? Federal? International?" the man asked.

"LAPD," Mingus said.

"What do you want here, Officer?"

"Your name for starters."

"You first," the man said, stone-faced.

Mingus hesitated. He couldn't remember the last time he'd let a weight lifter intimidate him, but this guy seemed a little too cocky. "We have reason to believe you're harboring a fugitive from justice," the detective said. "In there."

"No fugitives here," the man said. "Just sick people who don't need to be disturbed for no reason."

"We'll just come back with a warrant," Mingus said.

"Tell you what, champ. You get that warrant and I'll give you the tour myself."

"That kind of muscle-bound politeness has to be FBI," Mingus said, when they were back in Mercer's car.

"You handled your end pretty well."

"Go fuck yourself, Mercer," Mingus replied. "But first, let's find a sporting goods shop. If we're gonna drop in on that compound up the canyon, we're gonna need some stuff."

CHAPTER

FIFTY-SIX

As badly as Mercer wanted to see what Sellars and his crew were up to at the compound, in truth, he wasn't wild about Mingus's plan, which involved rappelling down a canyon and dealing with razor wire.

He suspected that Bolero might've been on to something with his immediate appraisal of Mingus as an original gangsta out to prove himself. That sort of I-can-still-carry-my-end attitude could explain why the big detective seemed so eager to get himself killed.

Or maybe it was just that he was tired of sitting back and taking whatever life threw at him. Like a bogus rape charge and a woman he loved who didn't trust him enough to stand by him.

Mercer was mulling over these thoughts while sitting at a table in the firm's conference room, fast-forwarding through the recording of people who'd entered his office during his absence.

Ladybug had done a fine job of hiding the camera in the cabinet. It was turned on by any motion in the room.

Judging by the time stamps on the video, from the camera's installation at 6:14 p.m. the previous evening until that morning at 8:52 a.m., the only visitor to the office had been the cleaning lady, who did nothing more than empty the wastebasket, straighten his chair, make a very fast run with a sweeper, and steal one of the Snickers bars from the emergency rations box he kept in his upper-right-hand desk drawer. He didn't consider the theft worth noting, except that it indicated she knew more about the contents of his drawers than he might have suspected.

At shortly before nine, his assistant, Melissa, had entered his office to place mail and messages on his desk. At a little after nine, the receptionist assigned the collateral duty of watering the office plants entered to maintain the health and well-being of the ficus in the corner.

He'd entered the office at 9:30 a.m. with Lonny Hootkins. Within minutes, Melissa had announced the arrival of Mingus and the three men had left for the clinic.

That was it until 5:18 p.m., when the recorder was brought back to action by him returning to the office with his afternoon purchases.

Satisfied that the disc held no crucial material, Mercer popped it from the player and carried it to his office. He'd just put it in the cabinet with the unused ones when Sidone arrived at the door.

"Hi," she said. "Long time no see."

"Been busy," he said, moving to his desk. "Sit down. Tell me what you've been up to."

She looked at the big bag from The Climber's Warehouse resting on one of the office chairs. "Thinking of taking on Mount Baldy?" she asked.

"You never know when you'll get the urge," he said. "What's up?"

"I wanted to apologize for removing the Baskin file," she said. "Kennard said you were looking for it the other night."

"No prob. We pulled another copy."

"I just didn't want you to think I make a habit of taking office files home. One of my roommates needed my help with something at the apartment and I hadn't quite finished making notes on the Baskin, so . . ."

"Your roommate okay?" he asked.

"Oh, sure. She was just . . . It was just a stupid thing. She needed cash for . . . something."

He saw her attention shift to the door.

Kennard was there. "Sid, you've got a call. Said it was important."

She got up.

"Roommate?"

"Some guy," Kennard said as if he weren't terribly happy about it.

"Oh. Okay. Thanks, Ken."

Sid and Ken, Mercer thought. Just friends.

She waved to Mercer as she headed out, almost dancing. And she was gone.

Kennard looked at Mercer. "New boyfriend," he said glumly.

"Maybe not. Maybe a cousin. Or just a friend."

Kennard shrugged. "We'll see."

When the associate left to mope in the library, Mercer asked Melissa if Hootkins had called in.

"Nope."

"That's not like him," Mercer said. "See if you can pin him down. Last I saw of him he was headed to the Olive Street lockup to talk to a desk sergeant named . . ." Mercer closed his eyes and summoned up, "Wolfman Bill Bardoo."

She was back in five minutes. "Sergeant Bardoo says he hasn't laid eyes on Lonny for months."

Mercer asked for the sergeant's number.

"Like I just told the girl at your firm," the sergeant grumbled with some impatience, "I haven't seen Lonny for some time."

"He was going to drop by to ask you about the Rightway clinic near Alvarado."

The sergeant took his time replying. "What's Lonny got to do with that?"

"It's something he's working on for the firm. I'll cut to the chase, Sergeant. The last I saw of Lonny, he was on foot outside the clinic. I'm worried about what might have happened to him."

"That goddamned clinic's got us all madder'n hell," the sergeant said. "I hope Lonny didn't get jammed up in there."

"Why not?"

"The clinic has been granted special privileges. I don't know why or how. The order came from on high. We are to consider it a neutral zone for the bangers.

"Like I say, we're not happy about it. But, so far, they've kept up their end. They're just there for the patchwork. Still, a lot of bad dudes go in and out. It's possible Lonny stepped on some banger's toes out on the street and got himself in a mess."

"Suppose I find out he ran into trouble inside the clinic?" Mercer asked. "Can I count on police help?"

"Man, you'd better have it on video and stereo and in three dimensions for anybody here to even consider going against a departmental operating order. But I'll put the street officers on the alert about Lonny right now. Find out if anybody saw anything in the neighborhood. They pick up anything, I'll let you know."

"Thanks, Sergeant. One last thing. If you knew that the FBI was involved with the clinic, would you tell me?"

"I've heard rumors of FBI, CIA, NASA—you name it. I'm just a cop on the desk, but I know that when it comes to things nobody can explain these days there's only one answer: homeland security. And the way I've seen that work, Lonny will be a hell of a lot better off if he's in the hands of bangers."

CHAPTER FIFTY-SEVEN

The sun was setting when Mingus found a parking spot across the boulevard from his apartment building. He pulled a large grocery bag from the backseat and was about to exit the vehicle when he saw Hildy McRae leaving the building. He wondered how long she'd been waiting for him—long enough apparently to have run out of patience.

He put down the bag and prepared to start the car and drive away if she spied him. But that didn't seem likely. She seemed so caught up in her thoughts she was barely conscious of her surroundings. She was carrying papers in her hand. Something she'd brought for him she'd decided not to leave? *Good.*

She walked with a slight limp but seemed to be on the mend. Her face was healing, too, though it was the color of a Spanish omelet with its yellow, brown, and purple bruises and red-raw scrapes.

She slowly walked down the block until she came to a pale green Accord in the row of parked cars. He watched her get into it, start it up, and drive off. Even then, he stayed put, suspicious that she might make a circle of the block before going away.

It wasn't just a verbal confrontation that he was trying to avoid. He was convinced she'd gone far enough off the deep end to be capable of anything. And he'd noticed she was wearing her police special. There was some irony in that—he'd had to turn in his official weapon while hers was still legally on her hip.

While he waited to convince himself she'd moved on, he dialed his home phone and hit the playback code. No messages at all. Two hours ago, he'd impatiently sampled and removed twenty-seven hits—twenty-five of them hers and two from telemarketers.

Still no word from Bettye. He didn't think time was on his side. The poets were wrong about absence making the heart grow fonder. Now that he thought of it, it seemed the poets were wrong about practically everything, judging by his limited exposure to poetry.

"A loaf of bread, a jug of wine, and thou." Well, he had the best two out of three in his bag.

He carried it into the building. He was rooting in his pocket for the mailbox key when he noticed the metal door was open. The box was empty. That was what that crazy bi-atch had in her hand—his and Bettye's goddamned mail.

He carried the grocery bag and his anger up the stairs and unlocked the apartment. The place grew lonelier and more depressing by the hour. He put the groceries on the kitchen counter and began turning on lights.

Sound. He needed sound. He punched on the CD player, turned the gain up a notch, and the room was filled with a pounding beat. Working through it was the druggy-sexy voice of India.Arie singing "Simple."

Walking to the beat, Mingus went into the kitchen and began putting some of his purchases away, popping the cap on a bottle of brew, trying to work his mood into some semblance of all right.

He layered roast beef on a thick slice of white bread, painted another bread slice with hot mustard, slapped the whole thing together, and carried it and his beer into the living room.

By then, India.Arie had moved on to another cut on the CD, the name of which he could only guess at. It was Bettye's disc. In fact just about everything in their living room was Bettye's—the sofa, chairs, rug, CD player, TV. Him, too. He was hers, the only one of her possessions she'd be leaving behind, probably.

The phone rang when he was about halfway through the sandwich.

At the sound of Mercer's voice on the monitor, he lifted the receiver and asked, "What's up?"

"There's a new situation."

"What?"

"Not on the phone."

"Okay. When and where?"

"I'll be in front of your place in twenty minutes. We can get some dinner."

Mingus looked at the last inch of sandwich on the plate. "Dinner sounds fine."

CHAPTER FIFTY-EIGHT

Lonny Hootkins was thinking about his daddy, how big and powerful Leander Hootkins had been before he took the bullet in his back that crippled him up. The Department was pretty good about it. As good as they could be with a cop who had difficulty working the right side of his body.

They'd offered to retire him with full benefits. But with his wife in the ground some five years and a boy who was gone all day and most of the night, Leander didn't particularly care for the prospect of spending the rest of his life at home, alone, with nothing but daytime TV for company.

They'd found desk work for him. That was fine at first, but he kept feeling like he was a charity case and, fact was, even doing filing or moving around a room wasn't that easy for him.

So he'd retired. And Lonny had watched his father, still young in earth years, shrink in on himself like a piece of fruit left to age on the ground.

He didn't know what had started him thinking on his daddy. He'd awakened not too long ago, lying on a bed in a strange room in his boxers and white T-shirt, without any memory of where he was or how he'd gotten there or what had happened to his clothes. Or his weapon.

He'd raised his head to confirm his suspicions that he also had on his black socks. Satisfied with that small mental victory, he'd let his head fall back against the pillow.

He always prided himself on his analytical mind, but, for the life of him, he couldn't come to grips with anything that had happened to him since morning.

He remembered walking in a vaguely familiar neighborhood and accompanying some boys to a doctor's office. Trying to reconstruct what happened after that was like trying to make a recognizable image out of a kaleidoscope that kept shifting and shattering.

The jumble only seemed to straighten out for memories that brought him pain. His daddy, shuffling around the house in his robe during the day. Or, at night, high on painkillers, screaming through another bad dream.

He thought about his partner, too, Charlie Logan, complaining about the cards life had dealt him, when in fact he'd wound up with a winning hand—a sweet woman and a great little boy—that he'd misplayed badly. He flashed on Charlie, face red as flame and wet as rain, riding the back of a big fat naked 'ho like she was some kind of beast of burden, getting himself so worked up he just blew apart.

Hootkins was fairly certain he hadn't been there when Charlie died. Why was he conjurin' up these awful pictures in his mind?

Something had to be wrong in his head.

He lifted a very heavy arm but there was no watch on his wrist. He raised up a few inches and saw enough of the sky through the window to know it was late. Dusk turning to night.

He wasn't sure he could handle night. Even at his best, he had a hard time coping with night's sorrow and despair. In his present mood . . .

The light in the center of the ceiling blinked on. The bulb was bare, but it emitted a soft glow that created its own halo effect around the man in the white coat who entered the room.

"How are we feeling, Lonny?" he asked.

"Not so hot." Hootkins remembered seeing the man before. Recently. Leaving the clinic with the fed.

"What's wrong, buddy?"

"My head's a little messed up."

"That's normal, considering what you've been through."

"What have I been through, Doc?" Lonny asked.

The doctor looked like a saint. It made you feel better just to rest your eyes on him. That was why his words seemed so hard, coming from that kindly face. "You've been betrayed by the person you trust most."

"Chet?"

"Yes. Chet betrayed you."

"I don't believe it."

"Chet told everybody your secret," the doctor said.

"What secret?"

"The secret only Chet knew, Lonny."

Hootkins's eyes started to tear. "How . . . how did he find out? I never let on how I felt about his mom. Not to her. Certainly not to him."

"Some feelings you just can't hide," the man said.

"I been lovin' that woman a long time, but she was married to my partner. An' when he died, then it was the race thing, her bein' white. So I kept my love secret."

"Chet knows, and he's told her and everybody."

"Why'd he wanna do that?" Lonny was crying now, tears pouring from his eyes.

"He hates you, Lonny. He resents your loving his mom and he's turned people against you."

"Who?" Lonny felt sad and angry and maybe a little afraid.

"Somebody you work with, somebody you thought was your friend."

"Not Mercer?"

"I'm afraid so," the doctor said.

"Mercer is my friend."

"He was only pretending to be. Now, Lonny, I want you to close your eyes and think about that."

"But Mercer—"

"Close your eyes."

Almost as soon as his eyelids shut, Lonny felt a cold breeze on his face and a slight stinging sensation in his nose when he inhaled.

He opened his eyes to see that the room was in darkness and he was alone. Alone in the room. Alone in the world. Chet and Mercer were plotting against him behind his back. They were good-hearted people. What damn fool thing had he done to make those closest to him hate him like that?

Lonny Hootkins rolled onto his side, drew his knees up close to his chest, and started weeping like a baby.

CHAPTER

FIFTY-NINE

Mercer was telling Mingus about Hootkins being missing as they headed east in his Benz.

"Could be the feds got him somewhere."

"His desk sergeant buddy didn't think so. And frankly, even with that asshole Pleasance's threats, I don't see the FBI taking a law-abiding citizen off the streets."

"These guys aren't exactly playin' it like Efrem Zimbalist, Jr."

"Who?"

"Used to be a TV show . . . never mind, you're too young. Where the hell we goin' anyway? LaLa's in the other direction."

"LaLa's isn't the only place I know."

"Anyway, point is, these feds don't much care how they get the job done long as it gets done," Mingus said. "An old PI wanders in the way of progress, tough luck, suckah."

"You're not sayin' they killed him?"

"I don't know how far they'd go. If they picked him up, it's more likely they got him in that hidden federal lockup Pleasance warned you about."

"We'll see," Mercer said.

He cruised along Little Santa Monica Boulevard, past the clutter of the Century City shopping area and into Beverly Hills.

"Goin' a long way for dinner," Mingus said.

"We're there," Mercer said.

He pulled to the curb and turned over the Benz to a waiting attendant.

He led Mingus toward an establishment with a completely dark display window that was unadorned except for a foot-high white neon martini glass.

The detective knew that the place had a name, even if it preferred not to show it: Martiniville.

The small clubby bar, done in deco black and white, was where young Hollywood tried to recapture the glamour and sophistication and decadence of the forties by dining and drinking from a menu limited to several varieties of caviar, several brands of champagne and martinis spiked with special flavors, like chocolate or avocado, that no one from that earlier period would have been caught dead drinking.

It was a few hours too early for the postscreening crowd and the room was empty enough for Mingus to spot Julio Lopez immediately, sitting alone in a booth at the far end of the club, nursing a martini that seemed to be the only clear one in the house. He was not particularly happy to be there or to see them.

"This place blows," he said.

"I figured Bolero wouldn't be dropping by here," Mercer said.

"This is true," Julio said. "The bartender don't even know how to make a good fucking martini. You'd think that'd be basic."

"Try the caviar," Mercer said. "It's straight from the Caspian. I know, because I defended the owner on smuggling charges."

A cellular sounded and all three men checked their phones. It was Julio's. "Ricky," he said to the others and took the call.

They listened while he dodged a barrage of questions about where he was and whom he was with. Finally he told the gang leader he'd see him in an hour and clicked off.

"Got you on a pretty short leash, huh?" Mingus said.

Julio glared at him, then turned to Mercer. "I gotta make this fast. The old man you asked about, Hootkins? He was picked up off the street. Ricky says it was something to do with the *clinica*. He only heard about it because these baby

Jaquecas, you know, *chaval* with Uzis, happened to be picking up some medication. Somebody at the *clinica* sent 'em to go find out why a black man was hanging around outside.

"When he wouldn't tell 'em, they took him into the clinic and turned him over to the head dude, big muscle they call Mr. Floyd."

"No wonder he wouldn't tell us his name," Mingus said.

"You know him, huh?"

"We met," Mingus said.

"Anyway, the *chaval* reported to Ricky that this Mr. Floyd gave your man a shot of something potent that put him out."

"Is Lonny Hootkins still at the clinic?" Mercer asked.

"It's where he was when the *chaval* split. And that's not good for him. The healing rate there has started to fall off."

"What do you mean?"

"All I know is what I hear from Ricky. The *vatos* get their bones fixed okay, but they been a little fucked up lately. Loco. Crashing cars. Whacking one another for no reason."

"What's Ricky's take on it?" Mercer asked.

"They doing the job treatin' his little bro'. So the doctors there can do no wrong." He stood up, eager to be gone. "And hell, Ricky's pretty fucked up himself to be judgin' the behavior of others."

"Why are you hanging with him?" Mercer asked.

"We're family," he said. "And I owe him."

"He have anything to do with your stepfather's murder?"

Julio smiled. "Old business," he said. "See you aroun', *mí abogado*."

"That clears the air a little," Mingus said, watching Julio's exit.

"Huh?" Mercer's mind was still on Julio's nonanswer about his stepfather's murder.

"What your *amigo* just told us clears the air," Mingus said. "We'd been wondering what to do next. I'd say it was to visit the clinic and see what's left of Lonny."

"Something I want to check at the firm first," Mercer said, getting up.

"No martini? No caviar? Damn."

"I'm sorry. I forgot about dinner." He started to sit down.

Mingus rose. "Naw. Caviar ain't my dish. I'm just fuckin' with you, Mercer. Let's go get in trouble."

DAY 11

FRIDAY, JUNE 25

CHAPTER SIXTY

It was shortly after midnight before they were ready to break into the clinic.

The delay had been prompted by Mercer's discovery that the sound-leeching bug had been replaced in the phone in his office and presumably in phones in the conference room and C.W.'s office.

He and Mingus had watched in silence as the disc from the spy cam transmitted its motion picture of the sneak entering his office and doing the misdeed.

Seeing the look of pain and dismay on Mercer's face, Mingus had started to say something but the lawyer had raised a hand, cautioning him to remain silent.

It was only after they'd left the darkened office and were walking along Wilshire Boulevard far from the bugs that the detective had ventured a comforting word. "You don't want to bust yourself up on this, Mercer. These spooks walk among us, bro'. Look like us. Talk like us. But they got some other goal in mind that don't include honor or friendship or anything comes close to that."

"Thanks, but I'm past the fact I was played for a fool by somebody I trusted. My bad. But it's done. Case closed on that. What concerns me is how much the bug might've picked up about our plans for tonight."

Unfortunately he'd been a little late checking the spy cam and discovering that the bugs were back. They'd walked into the office talking about breaking into the clinic.

"So we call it off for tonight," Mingus said.

"And let Lonny twist in the wind? Hell with that. We're gonna check out the clinic. But there're a couple things we got to do first. And one of 'em is gonna be a bitch."

According to Mercer's watch, it was precisely 12:15 a.m. when he and Mingus got out of the Benz in the alley directly behind the Rightway clinic. "I'm leaving the keys in the ignition," he said, "in case everything goes to hell and we need to get out fast."

"This ain't the kind of neighborhood you leave the keys in your car."

"All things considered, Lionel, worrying about a car thief is way, way down on my list of concerns tonight."

The warehouse district was deserted. There was minimal street lighting, an occasional bare bulb throwing a bright circle near a loading platform. Where they were, the alley was in total darkness.

Both men were wearing black trousers, shirts, and jackets. "Booster dress up," Mingus had called it. They paused to study the formidable-looking building. It was solid cinderblock and concrete. There were three cement steps leading to a back door that, considering their luck, was probably made of metal.

They both approached it, careful not to make a sound going up the steps. Mingus tapped the door with a fingernail. Metal.

"Maybe we should just go though the front," he said. "Hell with the cameras and what-all."

"Try your magic on this first," Mercer said. He hoped his nerves weren't showing. He felt uncomfortable. Dry-mouthed. His chest itched.

With a sigh, Mingus got out a little leather case that had been bequeathed to him by a wily old sneak thief he'd befriended in his moderately misspent youth.

While Mercer aimed a penlight at the lock, Mingus poked at it with two long thin rods, jiggering them, pausing, changing their positions slightly. He seemed to be having trouble.

"Hold the light steady," he whispered.

"Yassuh, boss."

Mingus left the two rods in the lock, removed another two from his case, and worked them in, too. Then he withdrew a gadget that resembled a mini monkey-wrench, maybe two inches long. He adjusted the wrench until it clamped tight on the rods. Then he twisted it to the right.

Nothing.

"Fuck this," he said.

"Try it again."

Mingus replayed the whole routine. Poking and shifting the rods. Seeming to get them in just the right positions and then securing them with the tiny wrench.

He twisted the wrench to the right.

And the door opened.

They were met by darkness and cool air that carried a hospital-like, medicinal-germicidal tang.

Mercer closed the door behind them, leaving it unlocked.

It was clear from the suffused light above them that the partitions separating the huge warehouse into a warren of rooms stopped at about seven feet, well below the unfinished ceiling. The place seemed abnormally quiet, except for a distant dissonant hum, possibly from the source of the light.

They clicked off their penlights and moved through a supply room, weaving around towers of stacked cardboard boxes containing paper products, cleansers, disinfectant soaps, latex items.

A door led them to a narrow hall that ran from one side of the building to the other. At its midpoint, it offered the option of a left turn toward the front of the clinic. Mercer walked past the turn to a door with a glass window.

The darkness beyond the window told Mercer that this room wasn't merely partitioned. It was totally enclosed. He clicked on his penlight and shined it through the window. X-ray equipment.

He backtracked to the turn.

The corridor led between facing doors, six on each side. Beyond that was an open area that housed the source of the ambient light.

Mingus was halfway down the hall, opening doors and

peeking in, then moving on. Following in his wake, Mercer glimpsed shadowy treatment rooms, some with expensive-looking gadgetry, some with just the basic examination table and basin.

After checking the last room, Mingus paused before stepping into the lighted open area. When Mercer was near enough, he whispered, "I'll go first. No sense making it too easy for 'em."

Mercer shrugged.

Mingus moved into the lighted area, looked right and left and waved him forward.

The light was coming from a shaded halogen bulb over a door that Mercer thought should lead to the clinic's waiting room. To the left of the door were a wooden table and a campaign chair. On the table was an empty Pepsi bottle, an open grease-stained pizza box with a single slice remaining, and a cheap digital radio the size of a cigarette pack that was sending out the annoying hum.

There had been a night watchman or a night doctor on duty, probably both. Were they snoozing somewhere? Or had they been sent home?

The radio hum was getting to Mercer. He turned the damn thing off.

The two men moved to a pair of swinging doors and pushed through, holding the doors and easing them back into position.

Finding themselves in another dark area, they once more employed their penlights. To their left was a row of washbasins and mirrors, powder-blue scrubs on hooks, metal lockers. Dead ahead was another set of swinging doors.

These led to the heart of the clinic, an operating arena with a domed ceiling of acoustic tile and recessed lights, a well-equipped room used primarily, Mercer assumed, for the removal of bullets, the suturing of serious knife wounds, the repair of cracked skulls and shattered limbs.

Mercer clicked off his penlight and stood there, listening. He heard the sound of heavy breathing. Not theirs. He wondered if Mingus could hear it, too.

A cough. Rubber soles squeaked against the tile floor.

The ceiling lights came on, filling the room with an intense brightness that blinded Mercer.

"You gentlemen have made a serious fucking mistake," Commander Tim Sellars informed them.

You sure as hell took your sweet time, Mercer thought.

CHAPTER

SIXTY-ONE

When his sight returned from Bright Light Land, Mingus surveyed the other people in the operating room. He recognized three of the six men who were pointing their weapons at him and Mercer—Mr. Floyd, the weight lifter who'd kissed them off during their more conventional visit to the clinic, and the two feds, Pleasance and Ivor. The other gunmen were unknowns.

Judging by their photos, the beautiful honeydip with the perfect ass had to be Mercer's heartbreaker, Annie, and the dude in the slick-looking green suede jacket doing the talking was the head dawg, Sellars.

That left the gray-haired man with the aging Angel Gabriel face. He was grinning like a bliss-ninny.

Okay, Mingus thought, *so far so good*. He and Mercer had figured on some kind of welcome, thanks to the phone bug. Having Sellars there was all to the good. At least he hoped so. Everything depended on Mercer getting the opportunity to lay down his lawyer jive to start them talking.

"You gents broke the law coming in here," Sellars said. "They'll say you were looking for drugs."

"You know what we're looking for," Mercer said.

"The other member of your gang? Hootkins? Well, you're looking for him in all the wrong places."

"How bad off is he?" Mercer asked.

Sellars turned to the saintly-looking dude. "What do you think, Alan? How bad off is Hootkins?"

"This one is Mr. Early?" When Sellars nodded, the man

called Alan added, "Mr. Hootkins is feeling a bit low, I'm afraid."

"You're Dr. Alan Donleavy, aren't you?" Mercer asked.

"You know me?" The angel-faced man seemed surprised.

Mingus relaxed a notch and sent Mercer a silent request to do his stuff.

"I've read about your amazing work with nerve transmitters," the lawyer said.

"Really?" Dr. Donleavy was on the verge of preening.

"In *The Sex Supercharger*."

Donlevy grimaced. "I hated that title."

"It hardly does justice to your extraordinary experiments with the effects of serotonin."

"That's exactly what I told the publisher," the doctor said.

"Alan, we don't have time for this bullshit," Sellars said.

"I suppose you're right," the doctor said with what sounded like genuine regret.

"You made the breakthrough, didn't you?" Mercer asked.

Dr. Donleavy frowned and stared at the lawyer. "What breakthrough?" he asked.

Okay, Mingus thought, *Mercer had the hook baited and it was in the water. Now, if only—*

"Do not encourage him, Alan," Sellars said. "These two are traitors, making this an RWEP situation."

Mingus knew the acronym. They were about to be Removed With Extreme Prejudice. And Mercer hadn't come close to reeling in the fish.

Sellars turned to Pleasance. "They're all yours, Arthur. Kill 'em and dump 'em."

"Why me?" Pleasance said, obviously caught off guard.

"Why not? You're fully committed, aren't you?"

"Of course."

"Carl, hand him Hootkins's gun."

"Give me one more day with the old gentleman," Dr. Donleavy said, "and he'll swear he did shoot them."

Pleasance took the offered weapon, returned his own to his belt holster.

"See you back at the ranch," Sellars said. He headed for the door with the other three men and Annie.

"Wait," Mercer called.

"No. Got nothing more to say to you, boy," Sellars said. "Annie, maybe you'd better stay and offer Arthur moral support."

"If you think that's necessary," Annie said.

"Yeah. He'll need help with the disposal."

"Wait a minute," Mingus shouted. "You can't—"

"Take it like a man, Detective. You lost."

The others waited for Sellars to exit, then backed away after him.

"Mercer?" Mingus said. "What now?"

"That's a good question," Annie said to Pleasance.

The green-eyed FBI agent glared at Mercer. "I ought to blow your fucking head off, you stupid, interfering son of a bitch."

"Maybe we have enough—" Annie began.

"No. We still don't have a connection to the big dawg. And now we have to figure out what to do with these assholes until we get the job done." He looked down at the gun in his fist. In disgust, he stuck it behind his belt.

"What just happened?" Mingus asked.

"Let me guess," Mercer said. "You two are some kind of FBI internal affairs? Checking out the operation?"

"Close enough," Annie said.

"So it doesn't strike you as a big coincidence Sellars picked both of you to do this job?"

Pleasance and Annie exchanged looks. Simultaneously they drew their weapons and began searching the shadow areas of the room.

"Too late, folks," Sellars said, as he, Ivor, Floyd, and two other gunmen entered from the scrub room. "Lose the artillery, now."

Annie and Pleasance dropped their guns.

"Okay, Al," Sellars said. "All clear."

Dr. Donleavy came into the room. He had a black metal box in his hands.

"Our turn to get fucked up, huh?" Pleasance asked.

The doctor gave a little negative shake of his head. "Not the way you think," he said, opening the box and withdrawing a hypodermic needle.

"This is a damned disappointing test result," Sellars said. "I've been suspicious of you for a while, young lady. But

Arthur . . . you cost me money. I had a five-dollar bet on you with Carl."

The doctor was filling the needle with something from a vial. Mingus hated needles even when they were used for a good purpose.

"It was a sucker bet, Commander," Carl Ivor said, breaking his usual silence. He looked at his partner. "You seemed a little too freaked when I told you I'd killed Grace Medina, Artie."

"I was freaked," Pleasance said. "I thought you and her had something going on."

"We did," Ivor said. "I cared for her, but she had to go." He pointed his gun at Pleasance's forehead. "You, you arrogant prick, I'll be glad to be rid of."

The doctor approached Pleasance. "This won't hurt," he said, jamming the needle through Pleasance's coat into his upper arm.

"Owwww," the agent yelled as Donleavy emptied the syringe into his bloodstream.

"So I lied."

The doctor jerked the needle free and Pleasance staggered away from him. Then his knees buckled and he fell to the floor. He writhed for a few seconds, trying to get words from a voice box that clearly had ceased functioning. Then he froze, eyes open.

"What the hell is that?" Mingus asked. He'd never seen a poison or drug act that quickly.

"A little something I whipped up in the lab. A paralytic potion that'll wear off in an hour or so."

"By then you folks will be the victims of a clinic fire," Sellars said. "The doc tells me every trace of the drug will burn off."

"Is that the same stuff you've been using on the Jaquecas?" Mercer asked.

"Of course not," the doctor said, as he refilled the syringe. "They've been treated to the full benefit of my greatest creation, a mist that causes dysregulation in serotonin synapses."

"I'm not sure what that means," Mercer said, "except that you've been using the Jaquecas as human guinea pigs."

"The little gangsta boys have proven the drug works. They've suffered such profound depression. They've killed their friends. They've killed themselves. It's the perfect weapon. A weapon that makes its victims blame themselves."

"Alan, if I may make a suggestion," Sellars said, "would you please shut the fuck up?"

Donleavy nodded. "Sorry," he said.

Mingus saw the doctor approaching with that goddamned long needle. He knew that his and Mercer's plan had now been put into play, but not soon enough.

Special Agent Ivor moved to within a few feet, aiming his gun at Mingus's head, keeping him in place.

The loony doc raised the needle and prepared for the jab.

"Doctor, before you do that," Mercer said, "there's something you and the commander should see."

Mingus was ready to make a move, but, unlike the others who were drawn in by Mercer's comment, Ivor remained focused on him. Sighing helplessly, the detective turned to see what the lawyer was doing.

"I got no weapon," Mercer said, using his thumbs to draw back the side of his black windbreaker. "I'm just gonna pull up my shirt, okay?"

Very slowly, he lifted his black T-shirt. The strip of white tape almost glowed against the blackness of his chest. It was being used to hold a small microphone in place.

"Oh my," the doctor said, mildly alarmed.

"So much for your plan to burn us alive," Mercer said.

"Lemme just shoot 'em," Ivor said.

Sellars shook his head. "A bullet to the head is not always the answer," he said.

"The best thing you guys can do," Mercer said, "is to start running right now while you have the chance."

"Mr. Early, I don't know who the LAPD underling is on the other end of that wire, but if they care to check with the office of the chief of police they'll discover I am acting with the full cooperation and permission of the Department."

"That sounds like bullshit to me," Mercer said. "But the point is moot, since this wire isn't going to the LAPD."

"I don't care who it's going to," Sellars said. "In matters of national security—and this is one—my authority is total."

"Except for those too lawless to give a shit about authority."

For one brief moment, Sellars's confidence seemed to desert him. Then it returned with a vengeance. "Alan, shut Early down right now. I'm tired of his babble.

"Floyd, you and Tupper get the gasoline."

Dr. Donleavy moved toward Mercer. He was still a few feet away when Mingus's attention was drawn to the doorway. Floyd had staggered into the operating area. His throat had been slashed and blood had turned his white shirt red and dampened the front of his dark suit.

"Jesus Christ," Ivor said, gawking at the dying man who was stumbling his way. "Who . . . ?"

The answer came with a roar of gunfire. A quartet of gangstas marched into the operating area, led by Bolero. The gang leader was screaming obscenities in two languages, the gist of which, as far as Mingus could tell, was that the white devils had killed and corrupted his friends and would have to die.

He had a gold filigreed gun in each hand that he fired at the domed ceiling, sending pieces of metal, glass, and soundproofing raining down.

Ivor shifted his aim from Mingus to Bolero, but before he could get off a shot, the detective shoved him forward and dove for the floor.

The landing rattled his bones, but not enough for him to ignore the bullets buzzing above him like a swarm of angry gnats. Embracing the tile floor, he opened his eyes to see, to his right, Ivor being spun and bounced and cut to pieces by gangsta bullets. There was some irony in that: the Jaquecas were giving him the same treatment that the SWAT team had handed poor Joe Mooney.

Then there was silence.

Mingus waited to see if he felt any pain, not quite convinced he could have totally escaped a second brush with massive gunfire.

Then a pistol barrel, hot as a branding iron, pressed against the back of his neck.

"Ow, goddammit," he yelled, pulling away.

"So, Señor *Boca Grande,*" Bolero said, "this how you do bid'ness, hidin' on the floor? Makes me think that badge story of yours is boolsheet."

"You *hombres* wasted enough of your bullets?" Mingus asked. He started to get up, but was hit by a dizziness and stayed where he was.

"Easy there," Bolero said. "Looks like your head got nicked."

Mingus felt a sting above his right ear. He raised a hand to it and checked his fingers. Blood. Lots of it.

The little gangsta leaned down to squint at the wound. "We need some tape."

The room was filled with bangers looting everything they could carry from the clinic. Bolero called out to one whose hands were empty.

He spoke in fast, heated Spanish. The man replied something and Bolero began yelling at him.

The man ran off and the gangsta turned to Mingus grinning. "He's in a *clinica* and he asks me should he go to the drugstore for the tape."

"I don't need tape."

"You do," Bolero said. "Now him. He don't need tape." He was pointing at Pleasance. A bullet had entered above the agent's left eye and blown off the back of his skull.

Mingus winced. "You sure dragged your feet getting here, Bolero. What'd you do, stop off for a taco?"

"Hey, I tole you guys I wasn't gonna do nothing till you make me believe your story. When the fuckin' *doctoro* admitted what he was doin', we came right in to save your ass."

"Great save on *his* ass. You're late and then you shoot up the place. Even the friendlies."

"It wasn't us shot him. Or you. I tell my men, no *neg-ros*.

"Manuel, you see who shot the *neg-ros*?"

Manuel had been on his way out with a case of latex gloves. He barely glanced at Pleasance's body. *"Gringo. Saco de verde,"* he said, and ran off with his spoils.

"Green jacket," Mingus said. "That'd be Sellars." He looked around the room. There were five dead on the floor beside Pleasance. Ivor, Floyd, and three men Mingus had never seen until that night. "Where the hell is Sellars? Or the doc? Or Annie?" Mingus was starting to panic. "And where the hell is Mercer?"

"Easy there, *amigo,*" Bolero said.

His man was headed their way with cotton, peroxide,

and tape. Bolero chuckled as he poured the peroxide onto a wad of cotton. "This gonna hurt like fire."

Mingus yelled while the gangsta dabbed at his wound with the peroxide. The detective kept twisting around, looking for Mercer, testing Bolero's patience.

The gangsta pulled a swatch of adhesive tape free from the roll. With one amazingly fluid motion, he slipped a gravity knife from his pocket, shook the blade into place, and sliced the tape until he had a piece the exact thickness he wanted.

He pressed it against Mingus's head, giggling demonically at the cop's discomfort. "No more fucking blood leakin' out of there," he said.

Mingus didn't seem to care about the wound one way or the other. "Where the hell is Mercer?" he repeated.

Julio Lopez entered the room through a rear door, a pistol in his left hand. He ran across the floor to them. "I missed 'em," he said. "In the alley. Mercer and four others. They took off in a Benz they had waiting."

To Mingus, that was simply the way life worked. "Mercer okay?" he asked.

"I was too far away. It looked like this white guy with a buzz cut hit him and threw him into the car."

"I know where they're headed," Mingus said.

"Fine," Bolero said. "Let's go get 'em and send the fuckers to hell."

CHAPTER

SIXTY-TWO

Mercer was in the rear of the Benz, jammed against the left side of the car. He was still woozy from the neck chop Buzz Cut had given him. Looking down, he saw that his shirt was pushed up and that the wire had been ripped from his chest. Annie was beside him and Buzz Cut was on her other side, taking up more than his share of seat, his gun pointed in her general direction.

The commander was driving. The doc, in the passenger seat, was fiddling with his instruments.

Some road trip, Mercer thought.

When Bolero made his dramatic entrance at the clinic, Mercer had been amazed at the commander's presence of mind. As if he'd worked it out in his head as a backup plan, he immediately shot Pleasance while simultaneously shouting at the doctor to run to the rear exit.

Annie rushed him, but was too late. Putting her in his sights, he forced her to accompany them to the back.

Mercer was only a few feet away. But as he ran to intercept them, he saw Buzz Cut about to fire a shot at Mingus. He plowed into the man just as his gun went off, sending them both to the floor.

By the time he got to his feet, bullets were flying around the operating theater and the commander, Annie, and the doctor were slipping away.

He ran after them, arriving in the alley as they moved in on his Benz. Cursing himself for leaving the keys in the ignition, he put on a burst of speed and arrived just as the commander was trying to push Annie into the rear.

He had his hand on the commander's arm when, suddenly, something struck his neck with incredible force, jerking his head back.

Another hit and he saw, heard, felt nothing until he awoke to a nearly unbearably sore neck and head and the thrum of the car's engine in his ear.

"Lawyer's awake," Buzz Cut said. "How you comin', Doc?"

"Nearly ready," the doctor said. "But, Tim, I don't know why you didn't just shoot him and leave him."

"We're making lemonade, Al. Maybe he'll add something to the mix."

"Well, I'm ready," the doctor said.

He undid his seat belt and turned until he was facing the rear. Mercer saw that the high car seat was frustrating his ability to use the hypodermic.

"You'll have to bring his arm where I can reach it."

Buzz Cut grunted and bent past Annie, reaching out.

Mercer played hard to get, holding his arm tight to his side. Buzz Cut prepared for one mighty yank and Mercer suddenly went with it, pushing off from the door, diving across Annie to ram his head into Buzz Cut's face.

He felt and heard the man's nose crack. Heard his garbled scream. But as he struggled to twist Buzz Cut's gun away, he felt the spike enter just below his shoulder blade.

Almost immediately, he lost control of his limbs. But he remained conscious. Just as Pleasance must have seen his fate approaching, he saw the blood seep through Buzz Cut's fingers as he clutched his crushed nose and yelled in pain and rage.

Annie was at the man's gun, twisting it from his fingers. Mercer saw the doctor's needle find her, too.

They both lay like two cut puppets, overlapping, helpless. Buzz Cut continued to wail.

"If you got any of that juice left, Al," Mercer heard the commander say, "hit that crying son of a bitch with it. I like a nice quiet drive."

CHAPTER

SIXTY-THREE

Lonny Hootkins was awakened by the slamming of doors and the sounds of people rushing in the corridor outside his room.

A bit fuzzy-headed and wobbly, he left the bed and turned on the light. He felt silly in the gown with his backside open to the breeze. He looked for his clothes, but they weren't in the room or in the closet.

He tried the door.

Locked.

He walked to the window and looked out on darkness. He thought he could make out blinking lights in the far distance. They were like stars, only too close to the earth for that.

Suddenly his door opened.

Two young white guys in dark suits entered, each carrying a body. He assumed the bodies, both African American, were dead. They sure as hell weren't moving.

The white guys dumped them on the floor and left, locking the door behind them.

One of the bodies was female. A good-looking woman whom Lonny recalled from a photo he'd seen. He didn't think he actually knew her. Her eyes were open, which was pretty damn creepy.

The other body belonged to . . . Mercer! He was staring up, too.

Lonny bent over him. He could hear breathing. Damn. Not dead, only sleeping. No, not sleeping. What then?

He went to the bed and got his two pillows. He put one under each head. It wasn't much, but he couldn't think of anything else to do.

He watched the two bodies for a while. When it appeared they weren't moving even a little bit, he shrugged and got back into his bed.

It wasn't long before the door opened again.

This time, it was the doctor and the guy they called commander.

They weren't interested in him at all. Not at all.

"Thanks to the bugs, we have a pretty good fix on what Early knows about OBN," the commander said, kneeling beside Mercer, going through his pockets. "But we have no idea how he managed to rally the Jaquecas like that."

"Is that important?" the doctor asked.

"Sorta makes one wonder what else he might have in his bag of tricks." The commander stood, examining Mercer's wallet.

"Sodium pentothal?" the doctor suggested.

"We're in no hurry," the commander said, tossing the wallet aside. "With Pleasance dead, there's no chance anybody'll be rushing out here to cramp our style. Let's think of something interesting for Mr. Early. Something especially punitive."

"And the woman?"

"I need her to do me one little favor. She's got a highly defined survival instinct and I think she'll do it."

He leaned over the woman, knowing she could hear him. "Otherwise, Annie, the doctor and I are gonna enjoy every orifice of your body and then dump you down one of the other canyons. I understand that's a pretty common practice around these parts.

"*Adios,* darlin'. Think about it."

He left, the doctor following. Lonny listened for and heard the door being locked.

He got out of bed and eased himself down on his knees next to Mercer. "I can't believe it about you and Chet."

He got no reaction. He raised his voice. "You hear what I said?"

Mercer just kept staring at a spot on the ceiling.

Lonny shook Mercer's body. The man was . . . limp. Nothing was connecting inside. He slapped Mercer's cheek, first softly, then harder. Nothing.

He crawled to the woman. Shook her, too, and got the same lack of response. "Well, ma'am, you might think about wakin' up, because they talkin' about molestin' you and killin' you. That'd wake me up."

When the doctor and the commander returned, they were momentarily stunned to discover Lonny in bed, alone in the room.

"They've escaped," Dr. D. said.

"You crazy?" the commander said. "They're paralyzed. The goddamned door was locked." He hunkered down and checked under the bed.

He got up, straightened the crease in his trousers, and looked at Lonny. "You're a funny old guy, aren't you?"

He went to the closet and opened the door. "There are your escaped prisoners, Al. Go get a strong back to carry Early out where we can have some fun with him."

When the doctor had left, the commander moved to Lonny on the bed. "This your idea of a joke?"

"No, sir. I didn't want to see anybody get hurt."

"Do you love America, Mr. Hootkins?"

"Yes, sir."

"So do I. The work we're doing here is crucial to the task of keeping this the land of the free. These two people are traitors. They probably don't see it that way, but we're at the point where anyone who isn't on the bus is part of the roadblock. Understand?"

"I guess," Lonny said, but it was a lie.

"A few people are gonna have to be hurt so that three hundred million Americans can live free. That makes sense, doesn't it?"

"Yes."

"All right, then."

A big man entered the room. He had his nose taped up, a sight that Lonny found so amusing he might have laughed if he hadn't been brought up to be polite.

The man also had blood all over his shirt.

He dragged Mercer from the closet by his feet and continued dragging him out of the room.

The commander nodded to Lonny and headed out.

"What are you gonna do with him?" Lonny asked.

"We'll just ask him a few questions. And then . . . we'll let him go." He winked at Lonny. "We'll talk again," he said. "See how good a patriot you are."

CHAPTER

SIXTY-FOUR

Mercer was naked, except for his boxers. And he was chilled. The ability to feel the cold was a good sign. Nothing else was good about his situation.

The tingling sensation that had started in his fingertips had progressed to the point where he could actually wiggle his fingers. He might have been able to move his arms, too, except that they, like his wrists, were held fast to his sides by rope with a tensile strength of 9,000 pounds.

His ankles were tied, too. The reason he knew the rope's tensile strength was that it had been a selling point when he bought it.

Another of his purchases at The Climber's Warehouse, the Special Ops rappelling harness—mil-spec black webbing, compact and ready-to-use, just $39.95—was digging into his crotch area.

It and more of the 9,000-pound rope were all that were keeping him from a very quick descent into Charleville Canyon.

Slowly he twisted in the wind, until he was facing across the canyon, eyes smarting and tearing. Shivering.

He had heard everything and observed everything that had been in his line of sight since the moment the contents of the doctor's syringe rendered him immobile. The arrival at the compound. The temporary stay in Hootkins's room. The commander's unhappiness at the discovery of the rappelling equipment in his car trunk.

"Did you know about this compound?" the commander had asked, slapping him angrily. "Nod for me, dammit. Were you planning on breaking in here?"

He'd been unable to speak, even if he'd wanted to.

"There were two harnesses. For you and your detective pal? Does he know where we are? Goddammit. Are we safe?"

The commander had ordered up more guards to check the road, then he'd asked the doctor, "You got something that can bring him out of it faster?"

The doctor had complied. Mercer hadn't felt the needle go in.

"You are a troublesome bastard," the commander had leaned in to say.

He moved away. "Let's soften this boy up to get him to answer some questions."

Mercer felt a tug on the rope. Then he was being pulled up, hard and fast. As his back was scraped and torn by the jagged side of the canyon, he tried to scream. That's when he realized there was something soft jammed in his mouth.

"Spin him around," he heard the commander order. He felt hands pushing him in a 180-degree turn until he was facing Sellars's shoes. Past the shoes, he saw the rope, his lifeline, stretching across the ground to the tow bar on the rear of a black SUV, maybe the Escalade.

"That cop Mingus know about this place?" the commander asked him. "Just nod yes or no."

Mercer kept his head still. In fact, he was too busy trying to fight the pain from his scraped back.

"C'mon. I know you can move your head. Are we safe here?"

Mercer remained rigid.

He saw the commander lift his foot, felt the tip of the shoe pressing against his forehead, then pushing him away from the side of the canyon. "Back 'er up," Sellars shouted.

Mercer heard the SUV's engine rev and then he dropped. Fast. Scraping his face this time. And shoulders and knees.

He jerked to a halt, dangling. The wetness in his eyes was something darker than tears. His forehead was bleeding. He hurt everywhere, the wind not helping.

He wondered if Mingus was still alive and in any condition to try and save him. In a way, he hoped not. The commander was expecting trouble.

While Mingus stood by feeling his anxiety edge into the red zone, Bolero spent precious minutes deciding which of four available vehicles to use himself and which was to be used by a second team that included Fuckhead and the man who could not speak English.

He finally settled on the black Blazer with red stripes along its hood and orange-red flames detailed on its side panels. The others would have to make do with a more conservative Suburban three-quarter ton.

Bolero tapped a very young-looking, very tall boy to be their driver. He and his associate had been carrying a leather couch to an open bed truck. He left the associate to drag the furniture away and climbed behind the Blazer's steering wheel. Bolero took the front passenger seat. Mingus eased his weight onto the rear seat as Julio slid in beside him.

As the Blazer zoomed along the freeway system, eventually heading north, Bolero said, "Our *chofer* is Tiago Almador. We call him El Tigre Poco. The Little Tiger." The driver didn't smile.

"His *fratello,* Luis, was El Tigre. Our leader. Much beloved. We see now that the sadness that overtook him was not of his own making. I want Tiago to be there when we find the *doctoro*. Okay?"

"Okay by me," Mingus said.

"I doan unnerstand how this *doctoro* can fuck up Luis so bad," Tiago said. "I lived with Luis, saw him get crazier by the day."

"Believe me, *amigo,*" Bolero said, "this *doctoro* not only did it, he laughed about it. They been testin' their boolsheet drugs on us because we outlaws, *esse*. They figure we got nobody we can complain to. But they forget: we don't need nobody. We got guns."

Bolero turned to Mingus. "How many gonna be there?"

"I don't think they'll be expecting anybody, so maybe a skeleton crew."

"Good. We turn them into real skeletons," Bolero said.

CHAPTER SIXTY-FIVE

Lonny felt somebody shaking him awake.

He'd been lost in a dream, reliving a trip to South Carolina he and his dad once took when he was fourteen. His room was dark, but he could see that it was the woman shaking him. "What?" he asked, annoyed.

"I need your help."

"Oh." He yawned. He looked past her. "The door's open."

"Yeah. I'm good with locks. Now come on. We don't have time."

"What do you need?" he said, sliding from the bed.

"There's another man here. I don't know what condition he's in, but I want you to take him out of here."

"Why can't you?"

"I'm going to be distracting the men out front so you two can leave."

"Then what'll happen to you?"

"Not a lot, if you guys get free. Once you're on the road, you've got to watch out, because they'll be coming after you. Just get to the next house down the canyon and beg them to call the police. Send them here. Tell 'em it's a home invasion. Got that?"

It sounded like a tall order to Lonny, but he nodded. "Home invasion," he said.

The woman led him into the hallway, which was empty. She opened the next door, closed it, and then tried the door after that.

Inside the lighted room was a white guy in bed, wearing a gown like his. He knew the guy. Some Department mucky-muck. Didn't look so high and mighty now, propped up on pillows, drooling on himself.

The woman tried to get him out of the bed, but he was a handful.

"Lemme he'p," Lonny said, taking the dude's arm. Between them, they got the man on his feet.

"Timmy?" the man asked.

"You better hope not," the woman said.

They moved him to the door and out into the corridor. As they headed toward the front of the building, Lonny heard a grinding noise that grew louder.

It was coming from a room to the right. Lonny saw a man in a white coat feeding papers and folders into a shredding machine. The woman propped the white Department dude against the wall and entered the room, moving up behind the guy.

She picked up a big, thick book from a table and drew back and thwacked the backside of the guy's head. The guy didn't go out, so she thwacked him again.

She took the folders that had fallen and shoved them under a carpet, like she was hiding them. Then she returned to the corridor and they continued on their way out.

They entered a long room that had chemical odors that made Lonny's eyes water. The room had basin-equipped tables on which rested test tubes in holders, small scales, an assortment of probes and other instruments, coils, and methods of heating the tubes.

"Some kind of lab?" Lonny asked.

"Yes," she whispered. "But we've got to be quiet now."

He nodded that he understood.

A door at the end of the lab took them outside, to a plot of land that separated the lab from a building in front. The night air felt good to Lonny. Chilly, but clean and invigorating.

The woman seemed nervous.

She was staring at something to their right.

He saw a group of men standing near the edge of the canyon. There was a big black SUV idling, a rope going from the back of it down into the canyon.

The commander was saying something he couldn't quite

make out. The white Department dude with them must've picked up on it, because he said, out loud, "Timmy," and jerked free of their grasp.

"Shit," the woman said under her breath. She grabbed Lonny's upper arm and damn near dragged him beside the front house.

She said, "Wait here until I go out there, then get the hell out of here."

"Where?" he asked.

"Through the house. Go. Remember, tell the cops home invasion."

He saw the commander turn, saw the surprise on his face as he discovered the white dude staggering toward him.

"Where the hell did you come from, partner?" the commander said. Then he smiled. "Annie? You out there somewhere? Damned if I didn't forget all about you, young lady."

"Wait, then get going," she whispered to Lonny. She stepped out into the moonlight.

Lonny remained still, crouched beside the house, while a couple of black suits moved in on the woman.

"Bring her over here," the commander said. "Show her how we do a little keel-hauling without a boat or an ocean."

Lonny didn't understand a word the commander said. But he saw that the others were all focused on the woman and not him.

He decided to do what she told him.

Only the back door of the house was locked.

Well, no matter. He preferred the free feeling of being outside under the stars.

"Did you give your boyfriend Early this address?" the commander was saying.

"No," the woman said. "When did I have the chance?"

Lonny was a pretty good sneak. Even as a boy. He smiled at some distant memory as he moved quietly around the outside of the house. The dewy grass felt nice under his bare feet.

At the front of the house, where cars were parked, he left the lawn and walking became more difficult. He had to cross a section with tiny stones and rocks that hurt like hell.

Then he was on the paved driveway. He followed it up an incline leading to the road.

He was halfway up the drive when an alarm sounded. He was aware of movement to his right and left. Men in suits had been hiding there, waiting for something. For him?

He started to run.

The front door of the house was thrown open and he heard someone shout, "It's an old guy making a run for it. Hold your fire, but get him."

Lonny reached the high ground and began running down the road, mindless now of the painful objects under his feet.

They were following, younger and faster men. But he'd promised the woman he'd get help. There were two SUVs parked just off the road. To him that meant a house somewhere, but he didn't see a house.

The men were right behind him. He felt a hand grab the flap of his goddamned hospital gown and jerk him back.

He tried twisting free of the gown, but they were all over him now. Three, no four of them, slapping him in the face, cursing him. One of them was laughing.

They started dragging him back up the hill.

"I thought this was an upscale neighborhood," one of them said. He was pointing at the parked SUVs. "That Blazer with the detail work looks like a piece of banger crap."

There was a grunting sound and suddenly Lonny wasn't being dragged anymore.

He turned and saw a group of men standing over the bodies of the men who'd been dragging him. Some of them were wiping their knives on the dead men's suits. The shortest of the men bent over one of the dead men and said, "I paid fifty grand for that 'banger crap,' you *maricon.*"

He spit on the dead man and said, "Throw this trash into the canyon."

"Hiya, Lonny." It was Mingus. Lonny wondered what he was doing with these bangers and why he had tape on his head.

"What happened to your head, Mingus?"

"Somebody tried to shoot me."

"You a little underdressed, ain't you, pop?" the loudmouthed banger asked. "Here, stay warm." To his surprise, the gangsta took off his leather jacket and put it around his shoulders.

"How many men they got in there?"

Lonny tried to count. "Maybe ten," he guessed.

The gangster grinned. "Piece o' cake."

"What about Mercer?" Mingus asked.

"He was in my room for a while. Then . . . I don' know. Maybe he's with Chet."

"Chet?"

"Yeah. Dr. D. tells me they been dissin' me."

"Mercer wouldn't do that," Mingus said. He turned to the little gangsta. "Lonny's not himself, exactly. His count may not be too accurate. There could be more."

"Ten. Twenty. Fifty. Who gives a shit? They waiting for those guys to come back. They got their alarms off. We go run down there now and kill as many as they got."

"Watch out for Mercer and the woman."

"Sure," he said. Then he opened a flame-covered door to one of the vehicles and said to Lonny, "Stay in there, *hombre,* till we done."

Lonny pulled the door shut and watched them move silently up the road. Then he lay down on his back across the two rear seats, knees tentpoled to make his lanky body fit. He could see the sky through the side window. But the window was smoked and he couldn't quite make out the stars.

He stretched a leg to the door handle and opened the side door. Now he could see the sky and stars and feel the clean fresh night. He pulled the little banger's jacket tighter around him. It smelled of good cologne.

There were popping sounds from the house down below. Lonny recognized the sound. Any ex-cop would.

CHAPTER

SIXTY-SIX

Mingus didn't bother to check the life signs of the two men lying on the drive, but he did pause long enough to pry a gun from one of their fists.

He was starting toward the house, when movement to his left caught his eye.

A big bozo with tape on his nose was hacking at a rope hooked to the tow bar of an idling SUV. He'd got about halfway through.

"Hey," the detective shouted. "Stop that."

The guy kept the knife to the rope.

"I shoot on three. One . . . two . . ."

The big guy drew back and threw the knife at Mingus. It didn't come close. The guy ran for the SUV, got the front door open, and started to slide in. Mingus grabbed him just as the vehicle started inching forward.

The guy flailed at Mingus and jammed his foot on the gas pedal. The SUV bucked. But as it did, Mingus held on to the man and yanked him from the vehicle. He head-butted the guy on his bandage and the man went limp.

The SUV rolled to a stop.

Curious, Mingus followed the taut rope all the way to the canyon, where he saw a bloody head poking up over the lip.

With a sickening feeling, he immediately knew who it was.

Pumped up by adrenaline, he had no problem lifting Mercer out of the canyon. The unconscious lawyer was a mass of scratches and scrapes and cuts. His breathing was ragged. In shock, maybe.

He unhooked him from the rope and carried him to the front of the house. He figured that by staying in the Jaquecas's wake, they'd be less likely to run into anybody to give them trouble.

Ignoring the two bodies in suits just past the front door, he carried Mercer across the living room, lowering him onto a couch. He took off his jacket and draped it over his friend's naked chest. Then he undid the harness and removed it.

Mercer's former client, Julio, came into the room. "How bad?" he asked.

"I don't know. Stay with him while I get a blanket." He saw the young man removing his coat to drape it over Mercer's legs.

Considering what he'd been through that night, he'd figured he'd just about seen it all. But the scene in a large, expensively appointed bedroom made him reconsider.

Bolero was perched on the arm of a stuffed chair in which sat LAPD Chief of Staff John Gilroy, drooling on himself. At their feet, quite dead, lay Commander Tim Sellars. "He was gonna cap my man here," Bolero said, indicating Gilroy. "I had no choice, bro'."

"You sure he's dead?" Mingus asked.

Bolero made a need-you-ask face.

"I got to get an ambulance for Mercer."

"Why? What's up with him?"

"They've been dragging him up and down the side of the canyon."

"Fuckers! Well, we don't get any ambulance here now. I got my *vatos* coming to help with the cleanup. When we done, your ambulance."

Mingus knew arguing would be a waste of time. He pulled blankets from the closet. "There must be some kind of painkillers and ointment around here."

"The doc's in his laveratory. With El Tigre Poco."

"Still alive?"

"The pretty ne-gro lady say not to kill the *cabrón*."

"Where is she?"

"Aroun' grabbing paper and shit she says she needs."

The detective ran back to the living room with the blankets. He was astounded to find Mercer sitting up talking to Julio, who'd used a towel to clean most of the blood from the lawyer's face. "How you feel?" Mingus asked as he wrapped the blankets around Mercer.

"I think I need something for these cuts. And for the pain, maybe."

"Take it easy. I'll go see what I can find."

"I made the tour," Julio said. "I'll show you."

There turned out to be several labs in the rear building. Julio led him past those to a smaller, more elaborate lab that was being used by Donleavy and El Tigre Poco. The doc was lying on his back on an examination table, arms and legs tied to the four corners.

The boy sat on a chair, waving a magnum in the general direction of the doctor's genitalia.

"You got a first aid kit in this joint?" Mingus asked.

"Cabinet," the doctor croaked. "Help me, please."

Mingus ignored the request.

Julio opened the cabinet, withdrew a large white box with a red cross on its lid.

"See," the doctor said.

Julio opened the box, showing Mingus a rich supply of ointments, gauze, creams, and sterilized cleansers.

"What about pain pills?" he asked.

"Good question," El Tigre Poco said, pressing the barrel of his gun into the doctor's forehead.

"There are some . . . darvon and Percocet in the desk drawer in the outer room," the doctor said, his voice showing just a hint of hope that by cooperating all or some would be forgiven.

Mingus went there quickly, found the pills, and took both bottles.

"Bring me what you don't use," El Tigre yelled.

"The doctor has problems enough with him sober," Julio said as they walked away.

They bumped into Annie in the hall. She was carrying an armful of papers toward another office. "Where's Mercer?" she asked. "I was on my way out to help him when I saw you had that under control."

"He's in the house," Mingus said. "He needs some doctoring. I think he'd rather it be from you than me."

"First I've got to secure an office," she said, "and put

these files and several others under lock and key. Meanwhile, you two big strong men can carry Mercer back here to one of the examination rooms to have him ready for me."

They watched her move off along the corridor.

"Got her priorities, huh?" Julio said.

"Seems like," Mingus agreed.

CHAPTER

SIXTY-SEVEN

Mercer awoke in a bright, warm examination room to find Annie cleaning and medicating his wounds. "Welcome to Gangland Central," she said.

"Hi. Didn't you used to be Lionel?"

"Detective Mingus got you to swallow a few pain pills, then he and your friend—Julio, I think is his name—turned you over to me."

"Where are they?"

"I think they're trying to convince the others not to start shooting the neighbors."

"I'm glad they're keeping busy."

"You're pretty resilient," she said. "No broken bones that I could find."

"Just a broken heart."

"Those pills must be more potent than I thought." She frowned. "There are two serious gashes—on your left thigh and your back—that a real doctor should look at. And a torn ear that I've taped in place, kind of. Everything else is just nasty surface scrapes and scratches."

"Do you suppose this table could hold you, too?" he asked.

"You need a reality check, brother. First, there are little gangsta boys running in and out of here with guns and knives. Second, my people are gonna be here any minute to try and contain the uncontainable. I got about four hundred things I'm supposed to be doing, including making sure nobody shoots Donleavy. If that's not enough, it'd take a kinder heart than mine to be knocking boots with a man whose body looks like a Salisbury steak in places."

"I get the message," he said. "So tell me what I don't know. Mingus fill you in on what happened at the clinic after we split?"

She nodded. "I saw the commander shoot Art point blank, but I was hoping there was a chance." She shook her head.

"Is the commander here?"

"The bastard is dead. I stuck a pin in him to make sure."

"I know he shot Pleasance to keep him from spilling the address of this place. But I've been wondering why he didn't shoot you."

The mood in the room turned chilly. "He needed me to make a final report to my boss at Criminal Investigation, clearing him of any misdeeds."

"What about your reports up to now?" Mercer asked. "Sellars and Donleavy have been testing a drug with suicidal and homicidal effects on a bunch of unsuspecting young men. Don't tell me you've been giving that the big thumbs-up."

"First off, with respect to these fine young men who are currently stealing everything that's not cemented to the foundation, they are gangstas. Outlaws. Killers. You might consider them this country's internal terrorists.

"Second, this is a very high level National Security project, which places it beyond the scope of most legislation I know of. Third, the business of testing was given the full approval of the Attorney General's Office."

This was all dismaying news for Mercer, made even more dismaying by Annie's obvious endorsement of it. "Well, hell," he said. "If we're at the point of lawlessness where loonies like Sellars are allowed to murder anybody without even a hint of due process, then what could you possibly be investigating?"

"The attorney general's order does not allow for the endangerment or death of law-abiding citizens, like Dwight Baskin," she said, dabbing nastily at an open wound with something on a cotton ball. "The Baskin incident hung a cloud over the whole operation. Even before that there were a couple of drive-by shootings of innocent people that, we have reason to believe, were prompted by the tests.

"Finally we have the situations with Merrill Gibbons, Joe Mooney, and Eldon Nunez. The best take on these events was that Donleavy and the commander were being sloppy. The worst was that, in their zeal to add more weapons to our antiterrorist arsenal, they'd stepped over the line into homicidal mania. That's when our boss at CI Division sent Art and me to become members of Operation Big Nightmare."

"OBN," Mercer said. "Is that all it is? Operation Big Nightmare? What a lame name."

"Don't blame me. I didn't come up with it."

In fact, it was not the name that annoyed him. It was her way of putting things: "the *situations* with Mooney, Gibbons, and Nunez . . . our antiterrorist arsenal." These suggested, at the least, an absence of empathy in her soul. Too damn bad.

"At first, Art and I felt that the Baskin incident was just bad luck. A cop with a hard-on for gangstas breaks into the clinic and performs an illegal search and seizure. He takes away one of the doctor's prototypes and—I'm guessing here—he examines it in his car and gets fully exposed to it.

"Mooney's exposure was a domino effect. When Baskin's car crashed, the canister sprung a leak. He got a whiff of it."

"And so did Merrill Gibbons, who removed the stolen box from Baskin's car," Mercer said. "And Eldon Nunez, who transported it back to Donleavy."

"All the recruits had got the word to be on the lookout for a box assumed to be in Baskin's possession," she said. "When Baskin's death was called in, Gibbons was unlucky enough to have been first on the scene. He phoned in that he'd recovered the box and Nunez was dispatched to take it from him."

"Why didn't Gibbons deliver the box himself?"

"Gibbons was a flake, bottom link on the need-to-know chain," she said. "He had no knowledge of Dr. D. or the clinic. He just did what he was told. Nunez happened to be in the neighborhood with an acceptable security rating."

"How'd he earn that?" Mercer asked.

"He was smart, aggressive and proved his patriotism by

bugging the D.A.'s home while she and his roommate were out having dinner."

He saw movement at the door behind her. Mingus was standing there. Being quiet about it so as not to interrupt their conversation.

"What brought you to my doorstep, Annie?" Mercer asked.

"It was the commander's idea for me to hook up with you. It was the most pleasant duty I've had."

He supposed she meant that as a compliment. He saw Mingus shaking his head.

"Who found out about the real Mercer Early?"

"That's not the biggest secret in the world," she said. "It took me fifteen minutes to discover the original Mercer has been in the ground awhile. That meant you had some kind of a past you were hiding. The commander wanted to know what it was. He thought we might be able to use it to keep you in line."

"That was some story you told me," he said, "about your husband George and all."

"It's a true story," she said. "It just doesn't happen to be mine. It was one of my best friends who married George. I have to say it was a classy tale and it usually gets results. Not with you, though."

He remembered how close he'd come to joining those who'd shared their past with her.

"Anyway, about the commander," she said. "Art and I still couldn't tell if we were dealing with a good man who'd had bad luck or if we had a rogue on our hands."

"You knew Mooney had been here."

"The commander said he'd caught a break and found the guy before he could do any damage. They were keeping him here, trying to reverse the effect of the drug."

"That can be done?"

"It supposedly worked for Mooney's partner. They took her off the streets one night, treated her to another of the doctor's little experiments, a sort of uptown roofie. Then they tested her and administered Donleavy's antidote. They took her home, put her in her bed, and she woke up with not even a hint of memory of any of it.

"I believe they pulled her in one more time, too, to make sure."

"Why didn't the antidote work on Mooney?" Mercer asked.

"Donleavy said he was too far gone. But as we discovered last night, that was a lie."

"Him being mowed down by SWAT didn't give you a clue?"

"No. The commander said he'd escaped. That tied in with the sloppiness theory."

"What happened last night to change your mind?"

"That oaf Carl Ivor had one drink too many and let slip to Art that he'd killed Grace Medina. Until then, we'd assumed, like everyone else, that Mooney had killed her. Art went ballistic and backed Carl into a corner and got the full story. Medina had discovered that Donleavy wasn't trying to cure Mooney; he was setting him up to be killed."

"Why?"

"Your client going to trial was worrisome enough. Another potential trial was out of the question. Mooney had to die and that was more than Medina had bargained for. She was ready to spill all, to the LAPD and to the media. Since Carl had a relationship with her, they figured it was easier for him to keep her quiet."

"What stopped Pleasance from reporting that right away?" Mercer asked.

"Something else Carl said. He told Art to relax, that they could kill whomever they wanted. There was someone close to the president who would 'make that problem go away.' Art was hoping to find out who that was before sending his report."

"Did you find out?"

"No." She turned and saw Mingus. "Oh. Been there long?"

"Just a minute. How's my man here?"

"With all modesty, I can say I saved his life. Actually, he's good to go. And that's what I suggest you do. I've got a cleanup crew coming in soon," she said. "You brothers might want to be missing when they arrive."

"How are you going to explain all this and the mess at the clinic?" Mingus asked.

"It's better to stay with simple truths. Commander Tim Sellars, continuing his proven bad fortune, allowed himself to get in a war with the Jaquecas. A war that he lost."

"They'll buy that without question?"

She smiled. "When I deliver the doctor's magic spray, complete with documentation, that's all they'll care about."

"Suppose you don't deliver it?" Mercer asked.

She hesitated only a moment before replying, "Suppose you don't get the antidote for your friend Hootkins?"

"What happens to the doctor?" Mercer asked.

"I imagine he'll be put to work developing something new."

"Jesus," Mingus half-whispered.

"The war we're fighting is never-ending. Just be glad this particular sick son of a bitch is on our side."

But as she and Mingus helped Mercer toward the front of the building, they discovered that Dr. Alan Donleavy was no longer on anyone's side. Bolero, Julio, El Tigre, and all the gangstas had cleared out, leaving very little of note except the doctor's corpse. His throat had been cut and the numerals "666"—the mark of the beast—had been carved on his angelic forehead.

"They do nice work," Mingus said.

"We're definitely leaving now," Mercer said. "What's the time?"

"Just after four," Annie said.

"Here's the deal," he said to her. "I'll be in the office in twelve hours. At that time, I'll need an official FBI document, signed by you, stating that my client Eldon Nunez participated in a government experiment that inadvertently resulted in the death of his friend Landers Pope. You'll probably also have to appear in court if the D.A. still insists on a trial."

"Why would I put myself in that position?"

"Because, in return, I'll tell you who at the White House was protecting the commander."

She smiled. "Is it the attorney general?"

"No."

"Then we may have a deal. You simply want Nunez cleared, right?"

"That's all I've ever wanted," he said. Not quite the truth, but it would have to do. "I assume there will be enough antidote to go around?"

"See you at four, counselor," she said.

CHAPTER

SIXTY-EIGHT

"Will this suffice?" Annie handed Mercer a type-written letter on Justice Department letter-head. It was short. Just a few sentences that said in effect that this was an official order that all charges, real or implied, against U.S. citizen Eldon Nunez be immediately withdrawn. It bore the signature of the attorney general of the United States.

They were sitting in Mercer's office.

"This really his signature," Mercer asked, "or did he just give you permission to forge it?"

She smiled and shook her head. "They don't play your games at DOJ," she said. "It's his genuine signature. Now it's your turn at show and tell. The attorney general is very anxious to know which of the prez's people was the commander's man."

Mercer took his time standing. At the emergency ward Mingus forced him to visit at 4:30 a.m., they'd done quite a job of sewing up his ear and taping up his thigh and back. Still, every shift in position was like a stab wound. They'd also sold him a walking stick that he secretly felt gave him a sort of war hero charisma.

Using the stick, he limped out the door. "Come on."

He paused to turn over the AG's document to his assistant, instructing her to make copies and place the original in the firm's safe. Then he led Annie to the library, where Sidone and Kennard were working on projects for other attorneys.

"Annie, I'd like you to meet two of our associates, Sidone Evans and Kennard Haines."

"That'd be Kennard Haines, *Junior*?" Annie asked.

"Y-yes," the young man stammered, obviously impressed by her beauty.

"I've met your daddy," Annie said. "Mercer, I must say, if it's his daddy we're talking about, I'm not exactly surprised."

"What about my dad?" Kennard asked.

"One thing," Mercer said. "He's got a conniving disloyal weasel of a son."

"Wh-what are you talking about?"

"I'm talking about you, sneaking in here and planting your bugs all over the place."

"I didn't—"

"Don't even try to deny it. I've got you on DVD. Must See TV."

"You did this?" Sidone said to Kennard. "You bugged us?"

"Has he been in your apartment?" Mercer asked.

She nodded.

"I bet he bugged that, too. He's a little bugger."

"You bugged me?"

Kennard wouldn't look her in the eye.

She turned from him to Mercer. "He's not going to continue working here?"

"No. He's gone. And he'll have to find some other use for that Yale law degree. There won't be a decent firm in the country that'll touch him when they find out what he pulled here.

"Annie, you must have known we were being bugged," Mercer said.

"Sure. The commander said he was handling it."

"That pompous jackass," Mercer said, watching Kennard.

"You don't know what you're talking about," the boy said. "Jackass? Commander Sellars is the finest American I've ever met."

He hadn't heard about Sellars's death. The news had not yet hit the media, though reports of an outbreak of gangsta activity was starting to surface.

"Did he ask you to plant the bugs?"

"No."

"Was it your daddy?" Mercer asked.

"Yes. That's how I knew it had to be the right thing to do."

"Did it feel right? Spying on your friends?"

"I . . . no. But I knew my purpose was correct. Patriotism is the key to survival."

"And bugging my apartment?" Sidone asked. "Was that patriotism or just being a sleaze?"

Kennard simply could not look at her.

"Where'd you get the bugs?" Annie asked.

"Dad sent a man to put them in my apartment mailbox. Now, is that all?"

"Get your ass out of here, sonny," Mercer said. "Do not pass go. And be happy you're not headed straight to jail."

Mercer and the two women watched as Kennard gathered his belongings. As soon as he'd gone, Sidone started to cry.

"That wrap things up?" Mercer asked Annie as he limped with her to the elevator.

"Sure. The AG will take care of Kennard Haines Sr. and see to it that his influence on the White House is brought down several notches."

"Justice of a sort, I suppose," Mercer said.

"That's why they call it the Justice Department," she said. "I'm going to grab four or five hours of sleep. After that, it'd be nice to spend my last night in L.A. with a friend."

He was surprised, but not really interested.

"I'm sorry, but I've got something else going tonight," he said.

"The associate?"

"No. Not the associate."

"Well," she said and hugged him, catching him so off guard, he dropped his walking stick. "It's been an adventure, Mercer, or whoever you are."

"Mercer. That's who I am."

CHAPTER

SIXTY-NINE

At a little after five C.W. Hansborough and Devon Olander returned from their business/pleasure trip to Vegas.

Devon stopped off at Mercer's office. "Okay," she said, placing a thick sheaf of papers on his desk. "That Hildegard McRae is some piece of work. She's like one of those explosives gets stuck to the bottom of a ship. You can't shake it and eventually it blows up. There is no way anybody is going to put any stock in anything the lady has to say after they hear about what went on in Vegas."

Mercer pointed to the stack. "Is there anything in there that'll explain how Lionel's pubic hairs got in her bed?"

"I sense you're testing me, Mercer, which isn't a smart thing to do, considering I just spent several days *and nights* in thc company of the senior partner of this firm. But yes, there is an explanation in there."

"Which is?"

"The lady's a lock expert. Her boyfriend in Vegas came home one night and found her in his bed. Not just *his* bed. He was married at the time.

"Our claim will be that she broke into Mingus's apartment, got the hairs from his bed, and placed them in hers."

"I don't know," Mercer said. "That still seems a stretch."

"Read the file. It'll knock your socks off. The woman is a stone freak. She shouldn't be allowed on the street, much less in the Homicide Division. I'm not sure what she had going with the lieutenant she was working for in Vegas, but he tried to blow me off. I had to get his chief to rain fire on his head before he turned over her file. The fire got hotter when I told the chief that most of Hildegard's bad behavior had been missing from the records sent to the LAPD, but there *had* been a glowing letter of recommendation from the lieutenant."

"Good work, Devon," he said. "I'll read this tonight."

"I wouldn't want it to cut into your romance time."

"No problem, there," he said.

When she'd gone, he picked up the phone and dialed Mingus.

The phone rang a few times, then the detective answered, "Hello."

"It's Mercer, Lionel."

"Mercer. I was thinking of calling you."

"Yeah, well that's . . . you okay?" Mercer had sensed something strange and scary about the way Mingus was talking, like maybe he'd had a snort of Dr. Donleavy's medicine.

"Me? I'm fine. Right on it. Perfect. See, I made up my mind to go to the store today and talk to Bettye. Turns out that was all she'd been waiting for. We patched things up easy enough."

"That's great, brother."

"Yeah. And her boss let her off early so we could, you know, celebrate. So we're planning on this big night out, but we came home first to get dressed. And Mercer . . . aw, shit, I need you, man."

Mercer could tell by his tone of voice that something unbearable had befallen his friend. "I'm on my way," he said.

Lionel Mingus used his left hand to replace the receiver.

He saw that the front door of the apartment was still open. He thought he could hear a siren in the distance. Maybe the paramedics, maybe the police.

He realized why he'd been holding his phone in his left hand. In his right was a gun. He'd used it on Hildy McRae, who was sprawled on the floor behind him. She was dead. He'd emptied his gun making sure of that.

She'd been waiting when he and Bettye walked through the front door. Ever the gentleman, he'd let Bettye go first, which is why Hildy's bullets struck her and not him.

It was possible, of course, that Bettye had been Hildy's preferred target, since, by killing her, she had effectively damaged him more than bullets could. Hildy may have been a psycho, but she knew how to twist a knife.

He sat down on the floor beside his beloved, reached out a hand to touch her light brown face. She looked like she was sleeping.

But . . . did she stir?

He'd been afraid to feel for her pulse, afraid to lose the slim hope that had made him tell the 911 operator to send the paramedics. Now he pressed anxious fingers against her neck.

There was a beat. A slight one, but steady.

The two wounds—in the shoulder and, more seriously, in the abdomen—were not showing an unusual amount of blood. That had to be good.

Her eyelids fluttered and she whispered, "Lionel?"

"I'm here, baby. I'll always be here."

"It hurts real bad."

"I know. But they're on the way to fix you up. It's gonna be fine."

"You just sayin' that."

"You gotta learn to believe me, woman."

"You sure?"

"Never been surer about anything," he said. "We're gonna be happy together for a long, long time."

He kissed her cheek and lay down beside her on the floor and waited for the medics and the lawyer who he knew in his heart would make it all come true.